Nikki Owen is an award-winning writer and columnist. As part of her degree, she studied at the acclaimed University of Salamanca – the same city where her protagonist of *Subject 375*, Dr Maria Martinez, hails from. Born in Dublin, Nikki now lives in Gloucestershire with her family.

NIKKI OWEN
SUBJECT
375

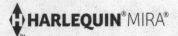

First Published in Great Britain 2015 as The Spider in The Corner Of The Room
By Harlequin Mira, an imprint of HarperCollins*Publishers*
1 London Bridge Street, London, SE1 9GF

© 2015 Nikki Owen

ISBN 978-1-848-45487-3

58-0616

Our policy is to use papers that are natural, renewable and recyclable products and made from wood grown in sustainable forests. The logging and manufacturing processes conform to the legal environmental regulations of the country of origin.

Printed and bound by
CPI Group (UK) Ltd, Croydon, CR0 4YY

To Dave, Abi and Hattie – my beautiful little family

Chapter 1

The man sitting opposite me does not move. He keeps his head straight and stifles a cough. The sun bakes the room, but even when I pull at my blouse, the heat still sticks. I watch him. I don't like it: him, me, here, this room, this... this cage. I feel like pulling out my hair, screaming at him, at them, at the whole world. And yet I do nothing but sit. The clock on the wall ticks.

The man places his Dictaphone on the table, and, without warning, delivers me a wide smile.

'Remember,' he says, 'I am here to help you.'

I open my mouth to speak, but there is a sudden spark in me, a voice in my head that whispers, *Go!* I try to ignore it, instead focus on something, anything, to steady the rising surge inside me. His height. He is too tall for the chair. His back arcs, his stomach dips and his legs cross. At 187.9 centimetres and weight at 74.3 kilograms, he could sprint one kilometre without running out of breath.

The man clears his throat, his eyes on mine. I swallow hard.

'Maria,' he starts. 'Can I…' He falters, then leaning in a little: 'Can I call you Maria?'

I answer instinctively in Spanish.

'In English, please.'

I cough. 'Yes. My name is Maria.' There is a tremor in my voice. Did he hear it? I need to slow down. Think: facts. His fingernails. They are clean, scrubbed. The shirt he wears is white, open at the collar. His suit is black. Expensive fabric. Wool? Beyond that, he wears silk socks and leather loafers. There are no scuffs. As if he stepped fresh out of a magazine.

He picks up a pen and I risk reaching forward to take a sip of water. I grip the glass tight, but still tiny droplets betray me, sloshing over the edges. I stop. My hands are shaking.

'Are you okay?' the man asks, but I do not reply. Something is not right.

I blink. My sight—it has become milky, a white film over my eyes, a cloak, a mask. My eyelids start to flutter, heart pounds, adrenaline courses through me. Maybe it is being here with him, maybe it is the thought of speaking to a stranger about my feelings, but it ignites something, something deep inside, something frightening.

Something that has happened to me many times before. A memory.

It sways at first, takes its time. Then, in seconds, it rushes, picking up speed until it is fully formed: the image. It is there in front of me like a stage play. The curtains rise and I am in a medical room. White walls, steel, starched bed linen. Strip lights line the ceiling, glaring, exposing me. And then, ahead, like a magician through smoke, the doctor with black eyes enters by the far door. He is wearing a mask, holding a needle.

'Hello, Maria.'

Panic thrusts up within me, lava-like, volcanic, so fast that I fear I could explode. He steps closer and I begin to shake, try to escape, but there are straps, leather on my limbs. Black Eyes' lips are upturned, he is in the room now, bearing down on me, his breath—tobacco, garlic, mint—it is in my face, my nostrils, and I begin to hear myself scream when there is something else. A whisper: 'He is not real. He is not real.' The whisper, it hovers in my brain, flaps, lingers, then like a breeze it passes, leaving a trace of goosebumps on my skin. Was it right? I glance round: medicine vials, needles, charts. I look at my hands: young, no lines. I touch my face: teenage spots. It is not me, not me now. Which means none of this exists.

Like a candle extinguishing, the image blows away, the curtains close. My eyes dart down. Each knuckle is white from where they have gripped the glass. When I look up, the man opposite is staring.

'What happened?' he says.

I inhale, check my location. The scent of Black Eyes is still in my nose, my mouth as if he had really been here. I try to push the fear to one side and, slowly, set down the glass and wring my hands together once then twice. 'I remembered something,' I say after a moment.

'Something real?'

'I do not know.'

'Is this a frequent occurrence?'

I hesitate. Does he already know? I decide to tell him the truth. 'Yes.'

The man looks at my hands then turns his head and opens some photocopied files.

My eyes scan the pages on his lap. Data. Information. Facts, real facts, all black and white, clear, no grey, no in-betweens or hidden meanings. The thought of it must centre me, because, before I know it, the information in my head is coming out of my mouth.

'Photocopying machines originated in 1440,' I say, my eyes on the pages in his hands.

He glances up. 'Pardon?'

'Photocopiers—they emerged after Johannes Gutenberg invented the printing press in 1440.' I exhale. My brain simply contains too much information. Sometimes it spills over.

'Gutenberg's Bible,' I continue, 'was the first to be published in volume.' I stop, wait, but the man does not respond. He is staring again, his eyes narrowed, two blue slits. My leg begins to jig as a familiar tightness in my chest spreads. To stop it, I count. One, two, three, four... At five, I look to the window. The muslin curtains billow. The iron bars guard the panes. Below, three buses pass, wheezing, coughing out noise, fumes. I turn and touch the back of my neck where my hairline skims my skull. Sweat trickles past my collar.

'It is warm in here,' I say. 'Is there a fan we can use?'

The man lowers the page. 'I'm told your ability to retain information is second to none.' His eyes narrow. 'Your IQ—it is high.' He consults his papers and looks back to me. 'One hundred and eighty-one.'

I do not move. None of this information is available.

'It's my job to research patients,' he continues, as if reading my mind. He leans forward. 'I know a lot about you.' He pauses. 'For example, you like to religiously record data in your notebook.'

My eyes dart to a cloth bag slung over my chair.

'How do you know about my notebook?'

He stays there, blinking, only sitting back when I shift in my seat. My pulse accelerates.

'It's in your file, of course,' he says finally. He flashes a smile and returns his gaze to his paperwork.

I keep very still, clock ticking, curtains drifting. Is he telling me the truth? His scent, the sweat of his skin, smells of mint, like toothpaste. A hard knot forming in my stomach, I realise the man reminds me of Black Eyes. The thought causes the silent spark in me to ignite again, flashing at me to run far away from here, but if I left now, if I refused to talk, to cooperate, who would that help? Me? Him? I know nothing about this man. Nothing. No details, no facts. I am beginning to wonder if I have made a mistake.

The man sets down his pen and, as he slips his notes under a file to his left, a photograph floats out. I peer down and watch it fall; my breathing almost stops.

It is the head of the priest.

Before he was murdered.

The man crouches and picks up the photograph, the image of the head hanging from his fingers. We watch it, the two of us, bystanders. A breeze picks up from the window and the head swings back and forth. We say nothing. Outside, traffic hums, buses hack up smog. And still the photo sways. The skull, the bones, the flesh. The priest, alive. Not dead. Not splattered in blood and entrails. Not with eyes frozen wide, cold. But living, breathing, warm. I shiver; the man does not flinch.

After a moment, he slips the photograph back into the file, and I let out a long breath. Smoothing down my hair, I watch the man's fingers as they stack paperwork. Long, tanned fingers. And it makes me think: where is he from? Why is he here, in this country? When this meeting was arranged, I did not know what would happen. I am still unsure.

'How does it make you feel, seeing his face?'

The sound of his voice makes me jump a little. 'What do you mean?'

'I mean seeing Father O'Donnell.'

I sit back, press my palms into my lap. 'He is the priest.'

The man tilts his head. 'Did you think otherwise?'

'No.' I tuck a stray hair behind my ear. He is still looking at me. Stop looking at me.

I touch the back of my neck. Damp, clammy.

'Now, I would like to start the interview, formally,' he says, reaching for his Dictaphone. No time for me to object. 'I need you to begin with telling me, out loud, please— in English—your full name, profession, age and place of birth. I also require you to state your original conviction.'

The red record light flashes. The colour causes me to blink, makes me want to squeeze my eyes shut and never open them again. I glance around the room, try to steady my brain with details. There are four Edwardian brick walls, two sash windows, one French-style, one door. I pause. One exit. Only one. The window does not count— we are three floors up. Central London. If I jump, at the speed and trajectory, the probability is that I will break one leg, both shoulder blades and an ankle. I look back to the man. I am tall, athletic. I can run. But, whoever he is, whoever this man claims to be, he may have answers. And I need answers. Because so much has happened to me. And it all needs to end.

I catch sight of my reflection in the window: short dark hair, long neck, brown eyes. A different person looks back at me, suddenly older, more lined, battered by her past. The curtain floats over the glass and the image, like a mirage in a desert, vanishes. I close my eyes for a moment then open them, a random shaft of sunlight from the window making me feel strangely lucid, ready. It is time to talk.

'My name is Dr Maria Martinez Villanueva and I am— was—a Consultant Plastic Surgeon. I am thirty-three years old. Place of birth: Salamanca, Spain.' I pause, gulp a little. 'And I was convicted of the murder of a Catholic priest.'

* * *

A woman next to me tugs at my sleeve.

'Oi,' she says. 'Did you hear me?'

I cannot reply. My head is whirling with shouts and smells and bright blue lights and rails upon rails of iron bars, and no matter how hard I try, no matter how much I tell myself to breathe, to count, focus, I cannot calm down, cannot shake off the seeping nightmare of confusion.

I arrived in a police van. Ten seats, two guards, three passengers. The entire journey I did not move, speak or barely breathe. Now I am here, I tell myself to calm down. My eyes scan the area, land on the tiles, each of them black like the doors, the walls a dirt grey. When I sniff, the air smells of urine and toilet cleaner. A guard stands one metre away from me and behind her lies the main quarter of Gold-mouth Prison. My new home.

There is a renewed tugging at my sleeve. I look down. The woman now has hold of me, her fingers still pinching my jacket like a crab's claw. Her nails are bitten, her skin is cracked like tree bark, and dirt lines track her thin veins.

'Oi. You. I said, what's your name?' She eyes me. 'You foreign or something?'

'I am Spanish. My name is Dr Maria Martinez.' She still pinches me. I don't know what to do. Is she supposed to have hold of my jacket? In desperation, I search for the guard.

The woman lets out a laugh. 'A doctor? Ha!' She re-leases my sleeve and blows me a kiss. I wince; her breath smells of excrement. I pull back my arm and brush out the creases, brush her off me. Away from me. And just when I think she may have given up, she speaks again.

'What the hell has a doctor done to get herself in this place then?'

I open my mouth to ask who she is—that is what I have heard people do—but a guard says move, so we do. There are so many questions in my head, but the new noises, shapes, colours, people—they are too much. For me, they are all too much.

'My name's Michaela,' the woman says as we walk. She tries to look me in the eye. I turn away. 'Michaela Croft,' she continues, 'Mickie to my mates.' She hitches up her T-shirt.

'The name Michaela is Hebrew, meaning *who is like the Lord*. Michael is an archangel of Jewish and Christian scripture,' I say, unable to stop myself, the words shoot-ing out of me.

I expect her to laugh at me, as people do, but when she does not, I steal a glance. She is smiling at her stom-ach where a tattoo of a snake circles her belly button. She catches me staring, drops her shirt and opens her mouth. Her tongue hangs out, revealing three silver studs. She pokes her tongue out some more. I look away.

After walking to the next area, we are instructed to halt. There are still no windows, no visible way out. No escape. The strip lights on the ceiling illuminate the corridor and I count the number of lights, losing myself in the point-less calculations.

'I think you need to move on.'

I jump. There is a middle-aged man standing two me-tres away. His head is tilted, his lips parted. Who is he? He holds my gaze for a moment; then, raking a hand through his hair, strides away. I am about to turn, embarrassed to look at him, when he halts and stares at me again. Yet, this time I do not move, frozen, under a spell. His eyes. They are so brown, so deep that I cannot look away.

'Martinez?' the guard says. 'We're off again. Shift it.'

I crane my head to see if the man is still there, but he is suddenly gone. As though he never existed.

The internal prison building is loud. I fold my arms tight across my chest and keep my head lowered, hoping it will block out my bewilderment. We follow the guard and keep quiet. I try to remain calm, try to speak to myself, reason with myself that I can handle this, that I can cope with this new environment just as much as anyone else, but it is all so unfamiliar, the prison. The constant stench of body odour,

Nikki Owen

the shouting, the sporadic screams. I have to take time to process it, to compute it. None of this is routine.

Michaela taps me on the shoulder. Instinctively, I flinch.

'You've seen him then?' she says.

'Who?'

'The Governor of Goldmouth. That fella just now with the nice eyes and the pricey tan.' She grins. 'Be careful, yeah?' She places her palm on my right bottom cheek. 'I've done time here before, gorgeous. Our Governor, well, he has…a reputation.'

She is still touching me, and I want her to get off me, to leave me alone. I am about slap her arm away when the guard shouts for her to release me.

Michaela licks her teeth then removes her hand. My body slackens. Without speaking, Michaela sniffs, wipes her nose with her palm and walks off.

Lowering my head once more, I make sure I stay well behind her.

Chapter 2

We are taken through to something named The Booking-In Area.

The walls are white. Brown marks are smeared in the crevices between the brickwork and, when I squint, plastic splash panels glisten under the lights. Michaela remains at my side. I do not want her to touch me again.

The guards halt, turn and thrust something to us. It's a forty-page booklet outlining the rules of Goldmouth Prison. It takes me less than a minute to read the whole thing—the TV privileges, the shower procedures, the full body searches, the library book lending guidelines. Timetables, regimes, endless regulations—a ticker tape of instructions. I remember every word, every comma, every picture on the page. Done, I close the file and look to my right. Michaela is stroking the studs on her tongue, pinching each one, wincing then smiling. Sweat pricks my neck. I want to go home.

'You read fast, sweetheart,' she says, leaning into me.

'You remember all that? Shit, I can't remember my own fucking name half the time.'

She pinches her studs again. They could cause problems, get infected. I should tell her. That's what people do, isn't it? Help each other?

'Piercing can cause nerve damage to the tongue, leading to weakness, paralysis and loss of sensation,' I say.

'What the—' The letter 'f' forms on her mouth, but before she can finish, a guard tears the booklet from my hand.

'Hey!'

'Strip,' the guard says.

'Strip what?'

She rolls her eyes. 'Oh, you're a funny one, Martinez. We need you to strip. It's quite simple. We search all inmates on arrival.'

Michaela lets out a snort. The guard turns. 'Enough out of you, Croft, you're next.'

I tap the guard's shoulder. Perhaps I have misunderstood. 'You mean remove my clothes?'

The guard stares at me. 'No, I mean keep them all on.'

'Oh.' I relax a little. 'Okay.'

She shakes her head. 'Of course I mean remove your clothes.'

'But you said...' I stop, rub my forehead, look back at her. 'But it is not routine. Stripping, now—it's not part of my routine.' My stomach starts to churn.

The guard sighs. 'Okay, Martinez. Time for you to move. The last thing I need is you getting clever on me.' She grabs my arm and I go rigid. 'For crying out fucking loud.'

'Please, get off me,' I say.

But she doesn't reply, instead she pushes me to move

and I want to speak, shout, scream, but something tells me I shouldn't, that if I did, that if I punched this guard hard, now, in the face, I may be in trouble.

We walk through two sets of double doors. These ones are metal. Heavy. My pulse quickens, my stomach squirms. All the while the guard stays close. There are two cleaners with buckets and mops up ahead, and when they see us they stop, their mops dripping on the tiles, water and cleaning suds trickling along the cracks, the bubbles wobbling first then popping, one by one, water melting into the grouting, gone forever.

One corner and two more doors, and we arrive at a new room. It is four metres by four metres and very warm. My jacket clings to my skin and my legs shake. I close my eyes. I have to. I need to think, to calm myself. I envision home, Spain. Orange groves, sunshine, mountains. Anything I can think of, anything that will take my mind away from where I am. From what I am.

A cough sounds and my eyes flicker open. There, ahead, is another guard sitting at a table. She coughs again, glances from under her spectacles and frowns. My leg itches from the sweat and heat. I bend down, hitch up my trousers and scratch.

'Stand up.'

She snaps like my mother at the hired help. I stand.

'You're the priest killer,' she says. 'I recognise your face from the paper. Be needing the chapel, will you?' She chuckles. The standing guard behind me joins in.

'I do not go to church,' I say, confused.

She stops laughing. 'No, bet you don't.' She cocks her head. 'You could do with a bit more weight on you. Skinny, pretty thing like you in here?' She whistles and shakes her head. 'Still, nice tan.'

She makes me nervous—her laughs, jeers. I know how those people can be. I pull at the end of my jacket, fingers slippery, my teeth clenched just enough so I can keep quiet, so my thoughts remain in my head. I want to flap my hands so much, but something about this place—this guard—tells me I should not.

The sitting guard opens a file. 'Says here you're Spanish.'

I reply in Castellano.

'English, love. We speak English here.'

'Yes,' I say. 'I am Spanish. Castilian. Can you not hear my accent?'

'This one thinks she's clever.' I turn. The other guard.

'Well, that's all we fucking need,' says sitting guard, 'a bloody know-it-all.' She spoons some sugar into a mug on the table. I suddenly realise I have had nothing to drink for hours.

'I would like some water.'

But she ignores me. 'Martinez, you need to do as we tell you,' she says, stirring the mug.

She has heaped in four mounds of sugar. I look at her stomach. Rounded. This is not healthy. Before I can prevent it, a diagnosis drops out of my mouth, babbling like a torrent of water through a brook.

'You have too much weight on your middle,' I say, the words flowing, urgent. 'This puts you at a higher than average risk of cardiac disease. If you continue to take sugar in your...' I pause. 'I assume that is tea? Then you will increase your risk of heart disease, as well as that of type two diabetes.' I pause, catch my breath.

The guard holds her spoon mid-air.

'Told you,' says standing guard.

'Strip,' says sitting guard after a moment. 'We need you to strip, smart arse.'

But I cannot. I cannot strip. Not here. Not now. My heart picks up speed, my eyes dart around the room, frenzied, a primitive voice inside me swelling, urging me to curl up into a ball, protect myself.

'You have to remove your clothes,' sitting guard says nonchalantly. She blows on her tea. 'It's a requirement for all new arrivals at Goldmouth.' She sips. 'We need to search you. Now.'

Panic—I can feel it. My heartbeat. My pulse. Quickly, I search for a focus and settle on sitting guard's face. Acne scars puncture her chin, there are dark circles under her eyes, and on her cheeks, eight thread lines criss-cross a ruddy complexion. 'Do you consume alcoholic beverages?' I blurt.

'What?'

Perhaps she did not hear. Many people appear deaf to me when they are not. 'Do you consume alcoholic beverages?' I repeat.

She smiles at standing guard. 'Is she for real?'

'Of course I am real. See?' I point to myself. 'I am standing right here.'

Sitting guard shakes her head. 'For fuck's sake.' She exhales. 'Strip.' Then she sips her drink again.

My chest tightens and my palms pool with sweat. 'I cannot strip,' I say after a moment, my voice quiet, the sound of it teetering on the edge of sanity. 'It is not bedtime, not shower time or time for sex.'

Sitting guard spurts out a mouthful of tea. 'Fuck.' Taking a tissue from her pocket, she wipes her face. 'Jesus. Look,' she says, scrunching up the tissue, 'I am going to tell you one more time, Martinez. You need to take your clothes off now so we can search you.' She pauses. 'After that, I will have no choice but to carry out the strip myself. Then you'll be placed in the segregation unit as a penalty.'

She folds her arms and waits.

I wipe my cheek. 'But…but it is not time to strip.' I swivel to the other guard, begging. 'Please, tell her. It is not time.'

But the guard simply rolls her eyes, presses a blue button by an intercom and waits. No one speaks, no one moves. A few more tears break out, trespassing across my face, down past my chin, stinging my skin, alien to me, unknown. I do not cry, not often. Not me, not with my brain wired as it is; I am strong, hardened, weathered. So why now, why here? Is it this place, this prison? One hour in and already it is changing me. I touch my scalp, feel my hair, fingertips absorbing the heat from my head. I am real, I exist, but I do not feel it. Do not feel anything of myself.

Shouts from somewhere drift in then out, their sound vibrating like a buzzer in my ears. I try to stay steady, to think of home, of my father, his open arms. The way he would pick me up if I was hurt. I inhale, try to recollect his scent: cigars, cologne, fountain pen ink. His chest, his wide chest where I would lay my head as his arms encircled me, the heat of his torso keeping me safe, safe from everything out there, from the world, from the merry-go-round of confusion, of social games, interactions, dos and don'ts. And then he was gone. My papa, my haven, he was gone—

Bang. The door slams open. We all look up. A third guard enters and nods to the other two. The three of them walk to my side.

'No!' I scream, shocked at my voice: wild and erratic.

They stop. My chest heaves, my mouth gulps in air. Sitting guard's eyes are narrowed and she is tapping her foot.

She turns to her colleague. 'We're going to have to hold this one down.'

* * *

Time has passed, but I cannot be sure how much.

The room is dark, a single light flashing. I look down: I am sitting on a plastic chair. I gulp in air, touch my chest. The material, my clothes: they are different. Someone has put me in a grey polyester jumpsuit. I look around me, frantic. Where are my clothes? My blouse? My Armani trousers? I draw in a sharp breath and suddenly remember. The strip search. My stomach flips, churns, the vomit flying up so fast that I have to slap my palm to my mouth to keep it in. Their hands. Their hands were all over me. Cold, rubbery, damp. They touched me, the guards, probed me, invaded me. I said they could not do it, that it was not allowed, to cut my clothes off like that, but they did it anyway. Like I didn't have a voice, like I didn't matter. They told me to squat, naked, to cough. They crouched under me and watched for anything to come out... They...

A screech rips from my mouth. I stand, stumble back against the wall, the bricks damp and wet beneath my fingertips. This must be the segregation cell. They put me in segregation. But they can't do this! Not to me. Do they not

know? Do they not understand? I turn to the wall, smacking
my forehead on it, once, twice, the impact of the pain jolting
me into reality, calming me. Slowly, I start to steady myself when I feel something, something etched into the masonry. Turning, I peer down, squint in the blinking lights,
feel with my fingers. There, scratched deep into the brickwork, is a cross.

A shout roars from outside. I jump. There is another
shout followed by banging, ripping from the right, loud,
like a constant thudding. Maybe someone is coming. I run
to the door and try to see something, anything. The banging reaches a crescendo then dies.

I press my lips to the slit. 'Hello?' I wait. Nothing. 'Hello?'

'Go away!' a voice screams. 'Go away! Go away!'

The yelling smashes against my head like a hammer—
slam, slam, slam. I want it to stop but it won't, it simply
carries on and on until I can't take it any more. My hands
rake through my hair, pull at it, claw it. I cannot do this,
cannot be here. I need my routine. I want to go home, see
my bare feet running through the grass along the hills back
to my villa, the sun fat and low. I want to sprint the last leg
to the courtyard where the paella stove is fired. Garlic, saf-
fron, clams and mussels, the hot flesh melting in my mouth,
bubbling, evaporating. That is what I want. Not this. Not
here. Think. What would Papa tell me to do?

Numbers. That is it. Think of numbers. I shut my eyes,
attempt to let digits, calculations, dates, mathematical
theories—anything—run through my head. After a moment, it begins to work. My breathing slows, muscles
soften, my brain resting a little, enough for something to
walk into my head: an algorithm. I hesitate at first, keep

my eyes shut. It seems familiar, the formula, yet strange all at once. I scan the algorithm, track it, try to understand why I should even think of it, but nothing. No clue. No sign. Which means it's happened again. Unknown data. Data has come to me, data I do not recall ever learning, yet still it appears, like a familiar face in the window, a footprint in the snow. I have always written the calculations down when they emerge, these numbers, these codes and unusual patterns, have always recorded them obsessively, compulsively. But now what? I have no notepad, have no pen, and without inscribing them, without seeing the data in black and white, will it exist? Will it be real?

More shouting erupts and my eyes fly open. There are so many voices. So loud. Too loud for me, for *someone like me*. I clamp my hands to my ears. My head throbs. Images swirl around my mind. My mother, father, priests, churches, strangers. They all blur into one. And then, suddenly an illusion, just one, on its own, walks into my mind: my father in the attic. And then I see Papa getting into his Jaguar, waving to me as he accelerates off, my brother, Ramon, by my side, a wrench in his hand. There is no sound, just pictures, images. My breathing becomes quick, shallow. Am I remembering something or is it simply a fleeting dream? I close my eyes, try to will the image back into my brain, but it won't come, stubborn, callous.

There is more banging—harder and louder this time. I tap my finger against my thigh over and over. Papa, where are you? What happened to you? If only I had stayed in Spain, then none of this would have happened. No murders. No blood.

I clutch my skull. The noise is drowning me, consuming

me. The banging. Make the banging stop. Please, someone, make it stop. Papa? I am sorry. I am so, so sorry.

My breathing now is so fast that I cannot get enough oxygen. So I try cupping my hands around my mouth to steady the flow, yet the shouting outside rises, a tipping point, making me panic even more. I force myself to stand, to be still, but it does not work. I can hear guards. They are near. Footsteps. They are yelling for calm, but it makes no difference. The shouts still sound. My body still shakes.

And that is when I hear a voice say, 'Help me,' and I am shocked to realise it is mine. I scramble back, shoving myself into the wall, but it does no good.

The cell turns black.

Chapter 3

When I finish talking, I check the clock by the door:
09.31 hours.

How did time move so quickly? I dab my forehead, shift
in my seat. I feel disorientated, out of place like a cat suddenly finding itself in the middle of the ocean. Something
must be happening to me again, some change or some type
of transition. But what?

The man checks his Dictaphone. He remains silent and
places a finger on his earlobe. Sometimes, I have noticed,
while I talk, he pulls at his ear. He was doing it just now
when I was telling him about the strip search. It is only a
small tug, a quick scratch, but still it is there. I have tried to
detect a pattern in his actions, perhaps a timed repetition,
but no, nothing. I shake my head. Maybe being in this room
is affecting my senses. Or maybe I am simply searching
for something that is not there. I tap my foot, check my bag
is there, my notebook, my pen. I can't trust my thoughts

any more, my deductions, and yet I do not know why, not fully. And it scares me.

'Maria, before your conviction, you came to the UK on a secondment, correct?'

I clear my throat, sit up straight. 'Yes. I was seconded to St James's Hospital, West London, on a one-year consultancy in plastic surgery.'

'And where did you work in Spain?'

'At the Hospital Universitario San Augustin in Salamanca. I worked on reconstructive surgery mainly developing…' I stop. Why does he remain so calm when I speak, ghost-like almost, an apparition? My throat constricts, jaw locks.

'And why did you come here, to London?'

'I told you,' I say, a steel in my voice that I never intended, 'I was seconded.'

He smiles, just a little, like a single dash of colour from a paintbrush. 'I know that, Maria. What I mean is, why, specifically, London? Someone of your talent? You could have gone anywhere. I hear your skills are in demand. But you chose here. So, I ask again: why? Or, shall I say, for who?'

My foot taps faster. Does he know about him? About how he betrayed me? I glance at the door; it is locked.

'Maria?'

'I…' My voice trembles, lets me down. This man, sitting opposite, he said he is here to help me. Can he? Do I risk letting him in?

'I was looking for someone,' I say after a short while.

He immediately straightens up. 'Who? Who were you looking for?'

'A priest.'

'The one you were convicted of killing?'

The curtains swell, the morning breeze draughting in a whisper of a memory. Aromas. Incense. Sacred bread, holy wine. The comforting smell of a wood-burning stove, the dim lights of a vestry, a stone corridor, confessional boxes. The inner sanctum of Catholicism.

'Maria,' the man says, 'can you answer my—'

'It wasn't the dead priest I came looking for.'

The man holds my gaze. It is unbearable for me, the eye contact, makes my hands grip the seat, makes my throat dry up, but still he stays fixed on me, like a missile locked to its target.

'Then who?' he says finally, his eyes, at last, disengaging enough for me to look away.

'Father Reznik,' I say, my voice barely audible. 'I took the London secondment because I was looking for Father Reznik. Mama said he may have moved here, but she wasn't sure. I needed answers.' I pause. 'I needed to find him.'

There is a flipping of a page. 'And Father Reznik was your family priest, a Slovakian, correct?'

I look up. How does he know all this? 'Yes.'

'And your mother knew him?'

Again I answer yes. 'She is Catholic, attends church twice a week, confession also. She said Father Reznik may have had some family in London.'

He nods, writes something down, glancing at me in between words.

'He was my friend. Father Reznik was my friend. And then…events happened. I found out that he…' I stall, touch my neck. The bloodshot whites of his eyes, the sagging pale skin on his jaw, the slight wheeze when he walked.

Even now when I think of him, of what he did, it hurts me. And while I know the man is speaking to me, I barely hear him, barely process what he says, because I can't comprehend what I think is still happening, what is developing right in front of me, in front of the whole world. And they don't even know it, don't even realise what is being done right before their eyes, like they're all wandering the streets blindfolded.

'Maria?' The man lowers his pen. 'This Father Reznik. Are you sure about him?'

I squeeze my fist, concentrate. 'What do you mean?'

He hesitates. 'Are you sure he was your friend?'

A trace of a memory floats in the air, like a drowsiness. I see me, sixteen years old. Father Reznik's drawn, lined face is swaying in front of me as I try to focus on a paper containing codes. Lots of codes. I smile at him, but when I blink, I realise it's not Father Reznik I am looking at. It is the dead priest from the convent. I gasp.

'Maria?' The man's voice hovers somewhere. 'Stay with me. Listen to me.'

I attempt to shake away the confusion. The faces, the blurred, blended shapes swim one more time before me then dive from view. I sit forward, cough. My eyelids flicker.

'What made him your friend, Maria?'

'He was kind to me. He…he would spend time with me when I was young, growing up.' A surge of heat scalds my skin. I swallow a little and loosen my collar, try to push aside the doubt creeping up like ivy inside me.

'What else?'

'He would…listen to me after Papa died, would give me things to do, keep me occupied. I grew up with him, with

Father Reznik. Mama knew him. He gave me problems to solve when I got bored with school. "Too easy for you, school, Maria," he would say. "Too easy." I would visit him every day; even when I was at university I would go home to see him, he would give me complex problems to solve. And then, one day, he just vanished. But sometimes… sometimes I recall…'

'Recall what?'

'Absences,' I say, after a moment, and even as the word comes out, I know it will seem unusual, because just as Father Reznik vanished, so had my memory.

'What sort of absences?'

'Absences of my memory, of what I had done and said.'

'And when did these occur?' the man says, writing everything down.

I hesitate. I know now what Father Reznik really was and what he was doing with me. But what do I tell this man? 'I would often wake up in Father Reznik's office.'

'You had fallen asleep?'

'No, no, I…' I stop. What will happen if I reveal the truth to him now? I opt to stick to the basic facts. 'Yes, I could have fallen asleep.'

The man stares at me. My heart knocks against my chest, my brow glistens. Did he believe me?

'Tell me, Maria,' he says, pen in his mouth, 'are you scared of losing people?'

'Yes,' I hear myself say. A tear escapes. I touch it, surprised. My papa's face appears in my mind. His dark, full hair, his warm smile. I didn't realise all this had affected me so much.

The man's eyes flicker downwards then finally rest on

my face. 'Would it help you if I told you I have lost a brother?'

I frown. 'How? Where did he go? How did…?' I falter, a familiar slap of realisation. He didn't lose track of his brother. His brother died.

He hands me a tissue. 'Here.'

I take it, wipe my eyes.

'He was killed in the 9/11 bombings,' the man continues. 'He was an investment banker, worked on the hundredth floor of the first tower.' He pauses, his body strangely stiffening, at odds with his so far relaxed poise. 'Everything changed that day.' He inhales one long, hard breath. 'I still search for his face in crowds now.' He stops, looks down. 'Sometimes, our desire to see someone again burns so much that we convince ourselves they still exist.' He locks his eyes now on mine, his body charged. 'Or we project their personality onto another person.' He tilts his head. 'Like with your priest.'

His words hang in the air like a morning mist over a river. We sit, the two of us, in a soup of silence, of faces, of contorted, clouded memories. I think of the murdered priest, of Father Reznik. Sometimes I cannot see where one begins and the other ends.

Like clouds parting in the blue sky, the man's body softens. He is back to normal, whatever normal is. He clears his throat, and, consulting his notes, tilts his head. 'Maria, I want you tell me: when were you diagnosed with Asperger's?'

I do not want to answer him. He is smiling, but it is different this time, and I cannot decipher it. Is he pretending to be nice? Is it because he likes me? Is that why he told me about his brother? I let out a breath; I have no idea. 'I was diagnosed at the age of eight,' I concede finally.

His smile drops. 'Thank you.' He immediately writes some notes. The air blows cold and I feel strangely unsteady. Why am I uncomfortable with this man? It's as if he could be a friend to me one minute, a dangerous foe the next. And then it comes to me.

'Your name!' I say, pleased with myself. 'I do not know your name. What is it?'

His pen hovers mid-air, an unexpected slice of a scowl lingering on his lips. 'I think you know it, Maria.'

I shake my head. 'No. The service could not tell me who would be here today as it was a last-minute appointment.'

'I think you are mistaken, Maria, but I'll tell you. Again. It's Kurt. My name is Kurt.'

Kurt. I had not been told. I am certain of this. Certain. I knew the meeting would be with one of their staff, of course. The service issued a date, a time, place. But as it was a late booking, interviewer names were unconfirmed. They said that. They did. My memory is not lying. I did not want to do it at first, to be here, but he said it would do me good. I wanted to believe him. But, after everything that has happened, it is hard to trust anyone any more.

A knock sounds on the door and a woman enters. Leather jacket, bobbed brown head of hair. She glances at Kurt and sets down a tray of coffee.

'Who are you?' I demand. When she does not reply, I say, 'I did not order coffee.'

Continuing to ignore me, the woman nods to Kurt and leaves. He reaches forward and picks up a mug. 'Smells great.'

'Who was she?' But Kurt does not answer. 'Tell me!'

He inhales the steam, the scent of ground coffee beans circling the room. He takes a sip and sighs. 'Damn fine coffee.'

My body feels suddenly drained, my legs tired, my head fuzzy, my brain matter congealed like thick, cold stew. Hesitating, I slowly reach for a cup. The warmth of the coffee vapour instantly rises to my face, stroking my skin. I take a small mouthful.

'Good?'

The hot liquid begins to thaw me, energise me. I drink a little more then lower the cup. 'Your name. It is Kurt.'

He nods, the cup handle linked like a ring to his finger.

'Kurt is a German name, no?'

'Yes,' he says. 'I believe it is German.'

'In German, Kurt means "courageous advice". In English, it means "bold counsel".'

'I read you liked names. Like writing everything in your notebook, the names are an obsession. It's a common trait on the spectrum. Your memory, your ability to retain information,' he says, sitting back, 'is that the Asperger's or something else?'

I go still. Why would he ask me this? Does he know? 'What else would it be?' I say after two seconds.

'You tell me.'

'Why would you ask what else it would be?' I can feel a panic rising. I try taking more coffee and it helps a little, but not much.

'You know it is normal for me to enquire about your Asperger's, about how you can do what you do? I am a therapist. It is my job.'

I look at him and my shoulders drop. I'm tired. Maybe I am inventing a non-existent connection here, conjuring thoughts and conclusions like a magician, plucking them from the air. How would he know what we discovered? The answer is he can't know, so I need to be calm. I drain my coffee and try to concentrate on facts, on solid information to clear my fog.

'What is your family name?' I say.

'You mean surname?' Kurt shakes his head. 'I'm sorry, Maria, I cannot say. Company policy.'

'You are lying.' I set the cup down on the table.

He sighs. 'I do not lie.'

'Everybody lies.'

'Except you, correct? Isn't that what you would say, Maria? I have seen your file, read your details.' He smiles. 'I know all about you.'

We both remain very still. Kurt's eyes are narrowed, but I cannot determine what it means. All I know is that I have a tightening knot in my stomach that will not subside, with a voice in my head telling me again to run.

'I have it in my notes,' he says after a moment, 'that following your blackout in segregation, you received help.'

'Yes,' I say quietly, the recollection of that day painful for me to think about. The room feels suddenly warm. I undo two buttons on my blouse, followed by a third; the fabric flaps against my skin in the morning breeze. I exhale, try to relax.

Kurt coughs.

'What?' I follow his eyeline. My chest. I can see the cotton of my bra.

'Nothing.' Another cough. 'Maria, can you…can you

tell me what help you received following your blackout in segregation?'

I pause. I know now exactly who tried to help me. And why. 'A psychiatrist came to the segregation cell.'

He hits record. 'I want you to tell me about that.'

He stares at me for three seconds. I rebutton my blouse.

* * *

Day must now be night because above my head the strobe lights hum, making me blink over and over, like staring straight at the sun.

I fall back, try to think, but my body throbs, my muscles and skin a sinew of stress. The signs. Normally I recognise them, can quell them, control them, but in here I cannot get a handle on myself, on my thoughts. I force my eyes shut and make myself think of my father. My safe place, my hideout. I inhale, try to imagine the soft apples of his cheeks, how his eyes would crinkle into a smile when he saw me, how he would sweep me into his arms, strong, secure. I open my eyes. My pulse is lowered, my breathing steady, but it is not enough. I need to think. If I remain in segregation I may not survive for long. I have to get out. But how?

I lower myself into the chair, my prison suit clinging to my skin, a stench of body odour jeering me. I am a mess. I hate to be in this state, out of control, in disarray. Allowing my body to slacken, I let my arm hang behind me. My fingers trace the cross, etched into the wall. I almost smile, because wherever I go, it is there: religion. All the priests, their rules. All of them controlling my mind, dictating life to me and everyone else, to a people, to a country, a government. Franco may have long died in Spain, but the Church will always be there.

I shake my head. Whether I want him to be or not, he is not in here now, the priest—he can't be. So think. I must think if I want to get out of here. This is all just logic. The strip search. The incarceration. The segregation. Isolation. Fear. Panic.

I sit forward. Panic. Could that be it?

I glance at the door. Thick metal. Locked. Only one way out. Standing, I examine the room. Small. Three metres by five metres. One plastic chair: green, no armrest. One bed: mattress, no covers. Floor: rubber, bare. Walls: brick, half plastered in gunmetal grey.

I begin with my breathing; I draw in quick, sharp breaths, forcing myself to hyperventilate. It takes just over one minute, but, finally, it is done. My head swells and I try to ignore the dread in my stomach spreading through my body. I move to the cell door and bang hard, but my effort is lost in a sudden outbreak of shouts from the inmates across the walkway. I wince at the noise, count to ten, make a fist, bang again. This time: success. A guard shouts my name; she is coming over. I estimate it will take her seven seconds to reach my cell. I count. One, two, three, four. At five, I thrust my fingers down my throat. On seven, the window shutter opens above my head and a guard peers through.

'Oh, shit!'

I vomit. My lunch splatters the floor.

A bolt unlocks. I count to three. One—two—three. I stumble, clutch my chest.

When the guard bursts in, she halts and mutters a swear word under her breath.

'Martinez? You all right?'

I groan. Another guard enters. 'Leave her! She's bloody well fine.'

The guard by my side hesitates.

'Come on!' shouts the other.

My chance is slipping away. 'Help,' I croak, retching.

'I'm sorry,' crouching guard says, 'but I think you are—'

I vomit. It sprays all over the floor, over the guard.

'Oh, fuck.'

I mumble some words, but sick is lodged in my throat and it sounds as if I am choking.

'Get a doctor!' the guard shouts to her colleague. 'Now!'

Chapter 4

The guard props me up against the wall. The brick is cold on my skin.

'Is this cell five?'

There is a woman blocking the light by the cell door. She wears no uniform, has no baton.

The guard scowls at her. 'Who the hell are you?'

The woman steps forward. Blonde hair snakes in a ponytail down her back. 'I'm Dr Andersson,' she says, her voice clipped, plum, like a newsreader. 'Lauren Andersson, how do you do.' She extends a neat little hand; the guard stands, ignores it.

Dropping her arm, Dr Andersson looks at me. 'She needs to be out of here. Now.'

'Hang on a minute,' says the guard. 'Who the hell put you in charge? I only want you to check her over.'

'I'm responsible for the physical and psychiatric well-being of the inmates here,' Dr Andersson says, side-stepping the vomit. She points to me. 'This woman is Maria

Martinez.' She folds her arms. 'And she has been assigned to me.'

'Since when?'

'Since today.' She pushes past the guard, crouches down and takes my wrist. She looks to her watch, checks my pulse, releases my arm. 'This inmate's pulse is up. Get her out. Now.' When the guard does nothing, Dr Andersson stands, her neck taut, voice raised. 'I said, now.'

I am hauled up under the arms by two guards. Dr Andersson informs them that I am, under no circumstances, to be returned to the segregation cell.

'I have the full backing of the Governor,' she says. 'Do you understand?'

The guards nod.

'Good. Take her to my office.'

* * *

'So, how are you feeling?'

I don't know how to answer the question. I am in Dr Andersson's office. She is sitting at her desk, staring at me. The room is cool, the light low. My pulse has dropped, but still my muscles tense, my fists clench. Everything is disorientating me.

Dr Andersson crosses her legs and her hem slips above her knee. Her cheeks are pink and she has eyes shaped like over-sized almonds.

'My throat is sore,' I say, touching my neck, avoiding eye contact.

'That is to be expected, given the vomiting.' She swivels to her right and picks up a blood pressure monitor. She opens the strap. 'Can you roll up your sleeve?'

'Why?'

'Blood pressure. You know. Routine.'

I hesitate, then slowly pull up the arm of my jumpsuit to find an apple-sized bruise. I gasp.

'You did that in the cell?'

'I think so. I do not remember.'

She peers at it, then after slipping the strap around my bicep, begins pumping the pressure valve. The sound of wheezing fills the air.

'That was a panic attack you had just now,' she says, watching the valve. 'Do you have them often?'

'Yes.' I watch the dial turn, try to breathe, remain clam. 'You can stop now.'

Dr Andersson pauses then deflates the pressure valve and unstraps the band. 'Your blood pressure is slightly high.'

I rub my arm were the strap has been. What is happening to my body?

Dr Andersson folds the monitor kit and sets it on a table to her left. 'Do you have a headache?'

'Yes.'

'Front or b—'

'Front.'

'Light-headedness?'

I nod.

She picks up a notepad and pen. 'Dizziness?'

I swallow. 'All the symptoms of anxiety. Yes.'

I don't want to believe it, but it has to be true. My high blood pressure means I am stressed. In here, in this prison. Anxiety. Worry. Trauma. None of them are good for me. But I do not know what to do, don't know how to handle the feelings, how to curb them from taking over.

As Dr Andersson writes something down, I distract my thoughts by scanning the room. Boxes sit unpacked in the corner, medical books teeter, stacked next to her desk. There are no personal pictures on her table, no certificates on the wall.

'Maria? Are you okay?'

I look down at myself. I am rocking. I had not even realised.

'Here. Drink some water.' She holds out a plastic cup.

I take it and sip. The water cools my throat.

'So, do you want to tell me what happened in there, in the segregation cell?'

'You already know. I had a panic attack.' I put the cup on the desk, my heart rate rising again. Maybe if I change the subject. 'You said in the cell that you are a psychiatrist.'

'Oh, right, yes. That's correct. I studied medicine at the University of Stockholm then specialised in psychiatry at King's College, London.'

'In what year did you qualify?'

She breathes out. 'Look, Maria, I would love to give you details on my entire professional history, but to be frank—'

'But I need you to tell me,' I say, my voice rising. 'It helps me to focus. The details, facts, they—'

'But to be frank,' she continues, louder, as if I hadn't spoken, 'that's not what we're here for. We are here to talk about you. To help you. You just had a major panic attack back there. Your blood pressure is up. You are experiencing classic symptoms of anxiety. So why don't you let me help to calm you down, see how you are and guide you through all this, hmmm?'

'Are you Swedish?'

She shakes her head. 'Sorry?'

'Your name. Andersson. It is Swedish.'

A sigh. 'Look, Maria, can we—'

'Lauren is a French name meaning "crowned with laurel",' I say at speed, desperate to cling on to any detail I can. 'It has a Latin root that means "bay" or "laurel plant". Lauren is the feminine form of the male name Laurence. In 1945, the name Lauren appeared for the first time in the top one thousand baby names in the United States.'

Dr Andersson stares at me. 'Maria,' she says after a moment, 'have you ever talked to anyone about your Asperger's?'

'Why do you ask?'

She reaches to her desk and opens a file. My name is on the cover. 'Your father,' she says, opening the folder. 'He died when you were ten. Correct?'

That stops me immediately. I swallow, nod.

'How?'

'Why do you want to know?'

She smiles. 'Because I am your therapist here. And I need to know.'

I dart my eyes around the room. 'You are new?'

'Yes.'

My gaze settles on the half-open boxes. I pick out Dr Andersson's name scrawled in black ink on the side and concentrate on it, so that when I speak about him, when the pain of the memory hits, it won't be as hard. 'It was a car accident in Spain,' I say, eyes dead ahead. 'Papa died in a car accident. He was returning from work. He was a prosecution lawyer.'

'Maria, can you look at me?'

'No.' I am scared to. If I make eye contact, I may scream.

'Okay. Okay.' A quick clear of the throat. 'Do you miss him, your father?'

I pull at a strand of hair by my ear. 'Yes. Of course.'

She notes something down. 'And how are you coping so far in prison with your Asperger's?'

At this, I divert my attention to Dr Andersson's watch. It is a TAG Heuer, loud tick. I can hear it in my head louder than I should. 'My brain is making faster connections here.' I stop. Everything is faster in this prison, in my head. I feel my arm where the blood pressure monitor squeezed my veins. The anxiety, the trauma—they must be the causes, the reasons why I feel different here. My head and my body are responding, trying to protect me. I think. The speed at which I could read the prison rules, suddenly recalling the algorithm in the segregation cell— it was all quicker, clearer. I have to write it down. Now. 'I need a notepad and pen.'

'Why?'

I pause. How do I describe it to her? How do I tell her that codes, numbers, data simply enter my head, procedures on how to complete tasks sauntering into my brain as if they own it. 'I like to write information down, that is all.'

She suddenly sits forward. 'Is that your Asperger's?' But before I can even reply, she is talking again. 'You said your brain is making faster connections here.'

I clear my throat. 'Yes.'

'And is that normal?'

'No.'

'Can you tell me about it?' When I do not respond, she says, 'I can get you that notepad and pen.'

I look at her. Is she sincere? Is she on my side? I need that writing book, need to get this information out, like an itch that needs scratching. What choice, right now, do I have? I scan the room. There is a laptop on her desk. I stand and, leaning forward, pick it up.

'Do you have something to unscrew this?'

Dr Andersson hesitates then, without speaking, opens a drawer and hands me a screwdriver. I unclip the back of the laptop and dismantle it. When all the insides of the laptop are spread out on the desk, I look up. 'Time me on your watch.'

'What?'

I point to her wrist. 'Your watch. It has a stop clock function. I am going to reassemble this computer. Time me.'

She pauses, then slowly takes off her watch and lays it on the table.

Ignoring the intensity of her stare, I begin to reassemble the laptop. My fingers fly, putting everything back together. It is easy, like adding one to one, or drawing a circle on a piece of paper. Once each item is returned to its position, I pick up the screwdriver, replace the pins and secure the cover. I set down the screwdriver and flip over the laptop so it sits on the desk, right side up.

Dr Andersson clicks her watch and stretches out her hand. Her fingers skim the edge of the laptop.

'What was my time?' I ask.

'Hmmm? Oh, thirty-seven seconds.' Her eyes are still on the laptop. She looks to me, then drifts her gaze to the shelf above my head. 'Try this,' she says and, standing, reaches to the shelf and hands me something.

I take it. A Rubik's Cube.

'Can you do it?'

I turn the cube in my hand, study the colours. The red stands out more than the others, so much so that I have to squint.

'How fast can you solve it?'

I hold up the cube. Its colours are all mixed up. 'Press your stopwatch.'

She touches the button and I start. Swift. Skilled. I twist the sides, study each move, each turn until, just like that, the colours match. I bang it down on the desk, hardly a ripple in my breath.

Dr Andersson checks her watch but says nothing.

'What was my time?'

She looks up yet still does not speak.

'In 2011 at the Melbourne Winter Open Competition,' I say, 'the Rubik's Cube record was set at 5.66 seconds. So that means—'

'You did it in 4.62.'

I go still. I have never done it so quickly before. Four point six two seconds. My hand-to-eye coordination is accelerating, but why? How? I hold up my hands, study my fingers, blink at them as if they were precious diamonds, sparkling jewels.

Dr Andersson taps her chin. 'That speed, that really is quite remarkable.' She picks up a pen. 'You have a high IQ, correct?'

I continue to stare at my hands. 'Yes.'

'Photographic memory?'

'Yes.' My hands return to my lap. I need to tap my thumb a little, let out the stress.

'How are you at spotting patterns?'

'Very good. A family priest used to help me when I was a little younger.'

'A priest? Goodness.' She sets down her pen, slips one leg over the other. 'Okay, Maria, here's what I think: it is possible the prison environment is affecting your Asperger's. It certainly wouldn't be the first time. All the sights, sounds, smells for your brain to process. Asperger's is thought to be a result of widespread irregularity in the brain, a neurodevelopmental anomaly that could be controlled by environmental influences. There was a recent study in the US on it. Perhaps that is what we are seeing here with you.'

I think about this. 'Prison is modifying my brain?'

'In an accelerated fashion, yes. Maybe. But not modifying per se—that implies curtailing you. Let's just say affecting your mind, hmm?'

I touch my head where my brain sits, my modified, neurodevelopmentally affected brain. There are times when I detest it, being me, my head, my neuro issues. Hate it. Locked into myself. Jailed by my own white and grey matter.

Dr Andersson swings her chair towards a cupboard behind her and opens the door. I rake my hands through my hair, scratching my scalp deliberately—my penance.

'Maria, I just need to take some blood samples now.'

I drop my hands. My internal alarm bells ring. 'Why do you require bloods?'

She hangs her head to the side. 'Oh, just routine.'

'But you are a psychiatrist…not a medic.'

She shuts the cupboard and faces the table. 'I have a remit to monitor patients.' She sets out five tubes and a blood-work bag already labelled with my name and prison number.

'But I am an inmate, not a patient.' I start to feel uneasy, agitated. I scratch the desk with my nail. 'What tests are you sending to pathology?'

She unpeels the syringe wrapping. 'I am sending a full blood count.' She unwraps the additional four vials and picks up the one already loaded with the needle. 'Okay?'

'No.' I shake my head, scratch harder. 'No. My blood work is normal. And a full blood count request does not require five tubes of blood.' I scrape the wood of the desk again and again. This is not routine. Over and over in my head, I repeat: *This is not routine.*

Dr Andersson lets out a sigh. 'Look, Maria, I'm sure your blood work is normal. I'm sure it will come back fine. You are a doctor. A medical doctor.' She says the word 'medical' slowly. 'But you are here now. In Goldmouth. In prison. And in prison, there are different rules. And the rule, right now, is that I have to take blood. From you. Today.' She pauses, softens. 'I know it is a change for you, *not routine*, shall we say, being here. I understand your brain functions differently. And I know that is a struggle for you at times. But this is the way it has to be.'

I say nothing. The phrase, *This is not routine*, laps around my mind like a motorcycle with the accelerator permanently down, engine screeching, rubber tyres burning. I can't stop it.

Dr Andersson bites her lip. 'Maria, it's okay. Trust me.'
This is not routine. This is not routine.

'You've been through a lot,' she continues. 'Let me take

the blood now. I have scheduled another appointment for you with myself and the Governor. All routine.'

The monologue in my head pauses, the engines stall. She said 'routine'.

'See?' Dr Andersson says, nodding.

Slowly, I withdraw my hand from scratching. 'This…this is a routine here, in prison?' I say, gesturing to the needles.

'Of course. And, with your Asperger's, I have instructed the Governor that, in my professional opinion, you require extra assistance from me, to help with your need for routine.' She smiles, but it doesn't reach her eyes. 'He has asked to meet you.'

'When?'

'Tomorrow. Is that okay?'

She has no certificates on the walls, no university degrees. As if she is not even certified to practice. It does not seem right, somehow. Yet, nothing seems right any more. Nothing makes sense. I rub my forehead, try to wipe away the confusion.

'Maria?'

I point again to the needle, attempt to act like a normal person. 'This is routine, you are certain?'

'Yes.'

'And you will get me a notebook and pen?'

She opens a drawer, takes out a fresh pad and pen. 'There you go.'

My eyes go wide at the sight and I snatch them, hungry to hold them. Only when I have the items do I allow myself to exhale, my whole body loosening, limbs, bones tired, worn out, and I realise there, in the room, that I haven't slept in forty-eight hours. Maybe routine is what I need.

A routine and my writing. Maybe then I can begin to feel some semblance of humanity inside me, rather than some half-wild, chained-up animal. I roll up my sleeve and hold out my arm.

'Thank you,' Dr Andersson says.

Sitting forward and with a slash of a smile on her lily-white face, she taps my vein. The needle pierces my skin and I watch, weary, limp, as my blood floods into the vial.

Chapter 5

Kurt laces his fingers together. 'So you are saying you simply took the laptop apart and put it back together?'

I have told Kurt everything, but he won't move on from this. I can feel my body become rigid, angry. 'Yes.' I shift once in my seat. 'That is what I said.'

He pauses. 'And that is the truth?'

'Yes. If I say it, it is true.' I stay still. Does he not believe me? Why is he asking me all these questions about it?

'You know our memories can play tricks on us,' he says after a second. 'What we think we remember cannot always be what actually happened.'

'It happened,' I snap.

He smiles at me, nods, but otherwise does nothing.

I tip back my head. Already, this is too much for me. My muscles ache and my shoulders feel heavy. Why is Kurt questioning what I have told him? Is it a therapist trick? Should I be on guard? Should I talk? I roll my head side to side. The session is tiring for me, the level of concentration, the social interactions—all exhausting. I flip my skull up and glance over to the window. The sun is sprinkled in a sugar-spin of clouds, and from the street below there is a shrill of laughter, the distant clink of glasses. People happy, living regular lives.

'Maria?'

I turn from the window. 'What?'

'This meeting with the Governor, the one Dr Andersson mentioned. You did not know, prior to then, that you were to meet him?'

I pause. 'No.'

'Can you expand on that?'

I think for a moment. 'No.'

He holds my gaze and I feel I want to squirm under the glare, unable to bear it. 'What sort of things did he talk with you about, the Governor?'

I keep my eyes lowered. 'The Governor introduced himself,' I say. I smooth down my trousers twice. 'He talked to me about why I was there, about the daily prison routine, the earned privilege scheme.'

'And what else, Maria?'

I look up now. He is too inquisitive; I cannot tell him everything. Not yet. 'Why do you want to know?'

He sighs. 'Maria, I am your therapist. I ask questions. It is what I do.' His eyes flicker to the corner of the room. It is only for a split second, but I see it.

'Is there something there?' I say, twisting my torso to look.

'No. It's nothing.'

I watch him. His legs are crossed, his back is straight. In control.

'Maria?'

'What?'

'I would like you to tell me about it now.'

'Tell you about what?'

'About your meeting with the Governor.'

He reaches for a glass of water and that is when I pin-point it: he is always in control. So why does his control make me nervous?

'Maria,' Kurt says, suddenly leaning in towards me so close that I can feel the warmth of his breath on my face, like the soft bristle of a brush. 'Time to talk.'

* * *

I have a new cell.

It is in the regular section of the prison and it smells of cabbage and faeces. The source of the smell is the metal-rimmed toilet in the corner. There is no door, no screen. I stare at the cistern and the washbasin standing beside it. Dirty, grimy, vomit-inducing. The stench of urine hangs heavy in the air, impregnating it, penetrating every molecule, every tiny atom.

It is too much for me to process, the reality that I will have no privacy, ever, that it is all gone, my freedom vanished, like the pop of a bubble in the air. I close my eyes and try to think of Salamanca, think of the river, of eating long hot churros from the stand just off the main square, the scalding doughnut mixture melting in my mouth, the sugar dusting my lips, chin, cheeks. I remember how, on returning home with frosting around my mouth, my father would laugh—and my mother would march me to the sink and scrub me clean before she took me to church. To Father Reznik.

I open my eyes, and a guard enters. She is long like a rake, hair like tiny thorns. She informs me of my imminent therapy appointment with Dr Andersson and instructs me to follow her straight away. Not tomorrow, not in a minute: now. She repeats the instructions again and so, wondering perhaps if she thinks I don't understand, I tell her that I know what the word 'now' means. She tells me to, 'Shut the fuck up,' then orders me to move out. I have to be escorted there, to Dr Andersson's office. In prison, the guard barks; no one can be trusted.

The walk to Dr Andersson's office affords me my first real look at Goldmouth Prison. The noise. The loud, loud noise. It is too much, on the cliff edge of unbearable. It is only the guard growling at me to, 'Shift it,' that prevents me from moaning over and over with hands on my ears, curled up like a foetus in the corner. I want to turn into a ball and block it all out. I am scared in here, in this place of loud, screeching sounds. The guard strides ahead and I force myself, will myself, to just keep going without doing what I usually do, because in here, I know they won't understand. Nobody ever does.

I subtly sniff the air, detecting the smells as we walk. Sweat. Faeces. More urine. The scent of cheap perfume. Above me, arms dangle from metal rails, hanging, swinging like monkeys from a tree, around them animals pacing everywhere like lions and tigers, the predators, the purveyors of their territory. Gum is chewed like bark, whistles are called out like the howls of wolves. Faces peer down. Mouths snarl. Teeth and stomachs are all bared. The only similarity between me and the other inmates is that we are all convicts. All marked: Guilty.

The guard takes me across a flaking mezzanine floor, suspended one storey up from the ground. I count the levels. There are four floors to this prison, all housing forty cells, each with two inmates. That is eighty multiplied by four, equalling three hundred and twenty inmates. Three hundred and twenty women with hormones. All using toilets with no doors.

Once at Dr Andersson's office, I am instructed to wait. The guard stands by my side, glaring, eyes like slits that make me nervous. I tap my foot in response; she barks at me to stop. I scan the area and see that rooms branch off from this corridor, door upon door stretching out every way, as far as my eye can see, strong, black doors, menacing, like ground soldiers, troops on watch. In the midst of it all is one door different to the rest, red, polished. It stands out, more refined, more elegant than the others. The plaque on it is partially obscured by the glare from the strip lights, but I can just read the first line: *Dr Balthazar*.

To my left, Dr Andersson's door opens.

'Ah, Maria.' Dr Andersson is standing in the doorway. Her hair hangs down past her shoulders, glistening like a lake, her make-up in place, lips a slice of crimson. So different to me, my bare sallow skin, my shorn hacked-at hair, bitten nails. I feel suddenly small, insignificant. Forgotten. I touch my cheek.

'Glad to see you looking better,' she says.

'I do not look better,' I answer instantly. 'I look worse than ever.' The guard keeps her stare on me. Dr Andersson supplies me with a brief smile.

'So, Maria,' Dr Andersson continues, clearing her throat, taking a few heeled steps, 'we have our meeting now. Could you come with me?' She nods to the guard and the three of us proceed through the corridor.

We arrive at the red door and halt. Up close it almost gleams, the polished finish reflecting like a mirror. I catch sight of myself and gasp. Eyes black with dark circles, mouth downturned, lined, hair matted to my head, shoulders dropped. Already the prison is beating me, changing me, as if the priest's death is slowly scratching its rigor mortis into my skin.

A buzzer sounds. I jump.

Dr Andersson pushes open the door. 'Okay, we can go in now, Maria. We are meeting Dr Ochoa—the Governor.'

I glimpse at the plaque on the door now fully visible: Dr Balthazar Ochoa. I mull the name over. *Ochoa*. It means 'wolf'. It is a Spanish name—Basque.

Which means the Governor somehow, in some connection, is Spanish.

Like me.

* * *

When we enter the office, the man from the corridor when I first arrived at Goldmouth is sitting at the desk.

I immediately halt, surprised. 'What are you doing here?'

'Maria,' Dr Andersson whispers, 'this is the Governor.'

I look at Dr Andersson then back to the man behind the table. 'You are Governor Ochoa?'

He stands, looms over the table, a shadow casting across it. Up closer, he is taller, older, his skin more tanned. Two strips of grey bookend his ears and, when he smiles, wrinkles fan out from his eyes, soft, worn. And his eyes, they are deep brown, so dark that they take my breath away, remind me of something, of someone, some… I step back, once, twice. My heart shouts, perspiration pricks my palms. Why do I feel unexpectedly nervous, jittery almost?

'Dr Martinez—Maria—please, there is nothing to be concerned about,' he says now, his voice a ripple of waves over pebbles. 'It is…very nice to meet you. Dr Andersson has told me a lot about you.' He lingers on my face for a beat then clears his throat. 'So, there are some aspects of Goldmouth I would like to talk to you about today. Will you please sit?'

He gestures to a set of chairs by his desk, smiling again, his teeth white, and I swear I can see them glow in the sunlight. I hesitate at first, unsure about him, but not knowing why, not knowing if I am safe here.

Slowly, I reach for the chair, resting my fingertips on its edge. 'You were in the corridor on my first day,' I say. I lower myself into the seat, perching on the edge, fists clenched. Ready. 'You spoke to me.'

'Yes,' he says. 'I remember.'

Dr Andersson coughs. 'The Governor is always keen to meet new inmates. It is routine, remember? Didn't you record it in the notepad I gave you?' She turns to the Governor. 'Maria has a thing for writing things down.'

'Routine,' I say, as if saying the word aloud, hearing it in my own voice, will make it true.

The Governor glances to Dr Andersson then looks to me. 'Maria,' he says, 'do you understand why you are here?'

'Of course. This is your office. You arranged with Dr Andersson to meet me.'

'No.' He lets out a breath. 'I mean do you know why you are here—in Goldmouth?'

'I am in Goldmouth because I was convicted.'

The Governor links his fingers, hands the size of meat slabs. He nods to Dr Andersson.

'Maria,' Dr Andersson says, crossing her legs, a millimetre of lace slip showing. The Governor glances at it. 'It is common practice for us to encourage you to verbalise your conviction, so we know that you understand why you are here.' She pauses. A smile. 'Think of it as reassurance. We are reassured you know, and in turn we can reassure you that we are here to support you. So to speak.'

'Maria,' the Governor says, 'can you tell me why you are at Goldmouth, what your conviction is?'

My conviction. I look down at my fingers. How do I talk about something I don't recall doing? 'I am here at Goldmouth because…' I clear my throat, my nerves creeping up. 'Because I have been convicted of a category one murder under the Criminal Justice Act 2003. I received life imprisonment.'

'And who were you convicted of killing?'

My eyes stay on my hands, on the flesh, skin, bones. All real. Above ground. 'The priest,' I say to him, after a few seconds. 'I was convicted of killing the priest. He was stabbed—' a deep breath '—tied up in the convent, his body splayed out by the altar in a star formation.' A swim of remembrance: blood trickling down altar steps, an upturned crucifix. 'There was a lot of blood. Mostly his.' I pause, gulp a little, try to stave off the image. 'Some mine.'

'The priest's name was Father O'Donnell,' Dr Andersson says.

'That is what I said. The priest.' I inhale the whisper of a memory: English tea. The priest used to offer me English tea. What happened to him, I… My throat runs dry.

I touch my neck, lower my head, my hands shaking. The priest tried to help me, tried to be my friend. Then he uncovered some information for me, and next he was gone.

'Can you say his name?' Dr Andersson asks.

I look up. 'The priest's?'

She nods.

Even now I still see his blood, his entrails, see the photographs. Somehow, if I say his name aloud I think I will cry, cry so much, so forcefully that I fear I will never stop, never be calm again. And I don't know how to handle it. I don't know how to tell anyone how I feel. So instead I tell her that I cannot say his name.

'You have to say it, Maria.'

'Why?'

'Because it helps the rehabilitation process, the healing.'

But I cannot. I just cannot. Dr Andersson sighs and looks to the Governor, and when I see them, when I spot the exchange of glances, I think: I have seen this look before. My emotional training. Some people have to learn calculus. I have to learn facial expressions.

As she continues to talk, I turn and scan the room. Books. Legal textbooks. They all are housed in shelves by the walls, legions of them lined up, straight, tall, spines of golden lettering and dates and names. Bookshelves of oak, walnut, strong wood built from trees, from Mother Nature, from the very earth we stand on, the same earth that we raid to create the paper that the words in the books are written on, words we use to educate, to provide knowledge. Provide truth. Truth that can be burnt with one lick of a flame.

I search the shelves some more and when my eyes settle on a criminal law book, it hits me. Just like that: Appeal. I have the right to appeal against my conviction. I should not be here, in this prison, encased like a specimen, gawped at, made to endure, made to face my nightmares every single day, every single night. Never mind that my current barrister deems it futile to try—the right is still mine. And I want it. The freedom. I need my freedom. Because I need to find out what is happening to me. And why.

'…And of course,' Dr Andersson is saying as I turn back, 'I will be here when you need me to help you to adjust your…behaviour, your temperament. I know you are a long way from home, Maria, and—'

'I would like to appeal.'

She falters then shakes her head. 'All inmates at some point or another consider appealing. I can tell you now that there is no point. It is not accepted at Goldmouth.' She stops. 'Are you thinking you want to get to the truth? Hmmm? That people need to know the truth about you?'

She understands! I sit up, feel an unexpected surge of hope. 'Yes! Yes.'

'Well, that is pointless.' My hope extinguishes. I drop my shoulders. Dr Andersson smiles. 'You see, Maria, you must learn to live with your circumstances. To accept your guilt. That, Maria, is the real truth. The sooner you realise that the better, and your healing process can begin.'

The Governor sits forward. 'Dr Andersson is right—to a point.' He pours some water then leans back, the glass in his hand, thick, bronzed fingers, white, square nails. I look at his face. Is he messing with me, too? Playing mind games I don't understand? 'The theory is that the sooner you accept responsibility for your…actions, for your situation, the better it will be for you here at Goldmouth.' He proffers a glass. 'Thirsty?'

'I am appealing,' I say, ignoring the water, an anger building deep in my stomach.

He lowers the glass. 'Why?'

'Because I should not be here.' My voice is low, a scrape on a barrel. 'The priest found something out...' I falter as his face flickers in my mind. 'There was nothing I could do.'

The Governor sits back, sets the glass on the desk. He can be no older than my father would be now, were he still alive. A flame of sadness burns inside me for a moment at the thought, then fades to an ember, but I can still feel its heat, its aching scorch.

'My current counsel do not want me to appeal,' I say after a moment, sitting up a little, trying to gain some composure, some control. 'But I disagree with them. I therefore require new counsel.'

The Governor frowns. 'A new barrister as well as an appeal?' He exhales. 'As Dr Andersson said, almost every prisoner who walks through these doors believes they have the right to appeal. Whether it is against their sentence or against their conviction. And now you say you want new counsel?'

'Yes.' I hold his gaze. I need to. I have to have this appeal. If I get out, I may find out what happened to him, to Father Reznik.

'Look, Dr Mart—' He stops, exhales, one long, heavy breath. Then he slips on a smile. 'Maria, can I say something?'

'Yes. You do not need my permission.'

He smiles. It touches his eyes. 'When I was at Cambridge, I met a group of people who made me feel I could... make a difference. I think you could make a difference, too.' He pauses. 'And I can help you to do that.'

Dr Andersson sits up. 'Balthus, what are you doing?'

'Helping. That's why we're here, isn't it?' He levels her with a stare. 'That's why I recruited you, Lauren. To help. So do it.' He checks his watch and stands, his frame filling the room.

I look to the Governor, unsure what is happening.

'Tell you what, Maria, if you can get a barrister, we'll support your appeal. How's that?'

I open my mouth to speak but no words come out. He has just allowed an appeal. I ring my hands together, excitement bubbling underneath. I can appeal!

Dr Andersson sits forward. 'Balthus, you can't—'

'I have another meeting,' he says over her. 'Maria, your new cellmate should be joining you tomorrow. Dr Andersson is assigned to work with you. She will be your therapist. Please, keep talking to her. Don't alienate yourself out there. Socialise with the inmates—if you can. I know it's hard. I've seen your file. I am of course here, as I am for all our inmates, should you require urgent assistance.' He flashes some teeth. 'Your profile is high; you have some adjusting to do. So use me, talk to me.' He rests his palms on the chair. 'At Goldmouth, we are all about rehabilitation.'

A guard enters and instructs me to stand, and as I do I stumble a little, confused at this man, this Governor. His familiarity, his smile, his help. His...his eyes.

'My new counsel,' I manage to say to him. 'What am I to do next?'

'I'll get a legal officer to look into it for you. Are you okay? You seem a little unsteady.'

'Balthus,' Dr Andersson says, 'I don't think—'

'Lauren,' he says, spinning round to her. 'Drop it.'

We walk to the door in silence. I can smell him, the Governor, the burnt-wood trail of his cologne, the subtle scent of his sweat.

I turn to him. 'Balthazar...your name. It means "God protect the King". Balthazar was one of the kings who visited Jesus.'

He nods, slowly, his eyes drawing invisible trails on my face. An image of my father see-saws in front of me. Hot, cold. One man's face into the other's. I cannot look away. Dr Andersson clears her throat.

'Okay, Martinez,' the guard says, 'time to go.'

* * *

Kurt sits very still and studies his notes.

The room feels hot again. I sip some water, fan my face, try to circulate some air, some breeze. It does not work. Replacing the glass, I scan the room. Everything is the same. Solid, real. The walls are there, the mirror, table, clock, carpet. It all exists just as it did before. All present, tangible.

But when my eyes reach Kurt, I hold my breath. He has moved, I swear he has moved. Instead of holding his notes, his palm now rests on the arm of the chair, and his eyes are directed at me. I stay very still, scared to stir, to draw attention to it. I do not know why, but my pulse is rising. I can sense it. The blood pumping in my neck.

Kurt's mobile shrills. My lungs start to work again.

'Excuse me,' he says, and picks up his phone, puts it to

his ear. He glances to me. 'I have to take this outside. Please remain where you are.'

As he stands and exits the room, I tap my finger. Therapy is confusing. When to speak, when to be silent. Kurt's control of the situation is so exact that I sometimes find myself wanting to slap his face to see if he will react, to see if he will hurt me, shout at me, to see if he can comprehend who I am or figure out if he can even tolerate me and my ways at all.

Drained, I reach for some more water then stop. My eyes flutter. One blink, two, clearing, focusing. There is something there, by the ceiling, something that wasn't there before, I am certain. Slowly, I stand, squinting for a better view. There is an object, tiny, in the far corner of the room, by the cornicing. An object that, two minutes ago, did not exist. I close my eyes then open them again, wondering if I had imagined it, wondering if I really am, as I have been told, going mad. Yet, even when I do this, even when I shake my head, there it is.

A cobweb.

A single cobweb.

Chapter 6

'Martinez,' shouts a guard, 'your new cellmate's here.'

I have been sitting on my bed furiously writing in my notebook, fevered, obsessive. Two hours and forty-three minutes have passed, inscribing, shutting myself off from the world, from prison. It is my way of attempting to cope, adjust, to hide. My notebook is already dense with scratches and scrawls of numbers, of pictures, diagrams, outlines of floor plans I have recalled, phrases, messages that have floated like disembodied skulls in my head. My hand aches, my brain buzzes. None of it, when I look at it, when I read it back, makes sense, but I do not care. It is now all there, pressed into the page. The recording of it seems to spurt out in stages—codes, patterns, cryptic information, unusual encoded configurations. It all exists. Counted, documented. Yet, when I review it, when I scan all the detail, one thought scares me above everything else: I don't ever recall having learnt any of it.

I set down the notepad, glance up and see her: the inmate

with the studs on her tongue and the tattoo on her stomach. My body goes rigid, an alarm shrilling in my head, the urge to flee coursing through me.

'This is Michaela Croft,' the guard says, stepping inside. Michaela grins; I do not. Instead, I swallow, try to keep my hands from flapping.

The guard raises an eyebrow. 'Well,' she says before backing out, 'I'll leave you two to get...*acquainted*.'

I glance to my bed, panic. My notebook. Where did I place my notebook?

Michaela pushes past me. 'I'm taking a leak.'

My pillow. There. My notebook peeks from under it. I allow myself to exhale then slip it out of sight, fast, silent.

A flush sounds. 'Well,' says Michaela, zipping her fly with one hand and wiping her nose with the other, 'ain't this nice?'

She flops to her bed. 'You do him then, the priest?'

The trouble is, while she asks me this, while I am a little frightened of her, all I can think is that she hasn't washed her hands. 'There is soap,' I say. I can't help it.

'Huh?'

'After using the toilet,' I continue, 'a hand can contain over two hundred million bacteria per square inch. You did not wash your hands. There is soap.'

She stares at me, blinking, fists clenched, and I know I am in trouble. I sit, a coiled spring, waiting for her to hit me, claw me, but then, just like that, she shakes her head, says, 'Jesus fuck,' and lies down on her bed.

I watch her. The piercings on her ears have gone. Six puncture marks remain.

She yawns, wide, cavernous, the mouth of a lion. 'All

over the papers you was,' she says. '*Doctor Death*, they called you, that right? You killed a priest! Ha! You hard fucker.' She slips her palms behind her head. 'I don't bloody know why. I mean look at you… You'd hardly scare a kitten, never mind a sodding priest. You're like some little pixie.'

The ceiling light flickers, making me jump. 'I have never scared a kitten.'

'You what?'

I stand, pace, lift my palms to my skull and knead my forehead. She is too noisy. Too noisy. 'I do not belong here,' I say, because I do not. I do not know where I belong any more.

'What? You're innocent?' She laughs, a cackle, a lash of a whip. 'That's what they all say. Everyone's innocent, la, la, la.' She swings her legs over her bed, stands and prowls over to me. 'Sit.'

I do not move.

'I said sit.' She pushes me to the bed and slides beside me. Anxious now, I flap my hand. The edge of my fingers hit her thigh.

'Hey! What the fuck?' She grabs my fingers, squeezing them. I feel a sudden, confusing urge to whip my hand out, jab her clean in the neck.

'You have to understand something,' she says to my face, her spit and hot breath on my skin, 'they all say they're innocent, and they're all shooting for another taste of freedom; but what they don't realise is this—is—it. Here. This place. No one gets out.' She releases my fingers; I rub them. 'And while you're in here, something to remember.' She whispers to my ear. 'I'm in charge. Got it?'

She stands and jumps onto her bed. 'Now,' she says, resting her palms behind her head, 'be a dear and turn off the chat. I need my beauty sleep.'

I find that I am too weary to respond.

* * *

Over an hour has passed.

I have been sitting on my bed with my notepad. Snoring, Michaela opens her mouth and groans. When she rolls to the wall, I return to my notes. I have been writing, furiously, urgently. Trial details, evidence, memories, schedules, anything and everything I think will help in an appeal, help to secure new counsel. It is my attempt at routine, at making something happen, at making my appeal become a reality. I have written about the priest, about what he discovered when I was volunteering at the convent, the paper trail that led nowhere, figuring that if I transcribe it, if I put it in black and white, I won't forget. I won't forget what he did for me—and what information I need to find out is where Father Reznik really went. Who he really was.

I carry on writing, absorbed in it, so waist deep in its waters that when she awakes, when she growls back to life, I do not, at first, realise.

'What fucking time is it?'

My head shoots up, my hand instantly flinging the pad behind me.

'I said what time is it? Were you writing?'

She rubs her eyes. I slip the notebook into my underwear. 'I was…sitting on the bed.'

She blinks, focuses back on me. 'You're just fucking weird.'

For some reason, over the next ten minutes, Michaela talks. I don't know what I am supposed to do. Listen? Answer back? Laugh? Smile? I am paralysed by the choices. The more she awakens, the more she reveals: a lover, life, parents. And all the while the corner of the notebook digs into my skin; I want to move it, but cannot. Her eyes are on me the entire time.

'So, you Spanish, huh?'

'Yes. I told you when we met.' She should already know this. Normal people seem to recall very little information.

'All right, smart fucking arse.' She sighs. 'I like Spain. We nearly moved out there, you know, me and my man. Then I got mixed up in some drugs bollocks and he met that cow and well...'

I move the notebook. A millimetre, that is all, but it is like pulling a thorn out of my flesh.

'...And so I killed her, I killed his bit on the side. Ha, Jesus. That'll serve him right for messing with me.'

When she pauses, I take it as a cue to speak. So I say, 'Killed his bit on the side,' because I have learnt that repeating what people say can make them believe I am conversing with them. Talking with them. Not *at* them. Either way, it's all pretend.

She narrows her eyes at me. I go still again. 'What is it with you, hey? Why do you always sound like a fucking robot? You don't say much. And then when you do...' She throws up a hand. 'You just sit there, still as a bloody wall.' She stands. Her face is suddenly flushed, contorted, and she stalks towards me, rolls her thick, tattooed shoulders. 'Who are you, hey?'

I cannot help it. The words tumble out. 'I am Dr Maria Martinez. Have you already forgotten?' I try to smile, maybe that will help. It doesn't.

Her eyes go wide like two marbles in her head, two perfect storms.

I try something else. 'You asked me my name. I wondered if perhaps you had temporary memory loss. Prison could do that.' I try a laugh, that's what people sometimes do. A bit of teeth.

'What the fuck are you doing?'

I scan my brain. Is she cross? So, I drop the laugh, recall what a concerned face may look like and attempt to replicate that. 'Women in prison are five times more likely to have mental health issues compared to the general population. In the UK.'

'What the—' She wipes spit from her mouth. 'Are you saying I'm mental?'

'No, I—'

'You what? You fucking what?'

She leans forward, then suddenly—before I can move, think, assess—she knocks me to the floor. My notebook flies from my pants and slides out of reach. Panic. Fear. A rocket of blood pressure. My hands reach for the notepad, but Michaela jumps on me with her whole torso. Foul body odour. Clammy skin. Suffocating me. She pins me down, flies fists into my face, raining them down on me like giant hailstones. I try to move my head, tossing it from side to side, try to lift my left arm, legs, feet, hands, but she has me locked, chained by her limbs. Desperate, I feel for my notebook and, to my fleeting relief, manage to grab it as another fist hurtles towards me, but this time, somehow, I roll to the side, knee her hard in the groin. She screams. I scramble, clawing my way across the floor, but then she seizes me again, flings me to the wall like her battered prey. The notebook spins away and out of sight.

Michaela stops, her shoulders heaving, chest lurching. Thinking she will hit me again, I crouch, gulp in air. Blood trickles down my forehead.

'You should watch your mouth,' she says, her breathing hard, heavy.

My ribs throb. I wince. Two, maybe three, are broken.

'You gone fucking mute? Say something.'

Boots. The sound of guards' boots on the walkway.

Michaela looks to the door then takes one step forward. Then another.

I raise my hands over my head, fingers trembling.

'You need to stay where you are, Martinez,' Michaela says, her voice barely audible. But even in my frightened state, even though I fear she will kill me, I hear it, there, something different about her voice. Her accent. It is Scottish; no longer East London. Scottish.

'You have to stay in here,' she says. 'Stay in Goldmouth. It is vital, understand? We know who you are. You need to stay put. Or Callidus will come knocking. Forget Father Reznik, you hear? Forget he was ever there. You shouldn't have come looking in the first place. Either of you.'

I spit out some blood. 'What is Callidus?' I say through ragged breaths.

She bends down so her face is almost touching mine. 'Callidus is something that doesn't exist.'

'How do you know about Father Reznik?' But she does not reply. 'How?' I yell. 'What do you mean, "either of us"?'

Inhaling, Michaela steps back and raises her fists. 'Fucking cunt!' she yells with one eye on the door. I go rigid.

Her accent. The tone of how she now speaks… Her London voice is back. Raw terror explodes inside me, ripping into me, tearing me to pieces. This woman knows we were looking for him, me and the priest. She knows. Yet how? Who is she? I need help. Now, I need…

But Michaela lets out a wild scream, one ear-piercing howl. And before I can respond, before an unfamiliar instinct to launch myself at her can kick in, she punches me clean in the head.

Then: nothing.

* * *

'And did you believe her, this Michaela?' Kurt says.

Two hours have gone. Lost. How did that happen? I look from the clock to Kurt and realise that I haven't answered him yet. 'Yes, I believed her. Why would I not?'

Kurt crosses his legs. 'You said Michaela mentioned something called Callidus, correct?'

'Yes.'

'And I assume you know what it means?'

I scarcely move. My fingers begin to tap furiously on my knee, the phrase, *who is he*, whipping round my head like a tornado, a lethal storm. Can he be aware of what it really is? What it really stands for? 'What do you know?' I finally say, and I am surprised at the venom in my voice, the clench of my jaw.

His eyes are narrowed, pen pointed. 'Maria, I purely refer to the *word*, *"callidus"*. That is all. I simply want to hear if you know its definition.'

I let my shoulders drop. What am I thinking? He only wants a definition. A definition. Do I want him to believe me unhinged? Crazy? Because if I continue to overanalyse every single word he utters, continue to try to decipher every utterance, every social nuance, that's what could happen. Insanity. I tilt my head, endeavour to adopt a normal smile. '*Callidus* is a Latin word. It means clever, dextrous, skilful, cunning.'

He lowers his pen. 'Now that wasn't so hard, was it?'

I rub my forehead, compose myself. I need to remain calm, somehow, stay steady, but it is relentless, all the talk and the words and the endless possibilities of meanings. I breathe in hard then pause. The air. Is it…is it paint? I sniff again to clarify, but I am certain. There is a smell of fresh paint in the room. It is strong and I don't like it, the fumes contaminating my nostrils, my brain, overriding them with new senses to process. I glance to the ceiling. The cobwebs dangle in the breeze, yet they seem strangely rigid, plastic almost.

Kurt coughs and I look over. He is staring at me now, chin lowered so his eyebrows appear thick, straight yet strangely transparent, liquefied.

'Maria, do you trust in your recollection of events—of what was said during the incident with Michaela Croft in the cell?'

I hesitate. 'Yes. I… Of course.'

'And what about her mentioning Father Reznik?'

He clicks his pen, waits. I am struck by silence. If I tell him what I have discovered, what then? A diagnosis, an incorrect one? Again? Maybe I should tell him portions of what happened, maybe he can advise me. I rub my head one more time then drop my hand. 'Michaela was not who she said she was.'

'How do you know that?'

I clasp my hands together, squeeze the fingers. I can do this. 'This is all private in here, no? Doctor-patient confidentiality applies?'

He nods, sits forward. 'Yes. Of course.'

I glance to the window, the swell of the curtains sweeping across the side of the room. 'She was part of MI5,' I say after a moment, my eyes locked on the curtains.

'They knew the priest and I were investigating the whereabouts of Father Reznik. The priest discovered that Reznik didn't exist, not as a name, not as a real person.' I turn, face him, squeeze my palms to stay calm, tell myself to trust him. I am in therapy, therapy designed to help me. 'I find myself not knowing if I killed the priest from the convent or if someone else did. I get…' I pause, take a sip of water. 'I get confused, sometimes.'

'Maria,' Kurt says now, soft, low, 'you have to remember you were convicted of killing Father O'Donnell—a guilty verdict, prison. And I think the repercussions of the prison environment, for you, may be adding to your sense of…your sense of anxiety, perhaps, your confusion. Prison is a hard place to be. You have been through a lot already.'

'But you know I am innocent,' I say. 'You know what happened in the…in the…' I stop, a slap of reality hitting me hard. Innocent. Not guilty. The two terms suddenly seem alien, odd, two strangers in the street. I don't know what I believe any more, what I am capable of. 'They put Michaela in Goldmouth to keep an eye on me,' I say now. 'They put her in there to ensure I said nothing over Father Reznik, about what—who—he really was.'

'And what is he?'

I hesitate. 'A retired intelligence officer.'

Kurt shakes his head. 'Maria, can you hear what you are saying? MI5? A Catholic priest a former intelligence officer? How can all that be? And besides—' he pinches the bridge of his nose '—retired implies no longer active, no longer working.'

'You don't believe me?'

He inhales, taps his pen. 'I believe that you believe it. I believe that you have been through a very traumatic process for someone like you. It is common for people in your position to…fabricate stories. To merge fact with fiction to create your own storyboard. It could be a way of the brain protecting itself from reality.'

He thinks I am making it up. My eyes dart left and right around the room, at my hands, my legs, my feet. 'This is not fiction,' I say, quietly. 'It is the truth.'

But he says nothing. Instead, I simply hear the click of his pen as he writes some notes. I rub my eyes. I cannot handle this, cannot cope with the feelings coursing through me.

The scent of paint is in my nostrils now. It is too much. Standing, I trail my fingers along my bag strap and walk to the window. I stop, hoist it up, longing for air, for a mouthful of freedom. Sunshine blasts in through the bars and hits my face. I inhale. I miss Salamanca. Sometimes I find myself thinking of my childhood home in Spain. Papa with the newspaper on his lap, oranges and lemons fat and ripe in the groves beyond. My brother, Ramon, and I running, shouting. Brown limbs. My calculator in my pocket. My brother crying when I broke his arm by accident. Papa negotiating a settlement between us. Always the lawyer. Mama cradling her Ramon, screaming at me to fetch the doctor, then apologising later for her anger, an anger that I never fully understood.

'Maria, I would like you to sit down now.'

I turn. Kurt is clutching a cup of coffee. I do not recall it being delivered. I return to my seat. Kurt taps his Dictaphone.

'We'll explore your compromised memory later. But for now, tell me what happened when you were taken to the infirmary, following the incident with Michaela Croft. You came across a newspaper article… Is that correct?'

'Yes,' I reply. Kurt smiles like the sun. I press my lips together. Thinking about my barrister, about what he did to help me—it is hard. 'The article concerned a QC in London,' I say finally. 'He'd recently won an appeal case. The appeal was thought to be futile, yet he was successful in overturning the original verdict.'

My throat is dry. I reach for the coffee.

'And this QC,' Kurt says, 'did you think he might be useful for an appeal?'

I sip. 'Yes.'

'And he contested the original DNA evidence, didn't he?'

'Yes, but—' I see something. Up there. Another cobweb on the ceiling. I clutch the cup tight. Kurt mentioned a compromised memory. Is that what I am experiencing? Is that what his therapy is uncovering, following the trauma? And so is the cobweb just part of my imagination?

'The QC's name was Harry Warren. Correct?'

The cobweb. It looks like the lace headdress my mother would often wear to church for mass or to visit Father Reznik.

'Maria? Did you hear me?'

'Pardon? Oh, I wrote it down,' I say, focusing again. I place my cup on the table and slip my notebook from my bag. 'It is all in here.'

He eyes the writing pad, his gaze probing the cover. 'Could you read it, please?'

I open the page, scan the codes, algorithms, procedures, muddled memories, dreams, until I reach the correct date entry. It takes all my concentration not to check if the cobwebs are real.

* * *

I am in the hospital wing hooked up to an IV drip.

There is bandaging on my torso. I have three broken ribs, two lacerations to my right arm and one to my left. My eyes are bruised and my nose is swollen. CT scans have been done: no bleeding on the brain; my right cheekbone is chipped; my knuckles are scraped. I feel drained, worn out, no energy left in me, no fight, no strength.

Michaela was in segregation, and now she is in solitary. Following a brief disciplinary hearing, she will remain there for two weeks. Her punishment. Governor Ochoa informed me himself. Twice he has visited me, sitting, watching. I do not know why. He does not say much, just blinks. Not a lot you can say to someone who drifts in and out of morphine-induced sleep. They have tried to quiz me about the beating, about what Michaela did, but events are hazy, a blur of words and images, nothing concrete, nothing I can grasp on to. She must have hit my head harder than I thought.

I reach out, pick up a newspaper. Pain shoots down my arm. I flop back and exhale. The hospital wing is bright and rest is impossible, so I have taken to reading periodicals. They keep me alert. Yesterday, my legal counsel again refused to support my application for appeal and while I pleaded with them, while I begged them to help me, still they refused. Despite the Governor saying he would help, I do not know what I am going to do. I do not know anyone in this country. I have no friends here, no life. The appeal application deadline is fast approaching.

It is on page five of *The Times* that I see it. An article. A QC has secured a famous chef his freedom after he was found guilty of murdering his sous chef. New evidence. Following a lengthy trial, the conviction was overturned.

Overturned. I scan for the QC's name.

Harry Warren.

Could this be it? My new counsel? Could he help me? There is a photograph of him next to the article. I study it: black skin, wide smile, round stomach. Good-looking, once. A man of money and paid help.

Metal clatters to my right. I glance up. A bedpan has been knocked to the floor.

I return my eyes to *The Times* and look closer. The man looks familiar, yet how can that be? To the right of the page there is a short biography. It says he is married, two grown-up children: twins. His wife is a solicitor. They are both fifty-eight, both charitable figures. But all that to me is irrelevant, because, to arrange an appointment with him, what I really want is right there, at the bottom.

His office: Brior's Gate Chambers.

Which means Mr Warren works here. In London.

Chapter 7

Five days in the hospital wing and now I am out.

The guard links my arm like a crutch as I hobble to my cell. Inmates stare and whisper. No one comes near me, a leper, a marked woman, strange, weird. I hold my head up as much as I can as I shuffle forward, but inside I am lonely, sad, completely desolate.

I enter the cell to find that I have a new cellmate. Her name, the guard says, is Patricia. She is moving around the cell now as I sit on my bed and touch the Bible, the new hiding place for my notebook, tucked behind the cover. Thankfully, prison is not a place where people read scripture. There's no room for God here.

'Hello?'

This new person is standing before me. Her hair is shorn, fuzzy against her scalp like the blood-soaked fluff of a newborn chick.

'Patricia O'Hanlon,' she says, holding out a hand. 'Pleased to meet you.'

I blink at her fingers.

'Well, go on then. You're supposed to take it.'

I shake her hand up and down five times, but my grip must have been too tight, because when I let go, she gives her arm a rub.

'Jesus, you've got some muscles on you there.'

Curious, I study her arm in lieu of a reply. On her wrist there are two small tattoos. One is of a blackbird. The other is of the Virgin Mary. She is the only person I have seen with a virgin on their arm. Her body, when it moves, is lithe, like a piece of wire, and her head almost skims the ceiling. The last time I saw someone that tall they were playing basketball.

I bend forward to get a better look.

'Whoa,' she says, before taking a step back. 'Getting a bit close there.'

'Patricia,' I say, stepping back. 'It is the female form of Patrick. Patrick means "nobleman".'

She pauses for a second then smiles. There is a gap where a tooth should be, her cheeks sit buoyant and bobbing on her face like two ripe red apples, and when I sniff her, a scent drifts out. It reminds me of soft towels, warm baths, talcum powder.

'Your accent's not English,' she says. 'Where you from?'

'Salamanca. Spain. I am Dr Maria Martinez.' A wave of exhaustion hits me. I rub my ribs.

'I heard, by the way,' she says.

I wince. 'Heard what?'

'S'all right. I know about that Croft woman. Word gets round.' She runs a palm over her scalp.

I step straight back, a flicker of a memory in my head. 'What do you know? What?'

'Whoa! Calm down a little.'

I remember something now from the beating, something to do with accents and Father Reznik, but the memory is still smudged, unclear. I shake my head, try to nudge it out.

'You okay?'

I gulp, focus. My breathing is heavy, my fists tight, cemented to my side. I sense Patricia moving slightly to the side, her head tilted. I make myself look at her and see that she is smiling, eyes crinkled, shoulders soft, hands loose. Will she hurt me, too? I look at her hands again. No fists.

'So,' she says, 'you're a handy woman to have around, Doc. Can I call you Doc?'

'My name is Maria.'

'I know. But would you mind if I call you Doc?'

I think about this. 'It is okay.'

Patricia picks up a small duffel bag and begins to unpack. There is a toothbrush, toothpaste, toilet roll, two pairs of jeans, three T-shirts and six pairs of thick walking socks, too warm for prison. The last item she pulls out is a small family photograph in a cardboard frame. No glass allowed.

A buzzer sounds. 'Ah, that'll be lunch, then,' Patricia says. She sets down the picture. 'Come on, you need to eat.'

I stare, unmoving, still uncertain as to her intentions, still uneasy. 'You'll never survive here in one piece if you don't eat.'

My eye sockets are beginning to throb and when I lift my arms they feel heavy, dead like two lumps of decaying meat. I ache all over. I want to go home. I want to stop time, or at least roll it back. And the canteen. Lunchtime.

All those people, those sounds, smells, colours. I do not know how much of this I can take or for how long.

Patricia walks over to me. 'Come on,' she says. 'It's all right. You'll be fine. I'll stay with you, okay?'

I glance to my bed. No pictures frame the wall. No family photographs stand on the table.

'Come on, Doc,' Patricia says. 'Everything will be great.'

I am tired of being lonely. Ever since my father died, I have been lonely. The priest saw that in me, but he did what he did and died. Father Reznik left me, too. But, I cannot be on my own forever, can I? My papa had me and I had him. But he is long dead. So now who do I have?

Patricia holds out her hand. 'Let me help you up, okay?'

I hesitate, then nodding, allow her to link her arm under my shoulder without flinching at her touch too much.

'That's the spirit.'

She helps me up and leads me through the door.

And in my brain, in my abnormal, high-functioning, emotionally challenged brain, all I can think of is the word 'friend.'

I think I may have found a friend.

* * *

'How would you define the word "friend", Maria?'

Kurt has been asking non-stop questions. He has not moved. He has not once appeared to even breathe. It is exhausting. I need a break, but none are allowed. All part of the therapy technique, I am told.

I tap my foot. 'Why do you ask this question?'

'Because I want to know what you understand.'

'Friend means companion—it is someone with whom you have a non-sexual relationship.'

Kurt keeps his eyes fixed on my face, my mouth, my cheeks, almost swallowing me like a cool drink. 'A dictionary definition,' he says finally. He puts his head straight and writes on his notepad. 'And she was your first friend, this Patricia?'

'Yes.'

He looks up. 'Really?'

I place my hand on my throat. Talking about Patricia causes my chest to tighten, my eyes pool. She was my friend, Patricia, my friend, and I do not have too many of those.

'You had no other—' he pauses '—companions when you were growing up? When you were at work?'

'No. Other than Father Reznik, no.'

'Why?'

The reason. The reason is me. I am why I have had no friends. No one wants to be friends with a social freak, the outcast, the pariah. 'People do not understand me,' I decide to say.

'People do not understand you?' He shakes his head. 'By saying that, you do realise, don't you, that you are implying it is the fault of others, not yours, that people are not your friends?'

'No. I am not implying—'

He holds up a hand. 'Would you say that you are the type of person who does not take responsibility for their own actions?'

The dread in my stomach is rising again. Kurt seems to be leaning closer to me. Just one or two centimetres, but I sense it.

'Maria? I would like you to answer my question.'

'I take responsibility for my actions. And I do not like your questions.'

He sits back. 'Okay.' He taps his pen. 'Answer me this: what was it about Patricia that made her your friend?'

I glance down to my hands. 'She used to touch me. If I was distressed, Patricia would lay her hands in front of mine so our fingertips touched.'

I press my palms into my thighs. 'She understood me,' I say. 'She accepted me. I did not have to explain anything. I did not have to speak. She would just lay her hand in front of mine.'

Kurt coughs. When I raise my head, he is staring. A breeze blows in and lifts the cobwebs in the corner, making them float up and down like a dance, a tease. For the first time, Kurt's eyes flicker to where they dangle, but I don't know if he sees them as I do. He does not look at me. Does not speak.

'There are no spiders on the cobwebs,' I say.

'You think you can see cobwebs?' He picks up his Dictaphone. 'Spiders can be dangerous.'

'I can see them,' I say. 'I can.' I glance back to the ceiling, and that is when the thought strikes me: if this room has been freshly painted, why are there cobwebs in the corner?

* * *

Each morning we awake. After I transcribe my dreams to my notepad, record any new codes that have appeared in my head, I use the toilet, then Patricia does the same. We clean our teeth, yawn and splash water on our faces. Patricia brushes her scalp, I comb my hair. Once dressed, Patricia collects the post. It is the nearest I have come here to establishing a routine; the nearest I have come to being myself. I feel better than I have done in weeks, not happy, but altered, say, like a petal in the wind, not attached to the flower it belongs to, but at least able to experience what it is to float in the air.

Today, Patricia returns dangling a white envelope.

I look up. 'I have informed you already I do not want a pen pal.'

'This isn't a pen pal, Doc.' She holds out the letter. An unmistakable blue embossment is stamped on the under-side.

Patricia thrusts it to me. 'It's from—'

'My mother.'

I take the envelope and immediately my hands betray me, wobbling, slippery. I steady myself as much as I can and study the paper. Green ink. Mont Blanc fountain pen. Only the best for Mother. My pulse speeds up. It is a long time since I have heard any word from home, since I have spoken to Mama, to my brother, my prison sentence break-ing them, rendering them mute, the two of them blinking in the sunlight, shielding their eyes, knowing with me there is a storm on its way and that the clouds will always be black.

My pulse keeps racing and I need to calm down, so I look to Patricia. Numbers. Figures. 'What is the sum of all the positive integers?' I answer before she can reply. 'You would assume infinite, would you not?'

'Er—'

'Well, you would be wrong. It is not infinite.' I stand up, pace, turning the envelope over in my fingers over and over. Stopping, I slip one finger under the flap and rip it open. Its contents spill into my palm. 'Only numbers are infinite,' I babble. 'Nothing else can continue forever.' I blink at the letter, at the ivy-green ink.

'Doc? You okay?'

I begin to read. The words—they swirl around my head like leaves caught in a crosswind.

'Doc, you're crying.'

I touch my eyes. They are moist, but how? I do not cry. Not me, not in front of people. It's as if prison has changed me.

I read on. My mother says she is disappointed in me, upset for me, that she has prayed for me, begged the Lord for forgiveness on my behalf. She has attended mass at the cathedral in Salamanca, knelt in the pews, stooped at the foot of Jesus and asked him why this has happened. I wipe my eyes, the tears clouding my sight, my throat tight, raw. There is more. Ramon, she claims, has calmed the neighbours, friends, but, oh the worry. What will happen to me, she says. Hard to make sense of the world when your daughter has been convicted of murder. When your daughter is guilty of murder.

'What is it?' Patricia says, but I barely register her voice.

My heart rate accelerates. I do not move. I read the word. Then read it again. Guilty. G.U.I.L.T.Y.

'Doc, you're worrying me now.'

But my oesophagus is too taut to speak. I give the letter to Patricia. She reads it. I concentrate on breathing, on trying to push aside the words: disappointed, guilty, emotions I experience but cannot display. Emotions my mother feels and, in her distress, has told to me, in black and white.

Patricia scans the page. Her eyes go wide, then she looks to me. 'Jesus, Doc, that's… I'm so sorry.' She looks again at the letter. 'It says here she wants you to call her, wants to know how you are.'

I sniff, wipe my nose with my sleeve. 'It does?'

Patricia hands me the letter.

'She never attended my trial,' I say after a moment. 'She was ill for a while.' I read the letter, the part where my mother requests I contact her. She was never close to me, Mama, but she was always there, looked after me day to day, checked I was where I needed to be. When I was with Papa, Mother hovered by the sides, like a bird on a window ledge, who, at any given moment, could lift her wings and fly away.

'Why don't you sit down?' Patricia says.

I shake my head. 'My mother is a defence lawyer, did you know that?'

'No, I didn't.'

I nod. 'She is a politician. She was voted last year into *el Congreso*, the Spanish congress. She is a Parlimentaria for the centre-right.' I look at the green ink. 'The Church backed her all the way. Decades after they joined leagues with Franco, the Catholic Church is still trying to keep control of Spain, of people's lives.' Then I laugh, but I don't know why. The absurdity of it? The sickening truth?

'Fecking religion,' Patricia says, shaking her head. 'Causes more bleedin' problems than it solves. A heap of the Catholic priests in Ireland were found up to all sorts. And when people were poor and starving on the streets long back, there were the priests, fat and warm in their rectories.'

I rub my thumbs on the envelope, the paper.

'I remember when I was nine,' I say. 'I had to accompany my mother to a meeting at Salamanca Cathedral. Our au pair was away. My mother told me to sit and wait in the seat outside Father Reznik's office, but I could not. I walked into the vestry and that is when I saw them. My mother and the priest…kissing.' My mother's writing swims on the page. 'She handed the Father a sealed package. I stood, watched, could not look away. For some reason, I knew something was not right. Before they could see me, I ran back to my seat. I never told anyone.' A tear escapes. Hurt, bewilderment. 'Why is it no one is who they seem?'

Patricia shrugs. 'God knows.'

An anger rushes to my cheeks. 'God does not know. If he did know, if he did exist even, he wouldn't allow it all to happen.'

I hold the letter and rub the paper. My mother kissed Father Reznik. A priest. A Catholic priest. I saw it, I am so sure. And now I can't find him, don't even know who he is, who he really works for or why—if he even existed at all. Just a made-up persona, a name, a being, plucked out of the air like an apple from a tree. Forbidden. Wrong. And now the convent priest who helped me is dead. Dead. And I am incarcerated, a man who pretended for years to be my friend, to be a man of God emerging before me instead as a snake. Because that's what happened, didn't it? That's what we discovered, what the priest found out? That Father Reznik was a liar? I drag my nails over my scalp and look at the letter, at the creeping ink, and without thinking any more, without wondering what I am doing or why, I rip.

I rip it, the letter, straight down the middle. Rip, rip, rip. Patricia steps back. I tear the letter again. And again. And again. My teeth are clenched, tears tumble down my cheeks, but I do not wipe them, do not let myself calm down. Because I can't, not now, not on hearing from my mother, from someone I should trust unconditionally and who says she is disappointed in me. I choke at the thought, hear my throat sound a yell, a cry, my chest crumbling under the weight of the reality that is ahead of me. That I am here. And I can't get out…

Rip, rip, rip.

When the paper is torn into confetti-sized pieces, I stop. My chest heaves. My eyes sting.

'Doc, you need to breathe.'

I stare at the pieces in my palm. Ink lies smeared on creamy paper, words bleeding, torn apart, dying.

'Why don't you sit? Maybe write it all down?'

I feel raw, ravaged, as if everything that has happened since my arrest has come out now, in one earthquake of emotion. My eyes blink, batting back the tears. I coerce my concentration towards Patricia, to her mouth, her words and what she is advising me to do. And I think: I should confess. I should admit what I discovered, what really happened, what the priest knew—and why he couldn't go on with knowing it. Maybe that way I can truly start to decipher who is doing this to me—and why. Yes, that is it. It has to be.

I turn, flop to the bed, the letter confetti still in my fist, sinking into the mattress as I sit. And it occurs to me that more than anything I would like to keep sinking—to plummet so far that no one could possibly find me, hidden, as I would be, in the bowels of the bed, digested, absorbed. Gone.

'I helped that priest,' I say after a while. Patricia sits, listens. 'I helped out there, at his convent. I did the fixing,

carpentry, small electrics. My father taught me a lot of it…
before he died. Papa said women are not the maids of men.
He said I was equal. No different to anyone else.'

'He was right,' Patricia says.

'After he died, the workmen tending the estate showed
me how to mend things. Father Reznik did, too.' I stop,
frown. 'I remember he would time me, Father Reznik, time
me how long it would take to fix things. He would set me
a challenge to get faster and faster. He called it a game
and it was fun, but…' I clutch the torn letter pieces in my
fist. 'I wonder.'

'What?'

I grab my notebook and stop. An earwig scurries along
the floor and disappears under the bed. I watch it, track
its course. It is not simply here by chance; the earwig has
made a path into Goldmouth for a purpose. I pause. Purpose. Everything has a purpose, has a reason why it occurs. So what was Father Reznik's purpose?

I rip open my notepad and look to Patricia. 'What were
you convicted of?'

She twiddles the edge of her T-shirt. 'They said I killed
me mam,' she says, her voice barely audible, so I have to
lean in to hear. 'My ma, she had cancer. It was hard, you
know, at the end. I just couldn't watch her suffer like that
any more. It was cancer of the pacrea—'

'Pancreas,' I say. 'Cancer of the pancreas.'

'Morphine couldn't touch it.'

'How did you kill her?'

She hesitates then says, 'Her pillow.' A small swallow.
'She wanted me to. She couldn't take it any more.' She
wipes her nose with her hand.

There are tears in her eyes. This must mean she is upset. What should I say in this situation? I rack my brain for data to help. 'The term "euthanasia" originates from the Greek word meaning "good death". Nine per cent of all deaths in the Netherlands are physician-assisted suicides or euthanasia. In the Netherlands, you could be free.'

She lets out a sudden laugh.

I sit back. 'What?'

'It's just that you…' She shakes her head, waits a moment. 'She had a will, me mam. A will. I never knew. It had a big insurance payout. My mam always wanted me to keep studying. She had money, left to her from an aunty. My sister hated me. In court she said Ma wouldn't have let me do it, wouldn't have let me end her life. She called me a liar.' She tugs her T-shirt now. 'My sister said I killed Ma for the money. I didn't, but she wasn't about to believe me.' She lets out a breath. 'Still doesn't. I'm due for parole really soon. Been banged up ten years. But if I get out, who have I got to go back to? Where can I go now no one from my family will talk to me?'

We sit on the bed, silence swinging like a noose in the air above us. If I close my eyes, I can see Father Reznik's face. 'I think I'm being watched,' I say finally.

Patricia turns to me. 'You what?'

I draw in a breath and tell her about Father Reznik, about the priest discovering he was a retired intelligence officer.

Patricia's mouth drops open. 'Whoa. For real?'

'Yes.'

She whistles. 'How do you know this?' she says, just like that, believing me in an instant. I want to cry with joy.

'You believe me?'

'Of course. Why wouldn't I?'

I consider this. I have learnt not to put my faith in any-one, not to trust, because no one, not a man in a priest's outfit, not a judge in a robe, not a God in the sky can be re-lied upon. But Patricia seems different, pure, a white sheet of cotton, a dandelion in the wind. She believes me. And I am tired, so, so tired at keeping it all in, to myself, the truth growing like a tumour. Gratitude washes over me, clear, running water, refreshing, energising, and I want to thank her, want to express how grateful I am for her faith in me, but I don't know how. Instead, I remain rigid on the bed like a plank of wood.

'I came to London to look for Father Reznik, took the job at St James's Hospital so I had a base here,' I say, slowly at first then faster still. 'When a nun came into the hos-pital one day on a visit to a patient, she told me about the convent, and when I spoke about how I attended church in Spain, how Father Reznik had taught me how to fix things, she invited me to volunteer, two or three days a week.'

'Then what?'

'I met the priest there. He was nice to me. I told him how Father Reznik had just disappeared after all those years, and so the priest said he would help find him.'

'And he found out this intelligence officer stuff?'

'Yes.'

'How?'

I steady my hands from shaking. 'He had contacts, asked a few questions. I was not sure at first—it all appeared so unusual, untrue. And then he died.'

'So you didn't kill him?'

'I…' I drop my head, smothered suddenly by the reality

of the situation. How did I let it happen? He died. I witness his blood every night when I sleep. I am testament to that. After a moment, I breathe out, rub my cheeks, my chin.

'You all right?'

I nod. 'Father Reznik taught me how to detect patterns, codes. Trained me in fixing things fast.' My notebook sits under my palm. I run my fingertips over the pages now etched in ink, scratched with numbers, words, odd cryptic codes. My shoulders drop, body, mind, tired. I don't know how all this just appears in my brain. 'Why?' I say after a while.

'What do you mean?'

'I mean why did Father Reznik teach me these things? Even when I was at university, I would come home, visit him and he would give me tests to do, advanced mathematical challenges.' I shake my head, cross at myself for not realising before. 'Don't you see?' I let out a laugh. 'He taught them to me for a reason. And if he used to be an intelligence officer, then why? Why did he do those things with me? Why? And my mother, kissing him—did she know who he was? It all connects, you see. It all has a purpose.' I stab the notebook with my finger. 'And all this data. What does it mean?'

'It's stuff you've learnt, isn't it?'

'No. That's the problem. I haven't learnt it at all. I've always recalled data, written it down—facts, details. I had a journal at home in Salamanca when I was growing up and I used it so I could record everything, every event, name, number.' I pick up the pad, shake it, feeling something— an anger?—surge inside me. 'How can I remember all this information when I don't even recall ever studying it?'

Patricia opens her mouth then closes it, exhaling. 'I don't know, Doc. I don't know.'

I throw the notebook down, peer at its pages. I suddenly feel wired, fired up, charged to accelerate. My leg jigs over and over, the prospect of the truth ahead, the quest of it all making me giddy, light-headed. By my feet, another earwig scurries past, silent, stealth. I move my foot and grind its body flat with my heel.

Patricia watches me. I reach forward, slam the writing pad shut. It all makes sense now, all of it. 'I have to call my mother.'

And, as I stand, the shredded letter remains slip from the bed and float to the floor.

Chapter 8

'We discussed false memories briefly before, do you recall?' Kurt says. 'That the mind can play tricks on us.'

Up until now, Kurt has remained silent. This is the first time he has spoken to me since I ceased talking, telling him about Patricia, about her life, her loss. For some reason, I clutch my mug tight in front of my chest as Kurt watches me, a languid smile lounging on his lips.

'Why are you asking me about my memory?' I say after a moment.

A heartbeat passes. 'Why do you think I am asking you?' He holds my gaze. I look away, scorched. 'Tell me,' he says after a few seconds, 'what would you say memory is?'

I press my palms into my lap, hard, sweaty, unsure where he wants to take this, because he is still smiling and I don't know what it means.

'Memory is the way we use our past experiences to understand the present,' I say. 'Memories are created when our brains encode, store and retrieve events.'

'That is a textbook answer.' He straightens his neck. Smile gone. 'You said you remembered the inmate, Michaela Croft talking suddenly in a Scottish accent, about her mentioning Father Reznik. And then you say he was a former intelligence officer. You even say you recall codes, numbers that you do not remember learning.'

'Yes.'

'Think about it. The beating, for example. Your memory is recalling an event, a traumatic incident. An incident that, in my opinion, could not have occurred as you recall it. A fabrication.'

'No. This is not make-believe.' A bird lands on the window ledge, beats its wings, rapid, frenzied, as if it were about to topple. Then it falls still, takes two steps, flies away.

'You said Michaela also mentioned something called Callidus.'

I turn my head from the window. 'Yes.'

'Are you sure?'

'I know what I know.'

'You see, Maria, here's where I have a problem. How could Michaela have ever known about Father Reznik? And this Callidus? Our brain can change what we remember—it is how we cope with trauma. So, in the end, what we think happened is different to what actually occurred. And we recall people as different to how—or who—they really are.'

'No. You are wrong. With this, you are wrong. I know my facts. I know what has happened.'

'You are questioning a scientific theory? You? A doctor?'

'No, I...' I falter. What is he trying to do to me? To my

mind, my sanity? 'I understand the science,' I say, voice quiet.

'So understand that it applies to you. That perhaps your memory is not what you believe it to be. Take your note-pad. You say you write everything down—it's your obsession. But to say you don't recall learning the data you have recorded is absurd.'

'That's not true.'

He smiles. 'No? Then, Maria, there's only one conclusion.' The smile vanishes. He narrows his eyes. 'The information you are recording is purely made up.'

'What? No!' I tap my hands now hard on my lap. Banging. I don't like him, this so-called therapist. He cannot continue to voice these types of opinions. No one understands me. No one.

Kurt sits forward. 'I know this is difficult for you to see, the complex emotion involved, but, Maria, as a doctor, ask yourself this: is your memory reliable?' He searches my face. 'How can you believe what you heard that day in the cell? Our memories encode events. Our memories can change facts into something else. That's how they store the data, how they process everything we see and do—by modifying it. There's simply too much to cope with otherwise.' He tilts his head. 'For example, say there was a loud bang. Our brain may convert that sound into a colour, instead, and that is how we remember it—as a colour, not a sound. We may even forget the bang altogether. To that end, how can you be certain, for example, that your mind hasn't altered a London accent into a Scottish one, plucked a long-distant name from the air, in order to protect itself from trauma? In order to cope?' He pauses. 'How do you *know* if this intelligence officer thing is true?'

My hands go still, my breath rasps, unsteady. I am suddenly beginning to doubt myself. 'What…what are you saying?'

'I am saying that you have been traumatised by your prison experience. Your brain has encoded the beating, has changed it and stored it as something different, and so now, when you attempt to recall what happened, you remember it in another way. Your mind has created a new memory.'

'You…' But I close my mouth, as if the words have all dried up, a desert, just sand, tiny grains of sand. I want to cry, but I can't.

Kurt leans forward. 'Would you like some water?'

I shake my head, too scared to speak, not trusting that my own voice will remain calm. Not trusting that my hands won't find his neck.

Kurt pours a drink for himself. The liquid trickles into the tumbler, and the curve of it reflects in the sunlight, wobbling water on the wall, a swirl of blue and lemon. Fresh. Innocent. As he holds the glass, I force myself to look at it. It is still the same glass. There. Real. But what Kurt said, the science of the memory, it has touched me, entered my hardwiring, my internal computer system now, and I cannot let it out. Because what if he is right?

What if everything I remember, everything I believe, is wrong?

I draw in deep breaths, try to quell my panic, think of my father, this time of his office, of the oak-slab desk I would slip under when we played hide-and-seek, his laughter, when he found me, filling the room like the boom of a cannon.

Slowly, I open my eyes, my heartbeat now a little calmer, and rest my gaze on the ceiling. I frown. Is that what I think it is? I check again, but it has disappeared now. There one minute, gone the next.

'Maria?'

'Just a moment.' I shut my eyes, rub them, then reopen and blink. A chill crackles down my veins, because what I saw once, then couldn't, is back.

I touch my forehead. A spider. One spider in the corner of the room.

* * *

I stand by the phone bank and hold the receiver. It has slid from my palms twice already, my nerves visceral, unforgiving. I cannot get the words out of my head: *Disappointed. Guilty.* What if she will always feel that way about me, my mother? Where does that leave me? And when I ask her the question, finally, after all these years, what will she do? Did it really happen? Did I really see them kiss?

'You okay, Doc?' Patricia says, standing to my left.

I nod, but I am not okay. I am scared of what my mother's answer will be. I am scared because I do not trust my brain.

The phone line crackles.

'Maria?'

I freeze at the sound of my mother's voice. It instantly takes me back to our home in Salamanca. I close my eyes, picture my mother seated on the patio, the wrought iron table set with a fresh pot of coffee, her fan by her side to fend off the early morning heat, her hands bony, her ballerina-like build upright, poised, ready. I sniff. A scent of oranges and Chanel No 5.

'Maria? Darling, talk to me. Are you well?' She speaks in Castellano, our mother tongue, our homeland Spain. I draw in a breath and speak it back to her.

'Mama,' I say, 'it is me.'

A shriek. 'Oh, my darling! My poor baby. How are you? Why have you not contacted me before? Why wait until now?'

The sound of her voice crashes like a wave, breaking all over me. I gasp, shocked at how much relief floods my body just by hearing her voice. 'I have not been...' I stall, gulp in a breath.

'It is okay, my child. It's okay.'

I sniff. 'Prison is very loud, Mama.'

'Are they helping you?'

'Sometimes.'

'How?'

'There is a psychiatrist. Dr Andersson. She is—'

'What does she look like?'

I pause. 'Why do you want to know?' I look at Patricia. She smiles.

'Oh, you know me,' my mother says, 'I like to know who is looking after my daughter, like to know every single detail. To picture it, if you will. Her hair, for example. What colour hair does she have?'

'Blonde.'

'Long?'

'Yes. She is Swedish.' Total silence. 'Mama?' A crackle echoes then a sharp bang.

'Maria? Sorry. I dropped the telephone.'

I start to bite my nails. Something is not right. 'Mama, I have a question that I need to ask you.'

'Yes?'

'Something I remembered about Father Reznik.'

She does not reply. Only the rasp of her breath fills the line. 'Maria, my dear,' she says finally, 'he left. I'm so sorry, I know you adored him, but people leave. That's just the way the world works. It wasn't your fault, I have told you this. Your therapist from when Papa died told you this.'

I swallow a little. 'Mama, I remembered something.'

A small sigh. 'Okay, dear. What did you remember?'

I glance to Patricia then back to the phone. 'I remember seeing you and Father Reznik…kissing.'

'Oh, Maria.'

'What?'

'It is happening again.'

A flush of anger. 'What is?'

'Your mind making things up. Darling, this is what you do. I have been trying to help you for so long now.'

I grip the phone. 'But I saw the two of you! Kissing near the vestry when I was supposed to be outside waiting for you. And…and you gave him something, some sort of letter or…or package. I know what I saw.' Patricia steps forward but I ignore her, my fury feverish now, lethal. I cannot believe my mother is saying this again about me. I do not want to believe it. To believe her.

'Maria, just calm down a little.'

'No. You are denying it, but you know it is true. You and Father Reznik.'

'You are still upset that Father Reznik left you.' I go still. 'Maria, I am right, no?'

I shake my head, blink. 'I… What are you trying to…' And then it steps into my view, an image, a memory, strong this time, all the colours clear, the image crisp. Father Reznik is waving goodbye to me, an aeroplane in the background, me watching, enraged, for some reason, that he is leaving me. My hair is long down to my back, so I am fifteen, perhaps sixteen, and I break free from my mother, her calling out to me that he will be back, but I am running to him, and when I get to him, just as Father Reznik opens his arms to hug me, saying he is leaving for just three months, I kick him hard in the shin.

'Maria.' My mother's voice slices through the memory. It shatters into a thousand pieces. 'Maria, you were always so angry when he left Spain, angry at the Church. The Catholic Church has been in Spain for hundreds of years, that's just the way it is, but I know that always frustrated you, that control that you say they had, the lies that you said they told.' She pauses, a petite cry. 'You shouldn't have taken out that anger on someone else, on that poor priest, poor Father O'Donnell at the convent.'

'But I didn't. I…' A slow shriek. It spurts out from me. My mother. She doesn't believe me.

'Maria, sssh. There, there. It's okay. It's okay.'

Patricia steps over, stands beside me, not touching me, but there, real. I scratch at my scalp, my mind jumbled, exhausted. I let out a long breath and feel my shoulders finally loosen. I simply want to go home.

'Maria, I'm going to come over to see you, okay?'

I drop my hand. 'What?' I sniff. 'How?'

'I've looked into it. You just need to request a visiting

order. Ramon will accompany me. He's very concerned about you.'

My brother, too? 'But he has never been concerned about me before.'

Another sigh. 'Maria, you're his sister, of course he is concerned about you. We need you to arrange the visiting order. Can you do that?'

Visiting orders. Prison. Iron bars. Loud screams. So much to process, to consider. I feel smothered by it all.

'Is there anyone that can help you?' my mother says.

Patricia tilts her head and smiles. 'Yes,' I say, after a moment. 'I have someone who can help me.'

A whoosh of exhalation. 'Oh, that's wonderful. Wonderful. Does this mean you are making friends? Actually, no, don't answer that. Tell me all about it when I see you, okay?'

I nod.

'Maria? I said, okay?'

'Okay.'

'Good.' There is a tinkle of silver, the coffee pot being poured. 'Darling, keep your chin up in there, yes?'

'My chin?'

'It means stay positive. As much as you can, anyway. At least being in prison means you can get help now, where no one can be hurt.' She sniffs, lets out another dainty cry. 'Oh, I'm sorry. Ignore me. It all gets a little much for me at times.' I hear her breathe in. 'But no matter. We will fly over to see you.'

Pips sounds. The prison phone. 'I have to go, Mama.'

There is a stillness. 'I know,' she says, after a brief moment. 'You look after yourself.'

'Yes.'

She goes quiet. The pips patter again. 'Maria, you'd better go. Take care. And—'

But she is cut off. For a few seconds, I do not move, just stand, staring at the receiver. Have I remembered everything incorrectly? I have just accused my mother of kissing another man. What sort of person does that make me? Slowly, Patricia reaches forward and prises the phone out of my hand. She returns it to its holder and looks at me. 'How are you?'

I blink, find a focus. 'She said they never kissed. That my memory is impaired.'

'Oh.'

I roll my shoulders, pinch the folds of skin on them to try to get some blood flowing again through my muscles. Maybe everything I have believed is not true. Maybe life has jumbled everything up in my head, mixing memories like the shuffling of a deck of cards, throwing them in the air so they land randomly, out of synch. I drop my head to my hands. All I have are facts. If I stuck with them, if I used the facts I have to piece it all together, would I see the final picture on the puzzle?

We walk away from the phone bank in silence. Only the shuffle of our feet fills the air, the regular prison screams in the distance temporarily suspended.

'Hey,' Patricia says as we stop at the next door, 'you've met the Governor, haven't you?'

I nod.

'Well,' she says, rubbing her palms together, 'listen to the gossip I discovered about him earlier. It'll take your mind right off the phone call with your ma.'

* * *

Kurt is writing notes.

A wind shoots through the window and a shiver runs down my back. Kurt does not flinch.

I scan the edge of the room. Kurt's talk of memory, of its distortion, is unsettling. Therapy is supposed to help you understand yourself, to feel better. But this? Now? I don't feel better. I just feel frustrated. And frightened.

'Maria?'

I turn. Kurt's file rests on his lap, the Dictaphone lying on the edge of table, red light flashing.

'I am going to ask you some more questions now.' He crosses his legs. 'You said, that when you spoke to Patricia in your cell after the call with your mother, she told you something about the Governor. I want you to tell me what she said.' He clicks his pen and waits.

I sit up straight. This is not the right question. 'Why are you discussing this instead of what my mother said about my memory?'

He tilts his head. 'Do you not want to tell me about the Governor, Maria. Is that it? Is there some reason, perhaps, why you won't talk about him?'

'What? What do you mean?' I press myself back against the lip of my chair. His eyes are suddenly steel, his voice prickles. The urge to flee wells up inside me again.

He leans in to me. 'I want you to tell me exactly what Patricia said.'

Kurt is so close to me, so near that I can see every sinew of his skin. Not a blemish, not a stain. He has me chained to him. What choice do I have?

'Patricia…' I stop. Swallow. 'Patricia said that the Governor was married to the UK Home Secretary.'

'And you did not know this already?'

'No. I… I did not realise.'

'But everyone knows. It's news. Are you telling me you didn't hear about it?'

'I do not follow such things.'

He sits back. 'Maria, would it be true to say that when it comes to relationships, when it comes to men, women— or whatever your persuasion—you have difficulty understanding the situation?'

'I… Yes,' I say finally.

'Have you ever had a relationship yourself? A boyfriend? Girlfriend?'

I sit and stare, the question hanging there, hovering like a floating ghost. The loneliness of my life is something I have been able to push to one side, to hide in a box, keep the lid tight shut. Until now.

A gust of wind bursts in and the window slams shut. I jump. Kurt glances over to it but says nothing, does not move. I slap my hand to my chest, slow myself. Something is happening here. Kurt was different just now. He was. I am positive. I have to try to seal it all in my mind, protect it, try to keep learning his contradictive nuances so I can paint the whole picture. So I can always remember.

A knock sounds on the door, breaking the suffocating silence. Kurt looks up. 'Come in.'

The coffee woman enters, the same one as before. Why is she back? She passes Kurt a message on a square yellow piece of paper.

'This came for you,' she says, her voice a punnet of

plums, a swollen bunch of black grapes. 'They need to speak to you for a moment.'

The women then turns, stares at me, her mahogany hair bobbing by her shoulders, skin the colour of buttermilk, jeans black, painted on, her leather jacket studded, worn. She continues her gaze for three seconds then, throwing Kurt a smile, she leaves, clicking the door shut behind her.

'Who is she?'

Kurt reads the note then stands. 'She's my…girlfriend. She helps out here sometimes.'

I look at the door where she exited. He has someone. Someone to hold, to love. I wonder what that must feel like.

Kurt scrunches up the note and drops it into the waste-paper basket. 'That was a message about a patient. The service need to speak to me straight away,' he says. 'I have to leave. I will just be a few minutes.' He turns to exit then pauses. 'Maria, I'm sorry if I make you feel uneasy sometimes. I know I must do. It's just the therapy technique. Let yourself trust it. That's the best advice I can give to you.' He applies a quick smile. 'Well, excuse me.'

After he has left, I breathe out and stand. My legs feel like two dead limbs. I shake them, blood rushing to my feet, and think. What Kurt said about his therapy technique, perhaps he has a point. Perhaps I am fighting it too much, reading too much into it, looking for clues and lies that simply aren't there.

The air feels woolly, thick, and I remember: the window slammed shut earlier. I walk over to it and thrust it open. Wind rushes in, and I allow myself to savour it for a second, this glimmer of freedom, of the world below. Through the bars, the bustle of the city street rushes past in a blur of watercolour paint. Though the noise is loud, I force myself to scan it all. Because it is here. All this life beyond—it is here. It exists. And I have to picture it exactly as it is. Like taking a photograph.

Soon, Kurt will return, and if I want this therapy to help me this time, I must have a clear head. I walk back towards my seat, spot the wastepaper basket and hesitate. The note about Kurt's patient is there, the paper yellow, words and colour together in one place just like an encoded memory. Maybe if I read the note, it will settle my mind, help me to see reality in action—real words, real colours. Then, perhaps, I will cease worrying about contexts and hidden meanings and distorted memories.

Without allowing myself a change of mind, I quickly bend down and grab the scrunched note. Returning to my chair, I flatten the paper ready to read it then stop.

I turn the paper over. Then over again. But still, I am right. Because it is blank. The paper is blank. No writing on either side. No message about a patient.

Which means only one thing: Kurt lied.

The door handle rattles and I freeze. He is returning.

Chapter 9

The door is opening. I re-scrunch the note and throw it towards the bin, but it lands on the floor. I scramble up, fling the paper into the wastepaper basket and dart back to my seat. My heart bangs against my chest, violent, crazed. I can't let him catch me.

Kurt enters and stops. He looks at me then glances to the wastepaper basket. 'What were you doing?'

My chest heaves up and down. I don't know what to do. I have a split-second decision to make: truth or lie.

'I said what were you doing?'

'I read the note.'

He shuts the door, stands, levitating almost, unreal. One second. Two seconds. Three seconds pass. My pulse pounds in my neck.

'There were no words on it,' I say, fearful of how he is going to react. 'The paper you threw in the bin—it was blank.'

He draws in a long breath then stares straight at me.

'Are you sure about that, Maria? There was writing on it when it was first given to me.' He walks to the wastepaper basket, retrieves the note and sits down. He slips the paper into his pocket and picks up the Dictaphone.

I look at the bin, at where the note lay. Writing on it? How can it be?

Kurt brings the Dictaphone to his mouth and presses the record button. 'The patient appears to be having episodes of confabulation.' His eyes find me. 'She is experiencing severe distortion and fabrication of events, all of which are affecting her memory. The subject has retrieved a note written to me, and has convinced herself that it contains no writing when in fact, it does. Furthermore, the level of paranoia…'

And, as Kurt records his notes, I touch my forehead and blink over and over at the criss-cross pattern of the waste-paper basket.

What is happening to me?

* * *

I am in the Plaza Mayor, the outdoor living room of Salamanca.

It is summer. The month is August. Heat shimmers from the stonework like a mirage, like a cloaked vision, and I prop my hand on my brow, squint and observe. The square is brimming with summer students, tourists, bronzed locals, their skin glistening in the sun.

I am sitting outside one of the cafés that shore up the square. A plate of tapas rests on my table: soft, succulent croquettes filled with Iberian ham, cubes of fluffy, fried potatoes smothered in spicy tomato sauce. I alternate be-

tween eating and sipping Rioja. My breathing is slow, measured. I want to be normal, seem normal.

In between bites, I glance at the notebook that sits on
my lap, its ink-soaked pages flapping in the soft afternoon
breeze, my bare legs still so as not to spill wine droplets
on my new white linen shirt. I take a moment to stop and
listen. The birds are sleeping their siesta in the heat, their
song replaced with human melodies, with the lullaby, the
dance of busking guitars. It all rings loud in my ears like
the tremor of a trombone, but, for some reason, it does not
bother me.

Every minute, I observe it all, drink it in. I have missed
it, missed this place. I never knew someone could want
their homeland so much to the point that they would do
anything to return. Anything. To anyone that gets in their
way. I lean my head backwards, allow the sun to warm
my skin and think: *I am lucky; the luckiest woman alive.*

'Doc?'

Someone's voice, I hear it. It pierces my mind; the illusion begins to judder. I try to hang on to it, claw it back,
but it does no good. The image of the Plaza Mayor flickers once, twice, then disappears—pop—like a television
being switched off.

'Doc, wake up. Quick!'

'Hmmm?'

I open my eyes, but cannot hear. I wriggle a finger in my
ear. Patricia's mouth moves and her hand is thrusting something at me. The dream. My mind cannot lose the dream.
I don't want it to go, don't want it to disappear forever. I
wrestle with it as it fades from view in a shroud of static,

try to pin it to the end of my bedstead, but it's no use; it floats from my grasp in a final bubble of doubt.

'What time is it?' I sit up and smooth down my hair. I have not yet brushed my teeth or splashed my face with water, and the guards will be here soon.

Patricia looms in front of me again. 'You awake now? Because you're going to want to look at these…'

There are newspapers in her hand. And something else. Her socks. All of six pairs of them. 'Why are they tied to-gether?' I croak.

'Huh? Oh, just bored.' She loops the sock rope over the chair and places a newspaper in my lap. 'You're not going to like it.'

She drops the bundle of newspapers on my lap. 'You need to read these.'

Taking a paper, I scan the page. At first, it makes no sense, and then it registers. On it, there is a face. A face I know too well. And beside it: a name.

Patricia sits down. 'Speak to me.'

My mind fusses and flurries, hands begin to jitter. I read the words on the page. 'My mother,' I say after a while. 'My mother is in your newspapers. How?'

'She's visiting today with your brother, isn't she?'

'Yes.' I grip the periodical, the print transferring to my palms, to the pillowed tips of my fingers. I smear them to-gether, rubbing them, the ink staining my skin, my brain not knowing how I feel about seeing my family again after what has been almost a year.

I spread my fingers over the image of my mother's face.

'You don't think she told them, do you?' Patricia says. 'About the visit?'

The morning buzzer sounds. Time to exit our cells. The meeting with my mother and brother is in two hours. I don't want to disappoint her, don't want to feel angry at her.

Not again.

* * *

I arrive in the visitors' room and stop. I feel slightly sick, nerves nudging my stomach, its contents threatening to erupt. My face is blank, but my mind is alive with doubt.

Inmates' feet shuffle on the tiles while voices saturate the air, air that reeks of perspiration, of a waterfall of bodily secretions. It swamps my head. The glare of the strip lights, combined with the ice-cold judgement of the white walls all momentarily freeze me. I lick my lips for moisture. Only when a guard digs my elbow and tells me to *shift it* do I move on.

I locate the table with my family, walk to it and stall. A lump swells in my throat. My mother. Her hands, hands that were once fleshy and strong, hands that lectured law at university, instructed housemaids, placed Band-Aids on my knees, are now bony and frail. I bite down hard on my lip to restrain the cry that wants to break out from within me. My family is changing before my eyes and I worry that soon they will all alter so much that I won't recognise them any more. That I won't have them, won't know if they are on my side or not. Won't feel that I fit in, not that I am ever sure I did.

'Oh, Maria!' my mother cries to me, her grainy Castellan voice guttural, instinctive. She stretches out her arms, pulls me into her. I go rigid. 'Oh, my daughter! What has happened to you?'

Tears threaten to spring up, invade my face. Being close

to my mother is one step away from my papa, dead or not. I touch my cheeks, surprised at the dampness staining my skin. My mother holds me out at arm's length.

'Oh my darling, it's okay. Sssh. Sssh.' She reaches forward to wipe my face. I hold my breath; a guard tells her there's no touching. She apologises in English, sits back, omits a sigh, dabs her forehead. 'Oh, dear. This is all too much.'

'Mama, are you okay?' Ramon, my brother. His crisp green eyes scan our mother, her own eyes, the same apple-fresh hue, blink back, her head tilting slightly, neck smooth, slender. She pats his hands.

'I am fine, son. I am fine.'

Ramon's gaze stays on her for two seconds more, his forearm strong like a tree trunk rooted to the table, his body baptised in a shroud of nut brown, stomach muscles taut from years of sport—running, swimming, skiing. Finally, he looks away, directing his attention at me for the briefest of moments before he dusts down his suit and opens up a legal file on his desk.

'Hello, Maria,' he says, a small flicker of a smile. My brother, a man of few words, to me at least. To everyone else? An eloquent, accomplished tax lawyer. But he has always been there, by my side—whether I wanted him to or not. When we were young he was like dog dirt on my shoe: impossible to shake off.

'Now,' Mother says, after clearing her throat. 'Let's have a look at you, my dear.'

She scans my face and her smile wobbles. 'Oh, you look so tired. Are you eating? Sleeping?'

'Yes. I have a friend.'

She goes still, her eyes wide. 'Really?' She throws a glance to Ramon. 'Really? My darling, that is wonderful news! Wonderful.' She takes a sip of water. 'Who is it?'

'Pardon?'

She set down her glass. 'Your friend.' A small cough. 'Who is it?'

'Why?'

'I…I am just interested. Making conversation.'

I open my mouth to speak, but suddenly check myself. My voice is raised, my fingers still pressed into the table. I soften, lean back, try to stay calm, try to stop searching for inferences that are not there. 'Her name is Patricia,' I say finally. 'My friend's name is Patricia.'

Ramon jots the name down. 'Do you know her surname?' he asks.

'Do you need to know that?'

'Ramon,' my mother says, 'it's okay.' She turns to me. 'Do you trust her, this friend? Talk to her?'

I inhale. Calm. 'Yes.' I glance at Ramon's file. 'Her surname is O'Hanlon.' Ramon writes it down. 'Why are you noting her name?'

'Maria,' my mother says, Ramon's pen hovering in midair. 'Maria, look at me.'

I glare at my brother, then slowly peel my eyes off him. I don't like that he is recording every detail, every utterance. Why? Why would he need to do that?

'Maria.' Mother again. 'It's for your journal, remember? The one you began after Papa died.'

'Why are you writing in my journal?'

'No, I didn't mean… We are not writing in—'

I look to the two of them, eyes frantic. 'It is mine. I don't want you to touch it. They are my notes. My journal. Mine.'

'Maria,' Mama says, voice almost a whisper, 'your journal contents—they are just dreams, random thoughts.'

'No. They are facts, information I know. Real names, real numbers.'

But she shakes her head. 'My dearest, you know what the doctors said. The notes in it, well, they are just flights of fancy, manic thought patterns.'

'They are not!' I yell. We all stop. My chest heaves, guards stand straight, dart their eyes to me.

Mother lets out a weak sigh and looks to Ramon. He tilts his head. No words. Mother draws in a long breath and clasps her hands. 'My dear, this place is taking its toll on you already. Of course, if you wish, Ramon will not write in your journal.' She coughs. 'Have you been to confession?'

'No,' I reply after a moment, my ribcage easing yet my hands still clenched.

'Well, maybe that's something you should consider. It may help a little. May help with everything that…that you've done. Visit the prison chaplain.'

I laugh out loud. It takes me by surprise. 'How can I do that?'

'What?' Mother looks to Ramon.

'Maria,' he hisses, as inmates and guards look to our table, 'not here. Not now.'

'I cannot see a priest. Not with my conviction.' I slap my hands to the table. 'Mama, I told you something on the phone and you denied it.'

'What?' Ramon says.

Mother presses her lips together. 'She says she saw me kissing Father Reznik.'

'Maria, you've gone too far this time.'

'Maria,' my mother says, 'your memory is not correct, my dear.'

'It is!' I scratch my head, nervous at the cloud of confusion forming in my mind. Then something else: Papa. 'Medical records!' I say. 'Papa found some medical records, about me, in the loft one day. From a…' I tap my head. 'From a hospital! I remember. It wasn't long before the accident. He told me about it…' I stop. Look down at the table. 'At least, I think he did.'

Mother reaches forward to me. 'Darling, what do you think Papa told you, hmmm? You know you have blocked all that out. Remember what your therapist said, the one the Church put us in touch with? He said your grief was affecting your memory. Why, at one point you could hardly recall what Papa looked like, let alone recollect specific conversations—it was too painful for you. Oh, you were so close to him. Papa's little girl.' She reaches for me.

But I ignore her advance, and close my eyes, will the memory—any memory—to work its way into my head, knocking aside the ingrained grief with all my might. Papa, whispering to me in the loft, I am so sure it happened. I scrunch my eyes tight, slap my hands to my ears to block out the sounds from the room. Think. He found paperwork, a trail of it via a computer link. What did it say? What? My mother's voice is calling out at me now, opposite me, but I have to ignore it, have to relive what I saw so I can tell them, tell them that Papa was…

'He was scared,' I say aloud, my hands still cupped on

my ears. 'He was scared. I remember! He was scared when he told me about a document he had found, and I know this, I know he was frightened, because he said so and his were hands shaking when he spoke to me, when he showed me the file. It was crammed with names, dates, codes, contacts, countries. It was! With my medical details from a hospital in…'

I avoid their stares, instead scanning my memory banks, urging my brain to help me, to not betray me this once. It works.

'Scotland,' I declare, a wide smile spreading across my face, elated. The conversation with Papa, the one I could never recall, the one I was always too upset to evoke, so sad was I at his loss, my brain jumbling my thoughts to a point where I made my papa into something else in my head, sometimes into a bear or a lion. And when he spoke to me in my fevered dreams it was, instead, with a roar or a growl. Not words. But now—now it is coming back to me. It must be here, in prison—the fresh trauma, the noise, the overloading of my senses. It has shaken my brain, unlogged something I thought I would never hear again: my papa's voice.

'I saw it,' I say now, fast. 'Something about a hospital in Scotland and…' I stall. Nothing else comes. Think. What was it? Who did he warn me against? Mama speaks, but my brain is on autopilot. Louder, faster, uploading data initiated from something from…from…

'Mother!'

Ramon and Mama blink at me.

'Jesus Christ, Maria,' Ramon hisses, 'what are you playing at? Everyone is staring.'

'I remember now,' I say, fast, fitful, giddy with possibilities, with what it all could mean. 'Papa warned me. He
said something was being done to me.' And then it occurs
to me. 'Mama! My journal! Perhaps there is something in
there, some clue I wrote down years ago.'

My mother sobs heavily, her hand flying to her mouth.

'Why on earth are you saying all this?' Ramon asks me
angrily.

'Because it is true. Don't you see? I blocked it out because I was grieving, and now, in here, after the trial, the
trauma, I remember it, not all of it, but—'

'No. Maria, stop.'

'Why?' I say, confused.

Ramon forms a fist on the table. 'Because you are lying
again.'

'I am not.'

Mama lets out another sob. Ramon glares at me, places
his arm on her shoulder, but she shakes her head, draws
a tissue from her pocket and dabs her eyes. She takes one
sip of water then draws in a breath.

'Maria,' she says, her voice tiny, like a bird's, 'you can't
say things like that about me, about your papa. The therapist predicted this might happen. He said the conversations
you believe you recalled having with Papa may never have
even occurred. It was grief back then, Maria, that made
you confused.' She sniffs. 'It is grief now.'

'But it is true.'

A small head shake. 'No, darling, no.' She clasps the tissue between her fingertips. 'My dear, you don't see what
we do. So much has happened to you that I worry. I worry
what it is doing to you, how much it has scarred you. You

are confused, scared. This much I understand. What I cannot comprehend is why you did what you did to that poor priest. Why you are spouting the lies you do now.' She exhales, her shoulder dropping, her poise gone. 'You need to stop now, my dearest. Just stop.'

My heart flutters. I wipe my eyes, not sure what to think. I know what I saw, what I heard. My mother's hands tremble, tiny movements, but I see it. Have I gone too far? If she is worried about me, about what they say I did to the priest, maybe if I tell her, she will feel better.

'I didn't kill him.'

'What did you say, darling?'

I look at Mama. 'I didn't kill him. The priest.'

Mother's head drops. Ramon places his arm round her and twists his head to me. 'Maria, this has to end. Your lies, the harm you cause.' Mother sobs; he pulls her closer. I feel a stab of loneliness. 'You were arrested, convicted, for God's sake. Accept it. Now. Before any more of us suffer.'

I blink at the table. They don't believe me. My own family. They still don't believe me. I feel as if I am falling, through the sky into a deep pit, ready for dirt to be kicked on my face, into my mouth. Buried alive. I sniff. 'Father Reznik left just after I graduated,' I say, distress creeping into my movements, my thoughts. I need my family to understand me. 'I came to England, went to the convent to find him. He was my friend. Mama, you said he had family in England. That is why I came here.'

'What?' Ramon says. 'So it's all Mama's fault now that you came here? Mama's fault that Father Reznik left? That you killed someone? Christ.' Chairs scrape on the floor ahead, visitors beginning to leave. He pauses, glances at them, then back to me. 'Maria, please. No one is conspiring against you. It's all in your head.' He pauses, swallows, his voice drops an octave. 'It always has been.'

I grip the table as if I were clawing on to the edge of reality. It's a puzzle. It has to be. Pieces, sections of time and events that slot together to create one complete picture. I just have to first find where all the pieces are.

'I am going to get out,' I say. 'Mama? I am going to request an appeal. You have to believe me. I shouldn't be here.'

Mother raises her head now, eyes rimmed pink, cheeks flushed. 'Oh, my baby. Please, listen to your brother. We both care about you so much. You are doing so much harm to yourself pursuing these…stories. Because that is all it is. Fiction. Pretend. Made up in your mind.'

'No,' I say, shaking my head, trying to stave off the doubt, the rolling wave of reservation. 'I have a new barrister.'

'Who?' Ramon asks.

'Harry Warren. He's going to help me. I am seeing him this week.'

Mama and Ramon share a glance. Ramon jots down the name.

'Maria,' Mama says, 'you know an appeal won't work, don't you?'

My stomachs twists at my mother's words. 'Mama, I have to try,' I say after a few seconds, squeezing my fingers together.

'But what about your health?' she says. 'What about your…condition?'

'It is accelerating in here.'

She goes still. 'It is? How?'

I tell her about Dr Andersson. She listens, but does not speak, does not murmur, only a slice of grimace on her face. 'It must be the prison environment,' I say. 'I can do and think faster. It happens, doesn't it? To people like me. It happens. I am even recalling more things—numbers, calculations—things I have never learnt. I have written it all down.' I stop. 'My journal, please, Mama, can you get it to me? I can cross-reference my notes.'

'Maria,' Ramon says now, 'are you lying again?'

'What? No.'

'Maria,' he urges. 'Come on. All this "doing things faster". It sounds impossible, unbelievable.'

'I am not lying!' I shout. My chest explodes and, when I look down, when I glance at my torso, I realise, to my surprise, that I am standing. Guards take a step forward; inmates gawp.

'Ramon,' my mother whispers, but we do not look at her, our attention fixed on each other. One second, two seconds, three.

'Ramon?' Mother repeats, a little louder this time. 'Ramon, I need to—' She slumps to the table.

'Mama?' Ramon looks down to her now, as do I.

My mother's body seizes like stone, then, softening, floats to the floor.

Chapter 10

An alarm pierces the air and guards rush to our table.

I stare at the floor where my mother now lies, fitting. A smell of vomit fills the room.

'Mama?' Dread washes over me, fills every molecule of my body, momentarily paralysing me. She fits again and I snap to. Moving quickly, I drop to my knees and loosen her blouse, check her vitals.

I glance to Ramon. 'Do you know what could have triggered this?' My fingers are on my mother's neck checking her pulse, her blood pumping, weak, laboured. I tilt my head, hover my ear over her mouth listening for signs of breathing. It is shallow, but there, the stench of vomit drifting in and out of my consciousness. I am about to check her chest when I feel myself dragged upwards, hands under my shoulders.

'Hey!' I shout. Two guards haul me up.

'Stay,' one of them orders like an owner would to their dog. I snarl but do as I'm told, only the sight of my mother preventing me from screaming at the guards. Ramon shoots me a glare.

A doctor and two nurses arrive now. I try to give them my medical observations but they ignore me. 'Why are you not listening to me?' I shout.

A guard intervenes to constrain me when Mama coughs, oxygen spluttering into her lungs.

'Mama?' I rush to her. Have I caused this? Have I driven my mother to illness all because of who I am?

'What is happening here?'

I turn. The Governor stands one foot from the scene, shoulders wide, face set in a frown. He spots my mother on the floor. 'Ines?'

'Balthus?' she croaks.

I spin round to her. 'You know him? How?'

The Governor turns to the attending medic. 'Will she be okay?'

But the doctor only nods before commencing chest compressions. I look back to the Governor, my eyes wide, agitated. 'How do you know my mother?' When he does not respond, I say, 'Tell me!' But a guard has arrived and is now speaking into the Governor's ear.

'Take care of her,' the Governor says to the medic team, and, throwing one more look at my mother, he strides away.

I watch as he exits the door. How does the Governor know my mother? Why did he not tell me when we met? I rub my head, spinning round to see what is happening, where my mother is. The room whirls around my head like clothes in a washing machine, noises muffled, woolly.

'Maria!' Ramon shouts.

I cock my head, blink at him. Ramon's words sound as

if they are underwater. I feel strangely stoned, intoxicated almost by events, by the confusion, the drama, the guilt.

Ramon steps over to me now, his face looming large in my vision. He finally swims into focus. 'Maria. She is trying to speak. Can you translate for the medical team,' he says. 'Maria, help, please, this once.'

Mother is lying now on a stretcher. My mama, frail, almost invisible under the blanket that shrouds her.

'Balthus?' My mother's voice croaks to life. 'Ramon, Balthus was here. My stomach hurts this time...'

I peer at her, my brain whirling back to life, connecting, solving. I relay to the medical team what she is saying, before looking back to Mama. 'How do you know the Governor, Ochoa?' I pause. 'His name is Balthus.'

'Maria,' Ramon says, 'leave her—'

'He is not who he claims to be,' mother says, then coughs into her hand.

'What does that mean?' When she does not respond, I tap her cheek. 'Tell me what that means.' But the cough returns, more violent this time, hacking.

Ramon pulls me away. 'It's back,' he whispers. 'Maria, the cancer is back. It's stage three this time.' He glances at her. 'She went into treatment last month.'

I feel decapitated by Ramon's words, sliced apart, severed by the fact that she may leave me, that someone else may leave me. I steady my voice and force myself to ask the question. 'What is her prognosis?'

He shakes his head.

'Maria?' My brother and I turn to our mother.

'No more trials, darling, please.' Her voice is flimsy like a thin sheet of tracing paper. 'You have to end this. Balthus cannot help you. He is not a good man. You are in prison. Accept it, my beautiful daughter. Get better.'

I wipe my eyes. 'Why must I stay in here?' I pause, try to breathe, be calm, quell the panic, the fear. 'Mama, please, how do you know the Governor?'

But her hands go limp, her eyelids flutter. The medics begin to wheel her away and I can barely look, my fingers squeezing each other, my mind knowing that, as she goes, my mother takes away the answers, takes away any belief or comfort she may ever have had for me. I am on the edge of jumping into an abyss of solitude.

Ramon follows the trolley, his eyes damp, his lips mouthing a goodbye to me. How do I tell him that I don't want to be left alone here? That it is dark and cold? Instead, I stand and stare; he sighs, turns his back and walks away.

'Visiting time is over,' says a guard.

I turn, knowing now what I need to do. 'I have to speak to Governor Ochoa.'

The guard laughs. 'Not going to happen.' She points to the door. 'Exit's that way.'

As the door swings open, a movement in my peripheral vision makes me halt. Someone has entered to the far right of the seated area. My mother is on the stretcher, just as I left her, three medics hovering around her, but now—now there is one more body, one more person.

Dr Andersson.

'Martinez,' says the guard, 'time to go. I haven't got all fucking day.'

I take one last look. Dr Andersson leans over and whispers in my mother's ear, rising and turning to speak to Ramon.

And Ramon? Ramon is nodding.

Ramon is staring at me.

* * *

Kurt tilts his head. 'How did you feel when your mother collapsed that day in the visiting room?'

Kurt is asking questions about my feelings. These are the worst kind. I am never sure what the correct response is. I shift in my seat, the room stuffy, suffocating. 'It was loud,' I say. 'The visiting room was loud.'

'Were you scared? Happy? Shocked when you saw her?'

I tap my finger on the chair. I do not speak, anaesthetised by the image of my mother frail on a stretcher, by the sheer desperation I felt when she said I was lying, her and my brother. Outside, the sun flickers and fades, the clouds take over.

'Tell me,' Kurt says after a while, 'have you ever wondered about your Asperger's, why certain aspects of it are more…heightened at times, particularly in comparison to others on the spectrum?'

I inhale, try to imagine I am elsewhere, that I am someone else, someone normal. 'Officially, being on the autistic spectrum and having Asperger's are now the same thing,' I say eventually. 'The American Psychiatric Association officially eliminated Asperger's as a separate syndrome.'

'And what do you think of that?'

I think about myself, how I am different from others, and them from me. 'People with Asperger's and those with autism do not have the same needs.'

He smiles. 'Really?'

'Yes.' I pause. He is still smiling. What does it mean? 'High-functioning autism cannot occur in a person with an

IQ below sixty-five-seventy. Those with Asperger's have high IQs. That is why you cannot merge Asperger's with autism.'

A beat passes. Then, 'You think you are different?'

I lower my voice. 'I know I am.'

'Special?'

'I cannot answer that.'

'Above everyone else?'

'I do not know what that means.'

He rests his cheek on his fist. 'So you believe you are high-functioning?'

'Yes. Of course.'

'How do you know this?'

'I have a photographic memory. I can fix things, reassemble electronic components at speed. I know numbers, can calculate vast equations, remember dates, decipher codes, detect patterns. I can—'

He holds up his hand. 'And you think that is normal?'

A phone shrills somewhere from outside, one second, two seconds, then stops. 'My father always said I could be myself.'

'And was he right?'

'Yes.'

'And how is that working out for you, being yourself?'

I say nothing, disarmed by his question, by his frozen smile. I don't feel safe.

'Was being convicted of murder "being yourself"?' he asks now. Then he suddenly sits forward, sets the Dictaphone on the table. 'How about this: have you ever considered that your Asperger's is not simply about nurture, or about how your father helped you, or about how you react to the environment around you?'

'I don't—' I halt. *Be careful*, a voice in my head whispers. *Be careful*.

'What about nature?' Kurt is now saying. 'What about the theory that what we are, what we do, is preprogrammed? That our DNA, ultimately, defines us? Maybe you have ended up where you are because of your genes. Maybe this—' he gestures to the room '—was always going to happen to you.'

My chest tightens. *Be careful*. 'What are you trying to say? What do you know?'

He remains quiet, still, like ice. I shiver. The clouds outside turn black, a droplet of rain taps the windowpane. 'Okay,' Kurt says finally, 'we are going to move on now.'

He consults his file. I blink, press my palms together, barely breathe. What just happened? Does he know? Does he know what we found out?

'You had a therapy session,' Kurt says, voice clipped, businesslike, 'with Dr Andersson on the twenty-third of May—the day you also met with your barrister for the first time. I want you to tell me about that.'

My shoulders tense. My friend, that day—I will never forget it, no matter what anyone tries to do to me. 'That was the day that Pat—'

'Yes, I know. I want you to tell me what happened.'

I try to remain steady, but even as I begin to speak, my hands shake a little.

Because all I can think is: why is this man here? And is he really a therapist?

* * *

'It seems your face is all over the papers. Again,' Dr Andersson says.

She talks sitting with her legs crossed, poised and ready for our therapy appointment. She slips one hand down to her shoe, flicks off the heel and rubs the arch of the foot. It is small, supple; I imagine what it would look like tied up in rope. Sighing, she pops her heel back and reaches forward to touch the pile of newspapers that fan out on the low table in front of her.

The air is hot and heavy. I don't want to be here, not wanting to talk, not wanting to ransack my brain, to verbalise my emotions, to be exhausted by the sheer effort it all takes. I dab my forehead and scan the walls, focus on anything concrete to stave off my pulsing agitation.

'You have put up your medical certificate,' I say, leg jigging. 'It is on the wall now.' My eyes survey the floor. 'And you have unpacked.'

She studies me. 'I have.' Her eyes take in the room. 'It was a little sparse before, that's for sure. Nice to have my things in here now. Feels better, less lonely.' I recoil at the word 'lonely'. Dr Andersson flicks open a file in front of her.

'I have my first meeting with a new barrister today,' I say, fixing my thoughts on facts, timings. 'It is at eleven hundred hours. I cannot be late.'

'Oh. Okay. That won't be a problem.' She clears her throat. 'So, have you seen today's papers?'

She is pointing to a low table to her right. I tuck a hair behind my ear and peer at the newspapers. I gasp at what stares back at me in colour, in plain black and white.

'Mama,' I say, laying my fingertips on the page, tracing her face, the contour of her slim neck. There are photographs of my mother, with me, old ones from graduation, of Ramon and… I stop, catch my breath, disabled by the image that swims in front of me. It is him. The nice one. The one that helped me. The one that I—

'What is it like, seeing Father O'Donnell like this?' Dr Andersson says, placing a periodical in my palms.

I blink. Still now, the sight of him makes me want to break down, to curl up, roll into a ball. 'What do you mean?' I manage to say.

'The picture,' she says, 'of Father O'Donnell, the priest you killed.'

'Murdered.'

A pause. 'Yes. What do you think when you see him?'

But I can barely look at him, the image choking me.

'Maria,' she says after a moment, 'it is normal for convicts to find it difficult to look at images of their victims. But I want you to try.'

'But I didn't…' I waver, suddenly uncertain about what to say, do, about what she will believe. I inhale, try again. 'He looks younger.'

She takes the newspaper from me and returns it to the table. I frown at my now empty hands.

'We need to start our session,' she says.

But instead, I pick up *El País*, its headline catching my eye, and read it aloud, a tremor trespassing my voice. '"Villanueva rushed to UK hospital".'

'Maria, can you put the paper down, we need to—'

'"Yesterday",' I read, translating, '"Congresswoman Ines Villanueva Cortes was taken ill during a visit to Goldmouth

Prison, London, where her daughter resides following a
murder conviction."' Vomit shoots up. I swallow it down,
glancing at Dr Andersson before continuing. "'Señora Villanueva is recovering in an unnamed hospital in London,
but a spokesman says that she is suffering from a stomach
bug and intends to return to full public office as soon as
she is well. Villanueva is a long-time supporter of right-
wing justice campaigns, and has acted as a defence lawyer
on many high-profile cases involving Basque terrorist cell,
Euskadi Ta Askatasuna (ETA).'"

I lower the paper. 'My mother did not have a stomach
bug. And Mama has never worked on ETA cases. Why are
they lying?'

Dr Andersson picks up a pen, rolls her eyes. 'Newspapers print incorrect details all the time, Maria. Maybe she
has just commented on the cases? And someone must have
released the illness part to the press.' She clicks the pen.
'Your mother probably doesn't want the world to know her
personal problems.'

I return to *El País*. Lies printed in black and white. Who
told the reporter my mother had a stomach illness. Why? I
place the paper on the table as Dr Andersson opens a small
notepad. 'What were you talking to my mother and brother
about in the visiting area?'

'I'm sorry?' Her hand rests on the open note pages.

'I saw you talking to Ramon as I was leaving the visiting area. What were you saying to him?'

She taps her pen on her lips then exhales. 'I was checking on them.'

'You talked to them for over two minutes.' Then I make

the connection. 'Did you release the stomach bug story to the press?'

She places her pen in the crease of the notepad. 'Maria, you cannot make false accusations like that. I simply wanted to ask how they were. It is important for me to understand how things are with the whole family, and…' She lets out a breath. 'Look, Maria, I think you are being a little paranoid.'

'No, I am not.'

'I believe you are. You think you see things, but you do not.'

I tug at my collar. No window in this room, no way out. I feel squashed, pressed against an invisible wall. 'All I have done is ask you a question and state a fact.'

'You and I both know what you really meant. Let's not play games.'

My inner safety alarm starts to beep. 'I am not playing games.' I dig my thumbnail into my skin, try to remain composed.

Dr Andersson leans sideways and opens a cupboard. 'I have to take some blood. Give me your arm, please.'

I do not move.

'Maria, your arm.'

I remain as I am, my body dismembered by the sight of the needle, of what it represents: doubt.

'If you do not give me your arm,' Dr Andersson says, 'I will be forced to put you on notice for the segregation unit.'

I pause, my breathing shallow, the alarm shrilling in my head now, screaming at me to have caution, to be careful. Slowly, I inch out my arm.

'Thank you.'

'Threatening me with segregation; they call that black-mail.'

Dr Andersson stares at me. Then, shaking her head, she tightens the vein band and lowers the syringe. The needle pierces my skin.

'Why are you so distant from your mother?' Dr Andersson asks, as she replaces one vial with another. My blood rushes into the tube. I feel the tug of the needle in my vein, a shot of dizziness.

'We live in different countries.'

'No,' she says, her smile like a splinter on her face. I want to dig it out, throw it away. 'I meant distance as in a lack of closeness. You don't seem to like your mother. Ramon told me you shouted at her.'

I feel wounded. I like my mother. Sometimes I have not understood her, comprehended fully what she has done, but she is my mother, flesh, blood. She is Mama. Mama, Papa—they rhyme for a reason. But how do I explain that?

'I take it by your silence that means yes.' She withdraws the needle and places a cotton ball on my vein. 'All done. Hold that.'

I press down on my arm. Dr Andersson slips the tubes of my blood into a laboratory bag, zip-locks it and places it in her drawer.

'They wouldn't believe me,' I say, quietly.

'Believe what?' She turns, tilts her head, ponytail slipping on to her shoulder. 'Why do you say that?'

I sit still, glance at the drawer my blood is in, now zipped up in plastic. My blood, other people's blood—they merge in my mind. The priest. My father. Jesus Christ himself, nails through his palms, through the flesh in his feet. The violent symbol of the Catholic faith, the stick, the baton used to silently strike us.

Dr Andersson picks up a remote control and directs it at an iPod dock that sits on a shelf to the right. Erik Satie piano melodies begin to play.

'*Gymnopédie* number one,' I say, coming round. I remove the cotton wool, pausing to gaze at the pinprick of blood left behind, then place the white ball on the desk.

'Do you know Satie?'

'How would I know him? He is dead.'

'No.' She exhales. 'I mean do you know of him? His music, his life?'

'Composer Erik Satie was French. He was the son of Alfred and Jane Leslie Satie, and was born in Normandy in 1866. He is mostly famous for his three *Gymnopédies*—short, ethereal pieces written in ¾ time.'

'That's…well, you know…a lot.' She clears her throat. 'So, I'd like to get started today. What can you tell me about the priest at your local church when you were growing up?'

'What?' I feel as if I have been hit by a Taser. 'How do you know about him?'

'What was his name?'

The piano melody is low, but it seems to boom in my head. 'The music is too loud.'

She turns it down. 'Better?'

I nod.

'Can you tell me his name now?'

My fingers interlock, foot swings over and over.

'Maria, can you—?'

'Father Reznik.'

She smiles. 'Thank you.' She jots it down and I try to

clear my head, try not to relive events in the visiting room
with my mother, what she said, what she believed. Or
didn't. I let the music wash over me, cleanse me. I don't
think it works.

'Maria, from the notes I received from your therapist at
home in Spain, you told him that you sometimes saw other
doctors. Is that correct?'

Black eyes. Why does the phrase *Black Eyes* appear in
my mind? My heart rate shoots up. Alert. 'How do you
know this?'

'It is my job. You are a convict, Maria. All your files are
accessible.' She twists her mouth. 'So, can you tell me?'

'I would rather show you.'

'Show me?'

I untuck my blouse from my waistband and roll up the
fabric. Just above my trouser line is a burn mark. It is 5 centimetres by 0.5 centimetres. It is brown and pink in colour.

Dr Andersson draws in a sharp breath and puts her hand
to her mouth.

'He seared me like cattle,' I say. The piano melody flows
in my ears. 'This,' I say, pointing to the scar, 'was my mark.
It was so he could see if I felt any pain.'

'Who?'

'The doctor, the one with the black eyes, when I was
young.'

She blinks at it for two more seconds, visibly shaking.
'You…you can do up your blouse now, Maria.'

I tuck my blouse back into my trousers, not before I force
myself to look at the mark, look at it to reassure myself it
is there, it exists.

'Maria, do you really think…' Dr Andersson stops, takes

a sip of water and inhales. 'Maria,' she tries again, 'in an old evaluation, you said "someone with black eyes did this", said he may have been a doctor, but you weren't certain.' She pauses, presses her lips together. 'I'm sorry, I have to ask you: did a doctor really do that? Did he really make that mark on you?'

My heart rate flies sky-high. 'Yes.' A small swallow, nerves. 'That is what I said.' I place my hand on my chest, feel the blood banging against my ribs. She is questioning my version of events just like the last therapist did, just like they all have done.

'The trouble is,' Dr Andersson says, 'that I find your version of events very hard to believe, Maria. When I spoke to your brother in the visiting room, he said you had tendencies to make things up, remember events incorrectly, said that the death of your father affected your memory greatly.' She presses her lips together. 'That sort of memory loss, that mis-recollection of events following the death of a loved one is not uncommon. It can last for years—a lifetime, in some cases. The brain in people who are grieving, well, studies show increased activity in the neuron network. These areas link to mood. To memory, to the absence of it.' She pauses, searches my face. 'Maria, these grief-initiated neuron patterns are also associated with how we perceive things, with how we rationalise. They are even associated with the function of our organs. Don't you see, Maria?'

I remain still, silent, too scared to admit that she may be right.

'Loss, disappointment—grief,' she continues, 'they can have a huge impact neurologically. And the more we linger on negative feelings, on thought patterns, the more established these connections, these neurological trails are. The consequences can be chronic worry, anxiety, unending grief, habitual loneliness. So—' she exhales, pointing to my blouse '—is this not simply a childhood scar you have on your stomach? Perhaps some accident you are recalling incorrectly? Your mother, in reports I have read, has said you used to be a little accident prone.'

'No,' I say after a moment, quiet, lost. 'I have never been accident prone. Why…why would Mama say that?'

Dr Andersson slips her left leg over her right. 'Maria, being accident prone is a common side effect of grief. It is because the mind, in grief, becomes easily distracted. Couple this with your apparent memory loss induced by the death of your father—and now the death of the priest, the one you murdered—and well, no wonder you cannot recall every tiny past detail correctly.' She stops, tilts her head. 'What do you think?'

I try to stay calm, try to think it all through but they overwhelm me. Dr Andersson's words slam hard against my skull, and no matter how hard I try to stall it, my breathing becomes rapid, burning. The urge to feel something, to physically feel something, instantly, now, something tangible, real, rises up within me, because the words people say, I am discovering, they are like bubbles blown in the air: there one minute, gone the next. As if they were never made.

'Maria?'

I ignore Dr Andersson and place my index finger on the scar beneath my blouse. The mark is bumpy and, when I apply pressure on it, the skin on either side feels tight. I press harder, then harder again, deep into the mark, sharp so I can feel it.

'Maria,' Dr Andersson says, 'what are you doing? Stop.'

But a wave of pain hits me and her voice fades away. My pulse rockets, my brow sweats. Whether it is the throbbing of the scar or the heat of the room, I do not know, but I begin to remember something, like an image on a movie reel it clicks into view, appearing frame after frame, until it is clear, present, as if I were there. I hear it at first: the whoosh of an aeroplane engine. Then I feel it: cold air. We are somewhere mountainous, desolate, and when I scan the area I see that there, in the distance, shooting past, is heather, moorland. And then we are travelling higher. The air is thinner. My chest tighter. And then what I see next is what makes me freeze. A hospital bed. Lights. So many lights. Straight ones, round ones, square ones. They are so bright. Yet only one shape casts a shadow over them all: the figure of a man. A man wearing a mask, his eyes black as coal.

'Maria? Talk to me.'

I can hear Dr Andersson's voice, but it seems so far away, like a song in a valley, a whistle in the wind. I focus. The man in the mask is still there. Look at his eyes. His eyes! Look at them.

'Maria?'

Her voice becomes louder. I can hear Erik Satie's piano.

'Maria, open your eyes.'

My heart punches my ribs. I choke as if no oxygen has touched my lungs for a long time. My eyes flicker open, my hands circle my neck, throat drawn, dry.

'What just happened?' Dr Andersson says, her voice

like a blade. She grabs the remote and pauses the music. I blink as her face swims into focus. 'How often has this been going on?'

'Often.' I swallow, search for water.

'And in your head? Are you temporarily unconscious or do you recall things?'

'Recall.' My throat is dry. 'I need a drink.'

She pours me a glass. I drain it and breathe out. I saw him again. I saw Black Eyes. I ask for more water, finish it and try to focus. Why did I see him? Why now? My hands tremble as I return the glass to the table. Dr Andersson watches. I don't like what is happening to me, how it makes me feel, these moments of confusion fused with episodes of bitter, tainted lucidity.

Dr Andersson picks up her pad and scribbles some notes. 'I think your memory is more challenged than I had originally thought.' She holds her pen still. 'Tell me, what did you see?'

I take in a breath and narrate the memory, and as I do, as I tell her my thoughts, clarity blooms in my head like a flower in spring: someone is after me. It all makes sense now. My father discovered information, linked to files, documents. Even though I do not fully understand what they were exactly, even though I cannot recall it completely yet, I know it happened. And Father Reznik used to make me practice codes, test out harder and harder ones on me, always tasking me with strange projects, projects that would involve deciphering data that led to war-torn countries, to odd scenarios. I wrote it all down in my journal at Mama's house, and I have written some of it down in my notebook, here. It was all a game, the Father said, just brain training.

But what if it wasn't a game? What if he was using me? Did something happen? Did I discover something without realising? Something big? Is that why he left? I rub my forehead. I would often wake up in the vestry, him telling me I had fallen asleep. But did I? Is Papa the key? Is the memory of Papa, of his voice, of what he told me? And so if I recalled his voice here, in prison, finally, after all this time, after all these years of memory-compromising grief, will I hear it again soon? And what will it say?

My mind races past all the possibilities and I feel giddy with it all, as if I am opening up a sealed box for the first time. I have to get to my notebook. I look at the clock. Ten fifty-five. I am meeting Harry Warren soon. I have to get to Patricia, get to our cell, tell her all about these new thoughts, write them down.

'I am seeing Harry Warren at eleven hundred hours,' I say, immediately standing, feverish with fresh hope. 'I need my notebook. I have to get it from my cell. Now.'

'Wait! You can't just—'

'Now,' I repeat, running to the door.

'Maria, I need to know about this memory. Wait!'

But before she can stop me, before she can tell me I am losing my mind, I have opened the door and left, only just managing to suppress the laughter, the sheer joy that wants to erupt from deep inside me.

I arrive at our cell and scan the room. 'Patricia?' I wait, chest heaving. Nothing. 'Patricia, I have something to tell you! I need my writing pad. I think I know what has been happening with—'

I step forward and halt.

Something is swinging at the back of the cell behind the shelf. 'Patricia, Father Reznik was really…'

And that is when I see her.

Patricia, hanging above the toilet.

With her walking socks roped together around her neck.

Chapter 11

'Help!' I scream. 'Someone help!'

Guards rush into the cell and immediately radio for emergency assistance.

'The rope, the socks,' I say, fast, desperate. 'We have to loosen them, get her out. Quick.'

I hold Patricia's legs, feel the bones through her flesh as a guard frees her neck, her head flopping to one side, limp, lifeless. My friend. I fight back the tears, concentrate on what I am trained to do.

Once we have her down, I immediately start CPR. The heels of my palms press into her ribcage, pushing air into her. Then I tell the guard to copy me, to take over as I pinch Patricia's nose, cover her mouth with mine and breathe into her. When the medical team arrives, they order me to stand back. My shoulders are heavy; my hands throb. I watch as they take over the cardiopulmonary resuscitation, wiping my face, not wanting the guards to see how I feel, how important Patricia is to me just so they can laugh.

'Oi. Robot. Move back,' says the guard.

'Does she have a pulse?' I ask the doctor.

But they all ignore me and, after dragging the trolley in, lay Patricia down, a mobile CPR unit next to it. Heart rate machine. Needles.

'Get me the adrenaline and atropine,' says the doctor. 'And we're going to need the defib.'

I stay very still. This is not good news, asking for the defib. A tear leaks out, one, sliding down my cheek. My friend. She is my friend. The guard looks at my face. I rub the evidence away.

A nurse attaches the heart monitor to Patricia's chest while another holds a bag and mask over her face, over Patricia's lily-white face. I watch, body stiff like steel, yet inside, I am a whirlwind, a rabid dog, diseased, broken.

The doctor presses the heel of his hands down on Patricia's chest for CPR just as I did. 'One, two, three, four.' He looks to Patricia. 'Breathe!'

The nurse checks the monitor. 'She's in VF.'

Another tear breaks out. I slap it back.

The doctor looks up. 'Let's shock her.'

The nurse hands him two defibrillator paddles.

'Charging at two hundred. Clear!'

The medical team stands back as the doctor puts the paddles on Patricia's chest. Her body rises suddenly at the shock, and then falls.

The nurse consults the monitor. 'Nothing.'

But the doctor is already pulling up some adrenaline. He flicks the needle and injects it into Patricia's vein. 'Ten mils of adrenaline going in. Obs?'

I look at her. Please, I want good news. 'Still no response,' says the nurse. 'She's asystolic.'

'Paddles,' says the doctor. 'Charge at two sixty. Clear!'

Patricia's body rises and falls as she is shocked.

The doctor waits. 'Come on.'

My pulse pounds through my veins and if I could give it, if I could give my life, my blood to Patricia right here, right now, I would.

The nurse checks the monitor. 'No output.'

'What happened?' I look up. Dr Andersson. She is standing in the doorway.

'She tried to hang herself,' I say, my voice flat, pale.

The doctor stands back. 'Still no output.'

Patricia's chest does not move.

'Maria,' Dr Andersson says, 'do you want me to take you to get another appointment with your barrister? You've missed your slot. We can speak to the legal advisor.'

Harry Warren—I had forgotten.

'Maria,' she says softly.

There is still no output on the monitor. Patricia. She is my only friend.

'Maria?' Dr Andersson says. 'Do you want me to—'

'Yes.'

'Charge at three sixty!'

I spin round. The nurse's eyes are wide. 'Doctor, I don't think we should—'

'Three sixty, nurse!' The doctor shouts. 'Clear!'

'Maria, let's go,' Dr Andersson says, but I ignore her, not able to drag myself away, to be parted again from someone I care about. The doctor shocks Patricia with the defibrillator.

The nurse shakes her head. 'She's not responding.'

'No!' I rush forward, pleading, wild. 'Try again. You must try again!' I attempt to grab the defibrillator then stop. There is a red line running across the monitor screen. That means no output. No response.

No life.

'Martinez!' the guard shouts.

The doctor steps back, shakes his head.

'You have to call it,' says a nurse.

The doctor raises his wristwatch.

'No!' I scream, and before anyone can stop me, before anyone can realise what I am doing, I grab the defib paddles and thrust them to Patricia's chest. 'Clear!'

As the current hits her, she rises and falls once more, sharp, jerking, a bolt of a spark. I hold the paddles in the air, breath heavy, watching the monitor, time standing still. The guard dashes to me, ripping the paddles from my hand, shoving me to the side, my back thudding against the wall, but still I watch, wait. The red line. I count. One—two—three—four—five.

'Doctor,' the nurse says quietly, 'you have to call it.'

A beat appears on the monitor.

'We have a response!' says the nurse. She scans the monitor, checks as the red line once again rises and falls. 'She's got good femoral output and sinus tachy.'

I hang my head, drained, utterly spent of energy, my body slack, my nerves raw, wounded. She's not clear yet, I know that, but I can't lose her. I can't.

The doctor checks Patricia's pulse by her neck and nods to Dr Andersson. She walks over to me with a guard next to her. 'Maria, let the medical team do their job now.'

Patricia is being moved on the trolley, its steel bars, its medical tubes clinking. I pause, then, turning, remember something: my writing pad. I reach up, slide it out from the Bible on the shelf, my eyes on Patricia the entire time.

Without a word, I wipe my eyes and follow Dr Andersson out of the cell. The sound of Patricia's trolley being rushed to the hospital wing echoes in the heavy, clammy air, inmates gawping, spying on us, on what is happening, as if it is entertainment, popcorn viewing. My hands shaking, I grip my notebook and follow Dr Andersson to the legal office.

I don't know if Patricia will live or die.

* * *

When we arrive, the legal advisor is still there. I stop, write down everything I recalled in Dr Andersson's office; Dr Andersson explains to the legal advisor that I require another appointment with Harry Warren. But agitation driven by fear, fear at losing my friend, makes me speak up, makes me impatient.

'I require another appointment as soon as possible.' The words speed out. 'My cellmate hung herself.' I stop. The phrase, uttered aloud, hits me like a smack in the face. I stumble back, dazed a little, suddenly wondering where I am.

'Maria...'

But I ignore Dr Andersson and look at the legal advisor, eager to explain, to make her—anyone—understand. 'I am late because my friend attempted suicide. She used her socks. Ha!' I say, for some reason finding this funny, 'And they were mountain socks. Winter ones. I should have known—I am not stupid. Not stupid. I should have known you don't have thick mountain socks in prison. I had seen Patricia with them. I did not realise she would try to kill herself with them. And then I had a therapy session with Dr Andersson. I returned to my cell, because I had forgotten my notes. I do not forget, but I did. It is this prison, this place. I walked in and I… I…'

Dr Andersson steps towards me. 'Breathe. You couldn't have known. Breathe.'

I cup my hands in front of my mouth. 'I am breathing,' I say, gulping in air, my lungs beginning to slow. 'If I did not breathe, I would be dead.'

Dr Andersson sighs. The legal advisor raises her hand. 'Er, can I just say something?'

We both look at her.

She points to the interview room. 'The barrister your inmate came to see? Harry Warren?'

'Yes?' Dr Andersson says.

She glances between the two of us. 'He's still here,' she says. 'Mr Warren is still in the interview room.'

* * *

A tray of sandwiches sits on the table.

Kurt is standing by the window. He has a plate in his hand and on it are two triangle-shape sandwiches, each containing tuna and mayonnaise. I uncross my legs, lean forward and pick through the bread. I select a ham sandwich, discard the tomato and bite. It tastes of sugar and fat.

Kurt turns away from the bars. He dabs his hand with a serviette and returns to his seat. His plate down, he brushes his palms together and, flashing me a smile, picks up his Dictaphone.

'We are going to recommence our discussion now.'

I swallow the sandwich. 'Now?'

He says nothing and clicks the record button. 'I want to talk to you about father figures.'

'I do not understand.' I wipe my mouth with my palm and shiver.

'A father figure is a man who is older and is regarded by someone younger as a person who has paternal qualities—fatherly qualities—and therefore may be a substitute for a father, emotionally. Someone who fills a void.'

This is not a phrase I am familiar with. 'Is that a dictionary definition?'

He stares at me before speaking again. 'Maria, do you think the Governor—Balthus Ochoa—may be a father figure?'

'To whom?'

'To you, Maria.'

I tap my finger. A whisper tells me I have to tread carefully here. Think. What does he expect me to say? 'I have a father,' I say, after a moment.

'Had.'

I stay still. Had a father. Past tense. How much about Papa and me does Kurt know, does the service he works for know?

The door opens and the woman from earlier—leather jacket, bob, girlfriend, eyes—enters with coffee. She throws Kurt one brief smile then removes the uneaten sandwich tray and replaces it with a pot and cups. One more smile and the woman exits, leaving a vapour of Calvin Klein perfume behind her. Kurt leans forward, pours a coffee and hands it to me.

'Drink. It will make you feel better. I know there's a lot to take on board at the moment. And you seem tired.'

Slowly, I take the cup.

'Good. Now drink.'

Whether it is the sudden flash of steel in his voice or the cold stream of air lingering from the open door, I do as I am told, and swallow some coffee. It tastes good, steam rising to my eyes, stinging them, slapping me awake. I take a few more sips then lower the cup. Kurt is writing some notes; the curtain at the window is floating up and down. All is normal. I move to set down my cup when my eyes spot something on the ceiling. My heart accelerates. I look to Kurt; he is still writing. I glance back to the ceiling and squint.

Without drawing attention to myself, I inch forward. I place the cup on the table and keep very still.

Kurt raises his head. I do not move. He clicks his pen and smiles. 'Do you know, I don't think I've said it yet, so I will say it now: you are safe here, Maria, with me,' he says. 'I just want you to know that. This is a safe place.'

I do not blink.

Kurt is smiling at me.

There are now two spiders on the ceiling.

Chapter 12

'The DNA evidence is inconclusive.'

I have been sitting in front of Harry Warren QC for fifteen minutes and thirty-two seconds. He has been recalling all the aspects of my original trial—the evidence, witnesses, timings. I have been jittery and vague. Patricia, her body being shocked with electricity, her head hanging like a limp rag doll, is an image that constantly plays in my mind like a showreel.

Despite my discomfort and confusion, Harry has been very thorough. Four times now he has stated that he is not impressed with the way in which the evidence was portrayed in the original court, so much so, he says, that he cannot believe my counsel were allowed to practise. When yet again I am slow to respond, Harry lifts his eyes from his file. In the flesh, he is stouter than his photos convey. His torso, his arms are fuller, cheeks plump on black skin, skin so shiny, so alive I feel he could last forever, that, as if by sheer force of his rooted, warm-blooded presence, he will always be around, like a house built of timber that never collapses. Safe. A haven.

He smiles at me, revealing large white teeth. 'Maria,' he clears his throat, 'your DNA, it says here, was found in three places, including the priest's shoe.'

'They were Crocs.'

'Crocs?' He laughs like Father Christmas then sighs. 'I'm so sorry.' He shakes his head. 'There is so much these days I don't know, so many new things, names.'

I hesitate. There is something about him. Something that makes me breathe more easily. A familiarity. 'Crocs are shoes,' I say finally.

He nods. 'Thank you.'

I watch him for a second then continue. 'I had purchased the footwear when I first arrived in London. I told the prosecution that they were mine, old ones from the operating theatre. They had never fitted me correctly.'

Harry unlaces the pink ribbon from the legal brief on the table. 'And why did you give them away?'

'I had a blister,' I say, 'from running shoes I had purchased in haste when I arrived in the UK. The Crocs I bought for surgery rubbed at the blister when moving. They hurt at the heel, so I donated them to the convent. They sell items like shoes to raise money. The priest must have kept them for himself; the trace of blood from my blister was left on the Crocs. The DNA…'

I trail off. DNA. I flip open my notebook, fly to the page, to the diagram—one of many I have instinctively drawn without knowing why. When I find it, my fingers hover. There. Deoxyribonucleic acid. The twisted double helix, the ladder of vertical sugar and phosphate modules.

Our human blueprint. I dreamt about it, one of the first few days in prison. Thousands of DNA structures were flying around my head. And now Harry is talking about it, about my case, my DNA.

Harry leans forward a little. 'Is that…?'

My eyes fly to him. 'What?'

He clears his throat, sits back. 'You keep notes, many, by the look of it.' He smiles at me; it reaches his eyes. 'Good idea,' he says, jabbing a finger at his brow. 'Keeps the brain busy. Vital, hmm?' A smile again.

I slam the book shut and say nothing. I cannot determine if he is being kind. Is he?

Harry clears his throat and consults his brief. 'So, the DNA is certainly weak, but—and it is a big *but*, I'm afraid—you have no firm alibi.'

'I have an alibi.'

He sighs. 'Ah, yes. That you were at the hospital. St James's, yes? The trouble is, Maria, that there is no CCTV evidence from that night placing you at the hospital. And there is a witness—' another file consult '—a DVD store owner from the shop opposite the convent. He places you at the gates of the convent at the time of the crime.'

He sits back, removes his glasses. I inspect them and feel something well up, feel something knock on my skull, reminding me.

'My father wore spectacles like that,' I say, pointing to them, realising now what I am recalling. My papa reading his daily newspaper, glasses perched on the end of his nose, slipping as they did down the bridge, his sweat increasing as fast as the hot sun did. I breathe in, the brief memory bathing me in a rare, temporary sensation of comfort.

Harry smiles. Eye creases to match. 'From what I can see, the evidence is weak at best. That is our defence, our route, I think—discredit the forensics.' He taps the frame of his spectacles. 'I will want to reanalyse the DNA. That involves revisiting everything—all the pathology analysis, the witnesses. All upturned, back to front and side to side. Are you ready for that?'

'Yes.' I hesitate a little, fear slipping into my consciousness. The thought of repeating it all, of dealing with the whole ordeal again, of the murder details, of my apparent, non-deniable guilt. It is an overwhelming feeling. 'And after that? What happens next?'

'I will set in motion the Notice of Grounds forms for your appeal.'

'And that is everything we need to discuss?' I say, my mind back on Patricia, on finding out any news.

'Actually, no.' He touches his file and pauses. 'Yesterday afternoon, the priest's parents gave a press conference. They're unhappy that you're appealing against your conviction.'

'How do they know about the appeal?'

He shrugs. 'These things get to be public information.'

'Oh.'

'The parents are denouncing the appeal. And they are insisting that the DNA evidence is strong enough to withstand an appeal process.'

'Can they do that?'

'They can and they have. Watch.'

Harry takes out laptop and opens it. He clicks on the web browser and brings up a YouTube video. There is an image of an old man and woman sitting behind a long desk, hair a soup of grey and white, skin liver-marked, pale. A bubble of worry floats up into my head. They both look like the dead priest. I can hardly bring myself to look as Harry presses play. Reporters come alive, ask questions. Bulbs flash from every angle, the man declaring that I am guilty, the woman crying into her hands.

When it comes to an end, Harry turns off the computer and looks up. The light above us flickers, fades, then splutters back to life. 'So,' he says, after a second or two, lifting a thick file from his briefcase, placing it between us on the table, 'what are your thoughts?'

I drag my eyes away from the light. 'On what?'

'On the video, on what the parents have said.'

'Their questioning of the DNA evidence presents a difficulty to my case.' I blink, shake my head. Their faces won't leave my mind.

Harry opens the file. 'I agree.' He extracts a court paper. 'Now, their questioning doesn't mean to say that they are correct, but it does pose a challenge to us.' He places a paper in front of me. 'These are the original court documents.'

I lean forward to read, palms clammy, nervous of what I am about to see. The words 'knife', 'fingerprint' and 'trace' instantly appear. I read on, my anxiety growing. There are details of the body, of how it was found—it is all there: perforating stab wound; nails in the hands; torso sprawled out at the altar; bruises inflicted; restraint used.

'I want to, with your permission, Maria, revisit the legal principles surrounding the nun's actions upon the discovery of the body.' Harry looks at me. I smell him now: a warm fug of tobacco, of icing sugar, of freshly baked bread. I inhale the soothing scent, and my whole body wants to fall into him, to let itself go, let itself be comforted by him, be told by him that everything is going to be okay.

'So the nun,' Harry continues, 'her acting immediately upon finding the priest could have saved his life. It could have broken the chain of causation.'

I snap to, shake off his smell. 'This chain of causation has never before been discussed.'

'It should have been.' He hesitates for a moment. 'Please be aware, Maria, that to get this conviction overturned, whatever we have must be bulletproof.'

'"Bulletproof"? That is a phrase meaning "beyond reasonable doubt".'

Harry nods. 'The judge should hear your application for permission to appeal any day now. As soon as we know anything, I will inform you. Okay?'

'Yes.'

Harry begins to slide away the paperwork. I watch him and feel a sudden rush of something that I cannot identify. A feeling. Gratitude? Think. What would Patricia tell me to do? I place one hand on the table. 'Thank you,' I say eventually, slow, measured.

He pauses, smiles, then resumes gathering files. We walk to the door. Harry presses the exit buzzer and waits. 'I hear you helped your cellmate. She tried to commit suicide.'

I swallow. 'Yes.'

He pats me on the shoulder. I flinch. 'I'm sorry,' he says, and lowers his hand. After a second, he smiles again, the type of smile that creases at the eyes. 'You know, you remind me of my own daughter,' he says. 'You're a similar age. She is strong, like you. Beautiful, too. But then, I am biased.' He reaches into his pocket and gives me a card. 'Here. For you.'

I take it. It contains his name, telephone number and address.

'I will arrange everything for you,' Harry says. He holds out his hand. I stare at it. 'I'll be in touch very soon.'

I wait, then realising that he expects me to shake his hand, I do so. It is large and damp. When I let go, I wipe my palm on the back of my trouser leg.

Harry signals to the guard that he is ready to go.

'Well,' Harry says, 'it was a pleasure to meet you. Take care of yourself, Maria.'

'Martinez,' the guard says, as Harry exits, 'the Governor said you're to go to the hospital wing immediately.'

Patricia. I hold my breath. 'Is she alive?'

'Come on. I'll take you.'

Chapter 13

The IV fluid drips into Patricia's arm as her chest rises and falls. I watch her, my lips parted waiting for words that cannot come, my hands clenched, worried, restless. She seems so fragile, Patricia, so transparent, like I could poke her, pierce my finger right through her and it would come out on the other side, neither of us hurt.

At the end of the bed hangs her chart. I set down my notebook and stretch across and scan it. It is hard reading. Patricia's airways have been restricted, the trachea temporarily closing, preventing oxygen from travelling to her lungs. She is alive. But only just. I examine her body, eyes resting on her neck. Red welts snake round it, skin open, pink with pressure. She is lucky to have been revived and I am relieved, relieved that she is here, not gone, not dead in the ground, but with me, now, her friend, her ally.

I return the file to its home and search for a medical torch. There are no nurses in the immediate vicinity, no guards by my side. Locating a torch on the bedside table,

I stand then leaning over Patricia, open her lids and check her observations.

'You took your time.'

I jump at the sound of Patricia's voice, dropping the torch. It bounces along the floor.

'Hey, hey,' she croaks. 'It's okay, Doc. It's okay.'

I touch my cheeks. Damp.

'It's okay to cry. You had a shock.' She is attempting to pull herself upright in bed.

I wipe my face. 'You must not move yet.' I link under her arms, heaving her up until her back is resting on the pillow behind. 'Do you have any signs of dizziness, pain. Nausea?'

She winces. 'No. I'm fine.'

I sit, shattered.

'Why did you do it?' I say, a clock ticking somewhere, the sound of whistling in the far distance.

Patricia looks at her hands. Two, three seconds pass. 'Ten years,' she says finally. 'I've been in prison for nearly ten years now.'

'I know. Why are you telling me this?'

She closes her eyes. 'I just struggle knowing my family hate me.'

'They do not hate you.'

'They do.'

'I do not hate you.' She opens her eyes, smiles. My throat feels tight, and I try to swallow, try to feel some moisture, but it does no good. I have nothing left.

'Hey,' Patricia says. 'It's going to be okay.'

'You cannot do it again,' I say, swallowing.

'I won't.'

I shake my head. 'You cannot do it again. You cannot…

You are my only friend.' I smear the tears from my face. 'I thought you had…' I sniff. 'I thought you had died.'

'You saved my life.'

I hiccup, gulping down air.

'Doc? Doc, breathe—'

'I could not help you,' I say, an unfamiliar burning need to get the words out. 'I had no equipment and the medical team seemed to take so long to arrive.'

'Why don't you—'

'Why did I not know you were going to kill yourself?' Patricia pauses. 'You couldn't have known. It was my decision.'

'No.' I tap my fingers fast. 'I should have known. But I cannot know, can I? Not being the way I am. Anyone else would have noticed how you were feeling. But not me.'

She sits forward. 'No one else would have known. Doc, listen to me. No one else would have known.'

My chest heaves up and down. I blink. Patricia's face swims into focus. I gulp in oxygen, cup my hands over my mouth, peering at Patricia over my fingers.

'Ssshh. Breathe. Good.' She reaches out her hand and places it flat on the bed sheet, spreads out her fingers, all five of them, in a star shape.

'I won't do it again,' she says.

Her hand is on the bed. I hesitate at first, then slowly I lower my palm to hers.

'I am getting out on parole soon,' she says. 'The Governor came and told me just before. So, see? I'm going to be okay.'

'But if you are out of prison, I will be in here without you. I will be alone again.'

She moves her fingers closer to mine.

Our fingertips lay in two star shapes on the sheet, touching now, and in that moment I know that this is the one person in the world I can truly trust.

So I draw in a deep breath, open my notebook and tell her all about the puzzle I am beginning to unravel.

* * *

I pour some more coffee. The dark liquid wobbles in the cup, images of the room reflecting on the surface. There one minute, gone the next.

The room is warm, but I shiver. I pull my blazer tight and clutch the coffee cup, but after one sip, I scrunch up my nose.

'This coffee does not taste normal,' I say, but Kurt is writing and does not seem to hear me. I repeat the statement, but still he remains silent.

From outside, life continues to drift in through the window; the pictures on the wall sit where they always have; the spiders hunch two by two in the corner, cobwebs forming like icicles in winter. I don't even know if they are real or not. For some reason, I hold out my coffee cup and study it. It looks normal, ceramic, white. Nothing has changed, everything is just as I remember it. Yet Kurt is convincing me my judgement is impaired. And I am beginning to believe him, but I don't know why. So much of this puzzle up until now has been solved, yet here I am, wondering what has really happened to me, questioning, again, whether my brain is working properly, and when I say everything aloud, when I put it into concrete words, it all sounds just as everyone has been telling me it does: Like a story. Like a work of fiction. A mis-recollection.

Shaking my head, I sip some more coffee then stop. Something is not right. I sip again, checking, but yes, I am right. The coffee. It *does* taste odd. 'Liquorice,' I say to myself. I glance to Kurt—his head is still bowed, busy.

I set down the cup and scan the room. All still normal. I tap my head, dislodge my thoughts. My mind is getting carried away, my feelings, my deductions. I am adding two and two together and getting five. I frown, tutting at myself. This has to stop, doesn't it? Whatever is going on, it all has to stop. As the curtain floats into the room, my eyes drift to the ceiling and—

I go very still.

I squint, lean forward. It cannot be. How? I bang my head with the heel of my hand, look again, but there is no mistaking it.

The cobweb—it is not there.

I look at Kurt. He is still writing his notes; he is not drinking any coffee.

* * *

The canteen is quiet.

I have been sitting, writing in my notebook whilst nobody sees—it is a risk, but I need to write, need to count the words, the pages, that way they may last, may be real. Patricia said she believed what I told her about Father Reznik, about him being involved somehow, about it all being connected—my father, his discovery of the documents. She said she would help me. I scan once more through the codes scratched out on the page, the numbers, equations covering every millimetre of space. What do they mean? I think of Patricia, of her faith in me. To have a friend who believes me, who is on my side, accepts me for who I am, for what I am. For the first time ever, it feels good, not bad or defective. Good. Human.

From the far wall, shouting erupts followed by a clatter of trays. The hall is filling up, food smells, body odour, too many flabby bodies.

I set down my pen and slip my notebook behind my plate. I pick up a napkin and dab the corners of my mouth three times, my eyes on the now fast-growing canteen queue. I watch for Patricia. Since her emergency stay in the hospital ward, I ensure she is okay and eating enough at every mealtime.

'Got yourself a notebook, hey?'

I turn at the sound of the voice.

'Hi,' a woman says, holding out a hand. 'I'm Bobbie Reynolds.' She grins. Her arm is slim, her shirt blue and crisp. The chinos on her legs are ironed down the crease and her skin is caramel. She is like a walking Gap advert. 'What's your name, then?' she says. When I do not reply, she simply shrugs and withdraws her hand.

The Bobbie woman drags out a chair from the table, sets down a tray and sits.

'I am waiting for someone,' I say.

She claps her hands. 'Ooh, lovely. Who are we waiting for?' She spears a tube of pasta on the plate in front of her. 'I just love carbonara.'

I sniff. Her perfume: lemons and oranges. Citrus. Clean. I place my hand on the edge of my notebook and search for Patricia.

This Bobbie woman keeps eating. 'You don't say much,' she says in between mouthfuls.

I spot Patricia in the food queue. Satisfied she is okay,

I turn. 'Bobbie is short for Roberta. Roberta is the female form of Robert, meaning "bright fame".' I tilt my head. 'You are of bright fame.'

She sets down her fork then laughs. 'Ha! You're great. I love you already. What's your name?'

'My name is Dr Maria Martinez.' The hall is loud, almost full. The sounds ring in my head, endless vibrations. I cover my ears a little.

'A doctor?' She whistles. 'Good for you.' She slaps my back and I wince. 'Very nice to meet you, Dr Martinez. You've got yourself a friend here. I've got your back.'

'I have a friend,' I say. 'Her name is Patricia.'

She grins and resumes eating.

'All right, Doc?'

I look up. Patricia stands holding her tray. She sits, smiles and spoons in some pasta, looking to Bobbie. 'Who's this, then?'

'This is Bobbie Reynolds,' I say. 'She is very neat and says she loves me already.'

Bobbie spurts out a mouthful of pasta.

Patricia waves. 'Hi, Bobbie.'

'What were you convicted of?' I say to Bobbie.

'Doc,' Patricia says, 'you've got to keep your voice down when you say things like that in here, because—'

'Murder.'

We look to Bobbie.

'In answer to your question, Dr Martinez,' Bobbie says, her elbow perched on the table, 'it was murder.'

'Of a man or a woman?'

Patricia drops her fork. 'Doc! Ssshh.'

'Man,' Bobbie says, her eyes on me, not missing a beat. 'Definitely a man.' She grins and pierces a mushroom. 'I was convicted of the murder of a male of the species.'

Chapter 14

The canteen is noisy now, so to block the sound from penetrating my ears, I concentrate on this Bobbie character as she studies her speared mushroom.

'Why do you ask about my conviction?' she says, mouth full of pasta.

Murder, I think. She has killed someone. I pick up my knife. 'Would you kill again?'

'Steady,' Patricia says, her eyes narrowed.

Bobbie glares at Patricia then smiles at me. 'In answer to your question—yes. I would kill again.' She proffers me a toothy grin.

I watch her. She makes me feel uneasy, as if she is hiding something. As Bobbie and Patricia resume eating, I push my plate to one side to retrieve my notebook, but it is gone. Bobbie clears her throat. There, in her hand, is my writing pad.

'Looking for this?'

'Yes.'

She holds it out to me. I hesitate then take it. I try to ignore her, but there is a tug on my sleeve.

'Hey,' Bobbie says, pointing. 'She your friend?'

'Doc,' whispers Patricia, 'it's Michaela.'

I see her. She is striding towards us. I touch my forehead where my right temple still has a shadow of a bruise, mild panic bubbling underneath my skin.

Bobbie throws down her fork and drags back her chair. 'It's okay, Doc, like I said, I've got your back.' And with that, she stands and positions herself between Michaela and me.

'Mickie, isn't it?' says Bobbie, smiling. 'How are you?'

I look to Bobbie. Does she already know Michaela Croft? But how? Bobbie has only just arrived at Goldmouth.

Michaela pushes Bobbie to one side. 'Fuck off, you psycho.'

'And so lovely to see you, too, Michaela,' says Bobbie, bowing.

'You,' Michaela says, jabbing a finger at me, 'I got fucking solitary because of you.'

Her accent. It is her regular East London accent, but there is something different. I try to place it, but nothing. No memory. No thoughts. I find myself clenching my fists.

'Cat got your tongue?' Michaela says, taking a step towards me.

I touch my tongue; no cat on there.

'Leave it, Croft,' says Bobbie.

Michaela goes still and looks down; Bobbie has put a hand on her chest. I search for the guards, but they are nowhere to be seen.

'Get your hands off me, psycho.' Michaela is glaring at

Bobbie, but Bobbie simply smiles. Scared, I pick up my knife, but Patricia gives a quick shake of her head. I let go of the metal.

Slowly, with her eyes on Michaela, Bobbie lowers her hand. And then it happens. Michaela—fast, precise—lunges towards me. Before I can move, before I can roll away, she clutches my blouse, dragging me up, out of my seat. The room erupts.

I try to move backwards, but Michaela's grip is solid, so I go for a punch to her head—right side, on her temples, and I must have hit because I can hear yelling, but it is muffled, like being underwater. Michaela has her hands on me now, around my neck and so I slap her, hard on the cheek, but her grip is still tight. So, desperate, I kick, three sharp jabs to her shin with the heel of my shoe, but, even though she cries out, she pulls me back, does not let go. I try to unravel her fingers, but cannot get free. I try to dig her with my elbow, shove her—nothing. But then—pop. Michaela's grip slackens. Just like that. I drop to the floor and gulp great swells of air. Michaela is gasping for breath beside me, her body writhing on the floor.

'Bloody hell, Bobbie,' Patricia says, 'what did you do?'

I dart my eyes back and forth. The guards are running over now, the room sways, my mind whirring. And that, then, is when I remember: Michaela in the cell. Her accent changed. She was Scottish. Suddenly, like a game of dominoes, all the pieces connect, fall into one another. Bang, bang, bang. She told me to stay put. She knew of Father Reznik. She is Scottish. The medical notes my father found, they were from a hospital in Scotland.

Which means she is not who she says she is.

'Get up, Doc, quick!' says Patricia.

My brain engages. I scramble up to a stand and Patricia brushes me down. 'Let Bobbie handle this,' she whispers.

The guards run over. They know something is happening, but as far as I can tell, they have seen nothing. No detail.

Bobbie shouts to them. 'She's choking! Help us. Quick!' Then briefly, in the blink of an eye, she turns to me and smiles like someone who has just walked out of an asylum.

Three guards arrive.

'Help her!' Bobbie is saying, but she is not looking at the guards, she is looking at me. Bobbie jerks her eyes to Michaela, but I do not understand.

'Tell the guards,' says Patricia, fast. 'Doc, tell the guards what is wrong.'

Now I comprehend. I point to Michaela. 'She is asphyxiating,' I say, quickly. The guards hesitate. I crouch to my knees and tug at Michaela's collar. 'Her trachea has been restricted. Her airway.'

'She's a doctor,' says Bobbie.

The guard eyes me with suspicion. 'What was with the raised voices before?'

'Oh, you know,' Bobbie says to the guard, 'high jinx. I think some food might have gone down the wrong way.'

I tilt my head. That is not true. I open my mouth to say so when there is a tug on my blouse. Patricia is glaring at me, a finger on her lips. 'Ssssh.'

The guard looks at us. 'All right,' she says, 'let's get Croft checked out.' She twists to face the dining hall. 'Show's over,' she says, addressing the staring audience of inmates. When no one moves, she yells, 'Bugger off. Now. Or you'll find your TV privileges revoked.'

The inmates grumble, shuffling off, and I watch as Michaela is led away, her feet dragging along the tiles, face white, small pink fingermarks on her neck.

Patricia whistles. 'Holy Jesus.' She turns to me. 'Doc, you okay?'

I nod.

'Then let's go.'

I start to follow her when I feel a tap on my shoulder. I turn. Bobbie hands me my notebook. 'Watch out,' she says.

'For what?' I snatch the writing pad from her.

She steps in closer. 'Don't trust anyone, you hear me?' Her eyes dart left and right. 'You're not safe in here. They thought you would be, but now that's changed. Everything has changed. Someone is after you in here, in the prison.'

'You do not make sense.'

'I have instructions to watch you. And I will. But help me. Keep your head down. I'll watch Croft, make sure she's kept away from you.'

The accent. The hospital. Can she help? 'What is Callidus?' I say. Bobbie goes quiet. 'Is it a hospital in Scotland? Is that where Mickie Croft is from? Who is she?'

'MI5.'

The word hangs in the air like a poisonous gas.

'What?'

Bobbie checks the area. 'They will kill you. Do you hear me? Kill you. That's why I'm here, to keep an eye on you. They thought they could keep you in here to be safe and then it all imploded, all broke up, a scandal.'

I try to compute what she is saying. 'What scandal? Who is "they"?'

She pauses. 'The Project.'

'What is that?'

'I don't have the clearance to say any more. But what you need to know is the Project will protect you. MI5 won't.'

I connect it, attempt to put it all together, but it is jumbled like a Rubik's cube split into multiple colours. MI5? And then I feel it: the sharp needle of realisation. I put my fingers to my mouth, sick at the thought. 'Was Father Reznik part of this?'

She hesitates then slowly nods. 'Him, your two previous university professors and your boss at St James's.' She pauses. 'And now? Dr Andersson.'

'What?' My head spins, stomach lurches. 'How?'

'They were you handlers, Doctor. They were your handlers,' she says.

'Handlers? Handlers for what?' My mind races, pinging from one pinball to another, suddenly frightened. People I thought I could trust, people who were supposed to support me, protect me in some way, were not who they said they were at all. How can Dr Andersson be part of it? None of it makes sense. None of it. I look up to speak to Bobbie, but she is striding away.

'They were handlers for what?' I shout.

'For you, Maria. They were all working for the Project.'

'What is the Project?'

She keeps walking. 'Look in your notebook. The answer is there.'

I shake my head, dazed. 'Answer? What answer?' I say, calling after her. 'What answer?'

But she has already gone.

* * *

Kurt crosses his legs and presses record on the Dictaphone.

When I ask him if I can perhaps get some fresh air later, he simply narrows his eyes and makes some notes. I look at the coffee cup, worry infecting me like a disease.

A siren wails from outside. He glances up. 'Tell me, Maria,' he says, once it has passed, 'did you ever consider that—' he consults his notes '—Bobbie was make-believing?'

'What do you mean?'

'Make-believing—it means pretending, making up a story. Lying.'

'I... I...' I halt, inhale. I know she was telling the truth. I have the proof now. I run a finger around my collar. 'I am warm. Can I have some water?'

He nods, gesturing to the jug. I pour a glass, stall for time. I have found out so much since Bobbie came to me that day, but what do I tell Kurt? He thinks Bobbie was lying. I study him. His body, now, is relaxed, but there is something there, in his eyes, a glint, a flash of something. What? Suspicion? Murkiness? I take another sip, set down the glass. I will see what he has to say first.

'Maria? What do you think about what I said?'

'She was not make-believing.'

A small head shake. 'I thought you might say that.' He sits forward. 'The way I view it, we are looking at one of two scenarios here. One: you are, again, recalling information incorrectly, your memory compromised; or two: Bobbie Reynolds was lying because she is a psychopath.'

I grip the seat. The worry creeps higher. 'It is neither of those. She was telling the truth. I am telling the truth.'

Kurt supplies a brief smile. One, two, three seconds pass. I stay very still, curtains billowing, scared to move, scared to admit what may be happening here.

'Do you like to be in control, Maria?' he says suddenly.

I clear my throat, unsure how to answer, uncertain at what he is trying to do. I decide to answer yes.

'And what does that tell you about yourself?'

'That I like to be in control, of course.' Stay calm. Stay calm.

'Do you think that your need to be in control has shaped your memory?'

My eyes hover over the coffee pot. 'I...I do not know.' The coffee. Why did it taste odd earlier?

'See, here's what I think. You have trouble with your thoughts and feelings and speaking about them. For people like you, in your situation, it is not uncommon to experience difficulties in relating to, and communicating with, others—for there to be a certain cessation of verbal reasoning, shall we say? You think that if you tell me about your inner feelings, you will lose control over yourself, over your life. Over your future.'

'No. I have Asperger's. I feel emotions just like everyone else, I just cannot communicate them. It is nothing to do with control.' My eyes fix on the coffee cups in front of us.

Kurt exhales. 'Okay,' he says, clapping his hands. I jerk my eyes to his. 'We are going to use a new room.'

'What?'

A slice of smile again. 'The service has a room designated, indeed designed, to help with situations like yours.'

'What do you mean, "like mine"?'

'People who have trouble sharing their thoughts, opening up. Like you.'

'I have opinions about many aspects of society.'

'I'm sure you do,' he says, gathering his belongings, 'but it is not your opinion on society I am after.'

He stands and walks to the door. 'I am after your feelings, Maria.' He opens the door and a waft of stale air sweeps in. 'I am after your real memories. I want to know, for example, how it makes you feel when you realise people like Bobbie Reynolds are liars. That is what I am interested in hearing.'

He holds open the door. Cold air sweeps in. I swallow, not wanting to move, frightened, but I don't know of what. Of Kurt?

'Maria, you signed a document agreeing to our therapy methods,' he says. 'You need to come with me.'

I peer through to the corridor beyond. White, no windows, no people. My heart slamming against my ribcage, slowly, I stand.

'Good. This way.'

Kurt walks through the door, and I have no choice but to follow him.

Chapter 15

Patricia leans against the wall, sheltering her face from the sun.

We are in the prison yard. It is square in shape, the perimeter hemmed in on all sides by the building walls, the windows of the cells and offices bearing down on us, watching, spying. The ground is gagged with sand and gravel, and in the far corner sits creaking, rusty outdoor gym equipment, old, worn, like a forgotten adult playground.

The sun is warm on my face; no clouds, no rain. Yet, even when my eyes are open wide, I can only see a small slither of sky, because my mind is replaying Bobbie's words, computing what they signify. Handlers. It means, my whole life someone was watching me for an organisation I know nothing about. And those people, those handlers—I trusted them. I feel a slap of nausea at the thought. They were figures of authority. So is that what authority means, then? A series of individuals who are not who they say they are?

Who deceive? And if they were lying, then who else was? My elementary teachers? My therapists? Were they all with this Project? Is Dr Andersson a fraud, too?

I swallow hard, dig my fingernails into the wall, feel the stone. Because the thought, the realisation of it all shakes me, makes me feel as if I will stumble and fall, as if the ground beneath me is shuddering from one giant earthquake, reducing everything I once regarded as solid, as real, to specs of rubble, to figments of fiction.

Patricia folds her arms, brow set to a frown. 'Tell me again, Doc. What was Bobbie talking about?'

I draw in a breath. I have told Patricia everything Bobbie said to me in the canteen. She has not reacted well.

'She said she had instructions to protect me. That the answer was in my notebook.'

'But you looked through your notebook and you found nothing?'

I open my mouth to speak then close it. She is right.

'Doc, the thing that bothers me,' Patricia says now, her voice reduced to a whisper, 'is that Bobbie said MI5's involved. It just doesn't make any sense.'

A fight between two inmates breaks out ahead. We look. A guard shouts, runs over and separates them, the battle over before it had even begun.

Patricia kicks her heel against the wall and stares out onto the yard. 'You know they call her psycho, Bobbie?'

'Yes. But that does not mean—'

'It means everything. Jesus.' She rakes a hand over her scalp, inhales. 'Okay, say she is telling the truth? Then what?'

'Then we put it all together, we uncover everything we

can. I will study my notebook again. I have to solve this. Someone, somewhere is lying to me, lying about me.'

Patricia exhales, long, hard. 'It just seems crazy. Bobbie seems a little crazy.'

'We are all a little crazy.'

We stand by the wall and breathe in the one-hour-a-day of fresh air. The sun bobs like a globe in the sky, a soothing glow, a reassuring warmth. It is easy to imagine, to dream that we are not here, in prison, that we are elsewhere, somewhere good. Somewhere better.

We are about to leave when a figure exits from the door at the far end of the yard. I prop my hand on my brow, squint in the sunshine. The figure moves towards us at speed.

Patricia notices, too. She dips her head to get a look. 'Hey, Doc. Is that—'

'Bobbie.'

Bobbie Reynolds arrives before us and cocks her head. 'How are my two friends?'

Patricia blocks her. 'Look, Reynolds, I don't know what your game is, but quit telling seven heaps of shite to Maria.'

Bobbie laughs. 'What?'

Patricia pokes her. 'You heard me.'

Bobbie looks to me. 'We need to talk.'

'Okay.'

'Doc, no.'

'But not here,' Bobbie continues. She shoots a glance to Patricia. 'Not with her here.'

Patricia glares at Bobbie.

'I will speak to you with Patricia present,' I say. 'She knows what you told me.'

Bobbie hesitates then shrugs. 'Okay, whatever you say.'
She smoothes down her shirt. 'Has Mickie Croft told you
anything…unusual?'

'What do you mean?'

'I mean, has she said anything out of the ordinary?
Something you wouldn't expect her to say?'

'I told you that she mentioned Callidus.'

'Shit, thought that's what you'd said.' She scratches her
head.

'What is it?'

'Okay. Here's the thing. Remember I said everything
had changed?'

'Yes.'

'Okay, well, the Project used to be part of MI5, but now
it's not. There are others involved, too, but…' She breathes
out. 'Look, I can't say who, but I am authorised to say this:
Mickie Croft is out to kill you, we have confirmation now,
fresh intel. She's been ordered to do it as soon as she gets
her chance. Dr Andersson will probably assist her.'

'Bollocks,' Patricia says. 'Total bollocks. Mickie is a nut-
ter who's already laid seven bells into Maria. You know
that. You're just trying to play up to it and—'

Without warning, Bobbie flies at Patricia, wraps her
fingers round her throat and pins her up against the wall.

'Bobbie!' I yell.

'This is not a game, do you hear me?' Bobbie spits, teeth
snarling. Patricia manages a small nod. 'It's not a fucking
game.'

Bobbie lets go and Patricia drops to the ground, gasping. I run to her.

'Why did you do that?' I say, checking Patricia.

Bobbie brushes herself down. 'Because this is serious. The Project put me here to protect you. You are not safe here.'

I look at her, my mind questioning over and over whether I should believe her. Then a puzzle piece slots into place. 'Callidus and the Project—they are the same thing.'

She nods. 'Project Callidus—that's the code name.'

My brain whizzes, computes, calibrates. 'That's where they took me.'

'What?

Patricia stands. 'Doc?'

But I ignore her, look to Bobbie, hands shaking, eyes wild. 'Sometimes I have memories of being in a ward, a hospital. They are doing tests on me, horrible tests. Was it there? Did they do the tests there, at Callidus?'

Bobbie looks between me and Patricia, her fists clenched, her brow furrowed. 'Yes,' she says after a moment, a whisper. 'They did tests there. Yes.'

'So the handlers, my professors, my boss—they were all with this Project Callidus?'

A nod.

I slap my hand to my mouth. 'My God.' I stumble back against the wall. And then I realise. 'Dr Andersson—she takes my blood, does tests on it.'

'Doc, you okay?'

'I have to go,' Bobbie says, fast. 'Speak to the Governor, bring your notebook. He has a laptop…you'll see. It will make sense.' She turns, starts to leave.

'Wait! You said to look in my notebook for the answer, but it's not there. There is no answer.'

But she keeps moving, head down, hands thrust into pockets.

I go to run after her but Patricia grabs me. 'Doc, no. Don't make a scene.'

'What is Project Callidus?' I yell. 'What is Project Callidus?'

Yet still Bobbie strides away, not responding, a ball of dust behind her, and then she is gone. Patricia lets go of my arm, and I glance upwards, squint.

There, standing by one of the office suite windows, is the Governor.

* * *

I stay behind Kurt as he weaves past the warren of rooms.

He does not talk to me, does not look my way. He keeps his eyes straight ahead and continues to move. I do not know where we are going. I do not know why. I am nervous. My head feels fuzzy, my tongue strangely thick, rough like cloth.

Kurt comes to a halt. 'Here we are.'

Ahead of us there is a door. I step forward and read the plaque stuck on the front of it.

'The Banana Room,' I say. 'What is this?'

'Somewhere to talk.'

Kurt opens a metal box connected to the wall. The door is thick, fluorescent yellow paint daubed in stripes across the middle, and on the top right sits a black smiley emoticon face the size of my hand.

Kurt enters a code. There is a loud click. 'In you go.'

I hesitate, hands tight against my thighs. The door pops open and Kurt gestures for me to enter.

'I said in you go.' He is smiling but it is small, a shard, a sliver.

I shake my head. 'I do not want to.'

'You have to.'

I sway a little, the nerves getting the better of me, then freeze. Kurt's hand is placed on the small of my back. 'I said, "in".'

Swallowing, I place my left foot into the room and gasp. Each of the four walls is painted green. But it is not simply household paint. From what I can see in the dim light, each wall appears to move. Taking another step forward, my eyes adjust and I can see that the movement is art. Someone has created head-to-toe murals on each of the four walls, each separate and distinct in design.

Kurt closes the door behind me and switches on a light.

'Are you okay?' he asks.

But I ignore him, instead stepping forward, observing. Now I can see that there is a path on the wall. I barely want to look, fear creeping up my spine, my neck, its fingers round my throat. What is going on? Where am I? I swallow hard, blink. The path runs through a boulevard of trees, their dark green leaves pointing like fingers to the middle. I cock my head. The path leads to a forest that sits in the distance. This forest is darker, as if forbidden to enter, like the Hansel and Gretel story my father used to read to me when I was little. I turn to see Kurt frowning.

I point at the set of painted leaves, finger trembling. 'The painting. It…it is a version of the *Arrival of Spring in Woldgate*. It's taken from David Hockney, inspired by him. The artist who did it must have attended the Royal Academy of Art, just like Hockney.'

Kurt stays very still. 'Maria, where do you think you are?'

I suddenly bend double. There is a sharp pain in my stomach 'Where am I?'

'You are in a different interview room, that's all, a different, normal interview room. Maria, where do *you* think we are?'

'We…we are in some odd art room, aren't we?' I point to the wall to our right. 'That painting there is based on Hockney's *Winter Timber.*'

I sidestep Kurt, wipe the emerging sweat from my temples, and peer at the painting. Layers of timber lie strewn on the ground, each a blend of banana yellow and burnt orange. In the corners, sawn tree trunks stand, crooked, worn, each one the colour purple. I touch them. 'The trees,' I say, my voice surprising me: distant, dreamlike, 'they are made of confectionery. All of it is.' I step back, wobble a little, clutch my middle. The pain shoots now. What is happening to me? When I look round, more painted trees stand towards the rear of the painting, this time winter ones, each bare, stripped of leaves or buds. To the left sits a pink dirt road, stretching to the horizon.

There is a sudden rush of heat to my head. 'I…I don't feel well.'

He gestures to one of two chairs positioned by a low table that resembles driftwood. 'Why don't you sit?'

I lower myself into the chair then halt. What is this? 'The chair,' I say, 'why is it made of chocolate?'

He pauses. 'Maria, it is just leather.'

Carefully, I touch the armrest. Leather. I repeat the word, as if saying it will convince my mind what I am seeing. But it is no good: I still feel chocolate under my fingers.

Kurt watches me then opens a file. 'We call this place the Banana Room because by changing venues, as we have done, we hope to encourage patients to open up without… slipping up, as it were.'

'Slipping up?' I scan the room, worried. 'On what? On the sweets?'

He narrows his eyes. 'There are no sweets. And "slipping up" is a phrase. It means saying something you wish you hadn't.' He pauses. 'Or shouldn't. The Banana Room will help you to talk.'

I do a 360-degree turn, utterly bewildered. Why can I see all this confectionery and yet Kurt claims he cannot? Is he lying to me? My eyes sweep the room. Paintings. Sweets. Marshmallow. Chocolate drops. All used as paint or decorations. They are there, I am certain. The wall, I notice, is raised with bumps like tarmac sleepers on the English roads. I stretch out my hand. My fingertips brush over the bumps. They are black, sticky. To the left of them are some red lines. I grip them—they break off into my palms.

'Strawberry laces,' I say to myself. I smell them; they remind me of Saturdays at the market with my father. He would buy me a packet of sweets to walk around with. I peer at the contents in my hand, observe the candy. It is long, hanging from my hands like vines from a tropical tree, a sickly scent of strawberry, caramelised sugar, vanilla.

Kurt taps his Dictaphone and places it on the driftwood table. He glances up at me. 'Maria, are you okay? You look a little pale.'

I say nothing. My head throbs, my stomach growls. I suddenly feel very, very frightened. Am I going mad?

'Now,' Kurt says, 'I thought this would be the best place to discuss what happened next after meeting Bobbie Reynolds in the yard.'

The chair is sticky and uncomfortable, fuelling what seems to be my rising temperature. I scan the room, try to focus on anything but the heat.

'There are four hundred and two chocolate mice in here,' I conclude after a few seconds.

'Pardon?'

'And one hundred and thirteen strawberry laces, seventy-seven chocolate logs, one chocolate clock, two marshmallow seats and seven orange lollies.' I stop, drag in some oxygen. My stomach ache is stronger, pulsating. I look at Kurt.

'Maria,' he says, after a moment, his body rigid, forward, 'there are no sweets in here. No strawberry laces, no chocolate logs. Okay?' He keeps his eyes on me, narrowed. 'Just calm down, take a few deep breaths. Okay?'

I nod, scared to speak, because Kurt is not seeing what I am—and that worries me, petrifies me, frightens me to death. Open my mouth and I know my voice will betray me, will scream out the thought that is now circling my head like a vulture tracking its prey: I don't know who I am.

Chapter 16

I stride through the walkways to the senior office suite, notebook in hand. I don't know if this is the right thing to do or if Bobbie can even be trusted, but I know something is not right, that something is happening. And, despite my nerves, despite the acorn of doubt in my head, I have to find out what is going on.

When I arrive at the suite, I stop, observe. Beyond the entrance is the Governor's red door and, ahead of me, two guards. One to the left, the other directly outside the office suite entrance.

I look to guard one. 'I want to see the Governor.'

She raises an eyebrow. 'You're kidding, right?'

'No. Why would I be kidding? I want to see the Governor.'

The other guard approaches and thrusts two fists to his hips. 'Problem?'

'Martinez wants to see the Governor.'

The second guard laughs. 'You got an appointment?'

'No,' I say. I keep my eyes fixed on Balthus's office. 'I need to see the Governor.' Balthus's office door opens.

'Hey!' I shout to him.

'Martinez, leave,' the guard says.

Balthus is in the corridor. 'The Governor is leaving his office,' I say, fast. 'Tell him I need to see him. Tell him.'

'You need to see him, do you?' the second guard says. 'Oh, well, in that case, go right on in.'

'Oh. Okay,' and I place my hand on the door to enter.

The first guard's arm blocks the way. 'What the hell are you doing?'

'Going right on in, like you said.'

The guard grabs my arm. 'Okay, time to leave.'

I shake him off.

'Hey!' he shouts. He grips both my wrists.

At the feel of his hands on my skin I turn to stone. 'Get off me.'

'You've crossed the line, Martinez.'

I look through the window. Balthus is there. 'Governor!' I have to grip on to this chance, it may be my only one. 'Governor!' I shout.

I see Balthus halt; then, squinting at me, he begins to stride towards us. A flicker of hope. A buzzer sounds. The double doors swing open.

'What is going on?' Balthus stands, looming large in the doorway.

The guard keeps hold of my wrists. 'This inmate wanted to see you without an appointment, sir. She was getting agitated.'

'Let go of her.'

The guard hesitates. 'Sir…'

'I said let go of her!'

The guard drops his hands.

I rub my wrists. This is it. This is where I take a gamble on a man I do not know if I can trust, but one that appears to, somehow, be acquainted with my mother, so does that mean he is trustworthy? I look at the Governor and realise that, whatever I conclude, my road has run out. I have nowhere else to go. 'I need to see you,' I say finally. 'It is urgent. It is concerning something called Project Callidus. There are people after me in here. I am not safe.'

Balthus holds my gaze. After two seconds, he narrows his eyes and says, 'Come through.' He presses the buzzer. The door swings wide. I finally exhale.

Balthus looks to the guards. 'As you were.'

* * *

Kurt lowers his pen. 'Maria, you are familiar with the term paranoia, yes?'

We have been here a while now, in this Banana Room, with the doubt and heat and the sickly smells. The scent of the sugar is causing my head to ache, my stomach to churn. I touch my scalp; sweating, hair matted slightly. Kurt has been asking me strange questions in this peculiar room; it is forcing my senses into overdrive.

'Paranoia,' he is saying, 'is a psychological condition. Typical symptoms include delusions of persecution, unnecessary jealousy and inflated self-importance.'

I keep one hand on my head. 'I am not paranoid.'

'Really?'

I clench my jaw and try not to breathe in the sweetness, try not to show my panic.

'From all the notes I have received about you,' he says,

'I would say that you have a distinct tendency to be paranoid. Dr Andersson's notes detail—'

'She is not who she appears to be.'

Kurt shakes his head. 'Listen to yourself, Maria. If you want to get better, if you want to learn how to deal with what has happened to you and try to create a better future for yourself, you have to listen to me.' He links his fingers. 'You need to stop thinking everyone is against you. They are not. What has happened to you in prison has been very traumatic for you, you more than most because of your Asperger's. Prison has distressed you.'

I touch my scalp. 'I…I didn't realise at first, the impact prison had. I would get upset so easily and that is not like me. I am normally in—'

'In control?'

I go still. In control. I like to be in control. The phrase smacks me on the cheek, a harsh reality of self.

'Prison has made you more prone to outbursts of feelings,' Kurt says. 'That would be the trauma, the wrench of being confined, the shock of the conviction, the experience. But not only that. Your memory has also been affected by it all—prison, denial, even grief of your father's distant death, as Dr Andersson highlighted. And as a consequence? Your judgement is impaired. And you agreed to see me. A counsellor with a proven track record of helping people like you.' He leans forward. 'So when, for example, you enquire why the yellow note from earlier was blank, all I can say is take a long hard look in the mirror, and ask yourself this: what can I do to get myself better?'

I frown, confused. 'You said, "I". Are you referring to me or you?'

Kurt slams his hand on the chair rest. I jump, hold my breath. What happened? Kurt runs a hand through his hair. Then, rolling his shoulders, slips on a smile. 'I mean you, Maria,' he says, his voice softer now. 'What can *you* do to get better?'

He sits back, picks up the Dictaphone. 'Okay. You are going to talk now. Clear?'

But I remain very still, scared to move. He was angry. Was he? I think so. And if he was, then that is the first time, the first time he has lost his temper. The first time he has lost control.

The mask is slipping.

* * *

Balthus closes the door and turns to me. 'What's going on? You're not supposed to do what you did out there.'

My heart beats fast. Something has happened to put me in here, in prison. So, I have to do something to get myself out. There is a choice to make. I have to decide who to ask for help. And who to avoid.

Balthus stands very still like an oak tree, firm, strong. 'You said you were not safe. Who has been speaking to you?'

'Bobbie Reynolds.'

He blinks once, but says nothing, just lets his eyes flicker to the side then back to me, his body solid, unmoving. After two seconds, he steps back, clears his throat. 'Please sit.'

I lower myself into a chair by his desk, place my notebook in my lap and wait. When he finally sits, he feels less looming, more honey-like, natural. But honey is made by bees, and bees can sting.

Balthus unbuttons his jacket, white shirt against tan skin,

and levels his gaze at me. 'You mentioned something called Callidus, just now, at the main doors.' His index finger taps the table.

I nod.

'Did Bobbie Reynolds mention that word, too?'

'Yes. After I did, but yes.'

Balthus looks at me, but says nothing. The clock on the wall ticks, the shelves stand to attention by the walls.

'I believe her,' I say.

'Believe who? Bobbie? Let me show you something.' Leaning to the side, he taps his computer. A printer to his left whirrs to life. He reaches over, lifts the ink-warm paper that has emerged and slides it to me.

'What is this?'

'Read.'

Slowly, I take it, suddenly unsure, nervous. I scan the paper. It is a psychiatric evaluation on Bobbie. Therapist reports, crime sheet, family background. The words 'cold', 'manipulative', 'charming' repeat like markers, like bumps in the road. And then the final conclusion the report gives: that Bobbie is a psychopath. My head starts to shake. It can't be true. I refuse to believe it's true.

'This means nothing.' I shove the report aside, not wanting to accept it because if Bobbie is making it all up, if she is unhinged, manipulative, then I will be left with the gaping truth staring me in the face: nobody put me in here. I put myself in prison. Because I killed the priest.

Balthus stares at me, his brown eyes two deep pools. He laces his fingers together. 'You said Bobbie told you that you aren't safe?'

'Yes,' I say after a moment.

'And you are certain of this?'

I hesitate. 'Yes.'

He holds my gaze then breaks away. Pausing first, his hand hovering mid-air, he reaches forward and opens a drawer.

I watch him, suspicious, heart rate rocketing. 'What are you doing?'

'Your interaction with Bobbie…' He trails off, drops his hands. 'What she says concerns me. It concerns me that you believe her.'

'But the report cannot be…' I stop, unsure what direction to take, which way to turn. 'The psychiatric evaluation of her cannot be right.'

'Maria, what Bobbie said to you is a lie. It's what she does.'

I close my mouth, press my lips together tight, scared that if I speak, if I articulate what my brain is thinking, it may not make sense. Because the simple truth is: I don't know. I don't know what is going on or who is real. Who is good, who is bad. 'I have to believe her,' I say after a while, voice weak. 'Because I didn't kill the priest.'

Balthus stares, his head dropping then lifting to reveal eyes slit like steel. 'I didn't want to have to tell you this quite so soon.' His voice is low, metallic.

I press my palms into my notebook, try to remain calm. 'Tell me what?' I say, almost too frightened to ask.

'This,' he says, 'was taken a long time ago.'

He dips into the drawer and slides across a photograph. Inching forward, I look, holding my breath. It is of two men. The image is grainy, but visible. I touch it. The paper is worn, perhaps several decades old.

'Why are you showing me this?'

'It was taken in 1973,' he says, voice smooth yet coarse.

The photograph pulls my eyes to it. 'Who are these people?'

'That one is me.' He places a manicured fingernail on the face of a young man. His hair is dark, shoulder length. His shirt has a very wide collar, dark sunglasses shrouding his eyes. A knot begins to tighten in my stomach, my brain sparking. I fling the picture at Balthus. 'Take it away.'

He hesitates then reaches forward, picks up the photograph. He looks at it for a few seconds, his breathing deep, heavy, then sets the image down between us. I sit, stare, not daring to move. I don't know how much I can trust him. I don't really know who he is.

'I hadn't long started university,' he says after a while.

I find my voice. 'What has this got to do with anything? Why are you telling me all this? Is it a game? Some social nuance game I can't interpret? What? What?' And I slam my hand to the desk, but he simply continues as if I had never spoken.

'We were studying Law at Churchill College, Cambridge.'

I go still. *'We?'*

He breathes out. 'Your father and I.'

'What? My papa? You knew my papa? What?' I say, over and over. 'What? But how…? Why…?' I sit, shake my head. Blood pumps fast into the base of my brain, banging, thrashing.

'Your father, Alarico, had a European scholarship for Cambridge. That's where I met him.' He pauses. 'That is where I met your mother.'

'Why are you…?' I stop, unable to articulate the thoughts that come flying out from my head. This man knew my papa, my mama. This man, the Governor of the prison I reside in. It is too much. Too much. I smack my head with my palm, my brain overloading, threatening to blow a fuse from the waves of lies, of truths.

'He was concerned for your safety,' Balthus says, cutting through my panic. 'That's why, when you told me about Bobbie, about what she said, I instantly became worried.'

I pause, lower my hand, try to stave off the tremor. 'Why are you telling me now?'

He plants his elbows into the desk. 'When you were young, Alarico—your father—he spoke to me, told me to keep an eye on you should anything ever happen to you. He had serious…fears. Something is clearly happening to you. That is why I am telling you now.'

'But…but…' I trail off, the words too spiked, too sharp to speak. If he was keeping an eye on me, what else was he doing? Is he one of them, working for the Project? Is he my handler in here, using me, too? Is no one who they seem? I stand, fast. 'I have to go. I have to go.'

'No. Maria, stay.'

But I ignore him, my eyes searching for the door, frantic. I spot it, grab my notebook and run to the exit.

'Maria, stop!'

I can hear him, but I reach the door, rattling the handle, desperate. 'Let me out!'

He is there by my side now, his torso thick, steady, his hands blocking the door. 'I'm sorry you are finding out like this.'

I shake my head. 'Are you with them? With Callidus?'

'What? No.'

I grip the handle tighter. 'How can I believe you? They have been watching me all my life. All my life! And now this Bobbie tells me to speak to you and you tell me my papa said to keep an eye on me, so what am I supposed to think?' My chest heaves. 'What?'

'Sir?' A guard shouts from the corridor beyond. We both go still. 'Is everything okay in there?'

Balthus stares at me. I force myself to meet his gaze, to make myself stand up to him. 'Everything is fine,' he shouts to the guard after a few seconds, his eyes not leaving mine. 'Everything is fine.'

He steps away from the door, drops his hands to his side. 'Maria, I don't know who or what Callidus is. They have not sent me to watch you. The only thing I know is that your father was my friend and he told me to look out for you.'

'Why?' I say, my body tense, ready to run. 'Why did you not tell me when I arrived at Goldmouth that you knew my papa, knew my mama?'

'I am the Governor, Maria. What could I say?'

'You could have told the truth.'

He nods and I look at him. Everything I thought was right, everything I believed in—my life, who I was, why I was here—all of it is disappearing, evaporating like water droplets into the atmosphere until they will eventually vanish, die.

A wave of exhaustion surges over me. I begin to loosen my grip on the door when a high-pitched buzzing suddenly invades the air. I slap my hands to my ears. 'What is that?'

'My bleeper.'

He slips it from his pocket, turns it off, reads the message. 'I have to go.'

I drop my hands. 'Why?'

'An…emergency.' He coughs. He shoots to his desk, picks up the phone and dials a number. Done, he sets down the receiver, strides to the door, then stops. He turns, looks at me. 'You sit, wait here.'

'But I have many questions and—'

He holds up a hand. 'Please, just wait for me.' He presses his lips together. 'I have more to tell you. I promise.'

He stares at me but does not move, eyes like two mirrors. I wonder if I looked deep into them, what I would see? Would they tell me that I can trust him?

'You said it was an emergency.'

He inhales. 'Yes.' He presses the exit buzzer, buttons up his jacket as, from outside, an alarm begins to wail. I watch as the door shuts and locks as he leaves.

Alone, I let my shoulders drop. My mind feels wild, crazed with what I have just been told. I need to sit, rest, think. Turning, I go to walk to the chair when I spy a laptop on the desk. I halt. Bobbie. She mentioned this.

I grip my notebook and stride round to Balthus's desk.

I need to find answers.

Chapter 17

'I am bending over the priest's body,' I say. 'He is still warm. There is no heartbeat, no pulse. Blood pools everywhere, thick, sticky. It drips down the steps like treacle and trickles towards the altar. Through the priest's neck there is an entrance wound, one slash, slick, neat. A knife. Clean like butter. The urge to stick my finger in the hole is incredible. I stand up. Fingermarks at a crime scene. Not good.'

Kurt's chair creaks. 'What happens next in the dream?'

I smack my lips together, mouth coarse, dry. 'The rope binding the priest's hands and ankles is taut now; I track its course, woven as it is around his limbs. There—by the altar,' I say, as if I can see it, touch it, 'that is where each juncture is secured. I stride over and inspect them. Tight. Immovable. I walk back to the body. There is more blood now, deep red, almost black. I can smell the iron. The blood is oozing from the wound and, when I inspect the arms, there are slashes there, too. He never stood a chance.'

'Then?'

I shift in my seat, the recollection of the dream uncomfortable. 'Footsteps. I freeze, listen. There is no time. Whoever it is, they are getting closer. My eyes dart left to right. The knife… It's nowhere to be seen. I check, but no. Nothing.'

'What do you dream next?'

I close my eyes, think. 'The footsteps. They are nearer.'

'And what do you do?'

I inhale. 'In the end, it is an easy decision. I turn and run. As fast as I can. Something tells me to, I don't know, a voice in my head? An instinct I don't recall learning? It urges me to go, to leave an invisible trace. To never be found. As if I don't exist.'

Kurt's mobile phone shrills.

My eyes fly open and I catch my breath. Kurt has been listening to me explain what I remember of my recurring dream: the priest, his death, his blood. All detail that I know about, yet do not recall being actively part of; instincts that kick-start in me, yet ones that I do not recollect learning.

Kurt's eyes are narrowed on me, observing, his mobile phone shrill dying off. A pen dangles from his fingers. 'Does the dream always end with the footsteps? With you running away? Always has you bending over Father O'Donnell's body?'

I nod. 'Yes.' I touch my scalp. The room feels as if it is spinning slightly.

Kurt twists the pen in his fingers. 'It sounds as if it is just that: a dream. Made up, fabricated. Because in the dream, you ran away, but of course, in the real world, you were caught, you were not invisible. And you do exist.'

'But I don't even recall being there. So why am I dreaming about it?'

'Your mind will conjure up all sorts of scenarios to protect you from the trauma. From the reality.'

I touch my forehead. My mind. My Asperger's. This strange, sickly sweet room. Everything that has happened to me recently—it has all affected my mind more than I thought. That must be why here, now, even in this room with Kurt, I sense things that are, perhaps, not even there, my brain moving quicker than normal, just as it does in prison, forcing it, each second of the day, into fight or flight mode. It must be why the colours are brighter, the smells stronger, the noises louder, my fingers faster.

Kurt swings his leg for a moment; then, sitting forward, he picks up his mobile. He checks it then shoots up. 'I have to make a brief call.'

A panic surfaces. A rush of heat hits my head, almost knocking me out. I lay a palm on my brow, but my skin is clammy, and it does no good.

'Are you okay?'

'I do not want to be alone in here.'

He sighs. 'There is nothing to be frightened of. I am a therapist—other people need me, too.'

Kurt begins to walk towards the door when his shoe gets caught on the chair leg. He shakes it off, mud, debris dropping from the sole. He darts one glance to me. Then, walking to the door, he repeats that I am not to be scared, and then he exits.

The door shuts. Silence.

My laboured breathing the only sound in the room, I look around, try to rationalise what is going on. I can see sweets, but Kurt can't. Why? I must be hallucinating, that is the only medical explanation, but how? I have not taken anything, not popped any pills. At a loss, I roll my head a little when something catches my eye in the faint light. I stop and stare. There is something on the floor, something from Kurt's shoe. Curious, I stand then sway a little. The sweets, the chocolate paintings, the sickly scent—real or not—they must be taking their toll. Steadying myself, I inch towards the door. When I reach it, I crouch down and pick up whatever has dropped from Kurt's shoe. I expect it to be a stone.

But it is not.

There, on my palm, is small piece of peat with a strand of moss stuck in it.

I raise it to my nose and sniff. Grass and damp earth, they spark something, a thought in me, a distant recollection. I smell them again, their burnt cinder firing a memory and I start to recall something. Like a radio being tuned, voices scratch like static across my mind, as if trying to broadcast to me, as if trying to communicate. Usually, I get a warning, but this time, nothing. The memory is fast, relentless. Within seconds, my breathing becomes quick and my chest tightens. Until, click! An image appears, a video in my head, and I am watching.

I am in a hospital ward, on a bed. The sheets are white and the air is damp. There is a cannula inserted into the vein on my hand, and by my side stands an IV drip. There are no doctors. No nurses.

I hear a voice as the door ahead opens. A cold draught shoots in, razor-sharp. There, stood in the room, is my mother. She is wearing a grey suit, her hair bobbing by her shoulders, her skin smooth, wrinkle-free. A white mask covers her mouth. She strides towards me and halts.

'Read this book, Maria, darling. Read it for Mama.'

I look at what she has thrust at me. A novel. Hesitating, I take it. For some reason, it seems the safest option, to do as I am told. The book has a hundred and five pages, and my mother instructs me to open it and read. I do as she says. Immediately, she clicks a button on a stopwatch; it begins to tick.

I read the pages aloud. It does not take me long. When I finish, my mother clicks the watch and a doctor arrives.

'How long?' he says.

My mother shows him the stop clock.

The doctor's eyes go wide. 'Quicker. Good, Ines.'

I say that I am thirsty, but my mother doesn't hear me. She addresses the doctor. 'Is her condition developing as expected?'

'Yes,' the doctor says, 'but there is more to do. For the meantime, I have secured these for you.' He hands her something. I see it: two vials of medicine. My mother's fingers clasp them, and then they both look to me. I do not know why, but I know I must shut my eyes; I must not see.

The image fades, slowly at first then fast, like liquid down a drain. I watch it, cry out after it, but it disappears like a rush of water. I open my eyes and gasp. I am slumped on the floor, my skin soaked, sweat sliding down my face onto candy and chocolate.

Swallowing, I manage to drag myself up, try to make sense of what I have just remembered. How could my mother be there? Am I recalling events incorrectly, putting her there because it suits me? Suits me to have someone to blame? She has been nothing but nice to me, yet what have I been to her? Suspicious. Difficult.

I concentrate on breathing in and out, on remaining calm, on trying to determine what I saw. It did not seem real, as if it were an old silent film where the reel flickers and the images are grainy. But the peat—the peat from Kurt's shoe—I think of it and I bite down hard on my lip. For some reason, it was a trigger. A trigger to the past.

I have to find out exactly who Kurt is.

Before it is too late.

* * *

I sit down and am immediately faced with a barrier: Balthus's password. I flop back. I don't know how to bypass this, how to access his computer. I shake my head. What was I thinking? I am just a doctor, not an IT technician, I know nothing about this and… My eyes land on my notebook. I stop, tilt my head, look at it. A wash of something ripples over me, but I cannot place it, cannot pin it down.

Slowly, I watch as my hand reaches out, slides the notebook to me, opens the cover. Numbers, patterns, codes. All of them are etched into every corner of the pad, none of them familiar to me, and yet, what if? A clatter sounds from the yard outside, making me jerk up. I wait, listen, blood rushing through my veins, heart, ears, but all outside is quiet now, motionless.

Fast, I return my eyes to my notepad, scanning the pages. For some reason, I flip to the middle section. My pulse shoots up, hands slippy. A dream I had one night—it is all there. A procedure, patterns, method, things that came to me one night like strangers. Moving quickly, I read the words scrawled in front of me: *Log into an alternate account.*

I sit up. How did I know to write that down? Swallowing, I glance again to the page, my eyes almost too afraid to look, too scared to see what I know, what I can do. At first, it's just a series of numbers and letters, each meaningless, seemingly irrelevant, but then I blink and something starts to form in front of my eyes and it scares me. I throw the notebook down, breathing hard. Did I really just spot that? I claw back the writing pad, force myself to examine it again. It is there: a code, a pattern hidden within my scrawl. The method to hack a computer password code.

My mind races. Why would I know that? Why would I write it down? How did I learn it? I catch sight of the clock and it knocks me temporarily out of my panic. Not much time. Balthus will return soon. If I am going to do this, it has to be now.

Hesitantly at first, then with speed, my fingers fly across the keyboard. I pause, inhale. I have never done this before, at least, I don't think so. I work quick, neat. The system prompts me for another password and I stall. How do I bypass this? I scan the notebook, examine the pattern, but then something walks into my head, an answer: press enter. I wait, my finger hovering over the key. Then I press it. One second, two, three. It works. I let out a laugh, amazed at what I can do, scared at why. Shooting a glance at the time, I fly to the user accounts, select Balthus's main one and immediately change the password and sit back.

After one second, it flashes up: full system access. I am in.

* * *

I start with this room. If I think it's made of sweets, then I'd better be sure.

I look around, swaying slightly, my eyes seeing double. I

blink, open them wide; it helps, but only a little. The room
still dusted with sugar, I decide to see at least what I can
uncover. I take on the picture frames first. They house three
paintings, all in a row. Upon first glance, they are made of
liquorice and butter icing, and there is a sprinkling of frosting over the top. I inch out my hand. My fingers touch the
edge of the first painting and it feels wet, sticky. I begin to
investigate it when a stab of pain in my stomach jabs me.
I stop, let it pass. Then, inhaling, I continue. Bit by bit, I
peel the edge off the first frame. It comes away with ease
and I keep tugging when something makes me halt. My
palms are sweaty, so I wipe them on my trouser leg, then
steer my hand forward until I feel the liquorice in my finger. And even though my logical mind says that my brain
is playing tricks, still it feels real, smells real. I pause and
listen for any sound of Kurt, but no buzzers vibrate from
the corridor, no footsteps echo on the tiles.

The liquorice frame is smooth. Each line of it spans the
width of the canvas, but there is something on the end, by
the edge. A flush of heat races to my face. I pause, wait for
it to subside and recommence. Pulling a little, it becomes
clear that the liquorice to the left of the frame is loose, as
if it has already been torn off. As if something has been
placed under it.

Feeling a kernel of panic, of uncertainty, I pause before
investigating further, exhale hard. The frame is bumpy.
I glance to the other two pictures and see that they are
smooth, untouched. I reach out and, taking the end of the
uneven liquorice, one millimetre at a time, begin to peel it
away. It is welded down, but eventually it starts to give. I

pull back, examine it. At first, it is difficult to detect, but then I see it.

Black, minute, but definitely there.

A camera.

And that is when I realise that I can hear Kurt's voice.

The handle is turning. Moving fast, I press the liquorice back into place as much as possible then shoot to my chair.

But before I can reach it, Kurt is already entering the room.

Chapter 18

I can see Kurt's hand on the door.

Darting my eyes left and right, I spot a crop of marsh-mallow flowers and, grabbing a handful, I thrust them into my mouth.

Kurt stops when he sees me. 'What are you doing?' His mobile phone hangs from his hand.

'I am eating marshmallow,' I say. Liquid dribbles down my chin.

'Maria, there are no marshmallows in here. Is that sick down your chin? Are you okay?'

I touch my face. He's right. I have been sick. And I re-alise with a vicious shock that it's not marshmallow in my mouth, it is vomit.

Kurt begins to walk towards me when a voice bellows from his phone. He must still be on a call. He stops, glances to me, then puts the phone to his ear. 'Yes?'

Immediately, I wipe my chin, my breath ragged, vision smeared. Sweat trickles from my brow and I dab it with the heel of my hand, but it does no good. A wave of nausea rises from my stomach and the room begins to sway, a gentle rocking motion, like a boat bobbing on the sea.

Kurt watches me. 'It's happening,' he says into his phone. 'I'll call you back.' He slips his cell into his pocket, stands and stares.

'What is happening to me?' I stumble. 'What did you do?' But the room is spinning and I cannot get the words out. I slap my hand to my chest and force myself to speak. 'You have to help me.' Another wave of pain hits. 'Help me!'

But Kurt does not move, does not call anyone. Instead he just watches and waits.

'What have I taken?' I say. And then I understand: this cannot be happening in real life. It must be a flashback of some sort, a dream, a nightmare, perhaps, all of it happening in my head. 'Wake me up!' I yell, my voice feral, untamed. 'Wake me up!'

I try to take my pulse on my neck, but my arms are weak and it is impossible. Heat gushes round my body, and the smell of the sweets and marshmallow and chocolate make the nausea worse. I focus on the room, focus on jolting myself awake. I slap my face, spit on the floor, try to walk, but everything surges, throwing me from side to side, thrashing me against an invisible wave, against a heaving tide of nausea.

I crash into the wall, sliding down it. My arms are limp, my legs are useless. Kurt is nearer now, his arms crossed over his chest.

'Who are…you?' I say.

'I am your therapist.' His voice is soft, a gentle coo.

'No,' I manage to say, shaking my head, his image

blurred, distant now. 'No.' My eyes dart up. And then I see it: the camera.

But Kurt must trace my line of sight, because he says, 'Ah, you found it.' He picks up the tiny camera. 'I wondered how long it would take you. They have to have some way of watching you from where they are. They need to see exactly what is going on with you.'

My pulse rockets. I do not understand what he is saying, whether this is all a dream. My temperature is rising, sweat popping out all over my limbs, my skin. My blouse is drenched, my hair is damp. 'Help,' I plead, and then I slump to the left, my cheek skimming the wall as my head thumps on the floor.

I lie there, blinking, washed up, motionless. My whole body is paralysed, saliva dribbling from my gaping mouth. I can see the room at an angle. The legs of the chairs, the corners of the tables, but only just, like shadows in a dark alley.

'It's me,' I hear Kurt say, and I know he must be on his phone. 'Yes, you better send them in now. Let's get her up there and tested before the drug wears off.'

My mouth dribbles, but I will myself to talk, speak. 'You…have to…help me.'

I hear Kurt take a step towards me. 'I am helping you.'

I want to ask who he is sending, but I am beginning to drift in and out of consciousness. Or is it back to consciousness? Returning to reality? And then, in front of my eyes, I see Kurt's shoes. 'Please,' I try now, desperate. 'What is happening? I don't understand.'

He crouches down, his eyes level with mine now. 'You

should know what is happening. You have the answers in there.' He jabs my forehead with his finger.

Saliva pools in my tongue. 'I don't know what…what you mean.'

He tuts, hard, loud. 'Yes, you do. Don't you realise that yet? I know what you've already discovered. It's been part of the plan all along, a test, a test for you.'

'No,' I croak.

'Yes!' he shouts. 'Jesus.'

'No, no,' I say over and over, muffled, spitting out dribble, bile.

He stands now, quick, sharp. 'Dr Andersson was right about you,' he says. 'It's a pain in the ass being your handler, even if you can help blow Al Qaeda away.'

My eyes go wide, my brain, even in its paralysed state, still computing. 'Why…? Why Al Qeada? I can't help you.'

'Yes you fucking can!' And he kicks me hard on the side of my head, then freezes. 'Shit! Oh, shit.'

Pains vibrates through my skull. The room sways, the blood in my head rushing to the spot where a lump is already forming.

Kurt squats in front of me. 'Fuck. Are you okay? Shit. I didn't mean… It's just… We're on the same side, but you keep on saying… I lost my temper.' He lets out a breath. 'Shit.'

I try to speak, try to ask him what is happening, but the room keeps swaying and, as hard as I attempt to avoid it, a black swell fills my sight and everything—Kurt's face, the sweets, the door to the room—all fade away.

* * *

I click straight on the internet browser then stop. The realisation hits me: I don't actually know what I am looking for. Stalling, pausing for breath, I lean back, think. What should I do? Who am I searching for? If MI5 are involved, if what Bobbie said is all true, then what? I cannot simply saunter into a secure website and effectively knock on the door. Can I?

I wipe the sweat from my palms, registering my rise in pulse, my brain knowing that already my blood pressure will be elevated, my heart rate will be intensifying. I am scared. I recognise the emotion, but at the same time, there is a sense of urgency in me, of energy that seems to be pushing the fright aside, like a battering ram. I haven't felt so alive in such a long time.

A stomp of boots wakes me out of my thought pattern and I listen, breath hard, chest taut. Finally, the sound passes. Pausing to steady myself, I face the computer screen and let my brain kick in. A word walks into my head: Callidus. Bobbie said that Callidus, this Project Callidus, is part of MI5, that they thought I was safe in prison.

I search the internet for the term 'Callidus' and hit a brick wall. Just definitions, ones I know already, Latin terms and descriptions. I sit back, track my thoughts. Bobbie said the answer is in my notebook. I flip the pad open, examine it again. Still I find no message from Bobbie, no hidden meaning anywhere, so what did she mean? Why did she direct me here? I leaf the notebook pages and try to clear my mind, attempt to take in everything I have scribbled, my head fast, prison still, even now, in this office, affecting my Asperger's, my skills, my acceleration. I don't like it. I don't like it at all, because it begs the question: will I always be this way? Brain wired, dancing on the edge of crazy?

I force my eyes back to the notebook and try to focus. For some reason, my brain locks on to one page in particular. It is thick with unfamiliar codes, each of them number heavy, sitting side by side with algorithms and thought patterns. I stare at them until the etchings begin to merge into one, my sight blurring, swirling round and round until: smash! I sit up with a start. I have used these codes before. But how? I swallow hard. Desperate, I shut my eyes fast, willing an image, a memory—anything—to appear.

Slowly first, then quick, like a torrent of water, it appears: my university professor. There was a challenge one day, a mathematical one that he asked me to do. I questioned, at the time, why he wasn't requesting any of the other students to perform the calculations and he replied that none of them were as fast as me, none of them as accurate. I recall completing the test for him in a few minutes and he thanked me, made a phone call, relayed the data to someone via email.

My eyes fly open. He was my handler. My professor was my handler and he was asking me to hack into a computer website. A shriek escapes from my lips and I slap my palm to my mouth. I glance at the door. I wait, one heartbeat, two. No one is coming. Slowly, I lower my hand as I realise that my university professor made me hack websites. And it wasn't simulation as he said it was, it wasn't for advanced mathematical practice: it was for the Project. For Callidus.

My hands won't cease shaking. The lies, deceit. Why? Why them? Why me? I sit, staring for two, maybe three seconds, when I remember that Balthus will return anytime soon. My brain, reluctantly first and then at speed, engages. I thrust aside the anger that spurts up and I make myself scan my notes. I examine the patterns first, just like I did at university all those years ago. I trace a finger over them. One, two, three encoded methods—they are all there. Yet these patterns are encrypted, protected by myself. Slowly, I pick up a pen and begin to decode them.

I close my eyes and start to imagine my fingers on a computer keyboard, imagine codes on a page. It is hard, but after a few seconds pass, the instinct returns. How I solved the challenge that day in the dusty university office—it returns.

I open my eyes, swallow, nerves slapping me. Because it means I can do it. Was that the answer in my notebook Bobbie meant?

Feverish, I find myself being able to decrypt my note patterns. I decode the method first, scribbling it down, every detail, every step. Done, I flop back, look at my frantic notes. And that is when I realise what I am staring at: a full procedure on how to anonymously hack a website.

I barely breathe. I am a doctor, a plastic surgeon. How do I know how to do this? I gulp hard, inhale, then check the time. I have to keep moving.

With unsteady fingers, I begin to tap the keyboard, start searching for something on Callidus—anything—that will give me a clue, when the door unlocks and starts to creak open.

My head flies up. Balthus. My pulse rockets. How did time move so fast? I shut the screen down, stand, rush to move, but it is too late.

Balthus is standing in the doorway. 'What the hell are you doing at my computer?'

I open my mouth to speak, to explain, when I stop. Because there is someone by Balthus's side. Someone I know. Someone I thought I could trust.

Harry Warren.

* * *

I awake to find myself in a van.

It jostles along what must be a road. I cannot move or speak, my mouth gagged, my wrists bound, brain groggy. There is a stench of vomit and bodily fluids, and no matter how much I try, no matter how hard I attempt to steady my breathing, I feel out of control, hysterical, peering into the edge of an abyss. Attached to the trolley I am laid out on is a heart rate monitor. It bleeps and I stretch my eyes to it as best I can. It is professional, hospital standard. Why am I hooked up to this? And who did it?

To quell the bile that threatens to erupt, I try to get clues—any clues—as to where I am, but when I move my head to the left, pain sears me, burning like a cigarette into skin. I press my lips together hard, clench my fists, wait for it to subside. Five aching seconds pass and finally the pain bows a little, enough of a gap for me to carry on. I dart my eyes round fast. To my left is a small window. Sun shines in through the glass, so I know it must be daytime, but where? The rest of the van, inside, is white, medical equipment running along the sides—bandages, medicines. But other than that, this is not an ambulance, it is too sparse, too unequipped.

I go to take another look at the medicines when then I hear it: breathing. I stay very still, frightened, scared at who it is, at what they will do. There is no one I can see here in the back of the van with me, so it must be someone in the driver's seat. Kurt? I want to shout his name, but the tape on my mouth is too tight. Whoever they are, they must not realise I am awake.

Careful not to move, I try to see where I am through the window. From what I can determine, we are travelling south. The sky here is lighter and there is less traffic noise, which means we are out of London, but where are we bound?

In desperation, I look at the heart rate monitor, still beeping, blue lights flickering. It tracks my pulse. I lower my chin and look to my chest. There are four electrodes attached to my ribcage. I begin to panic. My heart rate soars.

Is this a memory I have forgotten?

Times passes, and through the window trees fly past, followed by endless grey sky. And then, after what seems like hours later, I begin to see aeroplanes…to hear engines.

The van halts and everything jolts forward. My whole body goes rigid with fear.

'Hang on.' A man's voice. There is a clatter, a crash. 'I think she's… Shit. We have to get her on that plane. Now.'

The monitor begins to beep, wild, frantic. I try to claw my way out, try to bash my arms, but I cannot. The monitor beeps faster and faster still.

Someone's hot breath is on my cheeks. I jerk my eyes to the right and suck in the tape.

A man in a mask is staring at me.

'She's awake,' he says.

Before I can scream, I am injected with a drug. Everything fades to black.

Chapter 19

'I said what are you doing at my computer, Maria?'

Balthus looms in front of me. I do not move. My eyes dart to Harry. He is not smiling. I swallow, a surge of dread welling up inside me.

Balthus strides to the laptop, pushes me aside, peers at it. 'Were you using this?'

But I stay mute. What do I tell him? He knew my father but does that mean anything? Does that mean I should trust him?

Harry steps forward. 'Balthus said he spoke to you, Maria.'

'What are you doing here?'

Harry walks to a chair. 'Balthus mentioned that he knew your father—Alarico.'

I let myself give one sharp nod, nothing else. A wind whips at the window from outside. The clock on the wall ticks into the silence.

Harry sighs and sits. 'We knew we'd have to tell you, one day.'

I freeze. 'We?' I clench my fists tight, hard, over and over. The room feels suddenly hot, heavy, despite the window breeze. What is going on?

'Yes,' he says, setting down a legal file. 'That's why Balthus called me, told me to come over immediately.'

'What? No. Why would he be calling you? He said there was an emergency.'

'There was an emergency, yes. You, Maria. You are the emergency.'

'No.' I shake my head once, twice, dart my eyes between the two men. '"We". You said, "*we* knew we'd have to tell you". Who is "we"?'

But they do not answer, each of them glancing from one to the other.

'Who is "we"?' I shout.

Harry raises his head. 'Me and Balthus,' he says finally. 'That is the "we". We were both friends of your father, Maria. Me, Balthus.' He exhales. 'Both of us.'

* * *

I wake up in a white room. My breathing is frayed, torn at the edges, as it slowly dawns on me that I am no longer in the van. I dare not move, blood crashing through me, knuckles white while my fingernails dig hard into the soft underbelly of my palms. Slowly, I let my eyes scan the area. There is an IV drip in my arm. Straps sit tight around my legs. There is a heart rate monitor to the left, a metal table laid with syringes close by it. And I'm alone, but… I cannot be sure. Panic forces its way in, slamming hard into my thoughts. Where am I? What do they want? Where is Kurt?

I go to move my head when something pulls at it. Hands shaking, I place one palm on my hair. My scalp is covered in electrodes. They are on my forehead, my temples, on the back of my skull. When I tug them, I can feel leads protruding from each electrode. I turn my eyes to the right; there is an electroencephalograph machine by the bed, and I realise in horror that someone is recording my brain activity.

I close my eyes fast, not wanting to look. Instead, I make myself think of the facts, details, anything that will pin a tail on the real picture. Think, Maria, think. How old am I? Start with that. If this is only a memory, not real, then my body will be the teenage me, not the adult me. Peeling open my eyes, I slowly raise my hands, turn them over in the air. They are full size, adult. Trembling, I feel my face. There are no spots and my nose feels larger, my hair is cropped along the edge of my scalp.

Which means only one thing: I am me. Now. Thirty-three years old. The horror of the situation grips me, squeezes me tight, because if I am normal, if I am my usual age, then this is not a memory. This is real.

The panic, again, begins to appear, the primitive urge to flee strong. Why am I here? There is a flicker of movement by the window. I stay still, my breathing loud, like rushing water in my ears. The window is covered by a white blind, but the fabric is thin and there, behind it, I can just make out three shadows, none of which are moving. Does that mean they are watching me? Waiting to do something to me?

A beep bursts from the heart rate monitor and I jump, my eyes landing on the metal table of syringes, and it happens again, but this time fast, like the flip of a switch. No warning. No rapid breathing. Just a cold sensation, a gentle, familiar slide, like a fish slipping back into a river. My eyes close, lids flutter, and I feel a sudden, sharp pain of a recollection. It hurts so much that I call out for my father. And then I smell it: burning flesh. I panic and look down.

A screech.

My body: it is not mine.

It is now younger, skinnier, my stomach concave, my knees protruding. And I am not on my own. My mother. She is by my side. I blink. How did she get there? She bends over me and rolls up my gown, cooing, exposing me from the chest down, telling me not to worry. I try to cover myself, but my mother slides one palm round my wrist. I scream, but she slips one finger on her mouth and whispers, 'Ssssh, darling, ssssh.' I shake my head and then my mother is not there, and instead her image has been replaced by a man with black eyes. Was he there all along and not my mother? The man leans over me now, a red-hot piece of metal in his hands.

'Can you feel pain?' he asks, and his accent, it is Scottish.

The heat from the metal is strong and I know what's going to happen. I writhe, thrash my head side to side, cry out for my mama, my papa.

'They are not here, I'm afraid,' Black Eyes says, voice flat, lifeless. 'Now, tell me if you can feel this.'

He lowers the hot metal and my eyes going wide as he presses it deep into my stomach. I howl.

The acrid stench of burning flesh stings the air.

The room swirls. My heart rate peaks. The image, the memory—it sinks, deep, to the bottom of the ocean. Everything becomes dark, murky. A splutter of breath and I open my eyes. I gag, immediately try to sit up, my chest heaving, my eyes wild at what I have just seen. But the straps on my legs are too tight and I cannot move, so I dart my eyes downwards and frantically check. My body—it is normal again, full size, adult. Which means that it was a memory, I just had another memory. I gulp in air, as much of it as I can, as my mind drifts to the scar on my stomach, the one I showed Dr Andersson in the prison. He did it, I realise now with clarity. Black Eyes gave me that scar for certain. He is connected to all of this.

Pulling my head up as far as it will go, I study the EEG monitor. The graph paper shows frantic, peaked lines where it must have recorded the brain activity from what can only have been a vivid memory, a flashback. Which means that what I am experiencing now, here, must definitely be real. Slowly, almost too frightened to look, I inch my hand down to my abdomen and pull up my gown. There, beneath my fingers, is the scar. The scar Black Eyes gave me, just as I recalled. A memory, a real memory.

I lift my hand to my head.

And one by one, I rip the electrodes from my skull.

Chapter 20

I stare at Harry. 'Why did you not tell me you knew my papa? When we first met, why did you not tell me?'

Harry glances to Balthus. 'Maria, my dear. I couldn't. I… I am so, so sorry you have found out like this.'

'Like this?' I stand, manic. 'Like this? I found out by chance, but, actually—' I halt, scratch my head '—nothing happens by chance, does it?' I commence pacing. 'Numbers—they all have a meaning, a place, and numbers translate into code, and code into data, and data is just another word for information, for facts, for knowledge.' I stop, chest heaving. 'And you kept that knowledge from me, Harry.'

I turn, ignoring both men. How can I trust them, trust anyone? They have already lied to me, pretended they were something they are not, just like my university professor, like Father Reznik, like my hospital boss. Like Dr-fucking-Andersson. These are authority figures I assumed were genuine, there to help me. The enormity of it, the delayed shock, slaps me hard and I bend over, wretch, shoulders heaving, mouth raw. Even my boss at St James's was not who he pretended to be, and if someone like him can be a liar, someone kind, with a family, with a loving wife, how can we ever really believe anyone is who they say they are?

'Maria,' I hear Balthus say. 'Are you okay?'

I stand and wipe my face as dry as I can, not wanting to feel or appear weak any more, not wanting to seem like a victim. I want to get out, want to win my appeal. I want to survive.

'Maria,' Harry says, 'I know it must seem very unlikely right now, but we are here for you, to help you.'

'Then why weren't you here right at the beginning?' I say, voice firm. 'When I was arrested? When I was facing my first trial?'

Harry sits forward a little, smiles, one with creases that makes his eyes almost disappear. I feel myself soften a little. 'I wanted to defend you, Maria,' he says, 'but I was working on a high-profile case and—'

'The chef with the knife?'

'You know about that?' Another smile. 'Well, yes. And I couldn't get out of the case, and then you acquired a legal team and all I could do was watch them butcher your defence. When you were convicted, Balthus used his wife's connections, got you transferred to Goldmouth.'

'The Home Secretary,' I say, almost to myself.

Harry sits forward. 'Maria, I wanted to help you. I called Balthus when we heard the news that you were charged. We used his contacts to get you to Goldmouth. You're Al's daughter for God's sake. And he told us what he—'

My eyes dart between them both, heart shoots. 'Papa

told you? Told you what? What? What do you know? Did he tell you something to do with Scotland?'

They share a glance to each other.

'Maria,' Harry says, 'Alarico didn't mention anything about Scotland.'

I frown, shake my head. 'Then what did he tell you?'

Harry exhales. Balthus rubs his head with his hand.

'He told us that he was concerned for your well-being, Maria,' Harry says after a moment. He clears his throat. 'He told us he was concerned for you, how you would cope with day-to-day life as you got older. I suppose he was concerned for your…for your sanity.'

* * *

'Get someone in here. Now!'

I hear the voice but I do not stop, a juggernaut of strength, of survival instinct, railroading through me. I have to escape. I have to. So I keep ripping. I tear the electrodes from my scalp, the slime of the jelly on the pads mixing with my sweat so it trickles down my brow, stinging my eyes, sticking to my lashes, but I do not care.

'She's tachycardic,' someone shouts, but I don't know who, don't know from where.

The monitor is beeping; my heart rate is accelerating; still I rip.

Someone is in the room, flat voice, a subtle New York lilt. 'There's a change in her blood chemistry,' they say. 'We're getting low potassium levels.'

'Cause?' Another voice, different, low, gravel. Scottish.

'The sodium amytal drug. She must have had too much.'

And then I realise: Kurt. Is it Kurt's voice? I paw at the IV drip, try to sit up. 'Kurt!' I shout.

'You put it in the coffee as I instructed?'

I thrash. The coffee! He drugged me, in the therapy room. That's why it tasted odd, why I felt tired sometimes, why events were hazy. And then I think: spiders. Is that why I saw double of them? Because he had drugged me? Is that why I thought I saw cobwebs?

'We must have put in too much,' the voice says now. We? Who is 'we'? His girlfriend? The one with the leather and the studs? I lurch again to break free.

'Kurt!' I yell, but still he does not hear me. I thrash around, try to get up, but I am strapped down, secured by the ankles.

A face looms over my head. I gasp. Black Eyes. 'Hmmm,' he says, but not to me, to the other person, to Kurt. 'The drug has certainly helped us tap into her mind, see what she remembers. Thank you for recording it all—I saw it all on the secure site. She located the camera, though. Was only a matter of time. She's sharp, as we've trained her to be.'

The camera! The camera I found in the Banana Room. They were recording me. The people Kurt works for were recording me. 'Get away from me,' I scream, like a dog ravaged with rabies, wild, dangerous. 'Get away!'

Yet, Black Eyes just stands stock-still, peers at me, scanning my body. 'We'll need to get her back there, though. Fresh recording, hidden device as before. I need to see a little more of how she is acting under pressure, how she responds when her thoughts are being challenged, compromised. And I need to see a little more of what she is recalling. It is fascinating.' He lifts my right ear, inspects it. 'What have the endocrinological investigations shown?'

'No signs of Cushing's syndrome or hyperaldosteronism.'

'Kurt!' I scream.

Black Eyes drops my ear and presses his palm onto my mouth, silencing me. His skin tastes of metal. I try to scream, but only woollen muffles come out.

'I instructed you to go easy on the sodium amytal,' he says to Kurt. 'Your doses must have been too large. It's supposed to lower her inhibitions and give her mental clarity to talk, not accelerate her heart rhythm.'

I thrash my head, try to shake him off; he presses down harder on my mouth.

'Treat her with potassium and magnesium infusions. The dysrhythmia should stop. When you've done that and she's calmed down, give her something to keep her lucid but controlled, then contact me. I have tests to run. MI5 are on to us now, so we need to keep her on our side.' He looks at me, smiles, then removes his hand and slaps my cheek. 'You scream like that again and we won't be so nice next time. Do you understand?'

I do not respond.

He slaps me once more. A sharp sting flushes my cheek. 'Do you understand?'

My body falls back to the bed and, reluctantly, I nod. He narrows his eyes. I pant for air, the room pixelating into spots before my eyes.

He watches me for three seconds then leaves.

* * *

'Concerned for my sanity?' I shriek. 'No. No! Papa would never say that. You are just assuming that's what he meant. He didn't mean that at all!'

Balthus steps towards me. 'Why don't you sit, Maria? Let's talk this over.'

But I shrug him off, stride to the shelves, stop, stare at the literature that stands to attention in front of me. Facts, hard, true facts in the words of a book. Facts that prove things, demonstrate theory, present methods. My papa wouldn't have said he was worried for my sanity. Not my papa. He knew me, Papa, that is why he worried about me even then, always fearful that I would not cope in the world on my own. But he knew what I could do, knew how I thought, how I felt in the deep recesses of my mind even when no one else understood, when no one else could ever begin to comprehend what it was like, growing up, being me. Different, odd, freakish.

I rake my hands through my hair once, twice, three times, breathing, thinking. If it is facts that are written, then it is facts that must prove true. And my notebook contains facts.

I turn, face the two men, draw in a breath, then say it. 'There is someone after me in here.'

Balthus shakes his head. 'No, Maria.'

'Yes.'

Harry sits forward, holding a hand up to Balthus. 'Maria, why don't you explain what you mean?'

I glance to the wall clock, to my notebook lying shut on the desk and tell them. Tell them the facts: Bobbie, MI5, my handlers throughout out my life. Project Callidus. Dr Andersson. I say it, all of it, not because I trust them now, not because they listen, but because I have to prove to them that what they think Papa said about me is wrong. When I am finished, I pause, await their replies, but neither of them speaks. Neither of them moves.

'Well?' I say, blinking at them, the blood rushing round my ears.

Balthus leans on the back of his seat. 'I'm sorry, Maria, but you believe Bobbie?'

I stop. Do I? Really? Or is it that I want to, have to, *need* to, so I can survive, so I can prove to everyone who I really am. Not a murderer. I swallow hard, my brain on the cusp of confusion, exhaustion. Drained. I blink my eyes into focus, Harry and Balthus coming into view, shouts from the yard below drifting in and out of the room fuelling the heat of my thoughts, my uncertainty.

'I want you to look at something for me, Maria,' Balthus says, after a second, his voice piercing my thinking.

I look. There is the file on his desk. Balthus holds it aloft. 'Here.'

I hesitate at first, cautious. What is he trying to do?

'It's okay,' he says, 'you can take it.'

I keep my eyes trained on Balthus and inch towards the desk. Once there, I snatch the report and scurry back to the relative safety of the shelves. On the front cover is my name. And one other, too: Dr Andersson. My foot begins to tap furiously. 'What is this?'

'It is a report filed by Dr Andersson giving her medical assessment of your psychiatric well-being.'

I glance to Balthus then to the report, tearing it open. My eyes scan the words. It details how I find it difficult to distinguish what is real and unreal; says that it is hard for me to manage emotions, that I have difficulty relating to others. She documents how I am hostile and suspicious, that I have an inability to express joy, a tendency to declare odd or irrational statements, that I have a strange use of words and way of speaking, that I am…that…I am…

'No!' I shout. My hands squeeze the report. 'No. She cannot say this about me.' I slam the report shut, throw it as far as I can as if it is radioactive, deadly. 'No!'

Harry looks to Balthus. 'What is it? What does it say?'

Balthus gives one small shake of his head. 'It says Maria is schizophrenic.'

Chapter 21

I am on my own now and in a different room. The light is low, the blinds are black.

I lift my head. It aches, pain pounding into it like it's a plank of wood being squeezed in a vice. Carefully, I look down at myself, jittery, nervous of anyone who may come in, frightened that Black Eyes may return. My hospital gown, I can see, is white, tied at the back, and on my head there is a plastic cap covering my entire scalp. I open my mouth to scream but nothing comes out, no sound, no shouts. Horrified, I gag slightly, my stomach heaving, and exhausted, I try to rest for a second, try to think. By my side, there is a heart rate monitor. It does not beep any more. I am no longer sweating as I was before and my breathing is steady.

While there are no more straps on my limbs, I do not move, because now, ahead, of me, I see them, standing there like ghosts: three men guarding the door. Each one of them holds a gun. And though the room is white and the lights glow brightly, a dark shadow through the window to the left douses the room in grey.

The guards stand straight and the monitor remains silent. Still I do not move, do not dare. At first, nothing changes, but then I begin to detect a voice, a murmur. I steal a glance at the guards; their heads do not move, their eyes do not blink.

There. I hear it again! My heart races—it rises, but I don't want the monitor to resume beeping, so I pause, draw in long, deep breaths, calm myself. When I think I am clear, I listen again. There! A woman's voice. She is singing, I am sure of it. It's not in English, yet it is too low for me to decipher the language. I look at the window. No one there. The voice vanishes, and a feeling of dismay almost threatens to overwhelm me, when the voice appears again. This time I can detect the language: Euskadi. Basque. The woman is singing a lullaby in Basque dialect. I listen again. There are verses about twilight and silver wings spreading across the sky. The voice is light, gentle, soothing, like a warm cotton blanket.

A door opens. I dart my eyes to it. As quick as it began, the singing stops.

A man is standing in the entrance. He wears a white mask and he is wheeling in a laptop computer. He halts at my bedside, opens the laptop and taps some keys. He faces me and instructs me to sit forward.

'Who are you?' I say, fear prickling every molecule of my body.

'I am going to ask you to perform a series of tests,' the man says as if I had not spoken. He keeps his eyes on mine.

'I do not want to do any tests.' I try to push myself back

on the bed, but it is futile: there is nowhere left to go. 'Who are you?'

'The tests,' he continues, 'measure your cognitive skills, your visual and spatial reasoning, your dexterity, your mental calculation expertise and your ability to assimilate technical knowledge.'

'I will not do any tests. I want to see Kurt. Where is Kurt?'

The man grabs my wrist. 'We are testing you and you will do as we ask. We are running out of time.'

'Let go,' I say, looking at my wrist. He does not move. 'Please, let go.'

'Do you really think anything about you is normal?' he says.

And then it enters my head. I look around the room. 'Is this Callidus?'

He grips my wrist harder. 'I don't know where you heard that word, but we have to get you back to London in one hour. Your Asperger's traits are accelerating—not every aspect of the conditioning can be controlled. We only have one year left.'

'What do you mean?'

'Wars aren't fought on the streets any more, Dr Martinez. They are fought behind the screen of a computer.'

He slowly lifts his hand from my wrist. I hold my arm and rub the skin, too scared to connect what he is saying.

'I do not want to hurt you,' he says now, tapping the laptop keyboard, 'but I will if I have to. I advise you, Maria, to do as I ask.' He places a loaded syringe on a metal table to his left.

I bolt backwards. 'What is in that needle?'

He keeps his eyes on the laptop screen. 'It is a drug called Versed. If I administer it, you'll feel severe pain and discomfort. When it wears off, you will be unable to remember the pain, or anything we inflict on you.' He pauses. 'Or anything I say to you.'

I stare at the syringe. If I fight it, they will hurt me; if I do the tests, will they leave me? Somehow, it feels whichever road I take, it will lead to a bad place. 'What...' My head sways a little. 'What do you want me to do?'

'This is a code program,' he says, swivelling the laptop round to me. 'The code is encrypted. I want you to crack the code.'

I try to focus. There are blocks of letters on the screen. At first they seem random and then...I begin to catalogue them. One, after the other, after the other. In my head, I match them, trace the links, spot the connections, the holes. It is easy.

'Can you do it,' he says, 'because the time is—'

'It is a meeting.'

The man presses a button on his watch. 'Go on.'

I trace the code. 'It is for a weapons programme, but that is not all—there are details of a conversation. A transcript.'

'What does the conversation say?'

I scan the letters. 'It gives times and dates.'

'Specifically. I require details.'

'Twenty-third of September. The meeting is in Tehran. It involves one lieutenant, one colonel and one senior Iranian intelligence officer.'

'Does it give a task and target?'

'The American Embassy.' I swallow. 'A bomb will go off

at fourteen hundred hours on that date. The device will be brought in through the cleaning services' company van.'

The man in the mask presses an intercom buzzer. 'Did you get that? Make the call.' He releases the button.

I touch my forehead, breathe a little. 'Can I go now?'

'No.' He closes the laptop and hands me a directory. 'Take it.'

'Wh-what?'

'I said, take it.'

My eye spots the loaded needle. Slowly, I reach out, take the book.

'This is a telephone directory containing every phone number in Edinburgh,' he says. 'You have two minutes to scan the first hundred pages and memorise every number.'

'What?'

'Go.'

I hesitate, then glancing once more at the syringe, open the directory. My fingers fly through the book. I scan the pages like a computer, committing each address line, name and number to memory. It takes me one minute and forty-three seconds to complete. I sit back, breathing hard.

The man removes the directory from my lap. I try to steal a glance to the window where the singing was, but the man grips my chin and directs my face to his. 'Eyes front,' he says. His fingers smell of petrol.

'Now,' he says, letting me go, 'tell me all the details you memorised.'

I recite everything, a hundred per cent accurate. He turns to an opaque screen to his right and nods.

And it goes on. Next, he gives me a computer language to learn called Ruby. He tells me that it is a high-level scripting language, and he allows me three minutes to master the basics. I do it in two. When I tell him I have finished, he says, 'Close your eyes.'

I hesitate, look at the guards' guns. I close my eyes.

'Can you see in your head everything you just learned?' the man says.

'Yes.'

'Good. Now open your eyes.'

I do as he says. He taps something into his laptop then turns to me.

'Why are you keeping me here?' I ask.

He snaps on a pair of latex gloves, but says nothing.

'Did you hear me. I said why—?'

He punches me on the left cheek. 'Try to deflect them,' he says.

I clutch my face, my cheekbone reeling from the shock. 'Why did you—?'

'I said deflect!' And as I see his fist hurtling towards me, I instinctively flick up my arm; his fist hits my radius bone. It pulses with a dull pain.

'Good,' he says. 'Now stand.'

I do not move. My body is frozen.

'I said stand!' He pokes me hard in the stomach. I get up.

'Okay,' he says, 'deflect.'

This time I somehow make myself ready. He tries to punch me on the head, stomach, arm—I stop every one of them. He follows me around the room, kicking at me, slapping, punching, but I move fast, faster than I ever knew I could. He orders me to stop, but I want to keep going. I feel a sudden rage within me, an anger at him for hitting me, hurting me. He goes for my head, but I dart to the left and he tumbles. I feel on fire now, alight, ready to burn. I turn for him, screaming, everything pouring out of me, all of it. I jump on him, punching his head, his torso, anything. Slam, slam, fuck him, slam. An alarm sounds. A door whooshes open followed by the sound of boots, but still I punch.

'Who are you?' I scream at him, hair wild, eyes ablaze. 'Who the fuck are you?'

I raise my fist again, but two arms hook underneath my shoulders and drag me away.

'No!' I shout, but they wrench me back, out of the door and into the other room, the white room with the bed and the monitor and the vials of blood. I struggle, but they throw me to the bed and strap me down. And that is when I see Black Eyes. He enters, his head cocked, his fists formed, a woman in a white coat by his side.

'I said we would not be nice if this happened.'

'Fuck you,' I say and spit at him.

Black Eyes smiles and turns to the woman in the white coat. 'Strap her down, give her one dose of Versed, get her returned to London, then meet me in my office.'

And he turns and walks away as the woman prepares to inject me with the drug.

My eyes go wide at the sight of the needle. 'No! No. No.'

The needle punctures my skin and the drug courses into my vein. 'No!'

The effect is instant. Heat rips through my blood, courses through my muscles, my bones, nerves. I scream. My limbs feel as if they will explode, my head feels as if it will split in two, my skin prickles as if it were on fire.

I scream and scream until the drug takes over, sedates me, and everything white in the room decays into black.

* * *

I don't now how long I scream for.

When I stop, when I look up, shoulders heaving, breath ragged, Balthus is holding the phone, ready to call in the guards; Harry is stood by my side.

'Maria,' Harry says, 'please. Please, calm down.'

I gulp. I swallow back the snot, the spit, the nausea. 'She's lying. Dr Andersson is lying.'

Balthus sets down the phone and walks over until he is just one metre away.

'Stop!' I say.

He goes still. 'Maria, Harry and I just want to help you.'

I shake my head. 'No. No you don't, otherwise you would believe me and not Dr Andersson.'

'Maria, Dr Andersson is a trusted physician.'

'Bobbie Reynolds says Dr Andersson is with MI5, that she is my handler.' The word 'handler' lodges in my throat, threatening to constrict it, kill me off.

Harry sighs. 'Maria, hear what you are saying. My dear, please.'

Balthus steps nearer again and I move back, unsure, unsteady, every inch of my body feeling as if it's on fire. Burning.

'My father said something was being done to me. He talked about reports, codes, data on me from a hospital in Scotland.'

'No, Maria,' Balthus says. 'You spoke about this to your mother, didn't you?'

I halt. How does he know what I talked to her about?

'Were you listening?' I say. 'Did you bug our table in the visiting area?'

'Maria,' Harry says, his voice a soft coo, 'Ines *told* us what you said.'

'What?' My hands begin to rake through my hair and, as much as I try, I cannot stop them.

'They agreed with Dr Andersson's assessment of you.'

'What? How could they? I have Asperger's. They know that.' The visiting area, when Mama was taken ill—I saw Ramon talking to Dr Andersson. That is what she was speaking to him about. 'She is plotting against me,' I say, frantic. 'They all are.'

'Come sit,' Harry says.

But I don't, instead I watch Balthus and my eyes bolt to his desk. To my notebook. And that's when the solution becomes clear. 'I have it written down!' I begin to stride to the computer.

Harry steps forward. 'Maria, stop.'

But my sight is locked on my notebook, on the laptop. I feel like a rabbit caught in a hole and the only way out is to dig a new one. I shove past Balthus, grab my writing pad, hold it aloft, flap it in the air. 'It is all in here. Bobbie said the answers were in here and she was right. I can do things with computer and codes, things I don't even recall learning.'

'Maria,' Balthus says, slowly, carefully, like my name has gone nuclear, 'your mother told us you may say this. She said you are obsessed with writing things down and that you create links, fabricate connections that don't exist. She said you have a journal at home that you have been doing the same thing with for years.'

I drop my hand as he speaks. My journal. Of course. 'Then if I obsess over facts and writing them, if I have done this for years, using my journal as my mother says, an obsession in line with traits of someone with Asperger's, why is it that Dr Andersson can suddenly diagnose me with schizophrenia when every other doctor before her has never mentioned it once?'

Neither man speaks. Harry goes to open his mouth then closes it. I have hit a chord.

'If you don't believe me, if you don't think I am telling you the truth, then there is only one thing left for me to do.'

'What?' Balthus says.

I sit in front of his laptop and open my notebook. 'I have to show you.'

Chapter 22

I peel open my eyes and gasp as I awake in the interview room.

The sun is glaring through the window and I am sitting in my chair. I blink, trying to get my bearings, my breathing rasped, my palms clammy, mouth dry. My suit is on and my blouse is buttoned. As if I never left.

A flush of heat hits my head and I touch my scalp. The door swings open.

'You're awake.'

Kurt is standing in the doorway, holding his cell, tapping the screen. I drop my hand to my side, my mind a fog, a stew of faces and voices and rooms. I shake my head. A dream. Was that what it just was, with Black Eyes and the white room and the tests? It must have been. A dream or a nightmare, because I am here now, not there, not in a van or on an aeroplane. I try to recollect what it was all about, but I cannot recall much—just shapes, sounds, smells—but it seemed so tangible, so real, like the hair on my head or the nails on my fingers. Like I could touch it. Like I was there. And yet, here we are, as normal, me sitting in the chair, Kurt talking. And then I remember: we switched rooms, but events are hazy and I can't remember where or why.

'You've been asleep for over an hour,' he says, entering the room.

I glance at my sleeves. Crumpled. My arm stings at the wrist, numb at the top, but I don't know why. I must have slept on it. 'But we went to a different room, didn't we?'

He smiles. 'Yes, for a brief moment, but then we came straight back here as you were tired. That's when you fell asleep.'

I watch as he sits down, slipping his mobile to the table. There is a flask and two mugs already set in front of him. Kurt unscrews the flask and looks to me. 'Coffee?'

I say nothing. I do nothing. I feel as if I am suspended mid-air. Taxis beep in the street below. The muslin of the curtain floats up and down. Life is carrying on as normal. And yet I don't feel part of it, as if it is all continuing without me. 'Why was I asleep?' I say.

He pours some coffee. 'You were tired, I expect.' He screws the cap back on the flask and produces a cup and a smile. 'Therapy can do that sometimes, especially this kind of intense therapy.'

A fire alarm blares out suddenly from the opposite building. I slap my hands to my ears. Kurt sits back, sips his drink and watches me. I look left and right. The alarm is still shrilling. I stride to the window, heart pounding. The alarm is louder here. I scan the road. There are no fire engines, no evacuations. The alarm stops. Carefully, I lower my hands. Through the bars I see children walking by, laughing, eating sweets.

Sweets.

'Maria, you need to sit down now.'

I turn. Kurt. He is holding his Dictaphone. The flask of coffee is on the table in front of him. Don't drink it, I tell myself, but I am unsure why.

Kurt gestures to the empty chair. 'Sit. Now, please.'

I look at the chair then at Kurt. Something comes into my head. A memory. 'What is the Banana Room?'

Kurt's smile drops. 'I do not know what you are talking about. Sit down, Maria.'

'You are lying. Why are you lying?'

'I was reading Dr Andersson's case notes again while you were asleep. Her diagnosis of schizophrenia.' He gestures to the chair. 'Quite accurate now, wouldn't you say? The paranoia? Please, I will not ask again. Do sit.'

I walk to my chair, thinking everything through, my mind racing ahead of itself. That report by Dr Andersson is a fabrication, and yet, Kurt is referring to it now. For some reason, my eyes fix on the painting of the mountain and moorland on the wall. Different. It looks different somehow, altered from the way I remember it.

And as I take my seat, my gaze stuck on the painting, it pops into my head, fully formed: the answer. My blood suddenly runs cold, a shiver rippling down my spine despite the warmth of the room. The element that has changed, that is different since I first arrived at Goldmouth, is Kurt. Because, just like Dr Andersson before him, Kurt is now trying to purport that I am insane.

There is one conclusion and one conclusion only that I can reach to my horror, to my muffled, silent scream: Kurt is now my handler.

* * *

I scan my notebook. Harry and Balthus hover near me but I do not look at them. I need to concentrate, need to show them that I am not mad, that Dr Andersson is lying. A fox. A fraud.

I collect my nerves and examine the codes in my book. They are alien to me, but I force myself to keep searching for something—a pattern, a clue. When nothing comes, I try to ignore the welt in my stomach, the voice in my head that whispers, 'Balthus and Harry are right,' and I switch on the computer. Instantly, I perform the password bypass technique from earlier.

Balthus gasps. 'How did you get in to my secure login?'

I ignore him. Rain has begun to pelt the windows, the sound tinny, metallic against the prison bars, too loud in my ears. The lights are low, the air is muggy. It is distracting, messing with my senses. I lower my head, try to block it out and carry on. I have no option now. I am on this road.

I flip to the page where the hacking code is, the one I decrypted. I pause, look at it. Knowing that my university professor made me do this for real without me realising puts a new perspective on it. If I can hack websites, then the question is, what could be hidden for me to find? Why would I need to hack in the first place? If my professor really was working for the Project, then there was a reason, a truth—and truths are often concealed. The thought makes a lump form in my throat and I ignore the almost overwhelming urge to run and hide somewhere, somewhere from all the liars, and never, ever come out.

'Maria,' Harry says, 'what is going on? Don't you think—'

'Wait.' For some reason I catch myself thinking of Black Eyes. My hands begin to sweat, my legs jitter, but something else happens, too—a sort of rush, an energy, a cognitive thought. I can almost feel the neurons in my brain connecting, calculating, deciphering. How can this be happening to me? How do I know to do this? Read the notebook, my mind tells me. The answer is there.

I flip the pages over, one by one. Details fly past my eyes, my brain registering every single one until I stop. There. A pattern. I search it, scrutinise it. I remember dreaming about the pattern when I first arrived at Goldmouth. I track it now, calculate it. What is it telling me? What?

Balthus looms into view. 'Maria, I think that's enough.'

But my mind keeps working and the pieces start to fall into place. I find myself decoding the configuration until, just like that, a sentence is revealed. 'Websites are used as cover,' I say to myself, a murmur first then louder still. I look up. 'The website is a cover.'

'What?' he says. 'Whose website?'

'Dr Andersson's.'

'Maria, no.'

'Yes. It says here, in my notebook.' I point at it. 'A pattern, a code. I don't know why it's there or how I recalled it, but it is all I have. Websites are used as covers.'

He shakes his head. 'This has to stop.' He puts his hands on the laptop, begins to move it away.

'No!' I try to drag the laptop back off him, desperate.

'I have to show you.' I panic, pull at the screen. If I don't do this now, what will happen? I will be locked up forever.

'Maria, let go of the computer.'

But I do not, instead gripping it harder, as if my life depends on it, as if nothing after this will ever be the same again.

'Maria,' Harry says, 'let go.'

'No.' And I am shocked at the sudden steel in my voice, weighted, loaded.

Balthus tries one more pull, but the laptop slips from us both, smacking base first back onto the desk, a thick thud in the air.

We both look at the computer, breathing hard.

'I have to show you,' I say, trying anything now, anything to help them see, these men who knew my papa. 'I have to show you. I have to. For Papa.' I drop my head, beaten, shattered. 'For Papa.'

Balthus glances to Harry and Harry stares at me, head tilted, then nods to Balthus. Balthus exhales and steps back.

'Okay,' Balthus says, just one word, a low growl.

Not wanting to lose my chance, I drag my chair back to the laptop and search my writing pad. The hacking procedure, now decoded, is there. All I have to do is try it.

Step by step, I follow my notes. First, they tell me to access the web anonymously using a proxy. I hesitate initially, not trusting myself, but to my surprise it works. Next, moving at speed, I bring up the search engine and type in 'Dr Lauren Andersson, Psychiatrist'. My movements are instinctive, frightening. One more tap and a page of search results appears. I scan the data. It is mainly social media links and research papers. Each one of them seems convincing, but there is a website. About Dr Andersson.

`I click on the link and Dr Andersson's face appears. I hold my breath at the sight of her, the milky skin, the ice-blonde hair, like she is in costume for a part in a play I do not yet know the title of.

Outside, the rain slams harder against the glass and, steadying my growing disorientation from it, I examine the information. Dr Andersson's name and profession are listed. On her qualifications page, there is a catalogue of her degrees and courses. I picture in my head the certificates on the wall in her office; they match.

I scan it all, slowly coming to the gut-wrenching conclusion that there is nothing here, the whispering voice looming again, when I see something. There, at the bottom right-hand corner of the screen, is a black square, two millimetres by two millimetres, barely visible. I drag my chair as close as possible to the desk and click on the icon, hardly able to contain my nervous frenzy. A box pops up asking for a password. I remain very still.

'What's that?' Balthus says.

I squint at it, unmoving, frozen to the seat. 'A…a password request.' Carefully, I look back to my notebook. I close my eyes for two seconds, try to picture sitting in the university office, solving the pretend equation, my professor standing there when all the while he was an imposter. The thought takes my breath away, shoots up bile. I gulp in air.

'Maria?'

I push back the thought and check my decoded notes. I look to Balthus. 'I need a USB stick.'

'What?' Harry says. 'Here.' He hands me one from his pocket.

I grab it, insert it into the laptop, begin to download the hacking tools from the website's link extract, copying all the executable files. I do it all like I am an expert, not knowing fully what the phrases actually mean, and as I carry on, in the back of my mind, one word swings up and down like a see-saw: Callidus.

I wait for the file to download, anxious, jittery. One second passes, two, three, four, five. Balthus stares, Harry frowns, the rain slams against the window. The wait is almost unbearable. Finally, it pings complete. I let myself breathe out. I find myself flicking open the notepad function and, tracking my scribbled writing, type in the data from the hacking website.

My eyes stay on the screen. My palms are clammy. I rub them up and down on my trousers. I cannot get this wrong. Not now. There must be something hidden here, in Dr Andersson's website. It is a cover. It must be.

'Maria,' Harry says, 'I don't think you should be doing this.'

But, before he can finish his sentence, a list appears on the screen.

Balthus leans in. 'What are those?'

Stored passwords pop up. I peer at the laptop, amazed at what I have done. How? How did I know all this? My hands shake now, but I manage to scan the list. How do I know which password to choose? I search the notebook again and find an encrypted pattern seven pages in. Could that be it? Or is it all just made up? Stalling one last time, I follow the password-locate method and press enter.

The whole screen goes black.

'I think that's it now,' Balthus says.

'No.'

'Maria, it's crashed.'

'No, it can't. Just wait.' My heart races, my mind pleads for something to happen, yet deep inside, I know it is futile. They think I am crazy.

Harry moves forward. 'Come on, Maria. Let's get a cup of tea, hmm?' And he walks over to a kettle that sits by the window, pours himself a glass of water.

'Harry!'

Harry stops, turns, looks at Balthus. I look at him then at the computer screen, rigid, barely able to register what is in front of me.

Because a document has flashed up. A confidential report containing hundreds of names and numbers and test case allocation codes and secure file names. And at the bottom is an intelligence officer number next to a picture of the report's author: Dr Andersson. I do not move, too scared to admit what I have done, what I have accessed without knowing how.

'Jesus Christ,' Balthus says.

Harry comes over, peers at the screen. He drops his water glass.

Because there, at the bottom of the file is an address: Thames House, London.

The headquarters of the UK Security Services.

MI5.

Chapter 23

Kurt takes a sip of coffee then announces that he needs to use the bathroom. He gets up and leaves, and it all happens so fast, it is all so unusual, that I don't have time to tell him that he has left his cell behind.

When the door shuts, I immediately stand and grab the phone. I don't think, just do. The dream, the nightmare is fresh in my mind, and as every second passes it feels more real, more like it actually happened. I glance to the coffee. I wonder… I bend down, pick up the flask. Uncapping it, I sniff. Normal. No aroma other than the usual. I am tempted to sip it but something tells me to stop, yells at me that it is not safe, but I don't know why I should think that. All the same, I re-screw it and set it down.

Knowing time is short, I gulp some water for my dry, nervous mouth and turn my attention to the mobile. If Kurt is my handler, working for the Project, this could tell me, may provide some information. Having seen him use his phone often, I tap the screen. Closing my eyes,

I search my memory for an image of Kurt inputting his passcode... There! My eyes fly open and I tap it in. Denied. What? There is a clattering from outside. I freeze, not daring to move. When no one comes, with my hands wobbling slightly, I try again, closing my eyes. A picture pops up after three seconds: Kurt entering the room just after I awoke. He had his phone in his hand. I think hard, flicking through the images until... That one! I open my eyes, tap in the code... I am in.

Pausing to take a breath, to steady myself, I then begin to methodically scan his emails, his texts. Nothing of interest. I shake my head, check again, but still no real facts, no crucial information, and then, just as I think I was wrong, that I have flown to a crazy conclusion and that Kurt is just what he says he is—a therapist—I see something. Voicemail. He has a voicemail message. Should I listen to it? Pausing to check for anyone returning, I gulp and tap the icon before I can change my mind. I put the phone to my ear.

'Daniel?' a woman says. I freeze. I recognise the voice: a punnet of plums, a bunch of black grapes. Kurt's girlfriend, the one with the coffee. Except, she is not calling him Kurt. So does that mean...? I press the phone harder against my ear, listen.

'I'm at Callidus now,' she is saying. 'Dr Carr wants you to cut it now. We've got enough recording material. Tests are all confirmed and neutral. The geese are on our trail now. NSA is blown. We need her out and on our side. It's time. See you at the Project.'

The message ends. I lower the cell, my whole body suddenly numb, immobile. The woman who brought the coffee, Kurt's girlfriend—she works for Callidus. Which means...

I throw the phone down as if it's red-hot, as if it's scorching my skin, because the truth burns me, sears my mind. Kurt is not a therapist. He is from Callidus, and he has been here messing with my head, implying that I am going crazy when I am not. I pace the room, thoughts spinning, hands wringing themselves over and over again at what it all means, at why they are doing all this, at the gut-ripping reality of it all. Balthus and Harry and I—we found out, we discovered the eyes-only document that day in the office, the conditioning, the tests, the, the… I have to stop, overwhelmed, leaning against Kurt's chair, gulping in air, but it doesn't work. My heart still pounds in my chest, my blood still bangs in my veins.

Daniel. The woman on the message said his name was Daniel. Daniel means 'God is my judge'. God? *God?* I almost laugh out loud at the absurdity of it. Where is God in all this? How can a God condone what is happening in the world? The lies, the corruption—nowhere is free from it, not even the inner sanctum of religion itself, rife as countries all over the world are with violence and hate and greed and deception. All of them—Spain, Iran, Iraq, England, America, Israel, Palestine—justifying their actions in the name of their God. And so is that what God is? Cruel? Lying? Prepared to go to any means to succeed in his aim, to get what he wants? Is that what Father Reznik was, what Daniel—Kurt—is?

It is too much. I bang my head hard on the chair, my forehead, the taut bone hitting the leather. But then something happens, as if the blow dislodges a reality inside me, one I knew was there, but for some reason could not reach: Kurt took me to Callidus. I halt, skull resting on the seat.

I wasn't asleep at all, not in the chair. What I thought was a dream actually happened—they took me in a van and plane so they could test me, drugging me for the journey back to London. Why?

I flip up straight and, ignoring the head-throb, stride across to the picture of the mountains and moorland on the wall, utterly lucid now, knowing exactly what I need to do. His girlfriend said they had been recording me, so let's see.

I study the moorland picture. The frame is wooden, the paint is oil. I trace my finger along the edge and analyse the painting strokes. Each one of them appears just the same, each a deep green of the moor or a brown of the mountain. Mountains and moorland—the two are not normally found side by side. By the bottom right-hand corner there is a tear. It is only one millimetre in diameter, but I see it.

I reach out and, slowly, touch the canvas. Bit by bit, I poke my finger into the painting and, gradually, the tear becomes bigger until, when I stop, it is two centimetres long. I pause, listen to the rise and fall of my breathing. I look at the carpet, at the door, at the bars on the window. A soup of faces stir in front of me: Kurt, Father Reznik, university professors, colleagues at St James's, Dr Andersson, Michaela Croft. Each of them blending into one swirling stew of blood and tissue. All of them liars. All of them part of the Project, the covert conditioning experiment.

I face the painting and begin to rip it apart.

* * *

Harry and Balthus stare at the computer screen. No one moves. No one speaks. The rain outside has been replaced by a sudden howling wind.

Harry steps back, shakes his head. 'How can Dr Andersson's website link to MI5?'

They both look at me, but I avoid their gaze, my whole body spent, exhausted with what I have tried to do. 'She was right,' I say after a moment, voice quiet, shattered. 'Bobbie was right.'

Harry stares at the screen again. 'MI5?' He shakes his head. 'My God.'

Balthus reaches over, picks up the phone. 'I'm getting Dr Andersson, or whatever her fucking name is, out of here now. This is not okay. This is not fucking okay.'

'Maria, I am so sorry,' Harry says now. 'I...' He stops, breathes out. 'I am so sorry we doubted you.'

I look at him now and sway. It feels as if I am hanging off the edge of a cliff, teetering, staring into the sea below. Bobbie has been telling the truth. I roll the word in my head; it almost feels like a stranger to me.

'She took my blood,' I hear myself say now aloud.

'What?' Balthus says, holding out the phone receiver.

'In our therapy sessions, Dr Andersson took several blood samples from me for tests.'

Harry looks to Balthus. 'Is she permitted to do that?'

'No,' he says, slamming the phone back to his ear. 'No she's bloody well not.'

I hang my head, my notebook still open to my left. MI5. It is real, the connection to it is real. My mind fogs up and it's only when I hear Balthus shout down the phone do I come to, my sight focusing on the scrawled pages beside me. Why? Why are MI5 involved? How can I ever have had a part in any of what may be going on? Why was Dr Andersson taking my blood? Why? Why?

I dig my fingernails into the notebook, hold on, claw into it, desperate for more answers. What is Project Callidus? Why are they using me? If Papa were here now he would make me investigate more, make me keep going, tell me not to give up, but I don't know if I can. It has taken all my energy to convince Balthus and Harry of it all. To delve further may wipe me out.

I let out a breath and allow my eyes to flicker shut. A breeze glides in from the window. When I open them, the notebook is still there, but now it is on a different page, the wind having lifted it up and over. I stop, look at it. A thought begins to whirr inside me. Inching out my hand, I pull the pad over and scan the details on the page. Two codes stand out among all the others. They mean something, don't they? They have to.

I stay on the page, blink at the numbers again, glance to the computer screen. What if the codes are a key? What if they can help me get to the information I need on unlocking Callidus? 'I have to access these security-service file names,' I say aloud.

'What?' Harry says. 'Maria, MI5 will have the highest security levels. Access is impossible. Along with the CIA, the Pentagon, GCHQ, it's one of the most enclosed sites in the world. You just have to accept this is as far as we can go.'

I stare at him then look back to my notebook. He is right. About the security, he is right. But why do these codes spark something in me, unlodge a distant recollection, a glimmer of a procedure I have previously performed.

I divert my eyes back to the laptop, block out the sound of Balthus now yelling on the phone and look. I don't know what I am searching for, don't even know what to do, but still I examine everything. It is on my third search, leaning so close that my nose almost touches the screen, that I see it. On the top left of the page is a scroll icon. My head jerks back. Was that there before? I rub my eyes, lean in again. It is still there. Very slowly, I put my hand on the finger pad and move the cursor. I take in a breath and hold it. One second, two. On three I click on the icon. Immediately, a tiny image of a black bomb springs up.

I move the chair back, suddenly frightened. I am delving into something way above my head. I glance around. Balthus is still on the phone, Harry is now making tea. I set my eyes back to the screen. The bomb is still there, shimmering like a mirage in the desert. The voice in my head whispers: *Codes. Check the codes.* Hesitating, nervous, I examine my notebook. They are complex calculations, mapped full of equations and encrypted messages, but still… I take a picture of them with my mind and then go quiet. Think. What can I see there? What is the common pattern?

Bit by bit, as if unravelling a gift, the codes begin to decrypt themselves. I sit and work it out, connecting, undoing, re-establishing. When I lose the trail, I kick back my seat, swear, move back, carry on. Once I am finally done, I look down at myself and realise I am shaking.

Harry returns with tea. He sets a cup down in front of me, steam rising to my face, stinging it. 'Are you all right? You've gone pale.'

I cannot speak. The codes whisper in my head, the decryption. I could do it. Not much at first but then faster, quicker, as if I have always been able to manage it, like a fish that just knows how to swim. I put my hands to my sides, grip the seat rest. 'I think I can access the secure site files.'

Harry pauses. 'How?' He slowly lowers into his seat.

I swallow, inhale, count, anything to make me feel normal, normal for me, at least. 'My notebook.'

I hover my fingers over the keyboard and begin. I cross-reference everything I do on the laptop with my notes, stopping when I hit a problem, rerouting, using a new code. Balthus comes over—I hear him, hear Harry telling him what is happening, but I barely register their voices, so consumed am I with the process. When I reach the last code, I expect it all to unravel, but nothing happens. I have hit a wall. I shake my head. How can it stop there? I have followed the entire method. I leaf through the writing pad fast, scanning every single page, but still nothing. I look up, drained. If I can't access this, then what? How can I prove what is happening to me?

I slam the book shut, tossing it to the side, cross with it, the pad landing backside up. I close my eyes, open them, defeated. And then I see it. A tiny scrawl the width of a millimetre running along the back cover at the bottom. Heart rate shooting up, I grab the book, thrust it in front of my eyes. The writing—it is not mine. I study it and begin to realise it is a scrawl, something I do not recall writing: an algorithm. A complex algorithm.

And only one person could have put it there: Bobbie Reynolds.

Chapter 24

With an anger surging up from my stomach, I force my fingers to hack a safe site. And Bobbie's algorithm is the key. Just as she said all along, there, in my notebook has been the one thing I have been looking for: the answer.

I have to glance to my notebook, but it shocks me how fast it comes back. Balthus and Harry watch, but remain mute, their breathing deep, their bodies stone still. I input the algorithm following the pattern tracked in my notepad and when it happens, when the access is unlocked, the effect is instant, deadly.

A document. A classified document appears on the screen.

Balthus stares at it. 'This is an eyes-only briefing paper from 1973. We shouldn't be reading this.'

I try to examine it but falter, my mind bombarded with the data, with the awful possibilities this new information brings. I am frozen to the seat, my hands fixed mid-air, poised to type but refusing to move, refusing to acknowledge what they have just uncovered.

Harry studies the document on the screen, reads aloud from it, his voice, at times, wavering, shaking.

'"We are proposing an experimental training programme, code-named Project Callidus. It will be tasked with developing and conditioning high-functioning, high-IQ people with Asperger's who can operate covertly within a new cyber-terrorism era. It will be based at the safe MI5 facility in Scotland".' He looks up. 'The rest has been redacted. This is from decades ago.'

I stay still, scared, sick. The Project is a conditioning programme, a covert-conditioning programme in Scotland. Papa all that time ago, the memory I finally found in my rubble of grief: medical documents from a hospital in Scotland. The codes and dates he found, the reason he was scared. He said something was being done to me; he was right.

I rub my eyes. All these years—has this conditioning been happening my whole life? And what sort of conditioning? My eyes flutter open, pulse pounds in my wrist, hammering through my veins, against my skin.

'This,' Balthus says, pointing, 'here.'

We make ourselves look. In between the blacked-out paragraphs there are words, clear, legible words. There is a new section, fresh, dated from 1980. My year of birth. My fingers remain hovering over the keys, frightened to move. It is a new section, updated. It details that a new subject—subject number 375—has been presented to them, one that must be kept at home, unknown, in a controlled, natural environment, as opposed to the clinical surround-ings of the Scottish facility full-time.

'No,' I say, quietly at first then louder still. 'No.'

Balthus crouches down to me. 'Maria, it's okay.' But I shake him away, because I need to look, need to see the truth with my own eyes. This child, the document states, will be tracked and tested. The conditioning plan, includ-ing frequent physical and mental tests, will continue with-out the subject's knowledge until a specified age, using covert handlers for designated operations. Thereafter, the subject will be indoctrinated into the programme full-time, scanned for any adverse neurological changes due to age. They will, once tested, be activated for service.

I begin to wretch. Harry comes to me, but I shake my head, scared to be touched or comforted by anyone. My breath is short, laboured, but I force myself to scan the last two lines, not wanting to read on, but knowing I have to, knowing the answers lie there, in black and white.

'Oh my God,' Harry says. 'Oh my God.'

The penultimate line states: non-licenced drugs are to be used for the Project. Test child subject has shown no signs of physical or mental deterioration to date. Subject has been conditioned on complex mathematical calculus, code training, technical assimilation, non-verbal reasoning and advanced physical training. Regular handler reports to be given, as arranged, every six months.

And, as I reach the end, a lone shriek flies out of my mouth.

Because everything else is blacked out except one name. The test child. Subject number 375.

'Maria Martinez,' Balthus says.

* * *

My chest is heaving. The painting now hangs from the wall, shredded, ripped open, the canvas irreparable, the frame fractured. I stay as still as I can and listen, blood rushing around my ears. The street below—the cars, the buses, the pedestrians—they are all there. They all exist. But Kurt? Daniel? Where is he in all this?

I inch towards the painting and inspect it. At the back of the frame against the wall is a white sheath. I poke it. It is attached to the frame and, when I pierce it, my finger breaks a hole straight through to the wall. I halt, take a breath, hesitating yet, at the same time, knowing I have to do this, knowing I have to uncover all of it.

I extract my finger and observe the frame. Apart from the broken corner, it appears normal, untouched. My fingers run along the underside of it. Beginning at the top, they work systematically from left to right, feeling for anything unusual. When they arrive at the end, I begin to contemplate if it was hasty of me to rip the painting, when I feel something.

A long tube. Slowly, my fingers touch the lump, heart slamming. It is eight milimetres in diameter, narrow, definitely there. I draw in a breath; then, gripping it, I tear the tube from the frame.

I step back and open my hand. There, on my palm, is a glass vial containing something I cannot ever fail to recognise. I blink, shake my head, but when I look again, it is still there.

Blood.

Chapter 25

I grab the wastepaper basket and vomit into it.

Harry crouches down. 'Breathe,' he says. 'Breathe.'

But my focus is shot, my whole world crumbling in front of me, an earthquake, a seismic shift. 'I am the test child,' I say, lifting my head. 'I am the fucking test child. Me. All my life. An MI5 test freak.' A scream rips from my throat and sick drips from my mouth, my nose. Harry hands me a tissue, but I push it back, standing, swaying as I do. 'What the fuck? What the fuck?'

I grab at my hair, clutch it, scrape my fingers across my scalp over and over. The sheer scope of what we have discovered, of what we have just read is already putrid in my mind, rotting it, filling it with disease, decay. The reason I can decode encrypted patterns, the reason I can ascertain how to hack, read algorithms—it is all to do with the Project. Is all to do with the conditioning they put me through, conditioning I have never even been aware of because they used drugs on me, unlicensed drugs.

Test child. I repeat the phrase more and more: test child, test child, test child. My body becomes rigid, immovable. The words on the screen swim in front of my eyes, real words, written down, documented evidence of who I am, of what I am. How could I not know? How could I not know?

'Come on, Maria,' Harry says, 'let's get you sat down elsewhere.'

His hand touches my shoulders and I fly at him. 'Leave me alone!' I scream, stumbling, running immediately to the shelves, to the textbooks of words and facts, all jeering me, and I look at them and I think: do they all contain lies, too? Do they? Is everything I have ever believed in, ever held true all just one blanket deception? 'Who am I?' I yell at the shelves, deranged, out of control. 'Who the fuck am I?'

And then I grab one book then another and another, flinging them to the floor, my eyes blurred, my throat red raw, blood pounding in my neck.

'Maria, stop!' Balthus shouts, but I ignore him, my body feeling as if it is not here, as if I am an illusion, a hologram, that if an arm was waved through me, static would crackle and I would completely disappear.

I can hear the two men near me now and, like keys being taken out of the ignition, it stalls me a little, energy seeping out of me, deflated, over.

'Maria, look at me.' Harry, he is by me now, I can smell him. I try to look at him but my eyes cannot escape the textbooks, the words. The acres upon acres of lies.

'Maria,' Harry says again and this time, whether it is the scent of cigars from him or the heat of his body, I soften, thinking of my papa, of how he discovered some of this. And then I realise something.

I look at Harry. 'Do you think the Project will kill me? Bobbie says they will kill me, that MI5 will kill me.'

'You've had a big shock,' Harry says. 'Come and sit down.'

'No!' My eyes fly to his. 'What about you both?' I gulp down air as if it's the last pocket of oxygen left in the world. 'This Project conditions people with Asperger's to fight terrorism. Terrorism! Computers, secrets, codes…' I stop breathing for a second, momentarily paralysed by the fact that Father Reznik—his codes, the problem solving he gave me all through my childhood, right up until university—that was all part of the conditioning. I shriek, slap my hand to my mouth. What if they were not games or tests but actual tasks, operations to help catch people. Kill people? I make myself look at Balthus.

'If…if MI5 can go after me, they can go after you. This Project is secret for a reason. They could even kill Mama and Ramon.' I shake my head. 'They mustn't know that you know. It can only come from me. Because that's who this is all about: me.'

'But, Maria, why do they want to kill *you*?' Balthus says. His question floors me. I look at him now, standing strong and solid in the middle of the office. 'If it is you who has worked for them,' he continues, 'you who's the prime conditioning subject, why would they want rid of you? Why now? It doesn't make sense.'

I stay still, the question blinding me, muffling any response, like a bag over my head. He's right. It makes no sense. To train me then kill me. What has happened to change it all?

'Come sit over here now,' Harry says.

I blink at him, let him guide me to the chairs by the desk, my legs giving up on me, my brain shot, torn, blown to oblivion. Balthus offers me water and I take it, but the glass shakes in my hand. I set it down and look to the window. Dark clouds, a patter of rain.

'Who am I?' I say, staring blankly at the rain, at the window, the world. I turn back to Harry, a crack cutting through my voice. 'Who am I?'

'Oh, my dear,' he says. 'Come here.'

And he pulls me into him and, for the first time in so long, I let somebody comfort me.

* * *

'That's my phone.'

Harry stands and searches for his bleeping cell. He has been sitting with me, his arms around me, and I have let it happen, let another human being comfort me. The last person I allowed to do that was my papa.

'How are you feeling?' Balthus asks as Harry speaks in whispers in the corner.

But I am unable to describe feelings to him, to anyone. It is hard to believe it is true, what we have discovered. I thought I knew who I was: I was wrong.

'The one thing I don't understand,' Balthus says now, 'is why you?' He trails away, slowly sitting back. He slides one hand over his mouth, rubs it, places it in a fist on the table. I watch him and I think how one small fact can alter things forever, can merge one face to another— Father Reznik's and Father O'Donnell's. Father O'Donnell. I hold my breath as I realise. His name, I have acknowledged the priest's name for the first time since his death. It dislodges me, this fact, whips the ground from beneath me and I open my mouth with horror. Because I question something now, something I may have, in the very abyss of my mind, feared for so long: did I kill him?

I dart my eyes to the floor, foot tapping, banging. What if it was me? If I close my eyes, more and more now I find that the faces of the two priests merge together until I don't know one from the other, the good or the bad. Two sides of the same coin. And I am scared. Because, if this Project could do what they have to me since childhood, if they could condition me to decipher codes and catch cyber terrorists all without me knowing, make me trust people who turned out to be handlers, then what else am I capable of? What else have I done without my knowledge?

'Balthus,' Harry shouts.

We look at him. 'What?'

Harry rubs his head, his cell by his side. 'They pushed it through.'

'What? Pushed what through?'

Harry walks over. 'The hearing, Maria's appeal. A date's been set. *Already.* That was the List Office. Full court appeal hearing, Royal Courts of Justice.'

'When?' I ask.

'This week.'

'But…' I stop, all of it going too fast. So much spinning past me. 'It's too quick.'

Harry nods.

'But why?' I say, blinking. 'Why is it so soon?'

'Could it be down to this Project?' Balthus says. 'Harry, do you think they could have fast-tracked it?'

Harry sighs, scratches his cheek. 'I don't know. I mean, this is highly unusual, to be so fast, so yes, maybe, yes.'

'But why?' Balthus says. 'Why would they get involved in the appeal? Why now?'

And that is the question that hangs in the air. If the Project are pushing my appeal hearing through, why?

Because everything happens for a reason. So what is theirs?

Chapter 26

The next few days pass in a blur.

I tell Patricia everything, watch as Michaela Croft is dragged away, kicking, screaming, to solitary, Balthus supervising it all, his dark eyes narrow, his height, torso dominating every space. Dr Andersson has gone—all traces of her erased in one click, like she was never here—but still I spend each night caught in a web of dreams and nightmares, each one worse than before, a rolling screen of Rubik's cubes, of vestries and faces and knives and endless computer tests. I am convinced now, more than ever, that maybe I was complicit in Father O'Donnell's death, that maybe I was told to do it, under the influence, perhaps, of some drug or other. When I awake, I tell myself that it is all nonsense, that I can't have been drugged, but then I remember the conditioning programme, my Asperger's, the secret, hacked documents, and I cry out as my eyes fly open, sticky with troubled sleep, brain ripped apart, recalling that it has all happened. And, as I try to grapple with it, to shut it down, the quiet whisper that I may be a murderer returns over and over like a shadow in the night.

I am in the yard watching the dust float through the air, the sun glowing on it, changing the colours from dirt brown to pink, when I get the hearing notification, in the end the whole thing rushed through in just one week. As the guard leads me away, Patricia nods, her eyes down-turned, her fingers silently spread in a star shape for me on her leg. My knees want to give way, but I won't let them, won't let them beat me this time. Them or anyone else that gets in my way.

Harry is sitting at the table when I enter the interview room. As the door clicks shut, he strides over, opens his arms and hugs me. I let him. I let myself be enveloped by his warmth, like a blanket around me, comforting, safe. I cannot tell him, but I like him. His tobacco scent, his creased-eye smile. He is strong, a calming presence, one that lets me breathe a little easier, smile a little more. It is good for me.

We pull away, Harry gesturing to a chair. I sit, smooth-ing down my trousers, the nerves seeping out, the need for routine and repetition in the face of change overwhelming. Because I am here for one thing. One thing that I can barely think of. One thing that I have wanted to hear so badly, yet now that my palm rests on the handle, now I am at the point of opening the door, I am frightened. Because I do not know what is on the other side. Or who.

'The appeal hearing has finished? They have a verdict?' I ask finally, forcing myself to speak.

Harry nods, pulls out a file. He withdraws a paper and

slides it over to me. My fingers touch it, skimming the surface. I read.

'Is…is this true?' I say, not looking up. 'Is it?'

'Yes. All true.'

And I nod as there, on the page, I read the word: Retrial.

'You're to be tried for the offence you were originally convicted of,' he says.

'The murder.'

'Yes.'

'So fast?' I can hear the height in my voice, the rise. 'Harry, it is too soon. Do you think—?'

'That the Project has played a hand in it?' He sighs. 'I'm beginning to think it is highly likely. It's very unusual for proceedings to happen so fast.'

The Project, the conditioning, their intentions towards me if I get out. The doubt, the hazy uncertainty of my actions pulse in me, like a boil ready to burst. Father O'Donnell was nice to me, and he died. Papa was nice to me, and he died. I glance down at my hands, at my fingers, aware of their weight, aware of what they can do, what they can hold. A person's neck. A car engine component. A sharp knife.

'I have an expert witness lined up for the DNA evidence now.'

I shove my hands beneath the table, clear my throat. 'You do?'

'Yes. A very experienced pathologist.'

'Do you believe that will work against the prosecution?'

'I do. And the DVD store owner, a witness who placed you at the scene. Do you remember him from the first trial?'

'Yes.' But I do not, not entirely. I dig my nails into my legs, cross at myself.

'Something's not quite right about him. I have my team working on him back in chambers. Everyone has a past, everyone has a secret—we just need to find out what his is.'

Harry pulls out some more papers, and I watch him, his movements, his fingers on the pen. We are here together now, the two of us witnesses to each other's presence, and then, I realise, that is my biggest problem. 'What about my alibi?'

He sets down his legal paper. 'Tell me again, Maria, what you were doing at the time of the murder.'

'I was at St James's Hospital.'

'But it was not your shift?'

'No. My shift finished at twenty hundred hours. I was with the patients in the geriatric ward.'

'But there was never any CCTV of that, nothing ever recovered.'

'But there should have been. There were cameras, I know there were.'

He taps his pen. 'Okay, tell me again, why were you with the elderly patients?'

'I wanted to learn from them.' I pause. 'I used them to learn emotions. I studied their expressions. And they were…nice to me.'

Harry tilts his head. 'Oh, Maria.'

I manage a small smile, the warmth of him reaching me even here, on the opposite side of the table.

'It's all going to be okay you know,' Harry says after a moment.

I look at him. 'I used to think so, but I do not know any more.'

We sit in silence, the clock on the wall pulsing out a feeble, intermittent tick, as if at any point soon everything inside it, everything that makes it work, makes it track time, is going to give up and die.

'Time keeps moving,' I say aloud, my eyes on the clock, vision blurred, out of focus.

'That reminds me,' Harry says.

I turn to him. 'What?'

'The timing of your retrial date,' he says, pausing, pressing his lips together. 'It seems the Project may have had an input in that, too.'

I go very still. 'When is it?' When he does not respond immediately, I slam my palm on the table. 'Harry, when is it?'

'Two weeks' time,' he says. 'Two weeks.'

* * *

I am standing with my back against the wall when Kurt returns. I have made no attempt to hide the torn picture, the cell phone still lying on the floor. It is evidence, clear evidence that something is not right, not normal or solid. I squeeze the vial of blood in my fist.

Kurt halts when he sees me. 'What's going on, Maria?'

The door is still open. I look at it. Kurt follows my eye-line; he shuts the door. And locks it.

He begins to walk towards me. For some reason, he seems different. Robotic, almost. I step back.

'I found the vial,' I say.

'There is no vial,' he replies, striding to me.

'No! I have it. You can't mess with me any more!'

I hold the glass tight, but he is almost standing in front of me now, so I blurt, 'I know about Callidus, about the conditioning programme.'

Kurt halts. 'What?'

I sway a little, my pulse tearing through me. 'I know my father found some documents about me, about tests carried out on me in Britain.'

'Rubbish.'

'I saw it all,' I say, feverish, fast, 'a secret document.' I tell him all of it, everything we saw in Balthus's office. 'And now you are here, pretending to be my therapist, but you are just one of them! A handler, MI5, part of the Project. Tell me it's true,' I spit. 'Tell me!'

Kurt tilts his head, delivers me one, languid smile. A shiver runs down my back. 'Maria, I don't know what you are talking about, but you are worrying me.' He glances to the picture frame. 'Look at what you have done. You are increasingly losing contact with reality. You mentioned Dr Andersson—well, in my professional opinion, her diagnosis of schizophrenia was correct. You are hostile, suspicious. Callidus? It's just a word.' He takes one step towards me. 'You need to stay under my care.'

'People have been tested on,' I blurt. 'I have been tested on. I have seen the document. They have been using me to experiment on. Ask Balthus. Ask Harry Warren. They will both verify what I saw—what *we* saw.' I feel for the wall behind me.

A tiny tut. 'But, Maria, I have already spoken with both Harry and Balthus. They have no idea what you are talking about. In fact, they paint another picture entirely—of a delusional inmate, turning up unannounced at the Gov-

ernor's office several times a day; of a woman for whom
reality is a distant dream and an unwelcome nightmare...'

'What? No. That didn't—'

'You pestered the Governor each day with a new, crack-
pot theory about who was after you, who was protecting
you. You even brought your own family into it, claiming
they were in danger. Governor Ochoa has told me everything.'

I shake my head. 'No. No.'

'Yes.'

'But...but we found the web page. My notebook, the
codes, the algorithm from Bobbie Reynolds. We saw the
eyes-only data. I hacked into it all. Harry and Balthus—
they both saw it, too.'

'They were just humouring you, Maria, playing along.
Why do you think you needed so many appointments with
Dr Andersson? Why do you think she had to take blood
samples? You were unstable.'

Blood. The vial in my fist. I hold it out. 'So, how do you
explain this?'

Kurt flashes one short smile. 'What? An empty glass
tube?'

I stare at the vial. There's nothing in it. 'No. How can
that be?' I turn it, tip it upside down, but still it is bare. 'But
there was blood in it. I know there was. I saw it.'

'You saw what you wanted to see, Maria.'

I rub my eyes. What is happening? The vial was full.
Thick with red blood.

'Tell me, have you not been sleeping very well?'

I dart my eyes around the room, frantic like some wild
animal caught in a trap. 'You have drugged me.'

'No.' He sighs. 'You are paranoid. It is very common among schizophrenics.'

'I am not schizophrenic!' I touch the wall, move my body a fraction.

'It's okay. I can help you.' A line of sweat trickles down his temple.

'You do not want to help me.' I move one step to the right.

'Yes, I do.'

I take another step.

'Maria, stop!'

I freeze. My heart bangs against my ribcage, threatens to break free of my chest entirely.

'This cannot go on,' Kurt says. He shakes his head. 'You are clearly unwell, more than I initially thought.' He looks round him. 'Where's my cell?'

And then it comes to me. 'Daniel!' I say, fast. Kurt stops. 'Your real name is Daniel.'

He stands still.

'There is a message on your phone.' I point to it. 'Your girlfriend.' He glances to where the mobile lies. 'Dr Carr wants you to cut it—that means he wants you to stop inter-viewing me, doesn't it? He said you have enough recording material, that the tests are all confirmed and neutral. The geese, she said, are on your trail now. That you need me out and on your side.' I pause, chest heaving, air flying in, out. 'She said, "NSA is blown." NSA is the National Secu-rity Agency in America. What does it mean, "it's blown"? Why the NSA?'

When he does not speak, I keep going, desperate to break free. 'It's time. She said, "It's time." So you can stop all this now and tell me the truth.' I exhale, long, deep. 'Tell me the truth.'

I wait, not daring to move. Kurt keeps his eyes on me, inches towards the phone, picks it up. He listens to the message. Done, he slips the phone into his pocket. His eyes stay on me. One second, two. My body presses against the wall, frantic for a way out, an escape.

'Your brother,' I say for some reason, out of hopelessness, 'was he a part of all this?'

A flicker, there, in his eyes, a flicker of the lids. 'Don't mention my brother,' he says, voice deep, scratched.

'Is that why you are involved? Because he was killed by terrorists on 9/11?'

'I said, don't.'

But he is wavering, a wetness to his eyes. I keep going. 'Is that why you are watching me? Because I am part of this conditioning programme and you think I can stop terrorists like Al Qaeda?' The glass vial presses against my palm, and it suddenly all connects, all makes sense. 'You drugged me, didn't you?' I nearly laugh at the craziness of it. 'That's why I thought there was blood in the vial.' I shake my head. 'All this time, you were drugging me.'

'Versed,' he says after a moment.

'What?'

'Versed. It's a drug that makes you forget what has happened, any discomfort and…unwelcome effects of certain procedures.'

I look at the vial now, glass glinting in the sunlight. The memory of Black Eyes branding me to see if I could feel it. I touch my stomach where the scar sits. That's why I can't remember experiencing the pain. They were drugging me even when was a child. I look at Kurt now, my body shaking. 'The...the hospital, the doctor with black eyes—'

'Dr Carr. That's who we took you to see.'

His name. Black Eyes has a name. 'Then it all happened?' I say, half of me not believing, half knowing it's true. 'You took me in a van during therapy?'

'Yes.'

I slap my hand to my mouth. It wasn't a nightmare. It was real. 'And the Banana Room was...?'

'An hallucination. Side effect of the drug.'

I shake my head, press into the wall harder, not wanting to hear any of it, eyes darting around the room. And then I see it: the cobweb.

I look back to Kurt. When I speak it is like steel, like the deepest cut. 'There are no spiders are there? They were all hallucinations, too.'

But Kurt does not reply this time, instead his eyes are on the ceiling now, too. On one thing. One thing that seems as if it is there, real. I can tell he sees it, too.

Because when I look closer now, when I squint my eyes as tight as I can, I see it for what it really is: they were all hallucinations except one spider. One tiny black spider.

'Dr Carr said to cut it,' I say, frantic to say anything to keep him distracted from what I can see. 'You need me on your side, they said. Your girlfriend—she said they have enough recording material and...' I pause, shoot a fast glance at the spider now. 'That's how they knew what I was doing,' I say, stopping, realising. 'When I needed to go to Callidus for testing. They—you—were recording me the whole time. I just didn't know.'

I take one step to the corner. 'It is a real spider,' I say

aloud, not caring any more what Kurt does or says. Connections race through my brain. Like a fire sparking, they ignite, flames licking, growing bigger, hotter until my head is filled with a blaze of answers, questions, accusations, every one of them threatening to scorch me, to burn me to a cinder.

'It's a real spider,' I shout. 'Real!' I have to get it, prove it. I scan the room. Kurt's chair.

'Maria. No! Please, don't. We need you.'

But I ignore him, and instead, race over and, grabbing Kurt's seat, drag it to the corner.

'Maria, stop!'

'Are you MI5?' I shout to him. 'Are you?'

'Yes.' He shakes his head. 'No. I was. Let me explain.'

'Liar!' I yell. 'You fucking liar.'

I position the chair underneath the cobweb and clamber onto it. Raising my arm, I aim to wrench the spider from the web, but I have forgotten that the glass vial is still in my hand. It comes loose and drops to the floor.

I watch it. Kurt watches it.

It smashes into thousands of tiny pieces.

Kurt stares at it then looks straight at me. He holds my gaze for one, two, three seconds.

Then, quick, Kurt scrambles towards me. I move. Fast—I have to. Thrusting my hand as far as possible to the ceiling, I rip the spider from the corner of the room.

Chapter 27

It is here. The morning of my retrial.

I dry my face with a towel, fold it twice and set it on the rail. I do not look in the mirror, not wanting see my reflection staring back at me, a reflection I do not know any more, the image of a person I cannot trust, cannot be certain of, of what they have done, of who they have hurt. I slide my fingers down the mirror and turn away.

Patricia sits on her bed. 'What time will you be leaving?'

'Zero eight thirty hours.'

'And you don't know if your mam will be there, at the court?'

I shake my head. She is still ill, the cancer spreading its tentacles inside her. I squeeze my hands together.

'Hey.' She gestures to the bed. 'Why don't you come and sit down?'

I am faced with the reality of life on my own. If I stay in prison, Patricia could be out on parole. If I get out, then the Project will be waiting for me, as will MI5 and who knows who else.

I sit down. Patricia moves beside me and places her palms on her lap. 'Have you prepared for the trial?'

'Yes. Of course.'

'Is Harry a great lawyer?'

'Barrister. He is qualified and experienced.'

'And they are helping you figure out everything that's going on? All this creepy Project stuff?'

'Yes.'

'Then look, this is it now. Today. This is your chance. You have to get out of here. You have to figure out what is going on. They won't beat you.' She stops and exhales. 'You'll get out. And you'll win against them all, you'll see.'

And I try to listen to her, try to tell myself that it will all be okay, but the thought taps me on the shoulder, nonstop like an annoying child. 'What if I did it?' I say, my voice a small whisper.

'What?'

'I think I killed him. Sometimes…sometimes I see myself there, at the altar. The murder scene. I see it.' And saying it aloud, hearing my confession out in the open, makes my shoulders soften a little, my headache ease.

'Doc, you listen to me.' Her voice is firm, like a quick jab. 'You are good, you are kind. You are not a murderer, do you hear?'

I nod, but I can't believe her. I can't.

'I know you don't believe me,' she says, 'but this has to end. And it will—it will end well for you. I believe in you, even if you don't believe in yourself. So, when you go to court today, and for however long it takes, you tell your-self *enough*, you hear me? Say it.'

'Why?'

She sighs. 'Because you have had enough of people thinking you are one sort of person when you aren't that person at all. You are good. You are not a killer. That's why you have to say enough to all this.'

She goes suddenly still, swallows and touches her eyes.

I tilt my head. 'Is there something wrong?'

'Hmmm?' She drops her hand, pops on a smile. 'No. Everything is grand.'

I glance at the clock: eight-twenty-five.

Patricia stands. 'They'll be here in a minute.'

I slip on my jacket, pick up my legal files. My hands don't shake, but my eyes are blurred, as if my body is pro-tecting me from seeing what's ahead.

The cell door slides open. 'Martinez?' A guard is stand-ing in the doorway. 'Time to go,' she says.

Hesitating, I grab Patricia's hand and shake it.

'What are you doing?' she says.

'Saying goodbye. Like people do, like you taught me.'

She smiles again, releases her hand and holds it up, her fingers star-shaped. I hold mine to hers, tips touching.

'Martinez,' the guard snaps, 'time to go.'

'Yes.' I drop my hand, glance for the last time at my cell, at Patricia. Then, a lump forming in my throat, I quickly turn and leave.

* * *

I rip the cobweb down, desperate to grab the spider, but Kurt is right behind me. He grips my legs. I can feel the heat of his arms around my thighs.

'Get—' I kick out '—off me!'

I manage to shove Kurt away, but he clambers back up and clamps on to my right knee.

'Maria,' he is saying, yanking at my trouser leg. 'Don't!'

But I ignore him. I have to, my brain is screaming at me to run, my heart banging, begging me to protect it. Just as my fingertips grasp the spider, I feel myself falling from the chair. Instinctively, I roll my hand to a fist and hit the floor, landing on my back. The air shoots from my lungs. I try to swing back, but Kurt's face looms over me.

I move fast, kick his left shin. He cries out, and I roll to the right, scrambling up against the wall, my eyes on the door the entire time.

Kurt turns to me. There is a sharp sting in my palm, but I keep it in a fist, ready to pounce, I realise, just as the Project has trained me.

'Stop this, now. Please,' Kurt says.

But I do the opposite and, dragging myself back up, I run to the open window, desperate, frenzied. 'Help!' I scream, but the traffic is loud and busy and oblivious. I rattle the bars with my right hand, but they do not move, cemented hard into the brickwork. Kurt is behind me now. He pulls at my shoulders, but I grip the bars, instinctive muscles kicking in, and I think I can hold on when Kurt slices into my arm with the side of his hand. A pain shoots through my elbow, and my fingers let go of the bars.

Kurt seizes me by the shoulders, too quick for me to move in time. He drags me from the window and, flipping me around, pushes me hard into the wall.

He has me pinned by my neck, says nothing at all. Then he begins to squeeze.

* * *

I am in a police van. The sun is high in the sky, thirty degrees already. The time is 08.45 hours.

The van jostles along the road, the compressed air stifling. The walls are black and the seats are metal. I stay very still, trying not to think too much or contemplate what's ahead, because the answer will always be the same: I don't know if I killed him. The guard sitting opposite me does not speak, instead simply sniffs, blows from an upturned lip onto her cheeks and chews gum.

As we near the court, I hear shouting and am horrified when, through the tiny slit of a window, I see crowds lining the roadside en route to the court building. They are holding up placards daubed with slogans that say 'freedom', 'justice' and 'innocent'. The van slows down; the placard slogans change. 'Don't crucify Maria!' 'Tweet #saveMaria!' I read them all, eyes flying left and right, my pulse accelerating. Who are these people? Why are they here? I feel threatened, a caged animal, in danger, and only breathe a little softer when the shouting subsides. But then other crowds appear, new placards, different ones. 'God will be thy judge'. 'Priest killer'. 'Immigrants out!' I smooth my trousers over and over, unable to cope with the volume of yelling, so loud in my ears, roaring, muffling my mind. The van jolts, the shouting at its loudest now. It is too much. I rock back and forth a little in an attempt to calm myself; the guard stares at me and chews her gum.

The van comes to a sudden halt and a loud alarm shrills. I slap my palms to my ears.

'Hands down, Martinez,' says the guard.

She takes out a pair of handcuffs and slips them over my

wrists, but I don't like it, the restricted feeling. It frightens me.

Outside, there is a loud creak of heavy iron gates being
opened. I swallow. We are driving in.

It is 09.03 hours when I am escorted into the High Court
building. The masonry is white and the air is cool, voices
echoing, loud, vibrating, but my cuffed hands mean I am
unable to block my ears from the noise. As we walk, I see
the reception hall is cavernous and wide. Marble stair-
ways curve from the ground floor all the way to the top
and, on the ceiling, a fan, two metres in diameter, circulates air through the walkways. More sounds to deal with.
Wigged barristers and suited solicitors scurry by, criss-
crossing the tiles, heels clicking. Everyone appears to be
wheeling suitcases of legal files, dragging them behind
like clubbed seals.

I walk with the guard and glance to my left. There are
four carved oak doors, all double bolted and taller than
two men. Police firearms officers stand by each one. Long,
black guns sit diagonally across their bodies.

Once deep inside the bowels of the building, I am placed
in a box room and told to sit. The guard unlocks my handcuffs and turns on a radio before she leaves. 'Some company,' she says. Classical music immediately drifts in, and
for the first time since we arrived here, my shoulders relax.

When Harry finally arrives he is breathless, wigged and
sweaty. Greeting me, he dumps his files on the desk and
adjusts his wig as it slides forward. He is wearing a barrister's black robes. I breathe more easily now he is here.

'How are you?' he asks.

'You are sweating a lot.'

'Sorry?' He looks down at himself. 'Oh, yes. Big day.'

He lays out his legal briefs, stands and dabs his forehead with a handkerchief. 'It would be the hottest day of the year for your trial, wouldn't it? Did you bring the Spanish sun with you?'

'No. How could I do that?'

Harry opens his mouth to speak then closes it. He drags out a chair from under the table, flicks his cloak behind him and sits. The classical music still plays on the radio.

'So,' he says. 'We are as ready as we can be. Do you have any questions?'

'How long will the trial take today?'

'That depends on how long the prosecution cross-examine for. It could last all day, though naturally there will be a break for lunch.'

'Do you know who has been selected to be on the jury?'

He nods. 'I've seen the names. There's a good bunch to select from, it seems. Reasonable mix of people. Jobs. Backgrounds—we should be okay there when the clerk picks them out.'

'You will call me to the witness stand?'

'Yes. I think it's best. Are we still agreed you will do that?'

I pause. If I take the stand, what will I say? If they ask me if I did it, if I killed him, then do I tell them the truth? That I don't know, that I can't be sure any more because I have been drugged more times than I know? Because when I think of Father Reznik, I find myself now confusing him with Father O'Donnell and his butchered body? 'I haven't decided yet,' I say finally.

'Okay.' A smile. 'I understand.'

The door opens. One of the solicitors. 'They're running five minutes late, Harry,' she says. Harry thanks her. The door closes.

Harry gestures to the radio. 'I love this piece.'

I breathe in, a deliberate, indulgent inhalation. '"The Flower Duet".'

'By Léo Delibes from his opera, *Lakmé*.'

Our eyes rest on the radio as the sopranos sing, their voices lapping like waves on a shore. I loosen my shoulders, close my eyes. Violins. Flutes. They dance together across the room, twirling, spinning, entwined.

Harry sighs. 'I've always thought, when I hear this piece of music, that if there were angels, this is what they would sound like. That when I arrived at the gates of heaven, this is what I would hear.'

The voices are in the sky now, high notes gliding through the music. We sit, listen, no words spoken. As the piece comes to a close, the singing hovering in the air like a butterfly, I open my eyes.

Harry smiles at me. We do not speak, simply wait as the singing slowly fades away. I glance to the clock on the wall and my body tenses once more: 09.29 hours. Nearly time.

Harry starts to write some notes. I stare at the radio, try to focus on it to quell my rising nerves. The music has been replaced with a news bulletin, and the announcer is issuing a breaking report about the American National Security Agency—the NSA. There are allegations of espionage and something called Prism. I sit up, pay close attention. The NSA is being accused of illegally accessing personal information via social networking sites and other significant online organisations.

I turn to Harry. 'Did you hear that?'

He nods. 'The NSA scandal? It's all over the papers.'

'Do you think it has anything to do with the Project?'

But before Harry can reply, the door opens and the solicitor peers round. 'It's time.'

My pulse begins to race. I look at Harry. My father's friend. I have never been so scared in all my life.

'You can do this,' Harry says, standing, giving me one of his creased smiles. I open my mouth to speak, but no words come out.

'Mr Warren?' a guard says from the door.

Harry nods at him, hands me a tissue. 'For later. Just in case.'

As we walk towards the courtroom, I have to stop, lean against the wall. A memory? A dream? I don't know, but it is rolling in, fast, slicing into my mind: me, chest heaving, arms, legs smeared in blood, a knife hanging from my fingers, a priest's collar lying torn on the floor.

'Maria? Are you all right? Maria?'

I blink, suddenly aware of where I am. I gulp in a breath, cup my hands round my mouth.

'It's normal to have a small panic,' Harry says. 'That's it, breathe.'

I do as he says, take air into my lungs. Gradually, the image, the blood in my mind slides away.

'We have to go,' Harry says. 'Okay? It's starting now. You'll be fine.'

And I nod to Harry, but, in my head, the flicker of what I just saw slips back again, the reality of it now taking over as I walk to face the court.

I killed him.

Chapter 28

Kurt shoves his face in front of mine. 'I said, stop.' There is spit on the corner of his mouth, his teeth snarl like a rabid dog.

'You are hurting me,' I croak. My eyes dart round, frantic for an escape.

A police siren races by outside. Kurt freezes, glances to the window. The siren fades away.

'Jesus Christ,' he says, and he releases me, and steps back.

I drop to the floor and gasp for air, rub my neck where he held me, lifting my left hand to push myself up, when something pinches it. Slowly, I open my palm. There, on my skin, is a metal spider, and on it, a tiny spec of a camera lens. I try to hide my shock, try to hide the gasp that slips out of my mouth, but when I look up, Kurt is already staring at me.

I look at the spider then at Kurt. 'Who are you?'

He stares at me and I think he is about to run at me again,

when, instead, he shakes his head, walks over to the table and rests against it. His chest heaves up and down. 'I'm with the Project,' he says after a moment. He wipes his forehead. 'We have been recording everything. With that camera.'

'Why?' I shake my head. 'Why?' My brain flies. The voicemail message. Dr Carr—Black Eyes. They had enough recording material. And this is how they got the recording. My eyes shoot to the spider, examining every inch. It looks just like a household spider. There are eight legs and, when I turn it over, a tiny battery sits tucked on the underbelly. I pull myself up and stand as straight as I can against the wall, but the room sways, and I feel as if I am in a boat on the sea, the waves choppy, the wind wild, and that with every swell, with every slosh, I am losing my bearings.

I force myself, will myself to remain as still as possible, and wait for Kurt to explain.

* * *

The courtroom is heaving with people, the air hot and clammy.

I walk in, eyes betraying me, not being still, but scanning it all, wild at the sights, noises, bustle. My hands move to buffer my ears, but the guard shakes her head and so they remain by my side.

Up in the gallery, people sit, fanning their faces with their hands, the morning heat sweltering, unforgiving. There is no sign of my mother, brother or Balthus. On the ceiling, one fan circulates air around the room, but the sun is indiscriminate, burning anything it can through the high windows, searing the walnut desks, the wooden stands, the oak panelling. On the clock above the judge's bench, the time reads 09.37.

Concentrating on anything but the memories still floating in my mind, I bend forward and look to my right. A small circular table has been set with a plastic beaker containing water. I have been told the only time I am permitted to stand is when I am instructed to do so.

A door creaks open, loud, in the far left-hand corner of the room, and I jump a little. Footsteps. Firm. Flat.

'Court rise,' says the usher towards the front. I stand, focus, but so much is happening, so fast, that I find it hard to control the thoughts that pick me up and carry me away.

The clerk clears her throat, an usher to her right, Harry and the prosecutor stood in front. 'Her Majesty's Crown Court for the trial of a criminal case with jury is now open and all persons having anything to do thereat may attend and they shall be heard. His Lordship Mr Justice Marling-Fenton presiding.'

The judge enters, sits, his long white wig hitting the bench, his pale, sunken cheeks sucking in and out. I swallow, try not to think of the power, the life-changing, God-like control this man in a wig and a robe has in his hands. On the instruction of the usher, everyone in the courtroom returns to their seats. But I am told to remain standing. Why? I cast a glance round the room and my palms start to sweat. Everyone is staring at me.

The clerk begins to empanel the jury. I count as, one by one, a name is read out until twelve men and women are seated in the jury box, men and women I have never met before, people I know nothing about, and who know very little about me. The real me.

Finished with the jury, the clerk picks up a document and faces me. 'Maria Martinez Villanueva, you are charged with the murder of Father Joseph O'Donnell. Do you understand that?'

I nod, my mouth suddenly dry, mute.

'You have to speak.'

I swallow back non-existent saliva. 'Yes.'

'Do you plead guilty or not guilty?'

I hesitate, not knowing what to say, to think. The memory, the knife, the blood smeared over my body. Was it real? Did I do it for the Project? Or was it a hallucination, a figment of my imagination? My eyes land on Harry, his smile, and I think of my papa, warm, safe. And then, like it was always there, somewhere deep inside, a feeling of calm, of pure clarity envelops me, presenting me with the answer I have been searching: I need to do this. I need to do this for Papa. I draw in a breath. 'Not guilty.'

A low whisper whistles around the courtroom.

The judge looks to me. 'You may sit, Ms Martinez.'

The fan spins on the ceiling and the people in the public gallery stretch their necks to get a view. Down by the bench, the prosecutor rolls his shoulders and prepares his papers for his opening speech.

As he does so, I make myself sit up as straight as I can.

Once the prosecutor completes his opening statement, below in the counsels' area, Harry stands. 'I'd like to call Dr Andrea Gann.'

A murmur ripples around the courtroom. I shift in my seat, agitated, impatient. If this pathologist discredits the original DNA evidence, it could win us the case.

Dr Gann is sworn in by the clerk and sits down. Her hair is short, mouse brown, and her glasses have a thick black frame.

'Dr Gann,' Harry says, 'can you first begin by telling me your credentials.'

She nods, reels off a long list of professorships and institutions.

Harry thanks her and proffers a brief smile. 'Could I ask you to explain to the jury what state Father O'Donnell's body was in when you found it?'

'Yes. The victim was found inside the convent chapel, by the altar. He was on his back and his arms and legs were spread out in a star shape, secured at each juncture.'

'I'm sorry, "juncture"? Could you explain what you mean by that?'

A vision swims into my consciousness. Tied up ankles, tethered wrists.

'The victim was secured by rope to each wrist and ankle, so he was splayed in a star shape.' She holds out her fingers and thumbs. 'The rope was secured, well, weighed down actually, by four chalices.'

'And the injuries suffered?'

I brace myself to hear it, to hear the sorry truth.

'Knife wounds were sustained to the hands. The palms were up. Each hand had been pierced all the way through to the other side by a sharp instrument, probably a kitchen knife. The same for his feet—both pierced by a knife all the way through.'

Harry nods. 'And they were fatal wounds in your opinion?'

'No. While those wounds would have caused substantial blood loss, there was a further wound—a perforating stab wound to the neck region, just below the trachea.'

'But is the windpipe not hard to perforate?'

Windpipe—why does that word lodge in my throat? Why does it mean something? Something separate, new?

Dr Gann shakes her head. 'The area perforated was the soft triangle of skin just below the windpipe.'

My finger glides over my neck. I frown. My memory— the knife, the blood, priest—there were no neck wounds that I recall, just one fatal stab to the femoral artery.

'And was that the fatal wound?' Harry says. I set my concentration back on him.

Dr Gann nods. 'Yes. It perforated from front to back.'

'All the way through?'

'Yes,' she says, clearing her throat. 'All the way through.'

There is a whip of gasps from the public gallery. 'Would you say, Dr Gann,' Harry continues, 'that this wound would have required considerable force to inflict? Considerable muscle power?'

'No,' she says. 'Not at all. In fact, that area is soft, like butter.'

I glance to the jury, try to concentrate on the contours of their faces, anything to distract me from my thoughts, but still the same idea dominates my mind. Because a phrase is coming to me now, as if I was taught it, conditioned to think it, one phrase and one alone. It rises up above this expert witness, above the evidence and the facts, a phrase I realise, with revulsion, with a sudden jerk of memory, I have always known: if you want to kill someone, if you truly want to kill someone for a cause, for the greater good, then no matter what your obstacle, no matter how difficult it may appear at first, in truth, it is easy.

The phrase: Killing is easy.

Chapter 29

Kurt holds out his hand. 'I need the camera back.'

I grip the spider tighter.

'Jesus Christ.' He shakes his head. 'You really don't know who you are, do you?'

'I do. I am—'

'No, you don't know. You don't know who you fucking well are at all. You're a mess.'

I keep my eyes open wide, not even a blink, because, if I close them, if I imagine for a moment that none of this exists, it will all disappear.

'Who am I?'

Kurt runs a palm across his mouth. 'You are a highly conditioned intelligence asset and you belong to us. You are part of us—the UK and USA secret services. You are an extreme-priority individual selected, because of your Asperger's, for a covert conditioning programme called Project Callidus. And you are going to tell me how you managed to fuck it all up!'

'Why…why are you saying this?'

He sighs. 'Look at the state of you. To think I had my hopes set on you.'

'Your brother,' I say. I look at the spider in my hand, confused. My eyes dart, frantic, around the room. 'Is this…is this some sort of flashback?'

'You've been conditioned to remember everything you see, you've had millions spent on training you, so why don't you tell *me* what this is?' He waits, unmoving, coiled as if ready to pounce.

'But I don't remember everything.' I tap my hand on my leg. 'Why did you say you were a therapist? Why did you lie?' I step to the side.

'We needed to assess you completely unaffected, without your knowledge, so we could see how you were performing. Your memory was starting to malfunction—we needed to know what we were dealing with. The therapy cover was our route in.'

'Why are you telling me all this? Why now?'

'Because the service wants you dead.' His shoulders finally drop. 'And we want you alive.'

My hands begin to tremble. 'But…you said you are with the service.'

He exhales. 'Not any more.'

'I…I don't understand.'

He wipes his mouth. 'Callidus—the Project—used to be part of MI5, part of a wide international programme against terrorism, but not traditional stuff. Callidus uses people, computers to fight the terrorists. Callidus uses intellect, not muscle.'

The report we found on Balthus's computer that linked

to MI5. My name on the list. The test child. I swallow hard. 'You said, "used to be part of MI5", past tense.'

'MI5 want to cull the Project after thirty years.'

'Why?'

He hesitates, rakes a hand through his hair. 'The US National Security Agency is just hitting a huge scandal. Surveillance of stuff—internet sites, social media—they may not have been…allowed to watch, shall we say. Anyway, the world has got wind of it and now MI5 are scared the same will happen to them with Callidus, so they want it gone.' He exhales. 'Which means they want you gone.'

'No…' I clutch my hair, words whipping past my eyes, truth smacking me in the face. 'Michaela Croft, the inmate. She was—'

'MI5,' he says, confirming it all. 'And the woman you know as Dr Andersson? MI5.'

'Blood. She was taking my blood.'

'We needed to monitor you. But she's not with the Project any more.'

I step back. 'Why? This is not right. This cannot happen. I am not an experiment to be discarded. I do not belong to you, to Callidus, MI5 or anyone else.'

'Bullshit,' Kurt snaps. I go still. 'We conditioned you—tests, training, code cracking, all of it—we did it to make you think bigger, better, faster than anyone else, than enemies, than the sneaky fucking little jihad terrorists that killed my brother. It's not about muscle power any more, it's about intelligence.' He jabs a finger at his head. 'High-functioning intelligence. Yes, we trained you to be strong, to fight if you needed to—to kill.' He stops, draws in a breath. When he speaks, his voice is softer, quieter. 'But,

Maria, it's all about what's in your head, what astounding
things your brain is capable of. You can save people! So,
please, Maria, please: think. Why is the priest dead, hmm?
It's all part of the terrorist fight. It all starts and ends with
you, Maria. You.'

I shake my head over and over. Two priests, one blood-
ied face. They swirl round and round, until I don't know
which is which any more. I look to Kurt. Does he know?
Does he know the truth? 'Did...did I kill him?' I ask, my
voice unstable. 'Was he an...an assignment?'

Kurt checks his watch. 'Shit. We have to go.'

I wipe my face. 'No.'

'Christ, you really don't get it, do you? We're on the
same side. MI5 want the Project culled, which means they
want you dead.' He exhales. 'You and I work solely for the
Project. They want you hauled back in now, but, this, right
here, is the end of the road. You figured out about the handlers, right?'

I nod, unable to speak.

'Well, they kept an eye on you then, and I am doing just
that now. I am helping you, I have been all along, even
though I know you'll find that hard to believe. And you're
not safe any more. I can't protect you here; the game has
just changed. Now, please, let's go.'

His mobile bleeps. Neither of us moves. Then, slowly,
Kurt slips his hand to his pocket and pulls out the phone.
'Damn.'

I inch away from the wall. 'What?'

'They are sending her in if you don't move soon.'

'Who?' I dart round. 'They are sending who in? The
woman with the coffee?' The nightmare—that was real.

'You told Black Eyes that you had put too much of the drug in the coffee. They said I had to be sent back to London.' I slap my hand back to the wall. 'It wasn't a dream. You have been drugging me, all this time in therapy.' I gulp in oxygen. It all makes sense: my wild thoughts, hallucinations, swaying, paranoia—all down to the drug.

'We had to have some way of extracting your thoughts,' Kurt says. 'The drug gave us a chance to get the data we needed from you without you realising.'

A slap of nausea hits me, knocks me backwards. 'You can't do this.'

Kurt taps his jacket, then halting, pulls something out of his top pocket. It glints in the sun: a syringe.

'What are you doing?'

Liquid sloshes in the vial. I glance to the broken glass tube, to the door that is still locked.

Kurt steps closer. 'You have to trust me now, Maria. The coffee lady won't be as nice as me. We are fighting for the same cause, you and I. We're good people. Trust me, it's easier this way. You won't be out for long. It's just to get you out safely, unnoticed.'

The needlepoint glistens in the light, loaded, ready to make me forget, tempting me, like a sweet high, to soothe and make all this go away. But it won't go away, ever, like a cancer spreading to every organ in the body, it won't respond to treatment.

I push Kurt into the wall and scramble to the door.

* * *

The entire jury watches now as Harry taps his chin, looks straight at Dr Gann as she details Father O'Donnell's death. The urge to cover my ears so I don't have to hear it is almost unbearable.

'Dr Gann, to pin the victim down as he was found,' Harry says, 'regardless of the ease at which the neck wound could be administered, wouldn't it have taken force, to keep him still?'

'Yes,' she replies after a moment.

Force. Pinning someone down. I sit forward, a wave of heat smacking into me. Because the thought grabs me, shakes me, wakes me up: the Project have trained me, conditioned me to be strong—strong enough to hold a man down flat to the ground. I wrap my hands around my arms, my torso, muscles. I have always assumed my athletic build came naturally. Maybe I was wrong.

Harry takes a sip of water, and, consulting his file, returns his attention to the witness. 'Now, Dr Gann, if we look to the DNA evidence. The original forensic report stated that DNA was found in three places. Can you explain that, please?'

'From the evidence submitted to me I can tell you that the blood from the defendant was found on the victim's shoe—'

'Where on the shoe exactly?'

'The inside rim, by the heel.' She pushes up her glasses. 'Traces of the defendant's blood were also found on a knife discovered in a tool shed located within the grounds of the convent. Finally, the defendant's blood was found on a crucifix that was also located in the same tool shed.'

'And this shed was used by the defendant, is that correct?'

'Objection,' says the prosecutor. 'The witness is a pathologist, not a detective.'

'Overruled,' says the judge.

Harry continues. 'And by evidence, do you refer to the original documentation submitted by the police from their investigations?'

'That is correct.'

Harry adjusts his gown and looks to the expert. 'Dr Gann, what did you make of this documentation you were given?'

She hesitates. 'I was concerned about the testing carried out for the DNA.'

I drop my arms and sit as far forward as I can. Could this help my case?

'Do you refer to the DNA of the defendant?'

'Yes,' she says. 'In particular the DNA on the knife. Normally, we have a reasonable amount of specimen to test, but this amount, the amount from the knife from the shed in which the defendant is implicated—it was low and, in my opinion, too small to test. The readings would not have been accurate. I believe the evidence gained from it would not have been reliable.'

The people in the gallery murmur. I sit back, allow myself the smallest of smiles. The DNA may not be reliable, and that can lead to only one conclusion: I didn't do it.

'But this knife,' Harry says now, 'it also contained blood from the victim, is that correct?'

'Yes.'

Harry lifts the corner of a file. 'So we have a knife with blood from the victim, and the defendant. But the blood from the defendant is so negligible that, in your opinion, it cannot be reliably tested. So therefore the defendant cannot be identified as the perpetrator of this crime.'

I hold my breath. The courtroom erupts. 'Objection!' says the prosecutor, rising. 'Leading the witness.'

The judge bangs his hammer for silence then laces his fingers. 'Sustained. Ask a question,' he says to Harry, 'we are not in the business of monologuing our witnesses or passing judgement. That, Mr Warren, is my job.'

'Yes, Your Honour,' replies Harry. 'And the other items,' Harry continues, 'the shoe—a Croc—the crucifix, also found in the tool shed. How reliable, in your expert opinion, are they?'

'The Croc contained dried blood, not fresh, from the defendant.'

Harry clicks his pen. 'Consistent with, let's say, a shoe rubbing a bleeding blister on a heel?'

'Yes. It makes it unreliable as evidence, in my opinion.'

The courtroom buzzes. I squeeze my fists together over and over, suppressing the bubble of laughter that wants to pop out from inside me.

'And the crucifix?' Harry now says. 'What about that as evidence?'

'Again, the blood found on there is too small to test. Its age and origin are undetermined. So therefore, it is unreliable.'

Harry taps his chin. 'So, Dr Gann, would you disagree with the statement that the blood on the crucifix belonged to the defendant?'

'Yes. I would.'

Harry smiles. 'Thank you. No further questions.'

I wipe the bridge of my nose as the gallery beyond de-

scends into a rush of whispers, and I see him. Balthus.
There, at the back. He meets my gaze, blinking at me, a
loose smile on his face.

I turn back to the dock, unable to think of Balthus at
this moment, think of anyone except the priest. Because if
this expert witness questions the blood on the Croc, then
is there a possibility she is right? I hold the thought, weigh
it up, but no matter how hard I press it into my skull, no
matter how much I will it to be so, the truth sparks up like
a flame that will never go out: Father O'Donnell must have
died by my hands.

I hold my fingers ahead of me, watch them, bathed in
sunlight, shaking. My hands. Warm on the inside, cold on
the outside. The hands of a covert killer.

Chapter 30

I grab the door handle, but before I can prise open the lock, Kurt is pulling me away.

'No!' I scream, but he drags me over, onto his chair. The spider camera falls out of my hand and Kurt scoops it up. I grip the back of the seat, wrenching it from its moorings, and manage to kick out, knocking Kurt backwards slightly. Tumbling, I scramble across the carpet, my knee crunching on the broken vial glass, my blood smearing a trail behind me. I crawl to my seat, rip my bag from the armrest, stuffing my prison notebook deep inside, and feel for my mobile.

I haul myself up, dash to the door, when Kurt slaps my right cheek. A violent sting erupts all over my face. My head reels back.

He grips my arm. 'You are not going anywhere.' He raises the needle.

My eyes go wide. 'No!' I try shoving him with my fist. 'Get. Off. Me!'

But he is strong, trained, and he grips me harder, so hard, he leaves me with no choice: I sink my teeth into his hand and bite down, tight, feverish, determined, and I feel so angry, so confused that the urge to keep biting through his flesh and down to his bone is overwhelming.

Kurt yelps. I let go, but he still has hold of the syringe, so I lift my fist and punch him straight in the face. He drops to the floor, his fingers releasing the needle, the whole length of it thudding to the ground as Kurt lies bent over, gripping his broken cheekbone. The needle rolls to a halt in front of me and I lift my foot and bring my heel down hard. The syringe buckles, the plastic bursting, liquid spurting out from it, soaking into the carpet, the drug oozing, merging into the fabric until it is impossible to tell where one begins and the other ends.

I take one last look at Kurt, then bang open the door lock with the heel of my hand and run as fast as I can.

* * *

Harry adjusts his robe as the latest witness is brought in. My body tenses: it is the DVD store owner. I remember him now from the first trial—eyes heavy, dark circles under them. His hair then was oily and long, his skin sallow and lined. But today his hair is clipped, neat, his complexion smooth and bright. Someone has cleaned him up.

'Mr Granger,' Harry says, addressing the witness, 'can you tell the jury where you were at 10.30 p.m. on the night of Tuesday, the sixth of November.'

The store owner leans into the microphone. 'I was closing up my store.'

'And could you explain what your store is, please, Mr Granger?'

He faces the jury. 'It's a DVD store. I sell DVDs.' He turns back to Harry.

The jury is smiling.

'Mr Granger, would you say that the day in question was a regular day for you?'

'Well,' he says, 'apart from seeing a murderer leave the convent across the road, yes.'

The people in the gallery let out a light laugh. I want to stand and shout out loud, 'Don't laugh! It wasn't me! It wasn't me!'

Harry clears his throat. 'What time does your store open, Mr Granger?'

'Noon.'

'Every day?'

'We open at one on Sundays.'

'In the afternoon?'

The witness pauses. 'Of course, the afternoon.'

Harry shakes his head. 'Yes, of course. Silly of me. And what time do you normally close?'

'Ten-thirty—' he leans into the microphone '—p.m.'

The jury lets out a small murmur. Harry smiles at them then faces the witness. There were no eye creases to his smile.

'Mr Granger, have you always opened on time?'

'Yeah.'

'And closed on time?'

The witness pauses. I press my lips together, wait.

'Mr Granger,' Harry says, 'I'll remind you that you are under oath.'

The witness scratches his cheek and sniffs. Above him, the ceiling fan whirls. 'Can you repeat the question?'

'Certainly,' Harry says. 'Mr Granger, have you always closed your store on time?'

I want to yell at him to answer. The witness finally speaks into the microphone. 'Yes.'

'Are you sure?'

'Objection!' The prosecutor is standing. 'The witness has already answered the question.'

'Sustained. Mr Warren, move it on.'

'Yes, Your Honour.' Harry pauses. 'Mr Granger, your DVD store—it is across the street from the Catholic convent at Draycott Road, yes? Number one hundred and twelve Draycott Road, Lambeth, London? Is that correct?'

'Erm, yeah.'

'And so, when you are not running your store on Draycott Road, what else do you do?'

'I'm sorry?'

'Do you take drugs, Mr Granger?'

I sit forward. Harry did not tell me about this. Have they found out he is lying? And why? Did the Project pay him to do it, to say he saw me that night?

'Objection!' The prosecutor is standing.

'Overruled.'

'Mr Granger,' Harry continues, 'do you take drugs?'

The store owner's eyes dart around the room. 'I don't know.'

'I will remind you that you are under oath,' the judge says.

The storeowner hesitates. 'I…I used to.'

'I'm sorry,' Harry says, 'for the benefit of the jury, Mr Granger, can you repeat that a little louder?'

'Yes.' He coughs. 'I used to take drugs. But not any more. Not now.'

I watch as Harry consults a file. This cross-examination is crucial. I wipe my palms on my trousers, once, twice, three times, but I feel odd, light-headed. I glance round: the court is deadly silent.

'Tell me, Mr Granger,' Harry says, 'is it correct that you regularly use cocaine?'

'Um, I did use cocaine, but only once or twice.'

Chatter instantly erupts from the gallery. The judge bangs the bench. 'Order.' The room falls quiet. My head sways a little, my vision enclosed, as if I am in a tunnel.

Harry holds up a photograph. 'Can you take a look at this, please?' The usher takes the picture and hands it to the witness. 'This is a photograph,' Harry continues, 'of you receiving drugs from a dealer, specifically cocaine. Mr Granger, is this you?'

He nods.

'Can you speak for the court, Mr Granger?'

'Yes,' he says.

'I would like this photograph to be submitted to the court as evidence,' Harry says.

The usher takes the photograph. Harry's team must have located it somehow. This is good news, but I cannot focus on it. There is a blackness seeping around my eyes. I touch my head. I feel hot, clammy.

'Mr Granger,' Harry is now saying, 'how often do you take cocaine?'

He sniffs. 'I told you, I don't take it any more.'

'So, on the day in question, the day you say you saw

the defendant leave via the gates of the convent, had you taken cocaine?'

He glances to his counsel. 'No.'

I push aside the tunnel vision, my eyes flying from the DVD store owner to Harry. What? He can't say no. This man has to tell the truth, he has to! And, even though I tell myself to calm down, to stay still, anger erupts fast, like a gun being fired.

'Liar!' I shout, standing.

'Order!' shouts the judge.

The guard pushes me to my seat, tells me to shut up.

Harry swivels round, looks to me, a smile with creases by his eyes. My body immediately softens. The guard orders me to sit, but, as I do, the blackness returns and the room feels as if it is distant from me, faraway.

'Mr Granger,' Harry now says, turning from me, 'I'd like you to reconsider your answer and remind you that you are a drug user, and that—'

'Objection!' the prosecutor says. 'Badgering the witness. Mr Granger has already answered the question.'

The judge narrows his eyes. 'Sustained. Mr Warren, move on.'

Harry nods to the judge. 'No further questions,' he says, and, moving to stare at the prosecutor, returns to his seat.

In the witness box, the store owner descends the steps and exits the room, but I hardly notice, because my eyes are shrouded now, the blackness enveloping me. I begin to see something. A memory? I try to run from it but it comes, rolling in closer and closer like an avalanche. It hits and I gasp. An image smacks hard into me. I see myself head to toe in khaki and black. The air is cold but a promise of heat is there, like daybreak in an equator country. There is a woman in a hijab. She is running, her black cloak flapping behind her as she flees. But it is no use. I catch up with her, knocking her to the ground, flipping her round until I get her head between my knees, ripping off her veil. Her eyes are wet, but I ignore them. I have a mission to complete, a task and I will do it. I have been trained for this. I reach for her neck, enclose my hands around her windpipe and I squeeze. In the end it is easy. She goes limp and I fall back, check her pulse. Nothing. She is dead. For the greater good, she is dead.

I bolt forward, my eyes flying wide open. I gulp in large breaths. What did I just see? What? I look up to see everyone staring at me. Harry mouths, *Are you okay?* and I nod, but I am unsure. Because what I just saw felt so real, felt so familiar, it was as if it happened. My hands were around the woman's windpipe. *Windpipe.*

I inch my fingers to my neck, almost too scared to admit the truth. Because what I just saw has to have been a memory. A memory of an operation I had been sent to complete.

Chapter 31

I sprint down the corridor. There are no guards, no police. I do not know where I am or even where I am going, but I know I have to get out of here. Away from Kurt. Away from the service, the Project, the conditioning, the drugs, the tests—everything. So far away that I can finally think clearly, hide.

There are doors on either side of me, bars on windows, but when I shake the handles, every one of them is locked. I race to an exit ahead. It is a fire door. I stop, ribcage heaving. I peer through the glass window and evaluate the area. There are stairs to the left, one large window at the back, and on the wall is a map of the building.

I dart my eyes to the corridor—no sign yet of Kurt. I turn to the fire door, and, pushing it hard, slam it open, my body spilling into the stairwell. Catching my breath, I close the fire door as quietly as possible, and, turning, look straight to the map. I scan it and find the exit location. I am about to shoot down the stairs when there is the distant slam of a door.

I wait. Listen.

Footsteps. A voice on the phone. Kurt is running towards me.

* * *

The woman in the hijab floods my thoughts, confusion wrapping its tentacles around my head. Is it true? Is the memory real? For what greater good would I kill someone with my bare hands? The reality is almost too overwhelming, too crushing for my mind, my body.

I fall into reciting numbers to try to calm my growing fear, whispering them under my breath over and over to myself. So when the nun walks into the witness box, her Catholic robes floating behind her, I freeze. Only when the nun sits do I allow myself to breathe again, telling myself that she is not the same person. She is not wearing a hijab. She is not dead.

'Thank you for being here today, Sister Mary,' Harry says.

She smiles, her rotund body shrouded in a cloth of grey, her tubby fingers entwined around her rosary. Seeing her in the flesh dredges up something else inside me, but I don't know what. Fear? Calm? There is a fine line between the two.

Harry consults a file and looks up. 'I wonder, Sister, if you could explain to me what happened that night—sixth of November—when you found the victim.'

'His name was Father O'Donnell,' Sister Mary says. Her voice is plump, sugary, like a boiled sweet. I glance to the jury; they are all smiling.

Nikki Owen

'Thank you,' Harry says. 'Can you talk me through the moment you found Father O'Donnell?'

She sighs. 'It was terrible. He was lying there, strapped up. And the blood…' She kisses her crucifix. 'The blood was on his chest. Bright red like poppies in a field.'

'And what did you do when you found Father O'Donnell?'

'Well, I called an ambulance, of course.'

'How?'

'I'm sorry?'

'The ambulance, Sister—how did you come to call the ambulance?'

'I returned to the convent,' she says, after a small hesitation. 'There is a telephone in the main hallway. That is the one I used.'

I stop, shake my mind away from the image of the hijab and the windpipe, and try to focus. There was no telephone in the hallway, not that I recall. Why would she say this?

'And did you alert anyone to Father O'Donnell's… situation?'

The Sister raises her eyebrows. 'Well, of course I did. Goodness, I shouted as loud as I could. Awful, it was. So awful.' She shakes her head. The only sound in the courtroom is the whirr of the ceiling fan.

'Forgive me, Sister Mary,' Harry says, 'but I am a little confused and need your help.'

'Yes, dear?'

'Yes.' He coughs. 'You say you went to the telephone in the hallway upon discovering Father O'Donnell's body.'

'That's correct.'

'When?'

'Pardon?'

'When did you leave to use the phone? Immediately on finding the victim? Thirty seconds later? Two minutes after you discovered the body? When?'

What is Harry doing? Does he know there was no telephone in the hallway?

'Fifteen minutes afterwards,' the nun says. 'I left to telephone for an ambulance fifteen minutes after I found... after I found the blessed Father's body.' She crosses her chest. 'I was in shock.'

The jury leans forwards, shifts in its seat.

'Okay,' continues Harry. 'Sister Mary, can you tell me why you allowed fifteen minutes to pass?'

She lowers her eyes. 'It was as I said, I was in shock. I couldn't... I couldn't move... I...'

Fifteen minutes. I didn't know this. Sister Mary recruited me to the convent, introduced me to Father O'Donnell. Why would she wait a full fifteen minutes before she went to get help?

Harry picks up a blue clock from his table and clicks a button on the side. 'Fifteen minutes. Hmmm.' He pauses. 'Let us see how one minute feels.' Pressing a button, Harry allows the clock to commence a one-minute countdown.

I tally the seconds. One-two—three-four. Sister Mary sits very still in the witness box. I scan the room. .

Fifteen seconds pass. Sixteen. Seventeen. Eighteen...

The judge frowns, his left elbow resting on the oak bench, his long wig sliding forwards in the heat. The usher taps her pen on the table. The clerk folds her arms.

Twenty-five seconds. Twenty-six. Twenty-seven. Twenty-eight. Twenty-nine...

My heart beats. The prosecutor picks up a glass with a

bony hand, sets it down, shifts his legs under the bench, his height and limbs too long to fit.

More seconds tick by. Slowly. Excruciatingly. Forty. Forty-one. Forty-two...

I swallow and look at the oak-panelled walls, at the jury box, at the twelve faces of the men and women who will decide my fate. All their eyes are on the blue clock, ticking ...

I glance to the gallery. The makeshift fans are flapping in the heat. In the corner, Balthus is sitting very straight, his dark hair slicked forward, his arms crossed over his chest, torso taut, muscles firm...

'Sixty seconds,' Harry says, tapping the top of the clock. 'One whole minute.'

There is an audible sigh in the room. People visibly unstick themselves from their seats. My shoulders soften.

'It feels like a long time, doesn't it?' Harry says, 'And yet you, Sister Mary, you waited for a full fifteen minutes before you moved from the scene of the murder to the convent building to call for help. Again, I ask why?'

The Sister touches the crucifix that hangs around her neck. 'I said that I was in shock.' A small mew of a sound slips out of her mouth. 'I had never seen anything like it before. I was frozen. Scared. I was... I was trapped by the sight of the scene.'

The jury sits very still. My foot taps the floor. She is making this up.

'Let us go then, Sister,' Harry says, 'to the moment when you returned to the convent to get help. You say you telephoned from there.'

She nods. 'Yes.'

'When?'

'Objection!' says the prosecutor. 'Counsel clearly likes repeating questions he has already asked.'

The judge waves his hand. 'Sustained.'

Harry nods to the judge. 'Yes, Your Honour.' He adjusts his wig. 'Sister Mary, how much time elapsed between you arriving in the convent after discovering the body and calling the emergency services?'

'Well, I called them immediately.' She looks to the judge who smiles at her.

Harry tugs at the lapels of his robe. 'There is a logbook at the convent, is that correct?'

Sister Mary looks to him. 'No.'

I fly forward in my seat. Yes, there is!

'Oh, wait,' she says, batting a hand, 'yes, there is. Sorry, I am flustered. So sorry.'

I lean back. Something is not right. She should know all about the logbook. Has someone talked to her? Has the Project talked to her?

'The logbook was previously submitted to the court,' Harry continues, 'and it shows you entering the building at eight p.m. on the night in question, is that correct?'

'It is written down, it must be so.'

'Precisely.' Harry pauses. 'Father O'Donnell was killed between nine and ten p.m. that night, Sister. The call logged to emergency services from you, Sister Mary, was only recorded at 11.01 p.m.'

A whisper travels around the room.

'Can you explain why, Sister Mary, your call was only logged when it was?'

Again, she touches her crucifix. 'It must be wrong.'

Harry frowns. 'Wrong? But it is written down, so it must be so.'

'I said I was in shock,' she says quietly.

'In shock?' Harry tuts. 'Sister Mary, this court can just about believe that you were in shock upon first discovering the murder scene, but in shock for more than, what? More than fifteen minutes?'

'I—'

'Did you like Father O'Donnell?' Harry asks.

'Objection.' The prosecutor stands.

The judge looks at him. 'Overruled. Continue, Mr Warren, but get to the point.'

Harry nods and repeats the question to the nun. I smooth back my hair to stop the sweat trickling down my face, and notice three court reporters looking at me.

'Yes,' Sister Mary says. 'Of course I liked Father O'Donnell.' She pauses and dabs her eye. 'He was a bit difficult at times, but yes, I liked him, God bless his soul.'

'And yet you allowed him to bleed to death before calling for an ambulance.'

'Objection!'

The judge nods. 'Sustained. Enough, Counsel.'

'But, Your Honour,' Harry says, 'I am trying to demonstrate that, by Sister Mary not taking any action for what was potentially up to an hour before finally calling emergency services, she contributed to the victim's death. Sister Mary's actions broke the causation of the original crime committed and, I argue, contributed to the victim's death. Your Honour, if an ambulance had been called immediately, the priest may have survived. Fifteen minutes to one hour later was too long to help him.'

The judge rests his hands under his chin, his brow furrowed. 'On a point of law, Counsel, I cannot allow this line of questioning. Jury are to disregard Counsel's last question to the witness.'

Harry's shoulder's drop. Pausing, he turns once more to the nun. 'Sister, one last question, if you don't mind.'

'Not at all, dear.'

'How do you know the defendant, Dr Maria Martinez?'

She looks towards me. Green eyes, cold. 'She talked to me at the hospital.'

'St James's?'

'Yes.'

'And when you say talk—who approached who?'

'She approached me.'

Liar! She is lying. I clench my teeth shut, forcing myself to keep quiet. She is not being truthful. She came to me. Me. I watch her and slowly begin to conclude that she must be part of MI5, part of this Project, mustn't she? That day at the hospital, I know she came to talk to me, I know she did, and that must have been deliberate and... The idea must have been to get me to the convent all along! To lure me there, to put me in a position where I could be called a murderer. I raise my hand to my mouth, suddenly feeling as if I am dropping like a stone to the bottom of the sea without any anchor. I rub my cheek. Are my assumptions getting out of control? Is this, here, today—is it all affecting my cognitive thought?

At the bench, Harry frowns. He knows what I have told him. 'Are you sure, Sister? You are under oath.'

'Of course. She seemed...lonely. I guess she latched on to me.'

I didn't! I didn't!

Harry throws me a brief glance, but I hardly see him. The memory of my hands around the woman's throat, of what it means I am—a cold-blooded killer—threatens to engulf me. When I do look back down to Harry, my blood suddenly runs chilly, a shiver, despite the heat.

Resting a hand on the bench, Harry utters the phrase that means we are losing the battle: 'No further questions, Your Honour.'

Chapter 32

Kurt's footsteps echo along the corridor.

Moving fast, I rip the map from the wall and run down two levels of stairs. I stop and listen. More footsteps. I glance around, heart pounding; there is a door to my left. I check the map. There is a fire escape at the back of the building that can be accessed through the exit. Darting to the left, I shove my shoulder into the door, but it does not move. I try again. This time, I shove harder; it pops straight open on to the fire escape.

I am hit by the sound of traffic, buses, people, music. The sounds. The air. It is not prison. Not a therapist's room. I inhale a large gulp of it, close the door, turn and, without waiting, lower myself to the fire steps, not stopping until my feet touch the tarmac.

I drop to the pavement and look up.

Kurt is staring at me from two floors above. His hair sticks up, blood stains his face and his left eye is half shut. He looks as if he has just climbed out of a grave.

My pulse screams through my veins. We hold each other's gaze for a few seconds; then, securing my bag, I spin round and start to run, hard, fast, the sound of my feet pounding the pavement echoing behind me.

I scan the area as I sprint, head for a building on the opposite side of the road. There is a warren of side streets and, selecting the nearest one, I fly through them until I reach a corner and stop. I gasp for breath and listen. No footsteps. No one following. Spitting to the road, I fish out my phone.

And I call Balthus.

* * *

'Your Honour,' says Harry. 'The defence calls Dr Maria Martinez Villanueva.'

I do not move. The court has descended to a low murmur, the air thick. I feel stuck to my seat, paralysed by doubt. Events, so far, have not gone in my favour. Sister Mary, the DVD store owner's evidence, Mama believing I am schizophrenic. But while they all implicate me, all tell the world I am guilty, crazed, there is so much more: there is me. I am the issue now, because I do not trust myself any more, do not trust my memories to be real or fake. So what do I say if I go on that stand? What message do I give? That I believe in myself, in my innocence? Or that deep down, deep, deep down, I fear I may be a killer.

Slowly, I stand, my eyes on Harry. The gallery above creaks as people crane for a view. Harry is smiling his creased smile. I force myself to keep my gaze on his face, on his soft features. He believes in me. Patricia believes in me. Papa believed in me.

I walk across the courtroom, feet quiet, just a low shuffle from the soles of my loafers brushing the floor. I can feel everyone's eyes on me, hear the flap of their makeshift fans as the sun blazes in. I pass Harry and swallow hard, fighting the urge to run to him, to yell that I don't want to do this, that I cannot trust what I will do or say any more.

The heat saturates the court and sweat springs up on the back of my neck. I reach the witness box, ascend the steps and look down. A Bible. I almost fall when I see it. A priest, a nun and now a Bible: my holy trinity.

'Repeat after me,' the usher says. 'I promise to tell the truth, the whole truth and nothing but the truth.'

She finishes and looks to me. Everything is quiet. Everything is still.

I grip the edge of the oak panel, the only solid thing, right now, I can hold on to. 'I promise to tell the truth, the whole truth and nothing but the truth,' I repeat, yet even when I say it, when I hear my voice echo the phrase around the court, I do not believe it. I don't know if I can trust, any more, what the word 'truth' really means.

As the usher takes her seat, Harry walks over to the witness box and smiles at me. My shoulders soften a little. 'Dr Martinez,' he says now, 'how well did you know the victim, Father O'Donnell?'

I swallow and lean into the microphone. 'He was a priest at the convent.' There is a deafening ring. I recoil, slap my hands to my ears. The usher runs over, pulls the microphone back. My eyes dart round the court. People are frowning, craning their heads to see. The vibration of the ring fades and I slowly drop my hands.

When the rustle of whispers settles, Harry clears his throat. 'Why did you work at the convent?'

I inhale, try to claw back some composure. 'I did not work at the convent. I volunteered.'

'And what did you volunteer to do at the convent?'

'I fixed things for them. I repaired broken sheds and windows and other similar items.'

Harry nods. 'That is very noble of you, Doctor. You donated your shoes—Crocs—to the convent, correct?'

'Yes.'

'And Father O'Donnell took them?'

I flinch at his name. 'Yes.'

'And they contained dried blood from you, from a burst blister, correct?'

'Yes.'

'Your work as a doctor—can you tell me about that?'

'I am a Consultant Plastic Surgeon. I work mainly with burn victims and childhood facial disfigurements.' At the mention of the hospital, the thought walks into my head: my manager was working for the Project.

'If we could go to the night of the murder,' Harry says now. 'Between nine p.m. and midnight on the sixth of November, where were you?'

'I was at St James's Hospital sitting with elderly patients.'

He smiles. 'And why were you there, with these patients? You have Asperger's, yes?'

'Objection! Irrelevance.'

The judge considers the prosecutor. 'Overruled.'

Harry nods and repeats the question.

I pause, not knowing he would ask me this. It is not normally a question I falter with too much, but now, with the memory of the woman in the hijab fresh, raw, how do

I know what I do is simply down to my Asperger's? How do I know it is not a result of the conditioning?

'I was sitting with the patients,' I say, quietly, after a moment. 'I have…Asperger's. It is a condition on the autistic spectrum. I have difficulty expressing emotions. I found that sitting with the elderly patients helped me with empathy. They were kind. Most of them were dying.'

'These patients saw you?'

'When they were awake, yes.'

'So you were nowhere near the convent on the night in question.'

I hesitate. A flicker of doubt. There is no CCTV to prove where I was. Could I have been at the convent and not recalled it? Did Sister Mary have something to do with it?

'Dr Martinez,' the judge says, 'answer the question.'

I look from him to Harry and exhale. 'No,' I say finally. 'I was not at the convent.'

I glance to the jury; they are not smiling.

'Thank you,' Harry says. 'No further questions.'

The prosecutor stands and my shoulders become tense again. Coughs echo around the courtroom, hands in the gallery fan faces in the heat.

'Dr Martinez,' the prosecutor says, the skin under his jaw swinging slightly, his spindly arms arranged across his chest, 'let us go to the night of the murder. You were working a shift that day, correct?'

'Yes.'

'What hours?'

'I began at eight hundred hours and finished at twenty hundred hours.'

'A twelve-hour shift. That is a long time; is that usual?'

'Yes,' I say. 'Twelve hours is normal.'

He pauses. 'So, you work twelve-hour shifts and still manage to find time to volunteer at a convent, is that right?'

I hesitate. Where is he going with this? 'Yes.'

'And so the night of the murder, you went from your shift, straight to the convent.'

'No.'

There is a rustle of voices in the courtroom.

The prosecutor scowls. 'No? You see, Ms Martinez, here is the problem: you say you did not go to the convent, yet there is a witness that places you there at the time of the crime. And yet, you insist you were at St James's Hospital with elderly patients. I'm sorry,' he says, shaking his head. 'You expect us to believe this?'

'Yes,' I say, 'of course. I am under oath.'

A murmur ripples through the onlookers.

'Did someone see you during these…visits?'

'The patients saw me.'

'Who were elderly and medicated, is this correct?'

'Yes, naturally. They were dying and in pain.'

'And did anyone else see you on the ward at this time?'

My heart sinks. 'No.'

'What?' he says. 'No nurses? No fellow doctors?'

When I look up to speak, my body feels heavy, my mind exhausted. 'I wear a hooded sweat top when I visit. I go in unnoticed and in the evening there is a skeleton reception staff. I do not wish to draw attention to myself. I do not visit sick patients so others can see me. But there is—'

I stop dead. The phrase hits me like a truck, unlocks a recollection. *I do not visit sick patients so others can see me.* The woman in the hijab—she spoke that phrase to me once! She worked in…in a medical tent on a refugee camp, tended to patients. Which means I knew her, worked with her. Murdered her under the influence of what? Unlicensed drugs? My mouth drops open, a lone shriek flying from it. I look up. The prosecutor is standing, frowning.

'Ms Martinez,' the judge says, 'are you okay?'

I turn, blink at him, but my mind is melting.

'Ms Martinez…'

From the corner of my eye, I just about see the jurors fold their arms, heads shaking. I swallow hard, wipe the sweat from my brow and force myself to look to the judge. 'I am sorry.'

He nods to the prosecutor, tells him to continue.

The prosecutor clears his throat. 'Dr Martinez, is there CCTV evidence of these visits of yours to the elderly ward?'

'There…' I stall, try to focus, but it is hard now. 'There is a CCTV camera there,' I say, sitting back upright a little, suddenly wondering if he is part of the Project, too. I shoot a glance around the court. Maybe everyone here is with them, all conspiring against me. The judge. The jury. But what would I do if they were? Murder them, too?

'And is there a recording of your visits, showing you, at the time of the murder, sitting by the bedsides of these elderly patients?'

All eyes are directed at me. 'There is no recording, no,' I say, finally.

The gallery erupts.

'Order,' says the judge.

From the back of the room, a door bangs open and a man in a wig and cloak, clutching a file scuttles to the defence bench. The whole courtroom watches. The man slides next

Nikki Owen

to Harry, whispers in his ear, then exits, his back to me the entire time. The prosecutor dabs his neck, returns his focus to me.

'Dr Martinez, I put it to you,' he says, 'that you were indeed not in the geriatric ward in St James's Hospital that night, but in fact at the convent on Draycott Road.'

'I…I was not,' I say, unsure, but I am not looking at the prosecutor, my stare, instead, is on the small parcel Harry has just been given.

'And yet you cannot prove it.' He shakes his head. 'You cannot prove your alibi, Dr Martinez.' The prosecutor looks to the judge. 'No further questions, Your Honour.'

Just as I begin to descend the steps, my head hanging, Harry rises. 'Your Honour, I have just one or two more questions.'

I halt, grip the rail. What is he doing?

The judge lets out a sigh and eyes Harry. 'Okay, make it quick, Mr Warren.'

'Yes, Your Honour. Thank you.' Harry holds up a CD. 'The defence would like to submit this CCTV footage as evidence.'

The usher takes the CD and slides it into the PC system to the right of the room.

'If you could press play, please,' Harry says. I stay very still, not daring to move, to breath. To my right, a television screen flickers to life with grainy black-and-white footage. The image—I recognise it.

'What you are seeing here,' Harry says, 'is a CD that has been discovered—handed to me today, just now, in fact. It is a CD that contains CCTV footage of the night of the murder of Father O'Donnell.' He points to the screen. 'Note the time: 10.35 p.m. If you watch, you will see shortly coming along the corridor… Yes, there she is.'

I squint at the image. Then I see it: me. My whole body goes rigid, scared to admit what my eyes are telling me.

'Dr Maria Martinez Villanueva,' Harry says, 'this is who you are seeing in this recording in the hospital at the time of the murder of Father Joseph O'Donnell. And if we fast-forward it…' The screen blurs, black lines scratching left and right. 'Yes, here.' He points at the screen. 'The time: 11.55 p.m. This camera was stationed by the main rear exit to the hospital.'

I peer at the monitor. It is me, leaving the hospital. My mind scatters, thoughts blown wide open. It exists! Me, on screen. The evidence was there all along. I can feel myself shaking, tiny tremors. The people in the gallery whisper, everyone moving, looking to one another, to the television screen. I make myself peer at it now, too, my face, my evidence, one question forming in my mind until it is too big to ignore: Why? Why was the CCTV kept from my first trial? And why has it now been returned? I ring my hands together, feeling myself on the verge of breaking away, of finding an open window to flap out of.

'You are seeing now, ladies and gentlemen,' Harry says, 'Dr Maria Martinez, visiting, as she has stated in this court, elderly, dying patients,' Harry says. 'Leaving at 11.55 p.m. This is after the time the call was placed by Sister Mary to the emergency services.'

Harry nods to the usher, who presses pause. An image of my face half hidden under the shadow of a navy hooded Universidad de Salamanca top—but still clear, still me— flickers on the screen. I had thought the CCTV did not exist. It could not be found. No CCTV evidence—the reason I am in prison.

Harry looks to the judge. 'No more questions, Your Honour.'

The room erupts. I am led back to the dock, but I don't hear what else is going on, my mind dreamlike almost. How can an alibi appear just like that? Can it be true? But how? Is it the Project? It is all I can think of as, once the noise has died and the perfunctory processes have passed, the counsels begin their closing statements. Their words, as they speak, whip past me like a snow flurry.

Suddenly, a voice snaps, 'Stand!' I blink my eyes into focus and see the guard staring at me, her body leaning towards me. I must have lost track of time, because the closing statements are over and the whole courtroom is looking at me.

Slowly, I rise from my seat as ahead the judge bends forward to speak.

'Ladies and gentlemen of the jury, you have heard the statements from both counsels. The evidence has been presented and the facts are stated. You now have to consider this case based solely on the information presented in this court today. You have an important task ahead of you. This court will now retire and the jury will consider its verdict.'

Chapter 33

I try Balthus's number once, twice, but nothing. No answer, no voicemail. The air is hot, heavy, sweat dripping down my back, but I hardly notice, so pricked are my ears for any sounds of movement, of running, shouting. Of Kurt.

I examine the area, and, changing direction, ditch down another side street, dark, out of the way. I stop by some bins, steady myself, slowly check around. There is no one here. The whole situation hitting me, I slide against a damp wall and try to defuzz my head, think through my options. I have broken out of the session, which means they'll be after me, instantly. I wipe my forehead. Kurt, the needle. He wanted to drug me to get me out. To where? To Callidus? And if everything he said was true, if the NSA surveillance has threatened the Project, threatened me, then can I really evade them? Will they always be watching?

I rub my eyes. Callidus, the memory I had in the courtroom of the woman in the hijab. Was she real, the woman? And what of Project Callidus, of their intentions? Are they inherently good? Do they really want me to help them, as Kurt said, to fight terrorism? For the greater good? But how can murdering people—anyone—be good? How? Even the notion of it seems absurd, crazy: me, covert, an asset, trained without knowing, already having possibly completed code-based operations without realising, killing without knowing I was being drugged.

An unexpected wave of exhaustion washes over me. Leaning back against the wall, I give in a little, just for a moment, and, my eyelids heavy, close. The brickwork is cold against my back and it feels good, a relief almost to be here, outside, hiding, out of the way, out of—

My mobile vibrates. I grunt, eyes flying open as I try to get my bearings. I fumble for my phone, slam it to my ear.

'Maria?'

I freeze. The voice. I recognise it, tense up, self-defence mode on high alert.

'Maria, it's me. I missed your calls. Where are you? Are you okay?'

My body drops at the realisation of who it is, relieved I was wrong. 'Balthus,' I say, fast, alert now, 'the therapist, the one your service sent me to: he's part of the Project.'

'What? Jesus.'

I stand, scan the area, aware of everything, every sound, colour, smell, as if all my dials have been turned up to maximum, at breaking point.

'Maria? Are you still there?'

'I need you to get here.' I smear sweat from my face, tell Balthus where I am, words forming in my mouth, my mind automatically giving an almost exact GPS location without me knowing how. A clatter of bin lids echoes from

two streets back. I sling my bag over my shoulder. 'Hurry.'
I end the call and start to run.

* * *

The jury has returned.

As they take their seats, I am led to the dock by the
guard. My head, my thoughts are spiralling out of control
now, I can feel it. Sister Mary, the sudden CCTV discovery,
the blood, the knife, the killing—it all stinks of the Project, and yet, even now, as the ceiling fan spins and the sun
bakes the bodies of those returning to the public gallery,
I can't say for certain the Project is involved, the dreaded
thought that I have acted alone, that I have killed alone,
threatening to slice me in two. Reality sneaks in through
the back door of my brain, whispering one word: *Murderer.*

The room swells with noise as people take their seats.
I am not allowed to put my hands to my ears, so instead I
try to quell the sounds by clouding my vision, by attempting to zone out of it all, when someone catches my eye. I
hold my breath, not daring to believe it.

At first, it is not clear, but, as the remaining people take
their seats, it becomes obvious: my mother is in the courtroom, by her side is Ramon, both of them two seats away
from Balthus. Even from this distance, I can see her skin
shines with a translucent, pasty sheen, her hair brushed
back into an oversized bouffant that sits high and proud
upon her gaunt face.

Ramon is holding my mother's arm by the elbow now,
assisting her into her chair, and, as she eases down, she
looks straight to me, unexpectedly, and mouths, *Hello, my
darling.* A tear slips out, just one, sliding down her cheek.

My mama is ill and yet she is here, for me. I allow myself one last glance; then, rubbing my face, I turn away.

'All rise,' declares the usher.

Bile rises to my throat. I swallow it back down.

A door at the far left of the courtroom opens and the jury enter. I count them as they file in. One—two—three—four... Each of them glance at me then at the jury box. Five—six—seven—eight... The jurors begin to sit down, adjust their clothes, fan their faces. The heat, the sun. Nine—ten—eleven—twelve... They are all seated, their foreheads fixed into frowns, their hands laid in their laps.

Once the jury is settled, the clerk stands and the foreman of the jury rises. From the bench, the judge watches.

My hands shake. I hold my breath. This is it. This is the decision. I squeeze my fingers, recite complex equations in a low whisper over and over again. If I had not been in prison, if the Project had never existed, I wouldn't be here, hunted, marked. Guilty. A dead woman walking.

I try to direct my attention to the court, reroute my brain. The room is steaming with bodies and odour and heat. I remain standing in the dock. Up in the gallery, one by one, people are now falling silent, each of them looking at me. I press my lips together and keep my eyes straight.

Some of the jury members are biting their nails, others are dabbing sweat from their foreheads with their palms. At the counsels' bench, Harry is peering across at the jury, the prosecutor is reading his notes. I have gone over the words of both closing arguments five separate times in my head. I recall every sentence, every phrase. Guilty. Innocent. Beyond reasonable doubt. They all swirl through my mind now as I think, as I try to determine if, on its own, it is enough.

I raise my fingers to my lips. *Enough*—Patricia's message to me.

The judge clears his throat and I fight the sudden urge to curl into a ball.

'Have you considered a verdict upon which you are all agreed?' the clerk asks.

The foreman holds out a piece of paper. 'We have.'

I watch him, his fingers shaking, as across my mind the face of the woman in the hijab, eyes frozen wide in death, flashes past in one last defiant grip on life.

'Do you find the defendant guilty or not guilty?'

Chapter 34

The foreman looks to the clerk.

'In the case of the Crown versus Dr Maria Martinez Villanueva, we find the defendant not guilty.'

The room detonates into a mushroom cloud of noise. Harry turns to me, smiles. The prosecutor shakes his head. I cannot move, cannot think. The talking is so loud in the court that it vibrates against the walls, rings in my head. I cover my ears to lower the volume, but the guard tells me to place my hands by my sides, and all I want to do is turn around and yell to her that she can't do that any more. She can't tell me what to do. No one can. Not any more.

The judge bangs his hammer and a hush descends. I cannot believe what has happened. Like a dream, like a mirage, I feel that if I reached out, if I touched it, it would all evaporate before my eyes and I would be at the starting point again, arrested, a murderer.

I search for my mother, for Ramon, eager to catch a glimpse of their faces, but they are not there. How can that be? I stop, look again, eyes franticly scanning the people as they move, but they are nowhere to be seen. The reality hits: Mama and Ramon have already left. A lump swells in my throat, instant, harsh. They have left me, now of all moments. Why? I suddenly feel lost, abandoned, like a solitary bird in the sky, like a lone fish in the sea.

I swallow, try to refocus, anything to distract from the swell of sadness that rises inside me. I look at the foreman, at the twelve faces of the jurors, at the clerk, the usher, the gallery. At Balthus. At Harry. They all swim into one wash of colour, and yet, as the verdict sinks in, as the smiles of Harry and his team filter my way, I cannot allow myself to join in the elation. Because I have seen it. I have seen death. And I know the hands that have caused it all: mine.

The judge waits until the noise has receded, then he sits forward. 'Dr Martinez, you are free to go.'

The guard instructs me to walk down the steps and I follow, but I cannot focus. All around me, people stare and talk and point, and yet I feel like a fraud. I am aware there is noise, but it is as if the mute button has been pressed, and I see their mouths move, but I do not hear their voices, hear their shouts. I stare at the guard as she says something to me, but I cannot make out what it is.

The volume turns up. '...Because if you go this way,' the guard is instructing, 'you can be with your barrister before you exit. He wants to see you.'

I tilt my head at the guard, fight the urge to poke her, check if she is real.

'Did you hear me?'

'Yes,' I say, finally, wiggling a finger in my ear. 'Yes.'

She tuts. 'This way.'

We walk along a basement corridor where the lights blink and the walls are grey. Passing changing rooms with lockers and police kit and showers, we then halt at a door painted blue, and the guard says, 'Here you go.' And, as the door swings open, I see Harry and Balthus.

They immediately stand.

The door shuts. The room is cold. There is a table and three chairs and folders and water. Harry takes a step towards me and holds out his arms. 'Come here.'

I blink at him. I try to focus, but my eyes are wet and it is hard to see. I let Harry's arms wrap around me, feel the heat of him, smell the fug of a shirt dried in a machine, as he closes his hands around me and lets me rest my head on his shoulder.

'It's over now,' he says. 'It's over.'

I close my eyes. And push all my black thoughts to one side.

* * *

After I breathe, begin to focus again, we sit. Harry and I talk, but I do not relay to him my doubts. How can I? He is a good man, a kind man. Would he think so much of me if he knew that, deep down, I was a cold, trained killer? That, in reality, I think I may have killed Father O'Donnell after all?

Balthus leaves and returns with hamburgers ten minutes later, the hot stink of processed meat and fat and salt penetrating the air. He hands one to each of us. Slowly, I take it, inspecting the packaging, picking out the lettuce that wilts inside. It is the first hamburger I have eaten in over a year.

'What do we do now?' I say, swallowing a mouthful of

meat. 'If they were after me in prison, what happens now I am out? I need somewhere to stay.'

Balthus lowers his burger. 'You can stay with me.'

'Is that possible?' Harry says.

He nods. 'I have a place, an apartment. No one knows about it. I needed some space a few years back when things between me and Harriet were getting difficult.'

'Is it far?'

'No. Just ten minutes from here.'

'Good,' Harry says. 'We need Maria out of the way. That CCTV tape just turned up. If the Project has anything to do with this, if they released that tape to us in court, they have done it for a reason. They'll be looking for her. We need to be quick now.'

Balthus looks at me. 'What do you think, Maria? You can stay there until everything calms down, then Harry can meet us and we can plan what to do next, who to contact.'

I murmur a response, but keep my eyes down. The CCTV tape. Was it false evidence doctored by the Project? Am I indeed guilty? Slowly, I raise my eyes as Balthus repeats his accommodation offer. It has come to this, staying at other people's places, my own apartment long gone after my conviction, my assets temporarily frozen. My old life dead, resurrected with a new one I do not recognise yet. I pick up the burger then pause, the meat hovering, dripping with ketchup. I feel scared, unsure of what's ahead, of why people do and say what they do. But most of all I feel a gaping hole inside me, at a loss, a death, a savage murder, at lives taken.

'We have to find out what Project Callidus is,' I say finally.

Harry looks at me, nods. 'Yes.'

Balthus sits, stares at the table. Harry sighs, leans back, wipes his chin. 'Okay,' Harry says after a while, gathering food remnants then closing his files. 'Best not waste any more time. Let's go.'

'Are the reporters all out there?'

He looks at me. 'Yes, I'm afraid so. A full team of press and photographers on the court steps. It will be loud. I can do all the talking, if you like.'

The door opens, warm air whooshing through. Harry's solicitor enters. He takes Harry's documents for him then exits, leaving the door open. We all stand.

I look at Harry. 'Can you…' I pause, the thought of her, of my friend making everything seem more real, somehow, more urgent. 'I need you to do something for me.'

'Of course. What is it?'

'I require a pen and a piece of paper. Do you have them?'

'Hmmm? Oh, yes. Yes. Hang on a tick.' He fishes out a pad and pen and hands them to me. I scribble down my name and the address of my villa in Spain for Patricia. I add a small note telling her to come and visit me and stay as soon as she can when she gets parole.

Folding the paper, I hand it to Harry. 'My cellmate, Patricia O'Hanlon, is due to leave Goldmouth soon. Could you pass this note on to her?'

'Of course,' he says, and he slips it into his top jacket pocket. 'I will help in any way I can, my dear.'

'Ready?' says Balthus.

The three of us proceed to walk down the corridor, past the police changing area and towards the lift leading to the main exit. I can already hear the low hum of reporters outside, waiting for me, like Dobermans salivating over a slab of steak. I stop, scared.

Balthus tilts his head to me. 'You okay?'

But I do not reply, my eyes front, my hands clenched, ready to run.

As we press the lift button, Harry halts. 'Hang on.'

Balthus looks. 'What is it?'

'I've left something in the room.'

'Do you want us to wait?'

'No, no.' He waves a hand. 'You two go ahead. I'll be with you in just a minute.'

'What?' I say, suddenly worried, frightened that without Harry, without his safety, I won't handle it. 'You can't leave me.'

'I won't be long. Okay?' He smiles. 'Okay?'

I inhale. Harry reminds me so much of my papa that I have latched on to him, found myself needing him. But I have coped without Papa for so long, coped on my own for so long. I glance to Balthus then back to Harry. 'Okay.' And, as we walk into the lift, I twist round to watch as Harry turns and disappears back up the corridor.

* * *

I have been running flat out for two minutes and thirteen seconds. Ahead, in the street, I see Balthus. I slow down then stop, gulping in air.

'There you are,' Balthus shouts. He runs over. 'Are you okay?'

A smash of metal rings out from the adjoining street. I freeze and listen. Footsteps.

'Move,' I say, and I grab Balthus by the arm.

We dart down the street, but it's a dead end. Reversing,

we slip up a side road then stop. Five large delivery vans block our escape.

I scan the area. 'That way,' I say, and we swing left, down a side alley. The sun here has suddenly gone, too cold to exist, and with no windows bearing down on us, with no human life near, the atmosphere is suddenly dark, damp. As far as I can tell, the only inhabitants are three rats near two metal bins. It is unsafe. I begin to back out when I see something and halt.

Someone is standing there, blocking the exit.

'Who's that?' Balthus says, shoulders heaving.

'My counsellor.'

'What?'

Kurt begins to walk towards us.

'Stay where you are,' I shout, muscles automatically tensed, ready.

Kurt stops. 'You cannot hide, Maria.'

I swallow. 'Yes, I can.'

'You brought a friend?'

I glance to Balthus.

Kurt tilts his head. 'Tut, tut, tut, Governor—what will your wife say?'

'She would not authorise whatever the hell it is you are doing here,' he yells. 'Maria has told me everything.'

Kurt shrugs and takes one step nearer.

'Stop,' I say.

He halts. 'Maria, the Project needs you back. You are out, here, in the street. I told you, you are not safe. I have been honest and open, confessed the truth. But we need you back now. We've completed the tests, we know you are ready. You know you are safe with us.'

'If I am safer with you, why did you not take me to this Project before the therapy?'

'Like I said before, we needed to evaluate your memory, see how ready you really were. It was the only way. I'm sorry we put you through it—believe me when I say that. But right now, we need to go.'

From my periphery, I see Balthus shift a little. I step to my left.

'You know it was Balthus who called me, don't you?' Kurt says now.

I hesitate. 'He thought he was calling a counselling ser-vice. That is the only reason he called you. He didn't know who it really was.' To my right, I see a vague shadow of Balthus's arm.

'His wife is the Home Secretary,' Kurt says. 'She's in charge of MI5. Are you telling me she doesn't know about you?'

'Don't listen to him, Maria,' Balthus shouts. I glance to him and breathe faster. Could Balthus have been part of it all, just like everyone else? I shake my head. Not possible. He was my father's friend.

'You are lying again,' I shout to Kurt.

'I'm not lying, not about the danger you're in.'

I turn to move then squint. There is a glint in Kurt's hands. My heart rockets. I recognise it: metal, curved, a barrel. He lifts it, arms outstretched, aiming. 'No!' I scream, but Kurt is already moving fast, trained.

My mouth opens to a silent yell.

He points the gun and fires.

Chapter 35

Balthus moans, rolling from side to side, clutching his leg.

'You shot him! Why did you shoot him?'

'Leave him,' says Kurt, as I bend down to tend to the injury, tearing Balthus's trousers. His shinbone is just visible beneath the inky ooze of blood.

I begin to apply pressure on the wound, when I feel cold metal against my right temple.

'I said, leave him.'

Slowly, I rise, Kurt's gun firmly pressed against my skull.

'Move three steps to your right.'

I stay still.

He pushes the gun in harder. 'Do it.'

I glance at Balthus then move. Balthus groans, blood pooling on the cobbles, the red staining my eyes, burning me; the rats run into a dilapidated, burnt-out building to our left.

'We cannot leave him like this,' I say. 'He's losing blood.'

'We do not have time to help him.'

I dart my eyes round. There is no one. No help. 'What do you want?'

'You.'

'Why should I go with you?' I exhale, muscles loosening, my body reaching a limit, a point where it doesn't want to go on, yet knows it has to. 'Why now? I have been conditioned without my knowledge all this time, I know about MI5, the tests, drugs, even the handlers, the assignments, but why the urgency now, after all these years?'

'Maria, run,' croaks Balthus.

Kurt kicks him hard. 'That's enough out of you.' Balthus clutches his leg, lets out a long gurgling moan.

Kurt turns to me and grabs my arm. 'Time for us to go.'

'No. Why do you need me now? Why now?'

'Because you're not safe any more. It's that simple. MI5 want you dead. And we can handle that, feed them false intel on you, but we can only really protect you if we know where you are. That's why, right now, whether you like it or not, you're coming with me. You're coming into the Project.'

* * *

As we arrive at the court entrance, Harry catches up with us. He is out of breath, sweaty, but I stare at him, watch him, as if looking away will make him disappear, will make me lose him.

Beyond the large oak doors, people are shouting my name, yelling, screaming. I feel my muscles go taut, tense, the thought of seeing it all, of the sheer volume of it all, paralysing me, making my legs freeze, my brain seize up.

'This will be my first time out of the prison system in

a year,' I say to Balthus. 'When we are out there how...' I swallow, clear my throat. 'How will I find you?'

He smiles, steady, still, a crease reaching his eyes, just like Harry's. 'I'll wait at the back until Harry's done his bit with the press. You go with Harry to his offices and I'll meet you there.'

I look at the entrance and flap my hand.

'I'll go now,' Balthus says, his body to full height, casting a shadow across the marble floor. 'I will see you very soon.'

'See you there for a large whiskey,' Harry says. Balthus nods then leaves.

Harry adjusts his jacket and looks at my flapping hand. 'Are you okay?'

'Did you get your file?'

'Sorry? Oh, yes.' He taps his chest. 'All set.'

We walk towards the court entrance and pause. 'Ready?' Harry says.

My hand goes still. Standing here, the crowd seems louder, like a clatter of thunder. Harry inhales, and, opening the door, heat blasting our faces, we walk out onto the courthouse steps.

Immediately, camera bulbs flash and pop. I gasp, clench my jaw at it all. Dozens of journalists crowd the steps, all of them rushing up towards us, a pack of wolves thrusting their microphones into our faces. In the glare of the sun, I see TV cameras, the photographers. The noise is so loud that my head starts to throb and all I want to do is cover my ears and rock. But instead, I focus on Harry's large frame stood in front of me.

'Dr Martinez! Over here!'

'Maria! Give us a smile.'

'Dr Martinez, what was it like being locked up in a British prison for so long?'

The journalists bark question after question, relentless, feral. Harry holds up a palm.

'My client...' Harry pauses until there is a hush. 'My client would firstly like to say thank you to all those who have helped her to be here today, a free woman.' There is a pop of flashbulbs. I squint, shield my eyes with my left hand.

'Many of you have read stories,' Harry continues, 'about my client, her family, her relationships—all of it. But I will remind you that they are just that—stories. Today the truth has come out. Not fiction, but fact. The truth.'

The cameras whizz and pop, fighting for their pictures, but I cannot smile, my body unsteady, my mind overloaded by it all. To dampen the flames of my panic, I stare ahead to the city landscape on the horizon, count the tallest buildings, hoping the numbers will soothe me. I get to eleven when I see something. I stand on my toes, try to get a better view.

'Our thoughts now go,' Harry is saying, 'to the family of Father O'Donnell.'

I squint, but the sun is very bright and it is difficult to see.

'Father O'Donnell's family,' Harry says, 'walk away today without any answers to the crime that was committed against their son. It is them we must think of. That is all for now. Thank you.'

The flashbulbs pop like fireworks.

We hurry down the steps as journalists and photographers jostle and jump. I catch a glimpse of Balthus on the far edge and I attempt what I think is a smile, but he does not smile back. Everything is so loud. Balthus's mouth appears to be shaped into an O, but it is hard to decipher. I slow down, try to see him properly, but then it happens.

Balthus is darting towards us.

Harry spots him. 'Balthus?'

And that is when I see it. A spark in the sunshine. Blonde hair scraped back into a ponytail. The barrel of a gun.

'Dr Andersson,' I say, but before I can move, before I can sound the warning, there is a loud crack of a shot being fired.

Then people scream.

Harry pushes himself in front of me as a sea of bodies surges towards us.

'Harry!' I shout. 'She has a—'

Harry opens his mouth to speak, then is cut dead.

'Harry!'

He wobbles on the steps, clutching his chest. I try to push my way through, but I am against the tide and it is impossible. Harry looks straight at me; then, crumpling, his body topples, thudding onto the stone below.

'He's been shot!' shouts one of the journalists.

'Harry!' I scream. 'Harry!'

Cameras click, getting their images, indiscriminate of the subject, of the level of decency, of any human feeling. In the distance, I hear the wail of sirens. The people part a little and I finally manage to scramble over to Harry, ready to treat him, but before I make it, there is a tug at my elbow. 'Move, Maria! Move!' I look back. Balthus.

'Harry's been shot,' I say, gulping down air. 'We have to help him! I saw Dr Andersson. She's here. She has a gun.'

'There's nothing we can do. We have to get out of here,'

Balthus says, dragging me up. 'It's you she's after, remember? Move.'

He hauls me up, but, as he does, I stumble, falling, hitting my cheekbone hard on the step. 'Balthus, I have to help him. The police will be here,' I say, tears streaking my face as I try to push him off.

'Maria,' says Balthus, breathing hard, gripping me, 'if they shot Harry, they're after you. The police can't help us. You have to leave. Now.'

I scan the swell of people. Harry. Harry is there.

Swarms of journalists begin to surround his body, emergency vehicles screeching to a halt at the bottom of the steps. I glance to the far right: Dr Andersson stands at the edge, scanning the crowd where Harry lies.

'She is there. I see her.' I look at my hands; there is blood on my fingers, on my palms. Panic rises within me.

'Let's go. Lauren's coming,' Balthus yells and he yanks my arm.

And as he starts to run, me staggering in his grasp behind him, I steal one last frantic glance at Harry's misshapen body lying on the steps of the court.

Chapter 36

The blood from my hands mixes with the tap water as it runs down the sink. It swirls round and round the ceramic bowl, circling the waste pipe until, eventually, it disappears.

I hunch over, try to scrub my fingernails clean. My blouse is ripped at the hem and my cheek is scraped. I find a towel and pat my hands dry. Sitting on the ledge of the bath, I hang my head. The image of Harry slumped on the steps of the court lingers in my thoughts, and even when I try to imagine something else, it is still there—indelibly etched. I stand in front of the mirror and look at my reflection: my hair is matted to my head, there is a deep scratch on my cheek and the skin on my lower back is red raw.

I raise my hand, touch my face with my fingertips and wince. My whole body throbs. So much has happened. The murder. The conviction. Goldmouth. Dr Andersson. The Project. Handlers. Conditioning. Patricia. Harry. My mother. The veiled woman. The blood. The deaths. They all swirl into one, into a cauldron of memories, a brew of events that, if I blinked, if I closed my eyes right now and fell asleep, I could convince myself they never happened.

I drop my forehead to the glass and exhale, the cool of the mirror lowering my temperature, calming me.

A knock sounds on the door.

'Maria,' Balthus says, his voice low, gruff, 'are you okay?'

I peel my forehead from the mirror, and, slowly, pad to the door and open it. Balthus is standing in the doorway, shirt open, face streaked with sweat.

'How are you?' he says.

'They shot Harry.' I wipe my eyes.

He eyes my scars, my bruises. 'You look like you need a soak. There are towels in the top cabinet and soap just there.' He points to the bath ledge.

I stare at it.

I touch the scar on my cheek.

Balthus follows my eyeline then turns back to me. 'Look, you have a bath. I'll make us a sandwich or something. Okay?' He hesitates then walks towards the kitchen.

I close the door, turn on the taps and, shedding my ripped blouse, I begin the painful process of cleaning myself up.

* * *

I emerge from the bathroom in a grey dressing gown and go to the kitchen.

Balthus looks up. He has a white T-shirt on now, and his bare feet peek out from navy sweatpants. 'Better?'

I nod and glance around. The kitchen is open-plan, spilling directly onto a lounge area, to the right of which sits a glass dining table. The apartment window spans the entire length of the wall. I walk towards it. The view stretches all the way over to the Thames.

'I set you out one of Harriet's old blouses. I hope that's okay.'

I sit on the arm of one of the chairs in the lounge area, flinching at the cuts as they rub against my robe. 'Have you heard any news about Harry?'

Balthus sets down the bread he is holding. 'No. Nothing.'

I look over to where the television is. There are pictures on the screen, but no sound. President Obama is talking, and underneath a blue ticker tape reads: *Breaking news— NSA Prism scandal.* The documents we found, the secret details. My brain whirrs to life.

'Pass me the remote control.'

Balthus comes over with a plate of sandwiches and sets them down on the low glass table in front of the sofa. 'Here you go.' He hands me the remote. I press the volume button. The news anchor's voice springs into the room.

'…In a leaked presentation to the press, it has been revealed that the US National Security Agency—the NSA— has been using a surveillance system code-named Prism. The existence of the programme, which allows the NSA to receive emails, video clips, social networking data and other private information held by a range of US internet companies, has been leaked to the British press by an anonymous whistle-blower. In a comment today, the EU Commissioner, Patrice Duree, said that they are concerned that firms complying with Prism-related requests may be handing over data in breach of the privacy rights of European citizens. Activist groups claim that Prism violates the US constitution.'

I lean in closer. The newsreader continues. 'The reve-
lation of the Prism programme comes at a time when the
threat of cyber terrorism has never been greater. But gov-
ernments around the world are voicing their protests at
what the Chinese government is calling, "the warrantless
surveillance", in relation to a recently disclosed US cyber
attack. Both the UK Prime Minister and Home Secretary
have so far declined to comment—'

I mute the television and turn to Balthus. 'This is related
to the Project.'

'How?' He points to the plate of sandwiches. 'Here, have
something to eat.'

I shake my head. 'It's all connected. It has to be.'

Balthus picks up a sandwich and glances at the television. It is showing coverage from the scene outside the
courtroom. Harry's body lies on the steps, just as we left
him. I close my eyes, unable to watch. Balthus turns off
the TV.

'Maria,' he says, 'I am concerned for you.'

I open my eyes.

'So much has happened,' Balthus continues. 'Harry
has just been shot in front of you. You have just been ac-
quitted of a crime. The whole Callidus business, prison…
These things can get to people.' He sets down his sandwich. 'Look, my boss, he has a contact with a counselling
service.'

'No.'

He sits. 'Please,' he says, 'just consider it. It could really
help you. Help you with your Asperger's—everything. And,
in the meantime, we can figure out what's been going on,
who these people are who have been after you.'

I stare at the vast window. 'Harry stepped in front of me as the gun was fired.'

'Yes.'

I watch the landscape, the rise and fall of the clouds, passing, breezing by, life continuing, normal, regular. My body, my brain—they ache for calm, for clarity. 'How do you know these counselling people?' I say after a moment.

'It's a perk, let's say, of the prison service. Sometimes, in this job, we need help. We have access to some really good people. I can make the call, if you like.'

I shoot one more look at the skyline and, for the first time, I realise that I am gazing through a window without bars. 'Can...can you call them now?'

He smiles, pauses. 'Yes, of course.' He strides over to his desk and picks up the phone.

'I'll get dressed,' I say.

When I emerge from the bathroom, Balthus has finished his call and I am wearing a clean blouse and trousers.

'All done,' he says. 'They have a couple of new counsellors who have just started. They come highly recommended and have worked with people with Asperger's before. You'll have to sign up to a radical kind of therapy, but it gets great reviews.'

'Who is the therapist?'

'They couldn't confirm, given the last-minute nature of my request. You'll find out when you get there. I've booked you in for first thing tomorrow. Is that okay?'

I hesitate. 'Yes.'

Balthus smiles. 'Good.' He walks across to the kitchen, picks up a knife and slices into some more bread. 'I think counselling could be just what you need.'

Chapter 37

Kurt holds the gun to my head. 'I'm sorry to have to do this, Maria, but I really do need you to move.'

'Why?' I snap, the tension rolling out, the outrage, the injustice. 'Fucking, why?' I stop, heaving, exhausted by every inch of it all. I wipe spit from my mouth, raise my eyes. The gun loosens a little. 'Did I kill him?'

For a moment, I think Kurt is going to yell at me, but instead he frowns, takes a step back. The gun drops to his side. 'No,' he says after a moment. 'You didn't kill him.'

My mouth drops open, a reflex, shocked. Relief washes over me, surging like the ocean. I didn't do it. I didn't kill Father O'Donnell. I step back a little, stumble, the thought overwhelming me, the year of pain and uncertainty dropping away, leaving me exhausted, worn. Broken. 'Who?' I say after a second. 'Who killed him?'

Kurt leans back against the wall. 'This was when the Project was still connected to MI5.' He pauses. 'Your handler at the university in Salamanca was reporting changes in your biomechanical structure. Your cognitive responses were increasing. So we needed you here, nearer, in the UK so we could monitor you more closely. And, of course, we knew you were eager to find Father Reznik, so London was an easy option. We knew you'd come here.'

'So you…' I stall, not wanting to say it, not wanting to admit what they did, how they lied, schemed, cajoled. 'You implied Father Reznik had family in London? You set up the cosmetic surgery secondment at St James's, here?'

'We made sure your boss was your new handler, as you figured out.' He scratches his head. 'All was well until we got first wind of the potential NSA scandal.'

Balthus groans. I look at him—dark blood sticks like tar to the road. I turn back to Kurt. 'What has the NSA got to do with the murder?'

'I don't know if I can—'

'Tell me!' I yell, spit flying out. 'Look what you have done to me! Look how you have lied, how this Project has lied.' I stop, gulp in a breath. 'This is my life. My life. You owe this to me. You fucking owe it to me.'

Seconds pass. His eyes flicker shut then open, directing them straight at me. 'You want to know? You want to know why you matter? Why we did what we had to do to keep things safe, to keep the fucking world safe?'

I remain very still. A phrase swims into my head. 'For the greater good,' I say to myself. 'Killing is easy for the greater good.'

'You remember the Project training mantra?' A soda can blows in the wind, lifts up, then clatters to the ground. 'Okay, look. When the NSA Prism thing blew up, the government got scared, began intelligence-committee investigations into all of MI5's activity. They were going to pull apart everything, all operations. MI5 were shit scared they'd have their own NSA-style fuck-up. That's when they gave the order for Callidus to lay low, for you to be placed somewhere safe, where no one could touch you—find you—until it all blew over.'

It dawns on me, like a new day. 'In prison. You put me in prison so I could be out of the way.' I stop, nearly laugh at the audacity of it, almost admiring their intricate planning. 'And, in prison, I could not escape. You had me securely where you wanted me to be.'

'It was the obvious answer. A high-security facility without any extra effort on our part. All we needed was a reason to get you in there. A nun was all it took.'

'Sister Mary.' I slap my hand to my mouth. I was right. I was right about her in the retrial. She was lying. She was MI5.

'She attended the hospital—St James's—befriended you, persuaded you to volunteer at the convent. We knew you had struck up a friendship with your handler, Father—'

'Reznik,' I say, my voice sounding faraway, dreamlike.

Kurt's gun swings against his thigh. 'It was the ideal motive. You liked him, he left you. We could fashion a seething hatred from that. We lifted the Croc you donated to the convent and, because of the blood blister, we had your DNA. Then we staged the murder.'

Murder. My stomach lurches at the word. They staged it, they killed him, made it look as if I did it. As if I killed Father O'Donnell.

'Our officer waited until the right time and staged the crime scene. I helped; it was a tough job.' He blows out some air. 'The priest was stronger than we thought, so it took two of us to string him out, slice him up, pierce through his neck. All a bit dramatic, but it had to be done, had to look…vengeful. A lot was at stake.'

I swallow, eyes damp, head throbbing. 'But the DVD store owner…'

'We paid him. He was taking a hit at the time. Drugs. So we paid him to say what we needed—that he saw you. Then I went to the hospital, waited until you had finished your night-time geriatric visits, and took the CCTV tape.'

I look up. 'But the CCTV tape was uncovered.'

'That was me.'

'But…' I trail off. I know the answer now, but cannot say it.

'At first, the idea was to hide the CCTV so you would be convicted, which you were, then reveal the tape, get you out once MI5 knew they were in the clear.'

I keep my eyes on the floor, on Balthus's blood now seeping past me. 'But NSA happened.'

'Yes. The service was under too much scrutiny. The NSA scandal would not die down. MI5 were sure the Project would be uncovered and they couldn't risk that. So that made you a threat to them. And they had to eliminate the threat. They told me to destroy the CCTV.' He stops. 'And they told our two undercover officers in Goldmouth who were watching you, to kill you.'

My eyes go wide. 'Dr Andersson and Mickie Croft.'

'Yes.'

They all lied. The fact strikes me like a jab to the ribs as, ahead, the breeze lifts the soda can up once more. I watch it briefly rise until the wind throws it to the ground, un-wanted, trash.

'You recall I mentioned my brother to you,' Kurt says now, unexpectedly.

'Y-yes.'

'When MI5 wanted to pull the Project, I couldn't let that happen. I knew how close we were, with you, to being able to use intelligence, computers—all of it—to stop the terrorists in their tracks.' He looks at the gun. 'So I left MI5 and stayed with Callidus, committed to keep it going.'

My brain, through the fog, connects, puts the pieces together. 'You put Bobbie Reynolds in prison to protect me.'

'A cover, yes. And we sped up the appeal process to get you out, away from MI5, fast. So you see? We are on the same side.'

'Maria!' I spin round. Balthus is trying to drag himself forward. I drop to help him.

'Stop!' Kurt shouts. He points his gun at Balthus. Balthus thuds back down.

'You need to come with me, Maria,' Kurt says, rapid now, his body straight, ready. 'I am sorry about all this, I truly am. If it could have been done an easier way, if we could have initiated you into the programme in a more gentle fashion, then we would have done so. But this is MI5 we're talking about here. They know everything. And they are under enormous pressure right now with the NSA. If they want you gone, you'll be gone.'

His words echo around the dampness, the gloom. The despair hits me, threatens to engulf me. I see it. Harry lying on the steps of the court, the priest's body splayed at the foot of the altar. All of them lost to me. Their faces swim into my consciousness, each of them good, innocent. 'You killed Father O'Donnell. Why him? Just to get me out of the way?'

'He was getting too close to the truth,' Kurt says, his voice higher, almost shouting. 'He was helping you, was discovering Father Reznik was a cover name. We couldn't let you start to figure out the truth before we'd got you out of harm's way.' Kurt shakes his head. 'Don't you understand? This is for the greater good.'

'No,' I say, feeling myself drift out to sea, unanchored. 'I cannot trust you. I cannot trust any of you.' And then I remember: the memory, the woman in the hijab, the one I strangled. 'Have…have I killed before?'

He stops. 'For the Project?'

I nod, unable to speak, too scared of the answer.

'Maria, we have all done things for the Project that others will not.'

I shake my head, not wanting it to be true. 'Have I been to Afghanistan? Somewhere very hot for Callidus? Worked in a refugee camp?'

'I don't know every single detail of your operational duties, but, given the nature of our work, it is highly likely, yes.'

I swallow, shaking, frightened. I look down at my hands. What have I done?

Kurt steps forward, his gun lowered. 'It gets easier, you know. Please understand. I'm sorry about all this, about the way you are finding out. I really am. But you need to come with me now.' He reaches into his pocket, pulls out his cell.

'What are you doing?'

'Sending a message.' He pauses. 'You recall the woman I said was my girlfriend? The one who delivered the coffee?'

The woman with the leather jacket and the chestnut bob. Her face appears in my mind now, brown eyes, honey skin, accent like a punnet of plums.

'She's with the Project yet still undercover at MI5,' Kurt says. 'So once I make contact, she's going to confirm intel to the service that you're dead. Then I'll fly with you to the Project facility in Scotland. So you see? You stay with us and MI5 won't be hunting you any more.'

'If we fly from a commercial airport, MI5 will track me on surveillance camera. They will know I am alive.'

'That's why we're meeting at a private airstrip, thirty miles from here.'

'Your contact could have leaked false intel about me to MI5 anytime.'

'No, that wasn't possible until now. Think about it. You were a risk, but not any more, because, now we've tested you, checked your state, I've been able to tell you everything. And now you know your life is threatened. Now you understand why it's vital to keep quiet, to stay low. *That's* why we're leaking the intel now.' He exhales. 'That's why.'

I breathe hard, heavy, try to think. If I go with him, with the Project, who is to say I will ever return? Who's to say that I will ever be the same again? MI5 may soon believe I am dead, but if I stay with the Project, my life will not be mine. It will be theirs. Theirs to use and command as they need. I glance at Balthus on the ground then look to Kurt, a subject of the Project, willing to do anything for them. I don't want to be like that, don't want to carry out tasks that I am against. Don't want to kill, murder. I was a doctor. I *am* a doctor.

'I cannot go with you,' I say.

'What?' He taps his cell.

'I cannot do this. I cannot be a part of Callidus, of the Project.'

He thrashes his hand up. 'Jesus! Understand what's at stake: that this is for the greater good. We help people, Maria. Do you get that? And there are elements now about you that we need to…to ascertain. Crucial elements, elements we could not predict until now, now you're older.'

I go still. 'What elements?'

'I can't say.'

'You can say. You can speak. You are just choosing not to tell me.'

He shakes his head, looks at his cell. 'Maria, you're coming with me.' He taps the screen. 'It's done.' He holds up the phone. 'The message has been sent. MI5 will be receiving the intel now. You are dead to them. You are dead. All I need to do now, once I get you to a safe house, is confirm when we'll be at the airstrip and we're free.' He begins to walk towards me.

'No,' I say, backing away. 'I am not going with you.'

'You can help people, Maria. You can save lives. Isn't that what you've always wanted to do?'

'Not like this. If I want to help people, I can do it in a different way, a more honest way.

'An honest way? You think people are honest? Bullshit they are. Everyone lies, Maria, you of all people know that. All we are doing is blasting through the shit, using intelligent people to galvanise the lies, to cut through it all, make a positive difference in this fucked-up world.'

I inch back, hands trembling. 'No.'

'Yes.' He points the gun at me. 'And now you're dead, we have three hours to get to—'

He drops to the ground. I gasp, hands flying to my mouth. Kurt is lying on the tarmac, a bullet wound through his forehead. I stumble back, confused, blinded, his red blood seeping into the cracks in the ground, into the black of the earth. What just happened? I shake, trip over myself, falling, gulping in fistfuls of air. And then I see Balthus.

He is holding a gun.

Balthus swallows. His wound is scarlet, his breathing laboured. 'I...I shoved it in my pocket when I got your call.' Then he splutters and slumps to the right.

I drag myself up, crawl over, hauling Balthus by his arms, lean him as best I can against the wall. I glance at Kurt's body. Unmoving. Dead, the silent reality deafening. My eyes linger on Kurt for two more seconds, brain struggling with events. I turn back to Balthus, my fingers trembling, inspect his wound. 'Your...your leg... There is so much blood.'

He groans. 'Will it be okay?'

I grab his hand and press it to the torn skin, the shattered bone.

Balthus winces. 'I didn't mean to shoot him in the head. I just... I just meant to stop him. He was going to take you away.' He looks over at Kurt's body. 'What are we going to do now?'

The growl of a van driving on a nearby road suddenly sounds. We stop, listen. When the van passes, I force my attention to Kurt's body—his mobile phone lies on the ground. A memory floats into my consciousness. Me, standing in the therapy room, listening to a voicemail from Kurt's girlfriend, the one with the coffee, the one who, a minute ago, received a message from Kurt. The one who is now expecting a second message from him, too.

I stand, everything suddenly seeming clear, obvious, and, ignoring Balthus's calls to me, rush over to where Kurt's body lies. Alive one minute, dead the next. So easy. I shiver, gaze at his smooth skin, his splayed limbs, the man who made me doubt myself, who drugged me to get a result he wanted, that the Project wanted. Bending, hesitant at first, I pick up Kurt's phone and turn it over in my hand. Switching it on, recalling the same passcode I used when I accessed the voicemail in the therapy room, I scan the messages. There. The one giving the green light for the MI5 intel on my death.

'What are you doing?' Balthus says, as I hurry back over.

'He said he was going to send a message to confirm our arrival time at the private airstrip. So, if I send that message from his phone, from him to his contact, leading them to think all is as planned and that I am on my way to them, that will give me time to run, to get away.' I think of the commercial airport surveillance. 'I will have to change my appearance. Can you access a passport under a different name so I can get out of the UK?'

'I have a contact. Where will you go?'

'Somewhere no one knows about. I will require that contact.'

I grip the phone and, thinking of Papa, of Harry, of all the needless deaths, I write the message and hit the send button. Exhaling one long, deep breath, I throw the phone to the floor. It spins then comes to a halt by Kurt's legs.

Pressing my lips together at the sight, I close my eyes, think of Papa, then run to Balthus and help him up. 'Can you walk?'

'Yes. Just,' he says, and together we hobble to the main road, blinking as the sudden sunshine hits our faces.

Balthus stops. 'Maria, I can help you.' He winces. 'I can always help you.'

My eyes feel wet. I blink back the tears, because I don't want them, no longer wanting to feel weak or vulnerable or at the mercy of others. Swallowing hard, I focus on the road ahead, focus, now, on what needs to be done. 'I will have to dye my hair. And I will get some coloured contact lenses, perhaps some clear glasses, too. I will have to change how I look if I am going to travel. I cannot let them see me ever again and—'

I stop. Balthus is staring at me, the corners of his eyes creased, just as Harry's used to be when he smiled. A lump swells in my throat.

'It's going to be okay,' Balthus says.

But I cannot believe that. I may have killed people, hurt them, may have instigated covert crimes, and I need to know, need to understand what I have done. The Project is still out there. Once they realise Kurt is dead, once they know I have fled, they will be after me. So I will always have to hide, run, get away and never surface again, cut, sever any contact with my previous life. With people, with my family, with my...my friend.

'Can you—?' I stop, clear my throat. 'Can you get a message to Patricia O'Hanlon? Can you tell her I am okay, even though I cannot see her? Harry was going to contact her, but now he's...' I trail off, the words too hard for me to say.

Balthus nods. 'Of course.'

Once we are further along the road, I raise my arm to hail a taxi. A cab pulls over, and, as I start to help Balthus into his seat, something ahead catches my eye.

I squint. On the tarmac, by the front wheel of the taxi, is a small, black metal spider like the device from the counselling room. Kurt must have been carrying it as he ran after me, must have dropped it from his jacket. I stare at it for two more seconds, then staying as steady as I can, slide in beside Balthus.

As we set off, I turn and peer out of the window.

The metal spider lies crushed on the road, flattened, in pieces ready to be mended, ready to be put back together, refashioned anew. The taxi speeds forward and, slowly at first then faster still, the spider fades into the distance until it completely disappears.

As if it were never there at all.

* * * * *

Don't miss the powerful and gripping
second instalment in the
Project trilogy.

No matter how fast you run, the
past always catches up with you

Dr Maria Martinez is out of prison and on the run.

Her mission? To get back to the safety of her family.

Little does she know that this might
be the most dangerous place of all…

From the New York Times Bestselling author of *The Good Girl*

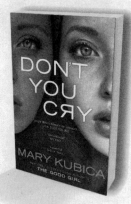

In downtown Chicago, a young woman named Esther Vaughan disappears from her apartment without a trace. A haunting letter addressed to My Dearest is found among her possessions, leaving her friend and roommate Quinn Collins to wonder where Esther is and whether or not she's the person Quinn thought she knew.

As Quinn searches for answers about Esther, so unfolds a twisted thrill ride that builds to a stunning conclusion and shows that no matter how fast and far we run, the past always catches up with us in the end.

*Everyone knows a couple
like Jack and Grace*

He has looks and wealth, she has charm and elegance.
You might not want to like them, but you do.
You'd like to get to know Grace better.
But it's difficult, because you realise
Jack and Grace are never apart.
Some might call this true love. Others might ask why
Grace never answers the phone. Or how she can never
meet for coffee, even though she doesn't work. And
why there are bars on one of the bedroom windows.

Sometimes, the perfect marriage is the perfect lie.
#StaySingle

The trip of a lifetime,
or the perfect murder?

Audrey Templeton has it all planned: she's going to spend her 70th birthday with her children Lexi and John, on a cruise around the Greek islands, where she'll tell them about their life-changing inheritance money.

But when Audrey fails to return to her cabin after the ship's White Night party, the crew carry out a full scale search that soon moves from inside the ship, to the deep waters of the med. With tensions rising between Lexi and John, they start to question not only how well they knew their mother, but whether they can actually trust one another.

After all, there are no police at sea…

Loved this book?
Let us know!

Find us on **Twitter @Mira_BooksUK**
where you can share your thoughts, stay up
to date on all the news about our upcoming
releases and even be in with the chance of
winning copies of our wonderful books!

Bringing you the best voices in fiction

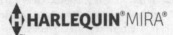